GOMEZ ARIAS; OR THE MOORS OF THE ALPUJARRAS.

A SPANISH HISTORICAL ROMANCE

By

DON TELESFORO DE TRUEBA Y COSÍO.

IN THREE VOLUMES

© 2011 Benediction Classics, Oxford.

Contents

VOL. I.

PREFACE.	i
CHAPTER I.	5
CHAPTER II.	9
CHAPTER III.	15
CHAPTER IV.	26
CHAPTER V.	31
CHAPTER VI.	37
CHAPTER VII.	51
CHAPTER VIII.	57
CHAPTER IX.	61
CHAPTER X.	72
CHAPTER XI.	82
CHAPTER XII.	87
CHAPTER XIII.	93
CHAPTER XIV.	104

VOL. II.

CHAPTER I.	117
CHAPTER II.	127
CHAPTER III.	136
CHAPTER IV.	145
CHAPTER V.	152
CHAPTER VI.	161
CHAPTER VII.	173
CHAPTER VIII.	179
CHAPTER IX.	185
CHAPTER X.	194
CHAPTER XI.	206
CHAPTER XII.	218
CHAPTER XIII.	223
CHAPTER XIV	232

VOL. III.

CHAPTER I. 245
CHAPTER II. 252
CHAPTER III. 257
CHAPTER IV. 266
CHAPTER V. 273
CHAPTER VI. 282
CHAPTER VII. 288
CHAPTER VIII. 301
CHAPTER IX. 309
CHAPTER X. 320
CHAPTER XI. 329
CONCLUSION. 339

VOL. I.

TO THE
RIGHT HONORABLE LORD HOLLAND.

My Lord,

It is with pleasure I avail myself of your permission to dedicate the following Work to your name, as a small mark of my respect for your Lordship's character.

As a Spaniard, I find an additional motive for addressing it to one who has uniformly shewn the interest he feels in the prosperity and literature of my country.
I have the honor to be,

   My Lord,

      Your Lordship's

   Most obedient and obliged Servant,

         TELESFORO DE TRUEBA Y COSÍO.

London, March 1, 1828.

PREFACE.

Let me intreat the reader not to be alarmed at the hacknied word, which generally augurs that a person is going to be very egotistical and prosy. This, at least, it will be my ambition to avoid. Nor is it my intention to assume its literary prerogatives in any way as a mask for a sort of mock humility, endeavouring to impose upon good-natured persons by protestations of demerits, want of experience and talent, with that long series of et ceteras with which a writer generally opens his first campaign.

The public has nothing to do with an exculpatory doctrine, which carries with it the aggravating circumstance of not being sincere; for I am sure that no man, with a moderate share of common sense, will suppose that an author really believes the accusation he so humbly utters against himself. Could he indeed persuade himself that his book was so very indifferent a performance, he might assuredly more justly accuse himself of acting the part of an unnatural parent in thus gratuitously exposing his intellectual offspring to the neglect and compassion of the world.

Besides, when an author presents his readers with this stultifying catalogue of demerits, he supplies them with the very best reasons to retort upon him:—"Good heavens; if the man has neither talents nor information, why does he write at all?" Having thus waved my claims to any similar indulgence, it only remains for me to say a few words respecting the origin and the object of the following Romance.

As an enthusiastic admirer of the lofty genius, the delightful and vivid creations of that great founder of English historical fiction, Sir Walter Scott, it often struck me, while reading his enchanting novels, as rather singular that he had never availed himself of the beautiful and inexhaustible materials for works upon a similar plan to be met with in

Gomez Arias; or The Moors of the Alpujarras.

Spain. It has, indeed, been generally admitted that Spain was the classic ground of chivalry and romance. The long dominion of the Moors—the striking contrast between their religion, their customs and manners, and those of their Christian enemy—the different petty kingdoms into which Spain was divided, with the consequent feuds, intrigues and battles,—all concurred to produce a succession of extraordinary incidents and character, highly adapted for romantic and dramatic illustration. Yet, while the less abundant chronicles and traditions of England, Scotland, Ireland and France, were successively ransacked by the great magician and his most successful imitators, they seem almost studiously to have avoided dwelling upon those glowing, luxuriant productions, replete with such variety of incident and character, which form the national treasures of Spain.

Conceiving, then, that I had the same right as any one else to spoil, if I failed to give attraction to a fine subject, I found that my ideas were further confirmed by the encouragement of some of the most eminent amongst my fellow-countrymen. I accordingly engaged in the undertaking, the result of which is the following Romance.

With regard to the hero, I cannot well determine whether he ever existed or not. In spite of my researches, I have no other authority for his reality than the well known comedy of the celebrated Calderon de la Barca, entitled "*La niña de Gomez Arias*." The probability is, that Calderon took the hint of this comedy, according to a generally prevailing custom in his time, from some legend or tradition now lost. Be this as it may, it is enough that such characters as Gomez Arias are unfortunately within the pale of human nature. I have endeavoured, however, to soften the character, as it is depicted, from that of an utterly abandoned libertine into a man of extraordinary ambition; for great passions, though they cannot palliate crime, are nevertheless not inconsistent with a dereliction of moral and legal ties.

To conclude my prefatory reasons for not writing a long preface, there is one point on which I am anxious to appeal to the indulgence of my readers. It is obvious that the work being written in English by a Spaniard, must bear some traces of its foreign descent. In extenuation of these unavoidable faults of style and language, I can only entreat that the English public will extend the same generous sympathy and benevolence to the errors of the author, which it has already evinced, in far more important matters, on behalf of his unfortunate fellow-countrymen.

CHAPTER I.

INTRODUCTORY.

The ancient city of Granada has ever proved a source of gratification to those who have occupied themselves with the investigation of its earlier history. It abounds with objects curious and interesting; and is no less celebrated for the conspicuous place which it holds in the page of Spanish history, than for the more pleasing associations of chivalry and romance. Situated at the base of the snow-capt mountains of the *Sierra Nevada*, and extending into the luxuriant plain of the *Vega*, it seems placed by nature as a barrier between an eternal winter and a constant spring—

> "Not as elsewhere with fervours frosts severe,
> Or clouds with calms divide the happy hours,
> But heaven than whitest crystal e'en more clear,
> A flood of sunshine in all seasons showers;
> Nursing to fields their herbs, to herbs their flowers,
> To flowers their smell, leaves to th' immortal trees:
> Here by its lake the splendid palace towers,
> On marble columns rich with golden frieze,
> For leagues and leagues around, o'erhanging hills and seas."
> *Wiffen's Tasso.*

Amongst the many architectural remains which adorn the city, the palace of the Alhambra is perhaps the most conspicuous. It was originally founded by one of the Moorish kings, after the conquest of the kingdom of Granada, and became, in process of time, the favorite residence of a long line of princes, by whom it was enriched with the spoils of conquest, and all the embellishments which wealth could supply. Nothing, indeed, that imagination could devise, or human industry effect, was omitted, to render it a retreat worthy of the Moorish sovereigns of Granada.

Ages have gone by since its foundation, kingdoms have been overthrown, and whole generations have passed away, but the Alhambra still remains a proud record of the Moslem's power. It is the last monument of their glory, amidst the changes that have long since taken place, and that still proclaim their fall.

The city commands an extensive view of the surrounding country, and the eye wanders with delight over the picturesque and varied scenery which opens on every side. Far as the eye can reach, a fertile plain teeming with life exhibits nature in her most lovely and fascinating forms; large flocks and herds are seen browzing and disporting amongst the luxuriant herbage, while the distant quiet villages interspersed throughout the landscape, are thrown out in bold relief by the dark green foliage in which they are embosomed. Here the orange-flower and the jasmin of the gardens, decked in all the pride of cultivation, load the air with their grateful perfume; and sparkling jets of limpid water, thrown aloft from fountains of alabaster, impart a continual freshness and beauty to the scene, whilst they contribute to dissipate the languor which in this luxurious climate softly steals over the senses.

After dwelling with delight upon this living landscape of happiness and tranquillity, the feelings of the beholder are aroused by the imposing aspect of the *Sierra Nevada*. The never-varying hue, the sameness of desolation exhibited by these gigantic mountains, offer a striking contrast to the glowing and lively tints of the surrounding country. On their lofty summits the clouds appear to have fixed their abode; and in their inhospitable regions no living thing can dwell.—Still barren and dreary they remain, in the very bosom of luxuriance and cheerfulness; throughout the vicissitudes of climate and season they are for ever the same.

Granada was the last strong hold of the Moors in Spain. They had for seven centuries defied the power of different Christian sovereigns, who by unremitted efforts slowly and progressively regained those territories which had been suddenly wrested from their ancestors. Indeed, it required the lapse of ages and a series of successes, wrought by the exertions of many a distinguished warrior, to recover those possessions which had been thus lost by the weakness of a king, and the treason of a prelate.[1]

Ferdinand and Isabella, happily uniting by marriage the crowns of Arragon and Castile, consolidated the power and gave a new impulse to the energies of the Christians. After a variety of minor advantages, they resolved to lay siege to Granada, fortunately at a time when that city was a prey to civil dissentions, occasioned by the rival families of the Zegris and Abencerrages. The Moors, gradually weakened by their domestic broils, offered but an inadequate opposition to the enemy, who pressed them, on this account, with increasing ardour. After a protracted siege of eight months, in which a host of warriors distinguished themselves, Granada, the royal residence of the Moslems for seven hundred years, surrendered, and the banner of the Cross streamed triumphantly over the turrets of the Alhambra.

The Moors seemed satisfied with their new masters, and the partial change of government which ensued; so that King Ferdinand returned to Seville, leaving the subdued city in apparent tranquillity. This calm was, however, but of short duration. Strong symptoms of disaffection were soon observable in the conduct of the vanquished Moors, and the murmurs of discontent which prevailed in every quarter, shortly terminated in open revolt.

The Archbishop of Toledo, in his intemperate zeal for the conversion of the infidels, had adopted measures which tended rather to increase their natural aversion to the Christian religion, than to wean them from a creed, the mandates of which were in greater harmony with their habits and inclination. The prelate seeing his designs thwarted by the inhabitants of the Albaycin, commissioned one of his officers to arrest those whom he suspected of promoting the opposition. This last ill-advised and imprudent step so greatly exasperated the malcontents, that no sooner did the alguazil proceed to the discharge of his duty, than he became a victim to their fury. Imprecations were first heaped upon him; menaces succeeded; and finally a large stone,

---

[1] The unfortunate passion of Don Rodrigo, the last of the Goths, for Florinda, surnamed La Cava, was the primary cause of the Moorish invasion, and the disastrous wars which followed. Count Julian, father of the frail fair one, highly indignant at the affront he had received, resolved to take the most signal vengeance. His views were warmly espoused by Don Oppas, Archbishop of Toledo, who was the most influential man in the kingdom. These two noblemen betrayed their country to the Moors, who, invited by them, landed in Spain, under the command of Tarik and Muza.

hurled from a window, stretched the unfortunate officer lifeless an the ground.

This murder was the signal for open rebellion. The Moors were aware that so flagrant an act could not escape an adequate punishment, and they accordingly prepared themselves for a vigorous resistance. Some of the most daring hurried from street to street, summoning their fellow-countrymen to arms, and exclaiming that the articles of the treaty, in virtue of which they had surrendered, were violated, since they could not continue unmolested in the exercise of their religious duties.

This untoward event was the occasion of great anxiety to the Count de Tendilla, who had been entrusted with the government of the city by the queen. He took active measures to subdue the increasing fury of the malcontents. But desirous of trying the effect of negociation before he had recourse to extremes, he set forth to the rebels, in the strongest light, the criminality and madness of the enterprise in which they had embarked, and the little probability of their ever again struggling with success against the Christian power. All his efforts to restore order proved for some time ineffectual. But the promise of amnesty and redress of their grievances, the well known integrity of the count, and his generosity in sending his lady and son as hostages for the fulfilment of the treaty, induced at length the majority of the rebels to lay down their arms and accept the proffered pardon.

The forty chiefs, however, who had been chosen by the insurgents, considered this conduct as pusillanimous, and despised it accordingly. Dazzled by dreams of ambition, fired with hopes of asserting their independence, and aware that the wild recesses of the mountains afforded facilities for conducting the war with greater security and success; they fled from Granada in the night, and succeeded in instilling their sentiments into the minds of the Moors who inhabited the adjacent country. The towns of Guejar, Lanjaron and Andarax soon rose up in arms; all the mountaineers of the Alpujarras followed the example, and the Christians were threatened with the loss of those acquisitions, which their valour and perseverance had so nobly won.

It is at this interesting period that the following romance takes place; and some of the subsequent events of the rebellion form the historical portion of its subject.

CHAPTER II.

We are up in arms,
If not to fight with foreign enemies,
Yet to beat down these rebels here at home.

Shakespeare.

Alarming accounts of the resolution taken by the insurgents being communicated to the queen, she lost no time in adopting measures for the preservation of her power. She summoned around her all those counsellors in whose judgment she had ever confided, and those champions on whose valour, in the hour of danger, she firmly relied.

At the upper end of the hall of audience in which they were now assembled, was seen the queen seated on a magnificent throne, over which was suspended a rich canopy of crimson velvet. Isabella could scarcely be considered at first sight as one born to command; her stature was not above the middle size; but there was a certain air of dignity which pervaded her every action. The mildness which beamed in her bright blue eye seemed rather to act as a persuasive to the observance of her mandates, than as a command, and her displeasure was manifested more by reproaches than by threats. Few women could boast of greater personal attractions—none a better regulated mind; if fault there were, it might be traced in the cloud which darkened her brow, when a consciousness of what was due to religion stood most prominently forward. At such times she became severe and abstracted; and yet her occasional austerity could hardly be condemned by her subjects, when it led to that firmness and courage, and that inflexibility in the decrees of justice, for which she was so remarkable. If the grave historian has stamped her character with these attributes of heroism, what scope may not be allowed to the writer of historical fiction? Distinguished by his noble bearing and his honorable station, on the right hand of the queen stood the renowned Alonso de Aguilar, the terror of the Moorish name. He had, like his brother, the heroic Gonzalo de Cordova, particularly distinguished himself in the wars against Granada, and was honored with the regard and unlimited confidence of Isabella. Of a lofty and imposing stature, he united with gigantic strength an air of dignity which well became the most accomplished warrior of the age. His noble countenance wore an expression of resolution and intrepidity, blended with openness and candour, that inspired the beholder with sentiments of awe and admiration. His fine athletic form was rendered more interesting from its still retaining the elasticity of ardent youth, unsubdued by the chill of fifty winters, which he had chiefly spent in the toils of the camp. His character bore out the impression thus formed in his favor. The active courage of his earlier days was chastened, not subdued, by the experience of a more mature age; whilst the furrows on his manly brow, and the few gray locks that slightly silvered his raven hair, heightened the feeling of respect and veneration which his many virtues were so well calculated to inspire.

On the opposite side stood Don Iñigo Mendoza, Count de Tendilla, Governor of Granada, a man who had numerous claims to the gratitude of Spain.—Nor was it the least, that of being father of a son, who afterwards served his country in the triple capacities of a valiant soldier, an enlightened statesman, and a profound scholar.

Near these warriors were seen the Master of the Order of Calatrava, the Aleayde de los Donceles, Count Ureña, and other renowned chiefs. The rest of the nobles, taking precedence, according to their rank, completed this imposing assembly.

An universal silence prevailed, and every one seemed impatient to ascertain the object of the council to which they had been so hastily summoned, the nature of which they could only conjecture.

But from these noble ranks, a gallant knight was absent—one who, though young in years, was already a veteran in military achievements, and whose brilliant abilities had won him the right of sharing with these distinguished personages the marked favor of his sovereign.— Gomez Arias was not there, and Alonso de Aguilar, who considered him already as his son, felt chagrined at his unavoidable absence.

This young nobleman was now a voluntary exile from court, and nowise anxious to appear at Granada, where his presence would be attended with danger. Neither his own merits, nor the influence of Aguilar, could induce Isabella to deviate from the path of justice, loudly demanded by the family and friends of Don Rodrigo de Cespedes, who, at that time, was stretched on a bed of sickness, in consequence of a dangerous wound inflicted by Gomez Arias, his fortunate rival in the affections of Leonor de Aguilar.

The members of the council, with this solitary exception, being assembled, the queen rose to address them.—"Noble Christians," she said, "my friends and brave defenders! You are no doubt already aware of the important motive which summons you to our presence. Unless a speedy remedy be applied, we are threatened with the loss of those territories for which we have so long toiled, and which have been purchased with the dearest blood in Spain. Again the noble patriotic fire which animates you must be called forth, and the redoubled strength of your arms be displayed against the enemies of our faith and native land. Scarcely had you, by courage and perseverance, reduced this last strong hold of Granada, and compelled the Moors to surrender the inheritance of our forefathers, when the seeds of discontent were sown, and sprung into open rebellion. Whatever may have been the complaints of the inhabitants of the Albaycin, it was by calm remonstrance, and by applications to our throne of justice, that they ought to have sought redress; not by the force of arms, in which they have had but too many occasions to acknowledge our superiority.—Our officers of justice have been insulted, and one of them has been murdered in the discharge of his duty. The prudent and active conduct of the Count de Tendilla succeeded in putting down the first commotion, but the leaders of the outrage have sought, in the wild passes of the Alpujarras, to conduct by stratagem a war which they are not able to sustain against us in the field. Let us then hasten to chastise their insolence before the evil gain ground. Not that I entertain any doubts of success, but for the purpose of saving the valuable lives which such procrastination might endanger. Amongst the rebel chiefs, who appear to possess in the greatest degree the confidence of their comrades, and most resolutely to defy our power, are el Negro,[1] of Lanjaron, and el Feri de Benastepar. The former, blockaded in the Castle of Lanjaron, will not long brave a siege; but the latter is a more formidable enemy, and being well acquainted with the innermost passes of those wild mountains, will offer a greater resistance. Against this man, therefore, our chief efforts must be directed."

---

[1] The Black.

She then took a banner, on which was splendidly emblazoned the arms of Castile and Arragon.—"To thee, Don Alonso de Aguilar," she said, "do we intrust the chief command in this expedition, and to thy care and keeping do we commit this precious gage, which thou must fix on the summit of the Alpujarras."

Saying this, she delivered the standard to the veteran warrior. He bowed on receiving it, and the fire of enthusiasm kindled in his dark eyes as he knelt, and kissed the hand of the donor; then waving the banner on high, he exclaimed—"All that human efforts can achieve, will I do. My Liege, from your hands Alonso de Aguilar receives this pledge of royal favor, and he will not prove ungrateful for the noble distinction. Yes, I will punish these accursed infidels, and this sacred standard shall not be separated from me till it streams in triumph on the summit of the mountain. Noble warriors," he continued with a burst of exultation—"if this banner be lost, search for it in the midst of slaughtered Moors—there you will find it, dyed in the blood, but still in the grasp of Alonso de Aguilar."

As he uttered these words, he again raised the banner on high, and the surrounding chiefs sent forth, simultaneously, a shout of approbation. Isabella then motioning with her hand to command attention, again addressed the council.—"Listen further to our sovereign decree. From this time let no one of our subjects hold communion or any intercourse whatever with the rebels. The least infringement of this order shall be accounted treason, and the transgressor shall be dealt with according to the law. Let an edict be proclaimed, that no one may plead ignorance of its purport."

The chiefs now gradually withdrew; and Don Alonso having made his obeisance, was likewise about to retire, when his royal mistress detained him.—"Stay, Aguilar. It grieves me much that the marriage of thy daughter should be thus deferred, nay, perhaps set aside, by the unfortunate adventure of her lover with Don Rodrigo de Cespedes. How is the wounded man?"

"Most gracious Queen"—replied Don Alonso, "I have received intelligence that he is even now considered almost out of danger. The issue of a few days will determine, and then if the result be favorable, I may safely welcome the return of Don Lope Gomez Arias."

"As good a knight as Spain can boast"—returned the queen—"and possessed of those accomplishments which insure the favor of our sex. But I hear he has a failing, which, as a woman, I ought rather to call a grievous fault. I am told he is of a very fickle character. Is not your Leonor alarmed at the reported inconstancy of her future husband?"

"Is she not the child of Aguilar?"—proudly cried the warrior—"And where is the man that dared wrong one of that name?"

"Nay," replied Isabella, in the most condescending tone and manner, "I do not mean that Leonor will repent her choice when once made; she has attractions to fix the most volatile and inconstant of men; and I sincerely hope that Gomez Arias will have discernment sufficient to appreciate them."

"Don Lope is not so fickle as some have wished your Highness to believe," observed Don Alonso. "Moreover, I use no compulsion; they love each other well, and I only am concerned that their marriage should not be celebrated before I march against el Feri de Benastepar. In the face of danger I would then feel tranquil, from the consciousness that there was one to protect my child, should aught happen to her father in this hazardous expedition."

"The daughter of Don Alonso de Aguilar"—replied the queen—"can never need one to supply her father's place whilst Isabella lives. She shall remain constantly with me, and I shall be gratified to manifest by my attention and kindness to Leonor, the high estimation in which I hold her father. But how does it happen that you are not the *Mantenedor* of the lists in the games of to-morrow?"

"One more capable than myself has already assumed the charge. Besides, I can feel little interested with the display of a tournament, when we are shortly to meet the enemy in mortal encounter. These sports suit well with gay young cavaliers, but not with veterans like myself. Those gallant knights have admiring ladies to look upon their prowess, and reward their success. But my only ambition is to sustain the laurels earned in bloody fray against the enemy of my country,—to gain the approbation of that country, and the favor of its greatest ornament,—my noble sovereign."

The resolute and manly tone in which Don Alonso spoke, perfectly accorded with the frankness and generosity of his character. He bent his knee as he pressed to his lips the extended hand of his queen.

"And well hast thou deserved that favor," she exclaimed, "my best, and most faithful friend: thy country will pay with gratitude thy long proved services. Go; prosper in thy brilliant career!"

The remainder of the day was passed in preparations for the games of the morrow. Gallant knights were busily engaged in preparing their accoutrements, and examining their armour, whilst many a fair hand was as anxiously occupied in ornamenting the devices, and arranging the colours of the favored knight. The city was thronged with visitors, the inhabitants of the adjacent country having been attracted by the fame of the reported games, insomuch that Granada could not hold her numerous guests. For more accommodation, numerous temporary tents had been pitched along the smiling plain of the Vega. The voices of vacant joy and revelry were heard on all sides, and the warriors and irregular groups, moving along in all the recklessness of anticipated pleasure, presented a gay and lively picture.

CHAPTER III.

> Cada uno dellos mientes tiene al so,
> Abrazan los escudos delant los corazones:
> Abaxan las lauzas abueltas con los pendones;
> Enclinaban las caras sobre los arzones:
> Batien los cavallos con los espolones,
> Tembrar quierie la tierra dod eran movedores.
> *Poema del Cid.*

The morning arrived, and the entrances to the lists were thronged by the inhabitants of Granada and their visitors; all anxious to witness a display which it was expected would surpass in magnificence any thing of the kind they had ever seen. A large piece of ground, perfectly level and free from impediment, had been appropriately chosen without the walls of the city, for the exhibition of the games of strength, valour, and skill, and a temporary gallery had been constructed, extending on either side to the extremity of the lists. At the end nearest the city, was erected a temporary wooden fortress, painted in imitation of stone-work, curiously fabricated, covered over with canvas, and capable of containing a number of men-at-arms. On the front turret of this castle streamed a large banner, on which was emblazoned a red cross decorated with gold, being the arms of the order of Calatrava, of which the *Mantenedor*[1] was the grand master. Other smaller banners were placed around it, and they appertained to the four knights, who had volunteered to support the *Mantenedor*, and who, in conjunction with him, were bound to accept the challenge of all knights adventurers disposed to encounter them. On each side of the castle were two

---

[1] Champion of the Lists.

tents, before which were placed the pennon and shield of the knights to whom they belonged, and at the entrance stood a squire, ready to meet the demands of all comers.

Directly facing the castle, at the other extremity of the lists, was pitched a large and magnificent pavilion, ornamented with little pennons, and numberless armorial devices curiously interwoven with gold and silver thread on green silk brocade. Before it were artificially grouped swords, lances, shields, and every description of armour, emblematical of the intent to which the pavilion was appropriated, it being set apart for the use of those knights who were willing to enter the lists against the *Mantenedor* and his assistants. About the middle of the gallery on the right of the castle, a platform had been erected for the accommodation of the queen and her retinue. It was covered with scarlet cloth, and shaded by a rich canopy of purple brocade, on the top of which were seen the royal and united arms of Arragon and Castile shining in burnished gold. The whole of this platform was occupied by the maids of honour, and other principal ladies, as well as the noblemen and gentlemen of the court. In front of the place occupied by the queen, were stationed the umpires of the tournament, whose duty it was to decide the merits of the candidates, and award the prizes. Other places on either side of the throne were allotted to the various nobility and gentry of Granada, whilst the two extremities of this gallery and the whole of the other were assigned to the public, without any claim to precedence, but that of a priority of occupation.

And now the ponderous bells of the cathedral filled the air with their tolling; and immediately the bands of martial instruments within the lists, struck up a glorious and enlivening strain, in signal of the queen's approach.

At length she made her appearance, surrounded by a numerous suite, and heartily was she welcomed by the multitude, whose joy at the sight of their beloved sovereign was equal to the anticipated pleasure of the tournament.

Isabella was sumptuously attired in a rich dress of crimson velvet, ornamented with pearls. A delicate and costly scarf, of the finest lace, was attached to the back part of her head, and covered with its graceful folds her beautiful neck and shoulders. On this splendid scarf were wrought in gold thread, lions and castles, and other insignia of the arms of Spain. The queen wore likewise the crosses of the orders of Santiago and Calatrava, richly studded with diamonds and precious gems of immense value.

The lists now offered a most dazzling and noble spectacle. On one side was displayed all the splendour of the court, and the sparkling jewellery, the costly attire, and the waving plumes indicated the spot where the rank and beauty of Spain was assembled in all its glory and magnificence. Indeed towards this part of the lists the attention was more particularly directed, as in all courteous exhibitions of martial prowess, the interest is chiefly centered in those objects, to win whose smile lances are broken and helmets shivered.—Nor was the feeling of enthusiasm on beholding this scene lessened by the appearance of the opposite gallery, which, though more humble, nevertheless contributed, by the variety and gaiety of their costume, together with the cheerful animation expressed in their countenances, to the general effect of the picture. Then the proud display of all the panoplies of the court; the rich waving plumage of the crests; the lustre of the burnished shields and polished armour, together with the neighing of the spirited charger that caracolled the lists, and the warlike strains that at intervals floated on the air, powerfully tended to strike the imagination and inspire the heart to deeds of chivalry and arms.

A flourish of trumpets and clarions now indicated that the tournament was about to commence. In a few moments therefore the lists were cleared, with the exception of the heralds, who, gorgeously equipped in suits of crimson and gold, and attended by trumpeters, advanced to the four corners of the lists to proclaim the challenge. It was couched in the formula of chivalric language, which it would be superfluous here to transcribe. The meaning, however, was, that the *Mantenedor* and his supporters, Don Manuel Ponce de Leon, the Alcayde de los Donceles, Count Cifuentes, and Don Antonio de Leyva, invited all knights adventurers to break lances, if they were hardy enough to dispute their right to the lists. As soon as the challenge had been pronounced, the heralds retired to their posts; when the trumpets sounded again, the gates of the castle were thrown open, and the five challengers came forward.

Nothing could surpass the richness of their harness, the splendour of their armour, and the gallantry of their bearing. The grand master was attired in a costly suit of steel, the corslet of which was entirely burnished with silver, and the ornaments chased with the same precious metal. Over this he wore a short mantle of white velvet, which was the colour he had adopted. On his shield, upon a field argent, was portrayed the red cross of Calatrava, which he also bore on his breast, and which was surrounded with the following device—"*Por esta y por mi Rey.*"[1]

Don Manuel Ponce de Leon next fixed the attention of the spectators; his armour was the same as the *Mantenedor*'s, excepting that the *ropa*[2] which hung from his shoulder was crimson. On his ample buckler were emblazoned the bars of the arms of Arragon, granted to his warlike ancestors by the kings of that country; and likewise quartered thereon, was a lion rampant, in field argent, a device which, tradition says, was adopted by the famous Trojan, Hector, from whom the old French chroniclers assert the Ponces de Leon to be descended. Beneath the arms was legible in red letters the motto—"*Soy como mi nombre.*"[3]

The armour of the other knights was made to correspond with that of the *Mantenedor*, the only distinguishing mark being the colour of the *ropas*, and the different device which each bore upon his shield, either as indicative of his feelings, or from the armorial bearings of his family. The colour of the spirited chargers of these challengers was snow white. Nothing could exceed the beauty of their proportions and the splendour of their trappings. They beat the ground with short quick tramp, and shook the white foam from their mouths, as they fretted at the discipline by which their fiery ardour was restrained. They were caparisoned with long housings of costly brocade, and ornamented with gold or silver, according to the colour of the rider's dress, and their manes and tails were decorated with knots of gay ribbons.

The five challengers now advanced at a stately pace, till they arrived before the queen, when, with a graceful and simultaneous motion, they made their horses kneel down; and after saluting the courtly retinue with their lances, they caracolled round the lists, as if to reconnoitre their dominions. At last, after various martial evolutions, in which they were accompanied by the animating strains of the music, they proceeded to the middle of the lists—there they halted, and, throwing down their gauntlets, retreated to the castle in the same order in which they had advanced. The trumpets then sounded, and immediately there was a rush of gallant knights, who pricked into the lists, all eager to take up these tokens of defiance. So upon retiring, five of their number, who had succeeded in securing the gage, came forward from the pavilion. The champions wore fine Spanish shirts of mail,

---

[1] For this and for my King.
[2] A kind of small mantle.
[3] I am like my name.

with a polished breast-plate inlaid with gold, and their pliant barbs of raven black, seemed to have been chosen to contrast with those of the challengers. The helmets of the knights were almost hidden in a shadowing plumage of white and red feathers. The chief of this gallant band declined giving his name, though he was known to his four companions, who pledged themselves for him. However, from the superior courage and address which the strange knight afterwards displayed, it was generally believed that he could be no other than the renowned Gonzalo de Cordova, who, from a pique in a momentary fit of passion, had withdrawn from court, and lost the friendship of the queen. The other four knights were easily distinguished by their devices and colours. Amongst them, the most conspicuous, appeared the young Don Pedro, son of Don Alonso de Aguilar. He carried himself with a bearing far superior to his years, and inspired a general interest, both on his own account and for that of his illustrious sire. On his shield he bore a golden eagle, emblematical of his name, flying towards heaven, and carrying in his claws a bleeding Moor. Underneath was the motto—

"Le subiré hasta el cielo,
Porque dé mayor caida."[1]

This shield belonged to Alonso de Aguilar himself, who was no less pleased than surprised that his son should have chosen such a device for the occasion. But every one applauded the young Don Pedro for that unconquerable hatred towards the enemies of his country, which he had inherited from his ancestors, and which engrossed their thoughts even in pastimes and games. By the side of Don Pedro, rode Garcilaso de la Vega, who was proud to bear the brazen shield which he had inherited from his father, and upon which was displayed the bleeding head of a Moor, hanging on a black charger's tail, and round which were the words—"*Ave Maria*"—a device which the Garcilasos wore in commemoration of the famous single combat which one of their house had sustained against the fierce Moor Audala, who, with impious insolence, had interwoven the sacred salutation to the virgin, in token of derision, in his horse's tail. The two other champions were the Count de Ureña and young Sayavedra, both equally renowned in that age of chivalry, brave and gallant knights.

---

[1] I will bear him to the skies, That he may have the greater fall.

Gomez Arias; or The Moors of the Alpujarras.

They now proceeded to the castle, and after the ceremony of striking twice the gong which was placed beside it, and selecting their tents, they again retreated. The five challengers next presented themselves, and a desperate encounter was anticipated. Indeed ten more valiant knights were scarcely to be found in all Spain, and their acknowledged skill promised a display of more than usual interest for the beholders.

At the signal given, they rushed impetuously forward, yet such was their perfection in horsemanship, and so well trained and disciplined were their chargers, that they all arrived at the middle of the lists at the same time, meeting in a shock, the abrupt and fearful clash of which seemed as if it had been the effect of a single but awful concussion. The lances were splintered to the very hilts, but the knights resumed their places amidst the loud applause of the multitude. Again they darted with the velocity of the wind, and again they met with the same precision, but not with the same success; for in this encounter the challengers were considered the victors—the two chiefs alone having sustained no injury—their lances broke as before, but they remained firm and erect in their saddle. Not so with the rest—for young Don Pedro was not able to withstand the superior force of Ponce de Leon's more manly age. Garcilaso was unhorsed by Don Antonio de Leyva, and the two others sustained great inconvenience from the Alcayde and Count Cifuentes.

The shouts of the spectators, and the flourish of instruments, proclaimed the victory of the *Mantenedor* and his supporters, who retired to the castle with their good fortune, ready to meet the demands of all other adventurers. The chief of the vanquished party who had so handsomely maintained his ground against the Maestre, now signified his intention of encountering that champion singly; but in this he was opposed by the marshals of the games, who declared that after the demand of his challenge had been acceded to, he could not, according to the rules, encounter again the same knight on that day. The matter was referred to the judges, who decided against the stranger chief, and he was accordingly obliged to desist from his purpose.

Great was the joy of the *Mantenedor* and his associates, who, having vanquished the most formidable knights, proudly imagined that all who might now appear, would afford an easy victory. Indeed this opinion seemed generally to prevail, as for some time no one shewed himself in the lists to dispute their supremacy.

Don Pedro, vexed at heart, now mounted a strong charger—rode up to the castle, and challenged the *Mantenedor* himself. Don Alonso de

Aguilar saw the noble daring of his son at once with pleasure and dismay; for although he was overjoyed to perceive him possessed of such undaunted courage, he yet trembled for the consequences of his temerity.

The gong sounded twice—the Maestre appeared, and was struck at the presumption of the young adventurer.—They took their places—the trumpets gave the signal—forward the champions started, and at the first meeting displayed such an equality that the whole place rung with acclamations. Indeed this was the most important encounter, and every one waited its issue in breathless expectation—the ladies in particular, always interested where youth dares against manhood, waved their kerchiefs and scarfs to animate the young knight, whose heart in sooth needed no such stimulus. In the second encounter, however, he was not equally fortunate; for the *Mantenedor*, jealous of his fame, now risked against a youth, stood more on his guard, and summoned all his might and skill to his assistance.—Don Pedro was unable to withstand the shock; the lance flew unharmed from his grasp, and he was compelled to leave the field honorably, but still in possession of the challengers.

The castle now sent forth a blast of clarions, in sign of triumph and defiance, whilst at the pavilion, no knight evinced any desire of renewing the engagement. In this state of suspense, some time elapsed, and the heralds, according to form, proceeded to summon the knights adventurers, but no one appeared—again ten minutes elapsed, and a second summons was pronounced, but again it met with no answer. The triumph of the *Mantenedor* now seemed certain, and the heralds were about to utter the third and last proclamation, when, lo! a knight was seen riding at full speed towards the lists, and, after thundering at the barrier for admittance, without further ceremony, was directing his course to the castle, when his career was arrested by the marshals, as no one could pretend to enter the lists against the challengers, without previously delivering his name and titles, or at least presenting a known friend to vouch for his being a true and loyal knight.

The incognito knight was accordingly obliged to give way; but making a sign to the herald not to proceed to the third summons, he rode up to Don Pedro and, taking him aside, conferred with him in secret. Young Aguilar immediately advanced with visible surprise and pleasure, and pledged himself for his new companion. This circumstance, no less than the general appearance of the champion in question, commanded universal interest and attention. He was completely accoutred in a blue steel armour, over which he wore a short mantle of black velvet, sumptuously adorned with gold. On his burnished helmet he wore a profusion of white and sable feathers, and on his lance streamed a pennon of the same colours. His breast was covered with a ponderous shield, bearing no device, but the solitary motto—*"Conocelle por sus fechos."*[1] The incognito knight brought with him neither squire nor page, and there was an air of mystery about his person that tended considerably to heighten the interest which his sudden appearance had already excited.

He now rushed impetuously towards the castle, when the charger seemed to be under no command, and the knight was apparently in peril of being dashed to pieces;—a simultaneous cry of terror burst from the surrounding multitude, when the incognito knight on the point of being hurled against the wall of the castle, and at the distance of scarcely two feet, suddenly reined up, and both he and his charger appeared rooted to the ground. A burst of admiration now superseded the terror which his precipitous career had occasioned, and every one was lost in conjectures relating to the incognito knight. The noble arrogance of the motto—*"Conocelle por sus fechos,"* made them better appreciate the feat he had just performed. He advanced to the gong, and sounded a redoubled and protracted peal, and flourishing his lance in the face of the castle and tents, indicated his willingness to do battle with all. This daring act excited a second burst of applause, and the astonished challengers appeared at the castle in a mood of mixed perplexity and indignant pride. The incognito knight, however, vaulted on his charger, and then retreated to await the pleasure of the *Mantenedor*; who, according to rank, was the first to engage. The flourish of trumpets acted as a signal, and the champions rushed against each other at full speed; the shock was tremendous—the lances were shivered, and the powerful chargers staggered with the violent concussion. The champions taking new lances, prepared for a second encounter, when the horse of the *Mantenedor*, either from sudden fright or other cause, swerved in the middle of its career, and its master, being obliged to deviate from his intended aim, would have offered an easy victory to his antagonist. The knight, however, generously refused to take advantage of this accident, and, making a demi-volte, returned to await the *Mantenedor*'s leisure. But the latter, overcome by the courteous behaviour of his adversary, declined a second encounter, and retired to the castle.

---

[1] Know him by his deeds.

Don Manuel Ponce de Leon next advanced, happy in the opportunity which chance offered him of gathering the laurels, which his principal had forgone. This knight, in the opinion of many, was the most formidable of the five challengers—the repeated single combats in which he had engaged against the Moors, and other feats of arms, having won for him very great reputation. He came therefore into the lists, as if conscious of his powers, and fully confident of success. In the first shock, there was a slight advantage on his part, having succeeded in striking his lance so forcibly, and directly on the breast-plate of his adversary, that the incognito knight was observed somewhat to stagger; while Don Manuel remained immoveable as a rock—however, as no decided advantage could be claimed, the two champions prepared to renew the engagement. Again the swift-footed steeds fly over the lists, and again the combatants meet with a terrific clash. It proved unfortunate for Ponce de Leon, who was dealt such a severe blow, that had it not been for the extreme goodness of his armour, the queen would have lost one of her most gallant warriors. As it was, the saddle girths broke, and the horse, unable to withstand the shock, staggered backward—tottered, and rolled over, throwing his rider, with a tremendous fall, into the middle of the lists. Ponce de Leon with difficulty arose, having received a sore contusion, and was assisted back to the castle, from whence the Alcayde de los Donceles soon issued forth, intent upon revenging the disgrace of his companion. He offered, however, a faint resistance; for the incognito knight, at every encounter, appeared to acquire new strength. The opposition afforded by Count de Cifuentes was still weaker; the unfortunate knight being fairly unhorsed in such a manner, that he seemed for a moment to be carried on the point of his antagonist's lance to the ground. The shouts of the spectators, and the peal of instruments redoubled at every new proof of strength and skill thus manifested, and the triumph of the incognito knight was hailed as certain. He had now only to meet the youngest; and, to the opinion of all, the least renowned of the challengers. Young Don Antonio de Leyva, however, by the martial and undaunted manner in which he came forward, showed that he was in no ways intimidated by the repeated and extraordinary good fortune of the doughty champion.

The trumpets sounded—the lances are couched—the horses started—the silence is intense—when, with one fearful resounding clash, the knights meet—the charm is broken, and all is converted into an uproar of wonder and delight.—The champions, though so unequal in all appearances, now proved to be fairly matched—both lances descended from the air in splinters, and the tremendous shock which the combatants had sustained, appeared to produce no other effect than to check their steeds in their impetuous course. The knights soon recovered and regained their stations.—Again the signal is heard—and again they speed with the swiftness of the arrow—the lances break, and both the horses recede with the violent shock.—Surprise and delight agitate the bosom of the spectators.—Hope inspires the drooping spirits of the *Mantenedor* and those of the castle.—Disappointment and vexation rage in the heart of the incognito knight. He made a movement of impatient anger, as he grasped firmly the lance which was now presented to him, and poised it as if to ascertain its consistency; then, making a circuit with his steed, he appeared resolved to put a termination to the hopes of his adversary in the present encounter.— With a desperate start he rushed headlong against his opponent, who, aware of the furious attack he was about to sustain, collected all his might to meet it with a suitable resistance.—The incognito knight inclined himself more forward on his horse, and turned his aim full at the breast of his antagonist, while Don Antonio, who perceived his intention, resolved to direct his lance towards his adversary's head, which, though a difficult manœuvre, would, if successful, insure the advantage.—The incognito knight, however, broke the tendency of the blow by suddenly inclining his head forward, while the anger that boiled within his bosom, so powerfully seconded his efforts, that the gallant Don Antonio fell, bearing, however, his adversary backwards on his seat, and carrying away, on the point of his lance, the plumage that adorned his casque.

The victory was now completed, and the whole place resounded with shouts of admiration. The incognito knight having thus vanquished the champions, for some time gallantly paraded the lists, making his obedient and tutored steed perform several graceful evolutions. Then suddenly advancing before the throne of the queen, he lowered the point of his lance and made his charger to kneel. Passing onwards to Leonor de Aguilar, he again made the graceful salute, whilst a shower of many-colored ribbons, white and highly-scented gloves, flowers, and other favors, fell profusely from fair hands—a due tribute to bravery and skill. Having performed this mark of courtesy, without waiting to receive the guerdon he had so well merited, he applied spurs to his horse and was soon lost to the sight of the delighted and admiring multitude.

The incognito knight became the subject of general speculation— he had overcome five champions to whom the court of Isabella could afford no equals—only one man perhaps might be capable of such valorous achievements, but he was now an exile whom the law pursued, and whose appearance in the lists would be attended with danger. Still the extraordinary prowess of the knight, and the circumstance of Don Pedro coming forward to answer for him when he entered the lists, left no room to doubt that he was that illustrious exile. Indeed the significant smile which the queen directed to Alonso de Aguilar, when the champion saluted his daughter, and the blush that mantled on the cheek of that lady implied a perfect recognition of her lover.

His absence from the lists gave the judges an opportunity of awarding the principal prize to Don Antonio de Leyva, by whom, according to their own, as well as the general opinion, it was more justly merited. The different bands now struck up a martial air; the queen departed with her numerous and splendid train, and every one retired from the lists, perfectly satisfied with the sports of the day, to spend the remainder of it in feasting and discussing the various merits of the knights who had afforded them so much pleasure.

CHAPTER IV.

> Poi la Vittoria da quel canto stia,
> Che vorra la divina providenza:
> Il cavalier non havrà colpa alcuna,
> Ma il tutto impulterassi à la fortuna.
> *Ariosto.*

The following morning shone equally bright as the preceding, and the expectations of the public were equally sanguine. The same pomp and ceremony presided in the court; the same precision and gallant deportment was observable in the knights, the heralds, and all other persons connected with the sports.

As these, however, as far as concerned the tournament, were but a repetition of the antecedent day, and more to be enjoyed by being an active witness than a passive reader of them, we will not dwell on the subject further than to observe, that those of the castle sustained the challenge most gallantly. Although many were the fresh arrivals of adventurers who fearlessly advanced to engage the *Mantenedor* and his comrades, none were sufficiently accomplished to bear away the palm. Indeed, the incognito knight, the most redoubtable of all the combatants, either from fear of discovery, or from some secret injunction, had abstained from making a second appearance in the lists.

The signal was now given, and the heralds proclaimed that the games of valour and strength were ended, and those of skill about to commence.

An interval of two hours was employed in clearing the lists, and preparing the ground for the *juego de la sortija*,[1] which was peculiarly

---

[1] The game of the Ring.

gratifying to the queen. This intermediate time was devoted by the assembled and motley crowd, to the rational, and provident purpose of a substantial repast.

A tall and slight pine tree, beautifully decorated with ribbons, was placed in the ground, and a gold ring of proportion suitable to the occasion, suspended on one of the projecting branches, under which the candidates were to pass at full career. The queen herself resolved to reward the victor with her own royal hand. Her portrait, superbly set in sparkling jewellery, and hanging on a ponderous gold chain of curious workmanship, was suspended by her side—a meet reward for the successful competitor. The nature of the guerdon, the quality of the bestower, and the circumstance that there was but one prize to be obtained, greatly stimulated the emulation of every knight to deserve an honor the more desirable from its admitting of no participation.

Chirimias, dulzainas,[1] and other musical instruments which are now grown obsolete, but which in those days were in high request, now filled the air with harmony, while the attention of the gay and motley concourse was arrested by the sudden arrival of heralds on horseback, gorgeously apparelled, and preceded by black slaves playing on the cymbals. These paraded the lists for a short time, and then retiring to their posts, gave way to beautiful pages, mounted on elegant palfreys, and attired in costly silken dresses of light blue, bedizened with ribbons, and bearing a turban of crimson velvet with white feathers. These pages carried before them the light and slender lances appropriated for the games, and having deposited them near the queen, they retired and took their stations opposite to the troop of heralds and black musicians.

The attention of the public was then simultaneously attracted to the four corners of the lists, from whence four quadrilles of equestrians proceeded, all vieing with each other in the richness of their dresses, the splendor of ornaments, and the gaiety of their bearing. These quadrilles were distinguished by the different colours which they wore, and out of each were selected three champions to dispute the prize. At the signal given, they started severally according to the order of prece-

---

[1] The Chirimia was a musical instrument made of wood, resembling somewhat a wooden flageolet, though much longer: it contained ten holes; the wind pipe was thin, and made of reed. Præcentoria tuba, fistula musica. The Dulzaina was an instrument like the Chirimia, only upon a smaller scale, and capable of producing sounds more acute and sharp.—Tibia.

dence, which had been obtained by casting lots, and in the first course seven candidates passed their lances clearly through the ring, carrying it along in their headlong career.

The music sounded a flourish, and the seven competitors underwent another trial, in which only two were successful—young Garcilaso, and Antonio de Leyva. The contest was now to be divided by the two, and pink and green were the colours that contended for the victory; accordingly their quadrilles, as well as the spectators of both sexes who had adopted those colours, awaited the result of the contest, with anxious suspense. Garcilaso now made a graceful curvet, and spring at once with the celerity of an arrow, in the middle of his precipitous career he extended his lance with perfect ease and dexterity, and again carried away the ring. Don Antonio next advanced; and having indulged for a short space in several feats of horsemanship, he sped towards the honored tree on which was suspended victory or defeat. His horsemanship was so perfect that, excepting the feather on his head which streamed before the wind, all appeared like the figure of a centaur, flying meteor-like along the plain. His lance, however, missed the middle of the ring, and touching one of its edges, such was the rapidity of Don Antonio's motion that the ring sprung high in the air, when the dexterous cavalier, to the admiration of the surrounding multitude, turned short, and before the ring had time to fall, he caught it fairly with his lance. This extraordinary feat excited universal applause, and some even vociferated that Don Antonio was deservedly entitled to the prize. However, as Garcilaso had likewise succeeded in carrying away the ring, the candidates were obliged to refer to another trial, which was decided in favor of young de Leyva, who was immediately escorted by the triumphant party to receive the reward amidst the exhilarating strains of the music, and the acclamation of the vast concourse.

As soon as the victorious cavalcade arrived near the queen, Don Antonio and the chief of the quadrille vaulted nimbly from their horses, when the conqueror knelt at the feet of his gracious sovereign, who, with a condescending smile, threw the portrait round his neck.

"Wear this," she then said, "in commemoration of thy skill, and the regard of Isabella. Remember that this gift is a gage of my royal word to accord to the bearer any boon he may have to demand. Upon the presentation of this token it shall be granted. My royal word is passed."

Don Antonio humbly kissed the hand of his queen, and mingling again with his party, they paraded the place in ceremonial triumph, previous to their departure. The feats of De Leyva, both in the tourney and the game of the ring, had secured for him the admiration of all the spectators, and more particularly amongst the fairer part. Many were the glances bestowed upon him by sparkling eyes and many a gentle bosom beat high with emotion as he inclined towards them his handsome figure in graceful salutations.—Even the proud Leonor could not entirely conceal the inward satisfaction she felt at the triumph of the young Don Antonio; for, notwithstanding her efforts, she could but ill disguise a latent feeling of interest and delight. Certainly it was not love; for, according to general opinion, she had irretrievably fixed her affections on another object. But yet she was in that state of mind which is more easily felt than described; a state too glowing to be called mere friendship—too cold to be denominated love; it was something between both—a tender sentiment of regard towards one whom she was taught to consider her inferior in point of rank and fortune.

Leonor de Aguilar had inherited from her warlike father that pride and loftiness of spirit which in some measure spurned the softer sensations of the heart. She scarcely believed in the existence of unbounded, unconquerable passion; her ideas were too much engrossed in the dazzling visions of glory and fame to descend to a minute analysis of the various gradations of tenderness, and the progressive workings of love.—She seemed to sympathize more with the lofty feelings of her father, than with those of her woman's heart. She had implicitly trusted to him the care of her happiness, and upon his slightest intimation she had consented to receive Gomez Arias as her future husband, and he had too many brilliant qualities not to meet with her approbation.

Gomez Arias possessed in an eminent degree great military talents, and an unbounded desire of glory and renown,—qualities which, in the opinion of Leonor, were paramount to every other consideration. Accordingly, she loved him, as she thought, in a manner worthy of the daughter of Don Alonso de Aguilar.

In this state of mind she awaited the marriage, which had only been retarded by the untoward accident which had unhappily brought the life of Don Rodrigo de Cespedes into mortal jeopardy.

Meantime the extraordinary valour and address which Gomez Arias had displayed in the tournament (for Leonor felt conscious that the incognito knight could be no other), tended considerably to increase her admiration for him, and to enhance her desire of uniting her fortunes to those of a man so well calculated to merit by his services the approbation of his country.

Gomez Arias; or The Moors of the Alpujarras.

The games being over, various chiefs, such as the Alcayde de los Donceles, Count Cifuentes, and others of equal merit, departed with the forces under their command, to act against the rebels, now daily increasing both in number and strength.

Meantime Don Alonso de Aguilar, on whom devolved the most dangerous part of the enterprize, that of penetrating into the heart of those terrible mountains of the Alpujarras, felt scarcely satisfied with his detention at Granada, as he considered every moment spent in inactivity as lost to glory and renown.

Great, therefore, was his satisfaction when he communicated to his daughter the perfect recovery of Don Rodrigo de Cespedes. Nothing now could prevent the immediate appearance of Gomez Arias at Granada, for the celebration of the nuptials, or throw any impediment on Don Alonso's departure against the rebel Moors. Intelligence, therefore, was sent to Don Lope, who lay concealed at Guadix, that he might repair with the utmost expedition to Granada,—an invitation which Aguilar entertained no doubt would be most anxiously welcomed by that cavalier. Under this impression Don Alonso now turned his thoughts solely to the object that was ever in his mind, and engrossed his every sentiment. Two or three days more and he would be marching against the enemies of his country, and adding new laurels to the flourishing branches that already graced his glorious name.

Meantime his daughter Leonor evinced an equal anxiety for the return of her lover, not so much for any selfish gratification of feeling as for the more noble ambition of claiming the prerogative to call by the endearing names of father and husband, the two first warriors of the land.

Thus impressed, both father and daughter awaited with impatience the following day, which, beyond the possibility of doubt, was to bring Gomez Arias to the city.

CHAPTER V.

Sterling. True, True; and since you only transfer from one girl to another, it is no more than transferring so much stock, you know.

Sir John. The very thing.

Sterling. Odso! I had quite forgot. We are reckoning without our host here.

Clandestine Marriage.

"What is to be the wonder now?" asked Gomez Arias, as he observed his valet and confidant, Roque, approaching, with an unusual expression of gravity upon his countenance, such indeed as was seldom discernible in the features of the merry buffoon.

"What is it you want?"

"I wish to leave your service, Señor."

"Leave my service! Surely, Roque, you are not tired of so indulgent a master?"

"Yes, Sir," answered Roque, "I am; and what is more, I have been so these three years—may I speak out?"

"Why," said Don Lope, "you never till now asked leave to be impertinent—but let me hear your complaints."

"In the first place you are not rich—a grievous fault."

"How can I help that?" demanded Gomez Arias.

"Señor, you could have helped it once; but that is passed. Then you play——"

"Here's the devil preaching morality," exclaimed his master, with a laugh. "Oh! most conscientious Roque, what are thine objections to this amusement?"

"To the amusement in itself, none; I am only discontented with the consequences. If you gain, you very composedly enjoy the whole fruits of your success; if, on the contrary, you lose, I get more than a reasonable share of your ill-humours, with which you most liberally indulge me. Now, Don Lope, I should like fair play, if play you will; to feel a little more the effect of the first, and not quite so much of the second."

"Thou art a pleasant sort of a fool, Roque," said Gomez Arias, as he leisurely twirled round his curling jet-black mustachios, and with much complacency eyed his fine figure in a mirror.

"Thank you, Sir," replied the valet, with a low bow; "but be pleased to consider, that the good opinion you entertain of my talents is unfortunately no adequate compensation for the privations and numberless perils which I undergo in your service. To continue, then, the list of——"

"My faults!" interrupted his master.

"I only say of my complaints," returned the valet: "next to your being a gamester, what I most deprecate is, your military profession, and the fame which you have acquired by your bravery."

"Good heavens!" cried Gomez Arias, "why thou art precisely complaining of the qualities that most become a gentleman."

"But I am no gentleman," pertinently observed Roque; "and I cannot imagine why I should be exposed to the dangers attendant on heroes, without likewise reaping their rewards."

"I glory in being a soldier," exclaimed Don Lope, a sudden burst of martial enthusiasm glowing on his manly countenance.—"Yes, I have laid low many of the enemies of my country; and before I die I hope often to try my good sword against those accursed and rebellious Moors of the Alpujarras."

"All that is very fine, certainly," said Roque; "but do you know, Señor, that I do not consider the country so much indebted to you, as no doubt you most complacently imagine."

"What!" cried the cavalier, with looks of displeasure.

"Pray be temperate, Don Lope; I do not mean to offend. You have unquestionably done great services to Spain, by ridding her of many an unbelieving Moor; but reflect, Sir, that your sword has not been less fatal to Christian blood. In battle you hew down infidels to your soul's content, and in the intervals of peace, to keep you in practice, I suppose, you take no less care to send the bravest of her majesty's warriors to the grave. Now put this in the balance, and let us consider whether the country does not suffer more by your duels in peace, than she actually gains by your courage in war. But now comes the most terrible of all your peccadilloes—of all my complaints, I mean."

"And which is that, pray?"

"The invincible propensity you have for intrigue, and the no less unfortunate attendant upon it—inconstancy."

"Inconstancy!" exclaimed Gomez Arias. "How should it be otherwise? Inconstancy is the very soul of love."

"I will not attempt to argue that point with so great an adept; my remonstrances are merely limited to the results, and I can truly aver that my life in time of peace is, if possible, more miserable than in war; for what with carrying love-letters, bribing servants, attending serenades, watching the movements of venerable fathers, morose duennas, and fierce-looking brothers, I cannot enjoy a moment's rest."

"Why, 'tis true," said Don Lope, "my life is solely devoted to love and war."

"I rather think it a continual war," retorted the valet. "It may be much to your taste, Sir, but I, that am neither of so amorous a temperament, nor of so warlike a disposition, cannot enjoy the amusement so well. Instead of passing the nights quietly in bed, as good Christians should do, we employ them in parading the silent streets, putting in requisition all the established signals of love, and singing amorous songs to the tender cadences of the love-inspiring guitar. Even this I might endure with Christian resignation, were it not for the disagreeable results which generally terminate our laudable occupations. It often happens that whilst you are dying with love, and I with fear and apprehension, we meet with persons who unfortunately are not such decided amateurs of music. Some surly ill-disposed brother, or unsuccessful lover of the beauty, is invariably sure to come and disturb our harmony; then discord begins—swords are drawn—women scream—alguazils pounce upon us, and thus the sport goes on, till one of the *galanes*[1] is dead or wounded, or till the alguazils are so strong as to render a prudent retreat advisable. Then by some ill fortune I am sure to be collared by the brother or the alguazils in question, and without further ceremony, by way of remunerating merit and encouraging a servant for faithfully serving his master, I am entertained with sundry hearty cudgellings, liberally bestowed on my miserable hide. When they have not left a single sound bone in my skin, they kindly permit me to go, telling me, for consolation, to thank my stars, and that

---

[1] Gallants.

another time I shall not escape so easily. With this pleasing assurance, I creep home as well as I can, and then my humane and grateful master, by way of sympathising with the misfortunes I suffer on his account, fiercely demands—'Roque! where have you been loitering, Sir?' Calls me a most negligent rascal, and other names equally gratifying, and upon the recital of my tragical adventure, very coolly, and as he thinks very justly, observes—'It serves you right—'tis all your fault—why did you not watch better?'"

"Roque," said Gomez Arias, "you have told me the same story over and over again, and I do not see the necessity of your repeating it now."

"I beg your pardon, Don Lope Gomez Arias," responded the valet, with most ludicrous solemnity, "but I am firmly resolved to quit your service in good earnest; for I perceive you are bent on getting into new difficulties, and I feel no inclination to go in search of fresh adventures. Lately you suddenly disappeared on some mysterious expedition, and I am sure you have been to Granada, to be a candidate in the tournament, notwithstanding the perilous nature of such an undertaking; for had you been discovered!—--"

"Enough, Roque—that danger is past."

"Very well, Sir; but there are a thousand others that are not. Will you be pleased to reply to a few questions?"

Gomez Arias, to spare any superfluous expenditure of words, nodded assent.

"How long is it since we left Granada?"—asked the valet.

"Two months or so," replied his master.

"We quitted that city," proceeded Roque, "in consequence of the mortal wounds you inflicted on Don Rodrigo de Cespedes, your rival in the affections of Leonor de Aguilar."

"True."

"We sought a refuge here in Guadix, to lie concealed until the storm blow over."

"Right."

"And you are now creditably employed in gaining the affections of a young and innocent girl, who knows no more of you than she does of his holiness the pope."

"Well?"

"I don't suppose you intend to marry both these ladies?"

"Certainly not."

"Then it puzzles me to decide how you can reconcile these matters; and as I foresee that mischief is likely to ensue, you must excuse me if

I prudently think of withdrawing before the evil is unavoidable. If fortunately both or even one of your mistresses were a plebeian beauty, I might be persuaded to hush my apprehensions, but as it is I cannot; two ladies of rank are concerned."

Thus far had Roque proceeded in his eloquent and moral remonstrance, when Gomez Arias turned round, took up a cane that lay near him, and walking very deliberately to his valet with the most perfect composure—"Now, Roque," he said, "you must allow I have listened very attentively to your prosing. I have had quite enough of your nonsense for this morning, so I beg you to close your arguments, unless you really wish that I should honor them with a most unanswerable reply."

Here to illustrate his meaning, he very expressively shook the cane, and Roque as prudently retreated; for he knew his master strictly adhered to his word on occasions of this nature.

"With respect to your quitting my service," continued Don Lope, "I have no sort of objection, provided that when you part with me, you are likewise disposed to part with your ears, for I have taken such a fancy to you, my dear Roque, that I cannot possibly allow you to quit me, without leaving me behind a token of remembrance. And now," he added in a more serious tone, "withdraw immediately, and mind your business."

Roque made an humble bow and retired. Gomez Arias in this instance, as well as in many others, took advantage of that uncontrollable authority which strong minds generally assume over their inferiors. The valet had indeed resolved several times to leave his master, for it happened that this same Roque had no particular relish for canings, and other favors of the kind which were liberally administered to him, as a remuneration for his master's achievements. Moreover, he had the nicest sense of justice, and he could not but feel the shocking impropriety of accepting a reward that was unquestionably due to his superiors. Indeed, it is but fair to add, he never acquiesced in the obligation, until it was actually forced upon him.

Roque was moreover blessed with a conscience—that sort of prudential conscience which must be considered as a most valuable acquisition. He certainly was not so unreasonable as to expect a spirited nobleman to lead the life of a sequestered monk, nor could he object to his master's intrigues, but he nevertheless found it extremely objectionable that these should not be kept within the bounds of common prudence. Now, could Gomez Arias have limited his gallantries to the seduction of farmers' daughters, or debauching tradesmen's wives, Roque would most implicitly have approved of the practice, inasmuch as in this case, his master would only be asserting a sort of hereditary right attached to those of his class. But to be deceiving two ladies of distinction was really too much for the delicate feelings of the conscientious menial.

Again, Roque could not urge anything against the courage of his master; he only objected to the effects of its superabundance; for this superabundance, together with Don Lope's unusually amorous disposition, were constantly in opposition with the nicety of Roque's conscience, by reason of the difficulties they gave rise to, in the fulfilment of the natural law of self-preservation.

It is an averred fact that Roque never wilfully put himself in the way of infringing so rational a precept, and most fortunately he was endowed with a quality highly favorable to the observance thereof. A quality which other individuals not blessed with the same scruples, would denominate cowardice.

This is not all: the valet was far from being of a romantic turn of mind; he evinced no taste whatever for moonlit scenery, and nocturnal adventure; and he was vulgar enough to prefer the gross advantages of a sound slumber to all the sentimental beauties of the silvered moon and its appendages.

These considerations dwelt strongly on the mind of Roque, and he had accordingly several times resolved to quit his master, but such was the dominion which Gomez Arias held over him, that the valet's resolutions fell to the ground, whenever he attempted to put them in practice.

CHAPTER VI.

Ma chi'l vede e non l'ama?
Ardito umano cor, nobil fierezza,
Sublime ingegno—Ah! perchè tal ti fero
Natura e il cielo?
Alfieri.

The bloom of op'ning flowers, unsullied beauty,
Softness and sweetest innocence she wears,
And looks like nature in the world's first spring.
Rowe.

Don Lope Gomez Arias was a man whose will had seldom been checked, and he placed the most unbounded confidence in the magnitude of his resources, physical and intellectual. Nature had indeed been lavished in conferring on this individual her choicest favors. To the most undaunted courage and quickness of resolve, he united the greatest powers of mind, and brilliancy of talent, but he was unfortunately divested of those genuine feelings of the heart, which alone can render these qualities desirable.

His courage, talents, and abilities, had rendered him an object of dread, not only to the enemies of his country, but to the rivals of his love or ambition. By the men he was generally disliked, feared or envied. Unfortunately the softer sex entertained for him far different sentiments.—Alas! they could not discover the void within his heart, through the dazzling splendour of his outward form, and habitual allurements of manner. Many had already been the victims of his seducing arts; were they to blame?—perhaps they were only to be pitied. He possessed every resource that professed libertines employ, to inveigle the affections of the innocent maiden, or attract the admiration of the more experienced woman. Besides his courage and resolution—qualities as much more prized by females, as they seldom fall to their share, Gomez Arias was engaging in his deportment and without any alloy of servility in his address; indeed he seemed rather to command attention, than to court it, and the general expression of his features was that of pride, tempered with the polish of gentlemanly bearing.

In his personal appearance he was remarkably handsome, being of tall and majestic stature, to which his finely turned limbs were in strict proportion. There was an intelligence in the piercing glance of his dark eye, and a smile of mixed gaiety and satire sat habitually upon his lip. To his other attractions he added a set of regular though somewhat large features, which were shaded by a profusion of black glossy curls, and the superb mustachios and *pera*[1] that clothed his upper lip and chin.

Such was the principal hero of this tale. Spite of all the resources of his mind, Gomez Arias found himself at the present moment involved in deep perplexity, and much at a loss how to extricate himself therefrom. He had received a letter from Don Alonso de Aguilar, father of his future bride, announcing the perfect recovery of his rival, Don Rodrigo, and urging a speedy return to Granada. But, unluckily, Gomez Arias felt in no hurry to return. Certainly, Granada was at the time particularly interesting, and far preferable to Guadix. Again, the beauty of Leonor was unrivalled at court—a great consideration to Don Lope. She was rich and of the first rank—greater consideration still; and bearing in mind the influence that her father, the celebrated Aguilar, enjoyed with the queen, a marriage with his daughter would open the road to the highest preferment, and yet our hero felt loath to return to Granada. The blooming Theodora de Monteblanco was then the reigning idol of the moment. She had fixed for a time his errant heart, and it was now that Don Lope perceived the great inconveniency of the unity of man; and certainly a lover of his description ought to be duplex for the opportunity of satisfying both duty and inclination.

In this state of irresolution Gomez Arias remained for some time. His sacred engagement to Leonor, and the brilliant dreams of ambition that sported before his fancy, could not all chase away the image of Theodora; for in this lovely girl he found all the perfections of his former mistresses, with an absolute exemption from their foibles.

---

[1] Pera. The military term is imperial; a small tuft of hair.

Theodora, at the tender age of seventeen, exhibited already the matured charms of a form voluptuously beautiful, blended with the delightful innocence of manner characteristic of that early stage of life, when the heart is yet unacquainted with guile, and unpractised in the deceits of the world. Her complexion was of a delicate white, without any other colour than that which occasionally mantled upon her cheek when called forth by the sensibility of her feelings, or diffused by the influence of some passing emotion. So lovely and yet so pensive was her countenance that but for the rapturous expression of her large dark eyes, partially revealed through their long silken fringes, and the profusion of sable ringlets which floated with unrestrained luxuriance over her exquisitely turned neck and shoulders, you might have thought that she had been a master-piece of some divine sculptor, who had successfully imitated, in the purest alabaster, the fairest work of nature.

Theodora loved Gomez Arias with all the enthusiasm of a romantic girl's first love. She felt the most ardent attachment, and could not,—would not conceal it from the object of her adoration. She loved him with the genuine simplicity of a heart incapable of deceit; and, unpractised in the school of worldly prudence, unacquainted with the arts to which more experienced women resort for the purpose of enhancing their own charms, or fixing more firmly the affections of men, she had surrendered her whole soul to her lover with the most confiding innocence, and an implicit reliance on his unbounded return to her tenderness.

This complete devotedness flattered the vanity of Gomez Arias. He beheld an angelic girl who centered all her happiness in his love, and in the ardour of her feelings was incapable of admitting the least alloy of cold calculating precaution. He was charmed with a character cast in the mould of nature, untutored yet by art, and, as amongst his former mistresses he had never met with one so entirely devoted, he returned her love with the warmest admiration.

Gomez Arias was fondly indulging in these pleasing reveries, when his man, Roque, suddenly burst upon him with a look full of information.

"Well, Sirrah!" cried Don Lope, "what means this intrusion?—Do you still stick to the wise determination of quitting my service? Are you willing to comply with the conditions?"

"No, Señor," answered Roque, with conscious importance; "I come loaded with fresh proofs of my inclination to serve you."

"Upon my honor," exclaimed Gomez Arias, "thou art marvellously complaisant, friend—thou hast seen the duenna, I suppose?"

"Yes, Sir, and I have seen some one else, besides."

"Let us hear first of the duenna."

"We must go to night—her master is engaged with a guest from Granada. I saw them leave the house myself."

Gomez Arias lost no time in preparing for the interview; and as night was now coming on, he girded on his sword, and, flinging his cloak carelessly round him, sallied out accompanied by his valet, on his nocturnal expedition.

"Art thou sure, good Roque," he demanded, "that you really saw the old gentleman leave his mansion?"

"Quite sure, Don Lope—my eyes seldom deceive me; indeed I feel perfectly satisfied with their capability. Never was there a more trusty pair, in descrying afar off a father, or brother, or any other kind of unwelcome intruder upon moonlight meetings. Argus, they say, had a hundred eyes, and yet was found at fault, whereas I have only two and——"

"They are sometimes as watchful," interrupted Don Lope.

"Seldom," replied Roque—"and when they unfortunately deceive me, I sorely feel for the deception. I am a man of very tender feelings."

"Argus," observed his master, "was punished for his negligence, and it is meet thou shouldst experience the same treatment, under similar circumstances."

"Aye," quoth Roque, "he was changed into a peacock—I wonder into what animal I shall be changed, since this sort of transformation is the retribution attendant on negligent scouts—I think the character of a jackal would suit me best, for I certainly lead the lion to his prey. But now, Sir, leaving jesting aside, I have a little piece of serious information for your ear. Do you know whom I saw in close converse with Don Manuel de Monteblanco when he left his house?"

"No, nor do I care."

"Don't you, indeed?—Well, it is very fortunate, for it happened to be no other than your rival, Don Rodrigo."

"Now, Roque," cried his master jocosely, "here's a convincing proof of the failure of thy boasted eye-sight."

"Why I really thought so at first myself, and I made the sign of the cross accordingly, but I soon perceived it was no delusion. Now it would be pleasant, should this same Don Rodrigo come upon an expedition similar to yours—it would seem as tho' the man was born on purpose to thwart you."

"Well," returned Gomez Arias, with a smile—"and it would seem also that I am born to chastise his insolence."

To this, Roque made some foolish reply; for in his capacity of *gracioso*,[1] he freely availed himself of the privilege allowed him of giving utterance to every thing that came into his head, whether to the purpose or not.

They proceeded with hasty steps towards the mansion of Monteblanco;—already they reach the spot, and the moon that sheds a partial gleam over yonder *reja*,[2] developes to the sight the outline of a female form. Gomez Arias approaches, and his penetrating glance discerns through the darkness the figure of his Theodora—her face is decked in placid smiles, and her frame evinces the soft flutterings of an anxious heart. The bolt of the entrance gently creeks, and the harsh sound thrills like the strain of heavenly music to the lover's throbbing breast—the door opens at length, and a comely matron far stricken in years welcomes the cavalier. Don Lope is not backward in his advances; a smile of grateful recognition plays upon his lip. He then seizes the good duenna's hand, and presses it in kind acknowledgment.

The trusty Martha showed in her dress and manner, all the outward signs of her state and condition. An imperturbable gravity sat upon those harsh features which were never known to relax into a smile, and in whose expression predominated a mixture of religious asperity and pride, vainly disguised under the cloak of humility. However, Martha was far from practising the rigid austerities her whole appearance seemed to indicate. She only assumed this outward demeanor, in the same manner that a dastard mimics courage, the better to conceal his cowardice.

Martha was dressed in an ample habit of black woollen cloth, girded her waist with the band of a monkish order, to which was suspended a rosary of huge black counters. A cap of the whitest linen adorned her head, and in all the rigour of female modesty, every part of her neck up to the chin was carefully concealed by a kerchief of the same material.

Gomez Arias rushes forwards, and the next moment finds him at the feet of his mistress. Theodora is happy in the Elysium of love; a thousand tender emotions swell that fond bosom, where an ardent flame burns under the cover of pure snow.—As she gazes on Gomez

---

[1] Jester.
[2] Reja, a small grated window.

Arias her melting eye is lighted up with unusual fire, and her whole frame appears gently agitated with a delicious tremor. The smile that quivers on her lip feelingly responds to the ardent glance of her passionate admirer, and the sudden rush of crimson that overspreads her lily cheek bespeaks the thrilling transports of genuine love in the first stages of youthful innocence and delight. Don Lope takes her soft yielding hand, and tenderly presses it to his bosom, he gazes fervently on her countenance; in sweet intoxication he inhales her youthful breath. Caressingly his arm encircles her sylphic waist. She gently inclines her head towards him, and both seemed overshadowed by the long beautiful tresses which float in wild luxuriance. From Don Lope's flashing eye the innocent Theodora drinks large draughts of sweet but deadly poison; a tear of tenderness starts to overwhelm her eye and falls on the lover's hand; a deep sigh escapes her bosom, and they meet in a fervent embrace. Happy!—thrice happy moments!—dear to the genuine sensibility of humanity, dearly cherished and oft alas! but too dearly purchased! Few words the lovers spoke, for when the heart is replete with rapture, there is an eloquence in silence far above the cold trammels of language. Gomez Arias forgot the dream of future ambition in the reality of present bliss. He was loved, loved passionately by one who was the most perfect pattern of innocence and beauty; loved more than he thought it was in the nature of woman to love. Hope assured its brightest colours, and Don Lope anticipated all the transports of delight possible for man to enjoy. He was supremely happy in expectation; for the expectation of bliss is perhaps even more gratifying than the reality. Thus the rose in its opening bloom, is sweeter than when its charms are expanded to the sight, for the hour of maturity is but the signal of decay. Alas! we eagerly follow the sparkling joy, snatch it with enthusiasm, and it withers in the grasp!

Time sped; yet the lovers still remained as if entranced in a delightful reverie of love, in the mutual interchange of soft sighs and eloquent glances, when suddenly the door burst open, and Roque rushed in with visible emotion. The faithful Argus came to announce the near approach of Monteblanco and his guest, Don Rodrigo. Gomez Arias, however, could not believe the danger to be so imminent, making due allowance for the valet's timorous disposition; but the good duenna, who had been unpleasantly disturbed at her devotions, now came forward to confirm the fearful intelligence.

Though these unpleasant interruptions are far from being of novel occurrence in the annals of love, and though Gomez Arias was familiarized with their danger, yet when he looked on the duenna's countenance, that faithful thermometer of intrigue, he could not but perceive the impending storm to be more than usually alarming. Deeper wrinkles furrowed her sallow visage; her eye was haggard, and the rosary shook in her withered hand.

"Holy Virgin! I am lost," exclaimed the affrighted dame. "Ah! Don Lope, this comes of my tender-hearted, complying disposition; there's my reputation sullied with a stain that not all the holy water in Spain will be able to wash away!"

"But, surely," observed Gomez Arias, "the danger is not so imminent as to preclude my escape."

"Escape!" quoth the duenna; "it is impossible; they are at this moment on the stairs."

"Villain!" cried Don Lope, turning fiercely to Roque, "is this the way you do your duty?"

Roque very prudently kept aloof from the contact of his master's hand; and, as if anticipating an explosion, began to stammer forth his excuses. Theodora's countenance was suddenly overspread with a deadly paleness, and the timid girl wrung her hands in an attitude of despair. Her critical situation, and the duenna's alarm, at first staggered Gomez Arias, but with the start of resolution which immediate danger inspires, he assumed a mastery over his emotion, and instantly bethought himself of an expedient to ward off the threatened discovery.

"If Don Rodrigo arrives with Monteblanco," said he, "we are safe; we shall have nothing to fear."

"Nothing to fear!" echoed Roque. "Methinks the danger is doubled when a man has two enemies to encounter, instead of one."

"Silence, fool!" cried his master. "Martha, be calm; affect not to know me; make free use of the organ with which nature has so liberally endowed you, and do not spare your reproaches and abuse. Theodora, keep up your spirits. Roque, be silent, you rascal."

The door opens—Monteblanco and Don Rodrigo enter, but are fixed to the ground in mute amazement at the group that presents itself to their view. The duenna had summoned the courage of despair, and was overwhelming Gomez Arias with a torrent of abuse. Theodora had receded from the light to hide her emotion from her father's sight, which fortunately was so impaired with age, as not to afford any material impediment to her concealment. Roque assumed an air of saucy assurance, and his master appeared leaning against the wall with the most perfect coolness and self-possession. Don Manuel and his guest stared at the intruders for some time, before either attempted to speak, till at length Don Rodrigo broke silence, with an ejaculation of surprise.

"Don Lope Gomez Arias!" exclaimed the astonished cavalier.

"Don Lope Gomez Arias!" re-echoed Monteblanco. "It is your rival, then.—What is the meaning of this, Martha?"

"Your honor may ask the gentleman himself," responded the duenna; "I know nothing of him, but that he is the most daring and impertinent man"—(Martha indulged in the privilege granted her by Don Lope); "the most unceremonious, head-strong, self-sufficient cavalier I ever met with—Virgen Santa!—What a disturbance he has raised in the house. Then there's that most impudent rascal of a valet; he is the principal cause of the commotion, and I humbly crave and hope your honor will give him ample reason to repent his impudence."

"Repent my impudence!" quoth Roque, "thou accursed *bruja*;[1] it would be more meritorious to chop off thy slanderous tongue!"

Here the duenna proceeded to pour forth a fresh volley of words, without any positive explanation, as is generally the practice when people are anxious to gain time, and collect their senses.

"Peace, woman!" interrupted Gomez Arias, in the middle of her harangue; "this disturbance, as you term it, is of your own doing; had you behaved with more courtesy to a stranger, you might have saved the impropriety my valet has been guilty of towards you; an impropriety for which he shall most assuredly suffer in due time."—Here he cast a terrible look on the astonished Roque, who perfectly well knew he was doomed to suffer for his master's vagaries; and that the failure of his adventures must recoil invariably on his unfortunate head. Yet he looked sorely puzzled how to find out the nature of the impropriety he had committed against the superannuated dame who dealt him such abundance of vilipendiary epithets.

All this time the good Don Manuel was patiently waiting for an explanation, and the more the duenna explained the more perplexed he found himself.

Gomez Arias at last, after several fruitless endeavours to stop Martha's tongue, availed himself of a momentary pause she made to take breath.—"Don Manuel de Monteblanco," said he, "is undoubtedly anxious to learn the object of my visit to his house."

"Visit!" exclaimed the duenna. "Intrusion—a downright taking by storm.—God bless me! a visit you call it—- a visit!"

---

[1] Anglice, a beldam.

"Silence, Martha, silence; let the gentleman proceed," cried Don Manuel, a little more composed, and feeling an inward dread at the matron's explanatory talents.

"Don Manuel," continued Gomez Arias, "I am exceedingly concerned for the confusion created in the mansion of so honorable a cavalier; but certainly I am not so greatly to blame as that good woman wishes to imply."

"Good woman, indeed!" ejaculated the duenna. "*Jesus me valga!* that I should live to be so called—*soy Cristiana vieja*[1]—and of as good a family as needs be.—No Jewish puddle in my veins.—Good woman, forsooth! My dear master, am I to be called a good woman?"

Don Manuel looked very grave, not so much perhaps at the difficulty of resolving the question, as at the probability of never obtaining a knowledge of the business so long as the duenna had the free use of her tongue; to quiet therefore her anger, the complaisant old cavalier kindly soothed her apparently wounded feelings, by allowing that she by no means deserved the appellation.

Silence being thus restored, Gomez Arias continued: "The cause of my apparent intrusion is simply this:—informed by my servant that Don Rodrigo de Cespedes was in active search after me, and not wishing to be backward in acknowledging the favor, I thought it incumbent on my honor to facilitate a meeting with the utmost expedition. I repaired to this house, from whence my servant had seen that gentleman issue, but before the nature of my business could be disclosed, that rigid dame assailed me with a tremendous storm of abuse, when my valet, in his zeal to serve me, or rather indulging in a propensity to retaliate, retorted the lady's freedom of tongue with rather too much acrimony."

"Now," thought Roque, "it is really too bad to accuse me of acrimony when I have not opened my lips."

"I attempted an explanation," continued Gomez Arias, "in the hopes of meeting with a more courteous reception, when this young lady made her appearance (turning to Theodora). I was then about to acquaint her with my intention, when fortunately the object of my search presents himself in person, a circumstance which I hail with the more pleasure, as I am assured that Don Rodrigo is particularly anxious we should renew an old interchange of tokens of our mutual regard."

---

[1] I am an old Christian.

Gomez Arias; or The Moors of the Alpujarras.

"Señor Don Lope Gomez Arias," replied Don Rodrigo, sorely incensed at the tone of levity in which he was addressed by his rival, "I likewise congratulate myself in thus accidentally meeting with Don Lope sooner than I was led to expect, and though the mock courtesy of his style plainly indicates the reliance he places on the constant good fortune that protects him, yet he shall find me more solicitous than ever for the immediate interchange of the tokens to which he so facetiously alludes."

"Señor Don Rodrigo de Cespedes," returned Gomez Arias, "I cannot but greatly admire that laudable ambition which stimulates you to deeds of noble daring, and an unworthy individual like myself cannot feel sufficiently grateful for the honor you wish to confer upon him."

These words and the sarcastic sneer that accompanied them, exasperated Don Rodrigo to such a degree, that turning to his rival, he pointed to the door, and without further reply intimated to him to follow. Gomez Arias was about to comply, when Monteblanco interposing, exclaimed,

"Forbear, *caballeros*, forbear; this is my house, and though I am far from desiring to withhold any gentlemen from the calls of honor, yet let it not be said that my mansion was made a scene of violence and bloodshed."

"*Valgame Dios!*" cried Roque, "Don Manuel speaks like an oracle. Nor do I think myself, this hour of night the most fit to decide such important matters. Broad day-light is certainly preferable to the glimmer of the moon and stars, for business like this."

Theodora was ready to sink with emotion and fear, but the very imminence of the danger inspired her with a sort of desperate tranquillity. She knew that her interposition would only increase the perplexities of her situation, without preventing the accomplishment of their design. Besides, she placed much confidence in her lover's courage and superior skill in the management of arms, and ultimately she possessed that nobleness of mind that shrinks from the imputation of cowardice in the object of its admiration.

Monteblanco's remonstrances were vain. Don Rodrigo rushed to the door with desperate haste, and Gomez Arias followed with the coolness of one to whom such scenes were familiar.

"Follow me," cried Don Rodrigo, as he bounded down the stairs with fearful alacrity.

"Stay, Don Rodrigo," said Gomez Arias, sarcastically, "not such precipitation, or you may perchance fall before your time."

This provoking sarcasm entirely overthrew the little remaining temper which Don Rodrigo possessed. His eyes flashed fire, his whole frame shook, and unable to restrain himself any longer, he furiously drew his sword, and fixed on the *Zaguan*[1] for the field of action.

"Defend yourself, Don Lope," exclaimed he, with frenzied rage.

"Look to yourself, fair Sir," returned Don Lope, as, unsheathing his rapier, he calmly placed himself in a posture of defence.

With impetuous fury Don Rodrigo darted on his antagonist, and commenced an assault with all the courage and address of a practised swordsman. Thrust succeeded thrust with mortal rapidity, but the active eye of Gomez Arias foiled their deadly aim with consummate skill and dexterity. A demoniac spirit seemed to agitate Don Rodrigo, and he continued for some minutes wasting his strength in the fruitless attack, and impairing his own means of resistance. The combat was too fierce to be of long duration, and a few moments would have brought it to a mortal issue (for Don Lope was now in his turn about to press hard his weakened adversary), had not Roque, in that tenderness of conscience for which he was so noted, very adroitly extinguished the light that hung in the *Zaguan*, as the most effectual way of suspending hostilities.

The place was thus plunged in utter darkness, and Don Rodrigo, afraid of being disappointed in his revenge, called out to Gomez Arias.

"I am here," replied Don Lope; "I am here, Don Rodrigo; the light is superfluous; we shall do perfectly well without it, for a mutual sympathy will lead our weapons aright."

The swords again met, and short, quick sparks of light, like the fugitive flash of a summer's exhalation, gave a momentary glimpse of the combatants' fearful countenances—then a dismal groan is heard, a body falls heavily on the ground, and a shriek of horror burst from the household, who had crowded round the entrance of the *Zaguan*.

"He is dead," muttered Don Rodrigo to himself, and sought for safety with the swiftness of lightning.

"Bring torches," cried Monteblanco; "let us afford the fallen *caballero* all the assistance in our power."

The state of Theodora baffles all description. Ignorant as yet who was the victim, her soul was harrowed up with the most fearful apprehensions, the reality of which would dash the cup of happiness from her lips, and embitter her future existence. This petrifying, this heart-

---

[1] A porch,—the entrance of a building.

rending suspense was happily but of short continuance. Theodora herself, with breathless anxiety, was the first to bring a torch, that might perhaps illume the pale ghastly features of him on whom she had centered all her felicity. The moment was awful, when the torch throwing a broad glare around the *Zaguan*, discovered Gomez Arias, tranquil and erect, in all the assurance of perfect safety. A faint scream escaped from the bosom of his mistress, for all the feelings which horrifying suspense had held imprisoned there, now sought relief in a tumult of sighs and tears. Her emotion, however, was scarcely noticed by her father, too much occupied at the time in ascertaining which was the fallen cavalier.

"Don Rodrigo is then the victim," sorrowfully exclaimed the old cavalier, casting his eyes around; for at this moment he spied a human body, lying in a dark corner of the *Zaguan*.

"It moves—it moves!" cried Martha, crossing herself.

"Then he is yet alive," returned Don Manuel; "let us hasten to succour the unfortunate young man; look to his wounds!"

"Aye," responded the duenna; "let us rather attend to his soul, and behave like true charitable Christians; run, Cacho, run, and call Fray Bernardo, or Fray Benito—no matter whom—any friar will do at such a moment."

Monteblanco and all his attendants hurried to the spot in their eagerness to render assistance to the fallen Don Rodrigo, when, lo! the body with a sudden spring bounds on its legs, and to the astonished eyes of every one discovers the person of Roque.

"What's this? Where is Don Rodrigo?" interrogated Monteblanco.

"Why," answered Roque, very unconcernedly; "some fifty leagues from hence, I should imagine, by his hurry to get away."

"Then he is not dead?"

"Not that I know of."

"Whence came that groan?"

"*De este humilde pecador.*"[1]

"*Jesus Maria*," ejaculated the duenna; "how dare this *judio*[2] throw a noble family into consternation?"

"Now, Señora duenna," quoth the valet, "I rather think I have been instrumental in preventing the noble family from being thrown into that consternation."

---

[1] From a poor sinner like myself.
[2] Jew.

"Roque," interposed here Gomez Arias, "thou art not wounded I perceive."

"No, thank God!" replied Roque.

"Then thou art a rascal."

"A rascal because I am not wounded! Good Heaven! here's a consequence with a vengeance!"

"This is an impudent interference," continued Don Lope, "and dearly shalt thou rue it."

"An impudent interference do you call it? A marvellous good one, in sooth, for I have saved the fruitless effusion of noble Christian blood, and I have separated two enraged combatants better than a whole posse of alguazils: and now, all the reward I am likely to obtain for such an important service, is threats and abuse. Here is my dear master sorely exasperated, because I have a greater regard for his safety than he has himself, and quite disappointed at not being run through the body by that sanguinary Don Rodrigo."

"Basta, basta," said angrily Don Lope;—then in a gentler tone he continued, "I am really concerned for Don Rodrigo,—full of anxiety for my supposed death, I venture to say he is now flying from the abode of man, to seek a shelter in the wilderness of the Alpujarras.

"It is very Christian-like in you, Señor," interposed Roque, "to show so much solicitude for the fate of Don Rodrigo. Well, the ways of honorable gentlemen are to me unaccountable. Here was my honorable master, but a short while since, eagerly seeking the life of Don Rodrigo at the point of his rapier, and now he is equally anxious that his adversary should not be exposed to the inconvenience of a nocturnal ramble into the mountains of Alpujarras."

Monteblanco could not but inwardly congratulate himself upon the fortunate termination of an adventure which threatened such serious results; for he by no means liked the idea of having a corpse in his house, with all the unpleasant appendages necessarily attendant on such an inmate. He certainly felt concerned for the safety and comfort of Don Rodrigo, but he very judiciously opined it was better his dear friend should suffer the inconvenience of passing a night in the mountains, than that he himself should be exposed to the unpleasant consequences which would inevitably attend a fatal result to either party, especially had the event occurred in his own *Zaguan*; for he would be thus compelled to take a part in the drama, with which he would very willingly dispense—that of explaining the catastrophe to the officers of justice. This consideration induced him to approve in his own mind the stratagem of Roque, although he would by no means audibly testify his approbation, thinking very properly that the conduct of inferiors and dependants should never be lauded, even when they are most successful in their services.

Acting upon this charitable principle, he would on no account interfere to prevent the taunts and abuse with which the luckless valet was assailed on all sides. Thus poor Roque had a fresh opportunity of discovering the little a man is likely to gain by following the impulse of a good heart, and the very extraordinary way men have of acknowledging a service, even when they are internally well pleased therewith.

"Begone, thou graceless dog!" exclaimed Don Manuel. "Thy impertinence justly deserves most exemplary punishment from thy master."

Saying this, he took his daughter by the hand, made a slight bow to Gomez Arias, and was about to retire, when Don Lope stept forward as though he wished to detain him.

"Stay, Don Manuel," said he; "I cannot leave your house, without again expressing my regret for the disturbance I have caused. I sincerely offer you my apologies as an honorable cavalier, and as such I am confident Don Manuel de Monteblanco will accept them. Moreover, I shall make all the atonement in my power; and as it is obvious that my servant is the primary cause of all the mischief, you may rest assured, Sir, the culprit shall not escape without condign and adequate punishment."

Don Manuel expressed himself perfectly satisfied with the apology of Gomez Arias, and most graciously accepted the atonement proposed; then making another bow, not quite so slight as the former, left the *Zaguan* accompanied by his beautiful daughter, who had already caught the eloquent parting look of her lover, and treasured in her bosom all the tender sentiments it conveyed.

Meantime, Don Lope, well contented with himself, haughtily called to poor Roque—the faithful valet was in a moment ready to lead the way. His master then very composedly returned to his apartments to muse over the adventures of the evening, and form plans for the successful accomplishment of his ulterior projects.

CHAPTER VII.

Pariome a drede mi Madre
Oxala no me pariera!—
Quevedo.

No ill luck stirring, but what lights on my shoulders.
Shakespeare.

"*Better be born fortunate than rich*," says an old proverb, and the correctness of this saying was fully exemplified in the life of Don Rodrigo de Cespedes. Indeed, his whole existence had been a series of mischances and unfortunate results; and he appeared especially reserved as a proper subject on whom the fickle goddess might exercise her caprice at leisure.

Why Don Rodrigo should belong to this class, is more than can well be resolved, for he was possessed of all those qualifications which are calculated to render a man brilliant in society, and amiable in private life. He enjoyed the advantages of birth and wealth; handsome in his person, and elegant in his address. A brave soldier in war, and a courteous cavalier in peace, it appeared natural that his fortune should be prosperous, and yet all those endowments availed him not. On the contrary, they only served to render the ill success of his undertakings the more remarkable.

These anomalies cannot be accounted for on any rational principle; but may perhaps be attributed to the absence of that requisite qualification, which sometimes serves a man in lieu of birth or fortune, and not unfrequently goes further than both these advantages;—it is that most enviable requisite, known under the appropriate, though somewhat vulgar, denomination of good-luck.

Gomez Arias; or The Moors of the Alpujarras.

Don Rodrigo had paid his addresses to three different ladies, with the moral and highly creditable intention of entering the holy state of matrimony. Perhaps in strict justice it must be confessed, this idea crossed his mind after having completely failed in his attempts to signalize himself as *un homme à bonnes fortunes*, a sort of ambition which, if not praise-worthy in itself, is nevertheless, when successfully pursued, conducive to the eclat of a man of rank, as well as gratifying to his vanity. Indeed it may be rather suspected, without any great affectation of discernment, that the unlucky Don Rodrigo bethought himself of marriage as a last resource, when ultimately convinced of his inability to succeed in his career of gallantry. But even in this instance, that unrelenting fatality which constantly followed him, could not be persuaded to spare him even in consideration of hymen.

Don Rodrigo had first for a rival a man whose stature was rather under than over four feet, whose features were of the most forbidding kind; his person distorted, and his fortune by no means superior to that of the Don; yet with all these disadvantages, this little monster, to the astonishment of every one, carried off the fair prize.

He next placed his affections on a lady of more humble pretensions, his inferior both in birth and fortune, and by no means remarkable for beauty. Don Rodrigo fondly imagined that his rank and affluence would insure him success; nor did he overlook the advantages nature had given him in a pair of fine eyes, an aquiline nose, well proportioned limbs, a carriage that shewed off these qualifications to advantage, and a degree of personal courage that even his rivals and enemies respected; but his Angelica must have been an admirer of the opposite qualities, as she chose for her husband an obscure plebeian, whom the very sight of a Toledo steel threw into an ague. Disgusted with the bad taste and vulgarity of those he had already courted, he boldly resolved to prefer his suit to the very first lady in the land. He accordingly laid siege to the heart of Leonor, but here his pretensions met with as decided a repulse as before, and though his vanity could not have been wounded by having Gomez Arias for his fortunate rival, yet, soured by his repeated crosses, he determined, if he could not by gentle means succeed in his object, to kill his rival or fall in the attempt: his success in this last exploit the reader will perhaps remember.

Nor was the ill-luck of Don Rodrigo confined to his amours; it extended to all his affairs. If he engaged in a duel, a wound was generally the result; or if he escaped unhurt, though he might have been the injured party, yet by some fatality he was sure to be accounted the aggressor. If he happened to say a good thing, it was invariably attributed to another person, while, if a piece of scurrility or a foolish remark circulated, he never failed to have the whole merit to himself.

We need not, however, go further for instances to exemplify the ill-luck that constantly attended Don Rodrigo. We see him at present a prey to his evil genius. He left the *Zaguan* of Monteblanco's dwelling with the utmost precipitation. Impressed with the idea that he had killed his rival; and, fully sensible of the necessity of speedy flight, he hurried to the inn for his horse and valet, anxious to put in practice his prudential resolution, before any impediment could be thrown in his way. On his arrival he asked for his man Peregil; but Peregil, as if on purpose to perplex him, was gone to evening prayers, which Don Rodrigo very naturally interpreted, to the tavern. So he sent a boy there, with instructions where he was to meet him out of the town. He then hastened to the stable, but found, to his unspeakable mortification, that Peregil, in his abundant care, had taken the key. Time being precious, Don Rodrigo, afraid of causing a disturbance, was fain to avail himself of the benefit of an ill-favoured looking mule that stood ready saddled in an outhouse. He doubted not that Peregil would bring his horse after him, and render compensation for the mule, which indeed, from the miserable appearance of the beast, would be no difficult matter.

Accordingly, after making his way to the place appointed, he waited two whole hours in a state of extreme anxiety and suspense, alarmed at every noise lest it should be a pursuit, and only consoling himself with the idea, that when his horse should arrive he could soon place himself out of the reach of danger.

At length he descried his valet advancing at a most leisurely pace, not mounted on his own strong horse, and leading a beautiful Arabian, but bestriding a miserable jackass, which required constant application of the whip. Of this Peregil was by no means sparing, to induce him to move at even the slowest pace a jackass is capable of travelling.

"Peregil, thou imp of Satan, where is my horse?" impatiently demanded Don Rodrigo.

"At the inn," sullenly answered the valet.

"At the inn, thou rascal! why didst thou not bring it, knowing, as you ought, that my life is in jeopardy?"

"For a very good reason," replied Peregil, "because they would not let me. You need only blame yourself, Señor, for since your honor scruples not to make free with the reverend friar's mule, you ought not to be surprised if his reverence takes the same liberty with your horse."

Gomez Arias; or The Moors of the Alpujarras.

"By *Santiago de Compostela*,[1] this is past bearing," cried Don Rodrigo. "How can the rogue of a friar conscientiously take my beautiful Arabian for this worthless mule? What! has the man of God no conscience?"

"I did not inquire that, Señor, but I rather think he is not overburthened by the manner he has dealt with me.—Oh! if I could catch his reverence by himself, I would so belabour his shaven skull, as not to leave it in want of razors for the future."

"Well, but how comest thou by that contemptible jackass?" demanded Don Rodrigo, angrily.

"Gently, Señor, gently; since the master shows such a predilection for mules, it is not to be wondered if the valet evinces a similar taste for jackasses."

"Villain! darest thou jest at this time and on such a subject?"

"Aye, 'tis no laughing matter, sure enough," quoth Peregil; "and in sooth I cannot perceive why I should be facetious on the occasion, for after all I am the greater loser of the two. Look for a moment at this vile beast! May the lightning of heaven and the curses of all the saints fall on him and his former master too;" and so saying he again belaboured the sides of the unfortunate jackass, regretting that its former master was not near enough to benefit by the energetic blows he so liberally dealt out.

"A truce, fellow, with thy profane foolery," said Don Rodrigo; "it is not seemly when the life of thy master is at stake. Prepare to give me a full and circumstantial account of this iniquitous business, or by my sword thou shalt severely rue the day thy master first bestrode a mule."

"Alack a-day," submissively rejoined the valet.—"You must know, Don Rodrigo, that the mule is the cause of all this. When I returned from church I was startled to see the inn thrown into the greatest confusion. The reverend fat friar was running round the place bellowing like a bull, calling for his noble mule, and vowing vengeance on the profane thief, which unseemly appellation he was pleased to bestow upon your honor."

"The friar must have been drunk," said Don Rodrigo, sneeringly; "why! did he not perceive that I had left my steed in the stable, which I think was sufficient security, till you could pay him the value of his beggarly mule!"

---

[1] St. James of Compostela, patron of Spain.

"Sure enough he did perceive it, but when I proposed to pay him for his loss, he demanded such an exorbitant price that it was out of my power to comply therewith. In his opinion, the steed was no adequate compensation for his mule; so to make matters even, and adjust the affair amicably, he proposed that I should give up my horse into the bargain, and then take this abominable ass as a present."

Peregil accompanied the epithet with another donation of his wonted favors.

"Thou miserable sinner," said Don Rodrigo, "how couldst thou consent to this nefarious arrangement?"

"Because I could not help it. Think you, Señor mio, I would have agreed to such an extortion had it been in my power to avoid it? But your precipitate flight gave me to understand that you had killed your adversary. Any delay in the town might have been attended with danger, backed as his reverence was by all the rabble of the inn."

Don Rodrigo was sensible of the force of this argument, and after bestowing sundry anathemas on the cheating friar and the inn, in which he was zealously joined by Peregil, he said in a melancholy tone, "Well, as there is no remedy, we must put up with this misfortune as well as we can."

"So we must, Señor," replied Peregil; "and at least there is some consolation in the reflection that we are already on such familiar terms with dame Fortune, that this new instance of her good-will ought by no means to take us by surprise.—But may I ask whither we are going?"

"To seek refuge in the mountains," gloomily answered Don Rodrigo.

"Well, may the help of God be with us!" ejaculated Peregil, "for we stand marvellously in need of it."

Saying this, they bent their course to the Alpujarras, as melancholy and slowly as suited the condition and convenience of the animals that bore them. Indeed, from time to time, the reverend mule actually stood still, as if pondering what he should do, and it required all Don Rodrigo's caresses (for he dared employ no other means) to induce her to proceed.

Thus the distressed master and his humble valet continued their march, for the space of three hours, in a most gloomy night. Observing at length that his servant made a dead stop, Don Rodrigo determined to assist him, and accordingly indicated his intention to the mule; but to his utter dismay he found that she had profited by the good example set by her companion the ass, and stood stone still. This obstinacy of their animals proved more than equal to the powers of Don Rodrigo and his man, who, after exhausting their strength in fruitless chastisement, prudently resolved to wait the leisure of their more determined companions. They took shelter, therefore, under the spreading branches of a large tree, and there they remained in anxious expectation of day-break, passing the tedious hours in silent and profound reflections on their miserable condition.

CHAPTER VIII.

O gran contrasto in giovenil pensiero,
Desir di laude ed impeto d'Amore;
Nè chi più vaglia ancor si trova il vero,
Che resta or questo, or quello superiore.
Ariosto.

At first a vague suspicion, a blind dread,
Then a quick feeling of the fatal truth
Instinctive flashed across her mind.
Wiffin's Tasso.

The first rosy tints of morning at length began to appear, and the heavy clouds of night were gradually rolling away before the splendour of the approaching sun, when Don Manuel de Monteblanco, who was already on the alert, received information that a party of horsemen were rapidly approaching the mansion. The old cavalier hastened to a spot whence he could descry his visitors, and form a judgment of their quality. The party consisted of an armed knight, and about half a dozen men-at-arms, bounding over the elastic turf, with the greatest buoyancy of spirits. Don Manuel, who stood watching their advance, was soon able to recognize, in the martial figure and gallant carriage of the knight, his young friend and kinsman, Don Antonio de Leyva, of whose arrival he had been in daily expectation. The youthful warrior was clad in a suit of polished steel armour, inlaid with silver; a quantity of massy and waving red plumage almost overshaded his shining helmet, and threw a crimson flush over his manly countenance, in which an expression of resolute courage was blended with an air of gaiety and frankness. The colour of his cheek was heightened by exercise, and the brilliancy of his dark blue eyes expressed an unusual degree of animation, whilst his blooming age and the gracefulness of his carriage tended to increase the interest of his commanding appearance. He was mounted on a fiery and slender barb, decorated with the most costly trappings, which appeared to participate in the buoyancy of the rider; for he champed the bit and shook off the white foam, requiring all the dexterity of his master to restrain the impetuosity of his nature.

The small party which accompanied the youthful warrior were arrayed in the military costume of the period. They served Don Antonio as an escort, and belonged to the body of which he was the leader. Upon their arrival the massy doors of the mansion were thrown open, and the venerable Monteblanco stood at the entrance ready to receive his noble visitor. The next moment Don Antonio, springing from his steed, threw himself into the arms that hospitably invited him to their embrace.

"Welcome, Don Antonio, thrice welcome to the abode of your old friend and kinsman."

"Save you, noble Don Manuel; it rejoices me to see that the hand of time has made so little impression upon you; your spirits are still young and ardent. How does the fair Theodora?"

"Blooming as the rose of summer, fair as the lily of the valley, and blithesome as the free tenant of the air," replied the fond father; "but come in," he continued, with joyful accents; "come and refresh yourself. Pedro," he then added, turning to his major-domo, a long, thin, grave looking personage, "mind that these cavaliers," pointing to Don Antonio's attendants, "are well entertained."

Then taking his relative by the hand, he led him into the mansion.

"Theodora," he then resumed, "is as yet at her morning orisons, in the company of good Martha, but on an occasion like the present, there would be no great sin in shortening her devotions."

"By no means," replied Don Antonio, smiling; "it is not my maxim to disturb fair ladies when so laudably occupied."

"Well, my young friend, as you please; but, good heavens!" continued he, surveying his guest from head to foot, with much complacency, "how you are altered! It is a goodly and consoling sight to see the improvement a few years bestow on a young man. You have distinguished yourself at the games," said Don Manuel; "this is a source of unspeakable joy to me, the more so, as it appears that the queen has been pleased to reward your merit. I have heard that you are entrusted with the command of a party of those gallant men, that are destined to chastise the rebellious Moors of the Alpujarras."

"In truth," modestly answered Don Antonio, "our great queen has condescended to honor me far above my deserts; but I trust that my future conduct will make me worthy of the confidence she has reposed in me."

"I suppose, then," said Don Manuel, "that your stay at Guadix will be but short?"

"Very short; as I am only allowed to wait the arrival of my party, and must then set off immediately to join the army under the command of the noble Aguilar."

"Then, my dear kinsman," observed Monteblanco, smiling, "the object of your visit must be accomplished without further delay."

"I shall never complain of too much expedition when the happiness of my life is so intimately concerned."

At this moment the door of the saloon was thrown open, and Theodora was ceremoniously ushered in by the stately duenna, who, after making a stiff and formal courtsey, sunk back, and kept a respectful distance.

"Dear child," said Don Manuel, "here is your kinsman, Don Antonio de Leyva, with whom you are already acquainted. He appears in our house as best becomes a gallant knight; his brow adorned with the wreath of triumph for the skill and prowess he has displayed in the games, a sure omen of his future glory in the field."

Theodora offered her hand to the salutation of her kinsman, with an attempt at cordiality; but it was evidently an effort to hide the real coldness she felt; for an involuntary tremor crept gradually over her, and her countenance betrayed strong symptoms of emotion, as she began to suspect the object of Don Antonio's visit. Indeed, the tone of ease and affection, in which her father and young de Leyva conversed, tended to confirm those suspicions, the truth of which she so much dreaded to learn.

As soon as Don Antonio withdrew, Monteblanco requested to speak with his daughter in his apartment. The trembling girl obeyed with a faltering step, looking like a criminal about to receive the sentence that is to seal her fate. The duenna remained somewhat surprised at this mysterious transaction, in which her family counsel and approbation had been so unceremoniously dispensed with. Her pride was mortified; in high dudgeon, she crossed herself with fervour; and then departed, muttering something between a prayer and a malediction.

A short time after, the conference broke up, and Theodora came forth, her eyes swimming in tears, and evincing the most lively emotion. She hied to her own chamber, and fastening the door, she gave a free vent to her grief.

"Alas!" she exclaimed, "the dreadful suspicion is confirmed, and the resolute manner in which my father has enforced his commands, affords me no room to hope for any alteration—any delay. Not a month—not even a week is allowed me to prepare—the measure of my misfortune is full—Lost! lost!—Oh! Lope! Lope!—-"

She could proceed no further; the tumult of sorrow impeded her utterance, and she gave loose to her feelings in sighs and tears.

Presently, however, a comforter came to proffer advice and assistance—in the shape of the duenna. As we have already seen, she was ruffled by Don Manuel's want of confidence, and proper regard for her judgment; and she had resolved to tender her assistance to another quarter. It is to be observed the duenna was of a most obliging disposition. She bestowed her good advice most liberally, and she had an inexhaustible fund of pious exclamations and admonitions at the service of her friends. She could not forego the idea of being serviceable, and therefore very properly desired to be consulted on all occasions. Yet with all these amiable qualities, the duenna, in the opinion of most people, would be entitled to no better appellation for her pains than that of a busy body.

"*Niña*,[1] how's this?" she cried—"What mean these tears?—Aye! aye! I see that your father has been guilty of some preposterous and tyrannical measure; I suspected as much from his carefulness in keeping the secret from me.—God bless the man!—what is the matter with him?—he will never be advised, and really I cannot imagine why I remain in his house. Well, child, unfold your sorrows and grievances to your kindest friend; you know nothing delights me so much as consoling the afflicted, and offering service to the unprotected."

"Yes, good Martha," replied the sorrowing girl; "I am fully sensible of your goodness, and I do trust you will not deny me your compassion. Alas! without your valuable advice and assistance, I shall never surmount the difficulties with which I am surrounded. I must see him—I must see Don Lope this very night!"

She then explained to Martha the nature of her distress, and the duenna, glad to find an opportunity of being serviceable, readily promised her co-operation in the accomplishment of her charge's wishes.

---

[1] Girl.

CHAPTER IX.

> Ye fair!
> Be greatly cautious of your sliding hearts!
> Dare not the infectious sigh; nor in the bower
> Where woodbines flaunt, and roses shed a couch,
> While evening draws her crimson curtain round,
> Trust your soft minutes with betraying man.
> *Thomson.*

In the most retired part of Monteblanco's garden, reclining on a rustic seat, under the fragrant canopy of the myrtle and arbutus, sat a female form enveloped in a loosely flowing dress of virgin whiteness. The air was cool and serene, and except the rustling of the surrounding foliage, when agitated by the breeze, or the soft plaintive voice of the nightingale, no obtrusive sound disturbed the solemn silence. The blue vault of heaven, glittering with countless stars, the rich perfume flung around by the orange flower and jasmine, and a stilly languor that pervaded the spot, all disposed the mind to gentle and loving thoughts.

Theodora, however, sat absorbed in silent sorrow and abstraction: her long clustering tresses fell in luxuriance over her white and polished neck, almost concealing in their profusion the traits of a countenance overcast with grief and despondency.

But a figure appears on the garden wall, and the sound as of some one falling is heard on the soft turf. Theodora starts, yet a sudden recollection seems to check her momentary fear. The nocturnal visitor was Gomez Arias, who had received a hasty summons from Theodora, and surmising that some unpleasant intelligence awaited him, he hurried in breathless expectation to the place of appointment.

What was his amazement, upon his arrival!—He beheld his Theodora, not in the joyful eagerness of affection springing forward to meet his embrace, but silent and dejected. Her intelligent countenance no longer beamed with that charming smile which his appearance never failed to create. Motionless and unmoved she appeared, amongst the flowery shrubs and verdant foliage of the garden, like some statue of chaste and classical beauty, placed to embellish and diversify the sylvan spot.

Gomez Arias is before her, and yet she seems hardly conscious of his presence. He gazes on her with surprise, and then gently whispers her dear name. The well known voice recalls her scattered ideas, and its magic sound awakens her benumbed sensations to fresh warmth and life. She raised her head, threw aside the rich clusters of her hair, and a stream of moonlight falling on her countenance revealed to Gomez Arias a picture of sorrowing love.

Her eye was swollen with grief, and the big tears in quick succession chased each other down her pallid cheek.

Don Lope approached her tenderly, and folding her in his arms, endeavoured to calm her emotion, by the most soothing and endearing expressions.

"Theodora, what means this sorrow? Whatever be the misfortune which threatens us, do not vainly yield yourself a prey to terror, before you know the means I may have of averting it." Then, as if struck by a passing thought, he added—"You surely cannot entertain a distant doubt of the singleness—the devotedness of my affection?"

"Doubt of your affection! Oh, heavens! do not even mention the appalling word; there is something more terrible than death in the very idea. No, no," she continued, with vivid earnestness; "I do not; I cannot; I will not doubt of your affection. If ever such agonizing——"

She could not proceed, for her imagination was so powerfully acted upon, even with the remote image of such a misfortune, that she was obliged to remain some time silent before she could control her emotions.

"No," she resumed; "I cannot doubt your affection. But there is another calamity in store for me that will assuredly render wretched the rest of my existence."

She again stopped, and her tears flowed more abundantly than ever.

Gomez Arias felt relieved from a heavy foreboding; for the idea that his engagement with Leonor de Aguilar had come to the knowledge of Theodora, had at first filled his mind with apprehensions. He was accordingly more at ease, feeling an inward conviction that however distressing the dreaded intelligence might prove, he should still find resources within himself to avert its dangers.

"Speak, my Theodora; unfold the cause of your extraordinary sorrow, and do not weep and tremble thus."

"Oh, Lope!" she despondingly cried, "I must renounce you for ever."

"For heaven's sake, calm this agitation, Theodora, and let me know the worst. But yesterday you were as happy as a heart teeming with genuine affection, and blessed with a most unbounded return, can make a mortal, and now——"

"He is come," she fearfully interrupted him; "my destined husband is come."

Gomez Arias appeared staggered at this unexpected information, but immediately recovering himself in apparent calmness, demanded the name of his rival. "Who is it," he cried, "that boldly claims the hand of my Theodora?—No doubt some noble and distinguished cavalier."

"Alas! your supposition is but too just," replied the weeping girl; "and it is that circumstance which adds to the poignancy of my grief: were he a less estimable character, were he divested of those amiable qualities that render man dear to the eyes of woman, my reasons for refusing his addresses would be unanswerable. In that case, if I were made a victim to parental authority, some consolation might be found in the conviction that the inextinguishable hatred which I bore him was grounded on justice. But the man that seeks an alliance with our house is one whose choice would confer the greatest honor on the most exalted of the land. Brave, generous, of noble birth, and alike distinguished for the superiority of his mind and person, he is in the highest favor with the queen, who has intrusted him with the command of one of the divisions which are now marching against the rebel Moors."

Theodora made these observations in the perfect simplicity of her heart, but she unconsciously excited an idea of the most galling nature in the mind of her lover. Not that he felt the pangs of jealousy, for he was too confident both in his own merit, and the unparalleled affection of his beloved; but yet he was inwardly mortified at the encomiums bestowed on another, inasmuch as they gave rise to a comparison which he could not easily brook. He, therefore, with some asperity of tone, inquired the name of this accomplished knight; and Theodora, who perceived the inward workings of his soul, with a faultering voice pronounced the name of Don Antonio de Leyva. The sound operated like an electric shock on the mind of Gomez Arias, and despite of his habitual self-command, signs of uncommon perturbation were discernible in his countenance.

"What!" he cried, "Don Antonio de Leyva,—that presumptuous, that detested youth!"

Here he checked his emotion; pride resumed the mastery over his irritated feelings, and with a forced gaiety of manner, he continued,—

"Certainly Don Antonio is a gallant cavalier, and well calculated to captivate a woman's affections."

He stopped; for his surprise had been too abrupt, and his manner too ill disguised to continue long in this constrained suppression of his real feelings. Gomez Arias hated Don Antonio on no other plea, than the fame he was daily acquiring for his valour and brilliant qualities. Besides, he could not forget his adventure in the tournament, when Don Antonio crossed him in his career, and well nigh endangered the reputation he had that day acquired. He looked on him, therefore, as a dangerous rival, and felt chagrined at the command with which the queen had invested him, as it would afford him opportunities of grounding his claims to her royal favor on the firmest foundation.

Theodora was far from suspecting the cause of her lover's agitation. She naturally attributed to a feeling of jealousy, what was in fact the effect of restless emulation. A long pause ensued, during which the state of Theodora became more distressing, as she perceived her lover's countenance gradually assuming an unusual expression of sternness. Various passions seemed to be contending for mastery in his bosom, but the feeling of wounded pride soon appeared to predominate. His eyes glistened with indignant fire, his lip curled with a bitter smile, and the flush of anger mantled on his brow.

"Theodora!" he said, fixing earnestly his eyes on the trembling girl; "Theodora, you have deceived me!"

"Deceive you, Gomez Arias!" She looked petrified at the bare supposition. "Deceived you! And can you for a moment harbour such a cruel, such a degrading suspicion? Oh! Lope, is it possible you can think thus basely of your Theodora?"

"Why was not I made acquainted with this engagement before?"

"I was ignorant of it myself; the marriage had been settled between my father and Don Antonio, without consulting my inclination. Alas! the first intelligence I received, was to bid me prepare for the ceremony, which is to take place immediately.—My dearest Lope," she added with tenderness; "Oh! never again harrow up my feelings, with doubts unworthy of our mutual passion."

She clung to Don Lope's neck, and pressing him with the earnestness of unbounded confidence and love—"Never," she continued, "had Theodora a single thought concealed from you; you, the absolute master of my heart, and the most secret wishes of my soul."

Then in a more composed manner, she proceeded; "It was but this morning that Don Antonio arrived, when my father immediately proceeded to announce the purport of his visit. My amazement at first knew no bounds; I remonstrated on the abruptness of the proposal, and endeavoured, by gentle expostulation, to ward off the threatening blow. But my entreaties, and my tears were in vain. My father, strenuously bent on the accomplishment of his wishes, left me the only option of yielding implicit obedience to his mandates, or passing the rest of my existence in the solitary gloom of a convent. My choice is made; I lose you, Lope;"—and here her anguish almost overpowered her utterance; "I lose you for ever, but your dear image shall be constantly before me in those dark abodes of penitence and woe. Thither must I go, and leave all these dear scenes, and the dearer sight of you, consigned to unrelenting misery. Not humbly, alas! to pray; not to abjure the world; for ah! I cannot abjure that world which contains the fondest object that links me to life. I go not in the humble mood of a repentant sinner, to weep over a guilty life, but in the desponding resolution of a fond woman, eager to keep her faith unbroken to him of her heart's first and only attachment. For you, oh Lope, my tears will flow; you alone will be the theme of my constant meditations—my fervent prayers. In my hopeless solitude, I may perhaps feel one glimpse of consolation;—the idea that you may be happy, and that even in the glittering scenes of ambition, you will sometimes revert to the cheerless abode of Theodora. This will afford me some solace in my affliction. And when the hand of death releases me from my odious chains, your tears will tenderly fall on the grave of her, whose greatest crime was that of loving you too well."

"Theodora!" exclaimed Gomez Arias, moved by the picture she had drawn; "and is this then the only remedy you can devise?"

"What!" cried she eagerly, "is there any other to be found?"

She paused, and gazed on Gomez Arias, with anxious expectation, breathless with hope.

Don Lope, after a momentary lapse, with a chilling coldness, observed—"You do not love me, Theodora!"

"Oh Heavens!" she cried in the hurried accents of terror—"Never, Lope, never utter those killing words;—what do you require of me?—

Speak, Gomez Arias, speak: I will do all, to convince you of the sincerity of my affection, and the cruel injustice of your words."

"You must fly then from the abode of parental oppression," calmly replied Don Lope; "and in your lover you shall find that tenderness, which a father denies; nay, start not, these words may perhaps alarm you, yet consider it is our only resource, and that imperious necessity is a law to which we must all submit. In a short time you shall be mine in the face of heaven, and now, you must resolve to follow me."

Theodora started at the proposition. She fixed her eyes on Gomez Arias, and with a deep but tranquil anguish exclaimed—"Alas, Don Lope! Is this the remedy you propose? Can you indeed tempt me to abandon my father in his declining years, to regret and shame?"

"You had already determined to abandon him," observed Gomez Arias.

"No, Lope," she replied; "by that step, I should only disappoint him in his expectations—not incur his merited hatred and malediction;—his grief would be tempered by resignation, not corroded with the sting of shame." "Don Lope," she then continued with dignity, "command my life; but oh! never, never require of me the commission of a crime, as the proof of my love."

"Stay, Theodora," interrupted Gomez Arias, with a composure that ill agreed with the terrific cloud gathering on his brow; "stay, you are right, and I must retract my words: the offer was dictated in the transports of sincere and ardent love, and as the only means left us in the hour of danger. But I perceive that I have mistaken your sentiments; such actions were only made for souls capable of feeling and appreciating the extent of a true passion; not for cold and timorous beings like yourself. I flattered my fond pride, that in you I had met with a miracle of deep and all-absorbing affection, but I am deceived, and sorely shall I repent my delusion; I now see you in your true colours; you are like the rest of your feeble sex, pleased with the gratification of their vanity, but incapable of a bold and generous resolution in favor of the man they pretend to love. I will not upbraid you; but from this moment cast you from me as a piece of inanimate clay, a painted thing, alike incapable of estimating and sharing my regard."

Saying this he rudely disengaged himself from her arms, whilst the unfortunate Theodora, affrighted at the violence of his manner, fixed on him a wild and vacant stare, the intensity of her grief depriving her of the power of reflection. But when she saw her lover actually receding from the place, her mind started from its abstraction, and her thoughts were fixed upon the dreadful desertion that now threatened her. She gave a frantic shriek, and fell lifeless on the ground.

Alarmed at the effect produced by his passionate and cruel proceeding, Gomez Arias hurried back to the spot, and raising the lovely victim from the ground, gazed on her with all the anxiety of returning affection. Theodora was in his arms, but, alas! her beautiful eyes were closed, her cheek was colourless, and a cold suffusion bathed her stiffened limbs. The vital spark had apparently deserted its frail tenement, for no sign of conscious life was there. Don Lope's angry feelings had given way to his fears for her safety, and as he wiped the cold dew from her face, he perceived blood trickling slowly down her marble brow. In the violence of her fall upon the gravelled walk, a flint had wounded her forehead, and the crimson drops that issued from it contrasted mournfully with the frozen paleness of her countenance.

Gomez Arias was moved as he gazed intensely on the angelic creature now before him. This was no artful fiction, no solemn mockery of woe: a few words had worked that dreadful revolution in her mind. Perhaps there is at times an indescribable cruelty in love that prompts a man, in a certain degree, to enjoy the misery which is wrought by an excess of affection towards him, and triumph now mingled with compassion in the abandoned lover's heart. He was, however, soon called to more generous sentiments. Anxiety and regret took place of vanity, while his passion for Theodora acquired new intensity as he scanned her beauteous figure and contemplated the distress he had occasioned. With the most endearing efforts he endeavoured to reanimate the lifeless form of Theodora. He ardently pressed the yielding burthen to his heart, placed his glowing cheek by the cold one of his mistress, fervently kissed the crimson stain upon her forehead, and then bound it with a scarf.

Theodora, however, for some time gave no sign of life. Don Lope called her by the most tender names, sprinkled her face with the water of a neighbouring fountain, and exhausted himself in efforts to revive her. At last she gently opened her eyes, a scarce perceptible motion shook her frame, and shortly after she raised her white fingers to her forehead, as if conscious of sensation. She heaved a deep sigh, and Gomez Arias watching with anxious gaze the progress of her reviving senses, strove with soothing fondness to hasten their return. Her eyes gently opened, and a sad smile played upon her lip, as she acknowledged the tender solicitude of her lover, unable as yet to express herself by words.

"Theodora, my dearest, don't you know me?"

Her abstracted senses awoke as if from a horrid dream, and with fearful and convulsive clasp she hung to Don Lope's neck.

"He is not gone—no, no, I have him here—" The rest of her sentence was lost in a hysteric laugh.

"No, my love," tenderly said Gomez Arias, "I am not gone, nor ever will. I am a barbarian to treat you thus. I do not merit such excellence as thine, and, I crave thy forgiveness for the misery I have inflicted."

Theodora, now perfectly restored, saw the stain of blood on her lover's lip, then she felt the bandage on her forehead, and when Gomez Arias explained the nature of her wound, the fond girl rejoiced at a cause that had called forth her lover's anxiety and caresses.

They remained in profound silence, which they were both afraid to break, for they trembled to renew a subject which had produced such melancholy effects.

But time was swiftly flying, and Gomez Arias again urged the necessity of adopting some resolution.

"Theodora," he said, "the night is wearing fast away, her friendly shade will but for a short time longer favor us, and the morning must, alas! throw still darker shadows over our brightest hopes."

Theodora sighed deeply, but was unable to reply.

"What is to be done?" demanded Don Lope. "Is it your wish that we should part for ever?"

"Part for ever!" cried Theodora; "Oh Heavens! the idea is more than I can endure."

"There is no other alternative left us," said Gomez Arias, "unless you feel yourself courageous enough to—" and here he cast an inquiring glance, and waited her reply; for though the purport of his meaning was obvious, he felt almost afraid to convey it by language.

Theodora's distress increased, and her fond arms that had till now encircled her lover's neck, loosened their hold, whilst her head drooped despondingly upon her bosom.

After a short pause—"My love," continued Gomez Arias, "you must decide, and instantly, we have but a short time more to remain."

"Don Lope," exclaimed the afflicted girl, with impassioned eagerness, "pity! oh pity my horrible situation, and do not tempt me with a crime, to which my own fond woman's heart urges me but too strongly. No, do not exert that uncontrollable power which you possess over my very soul, to sink me deeper into the abyss of misery, that must embitter my future existence. Do not force me to destroy the tranquillity and comfort of a venerable parent—of that parent, whose greatest fault is his excessive fondness and solicitude for his child. Though by his last determination he has completed my misery, he is nevertheless more deserving of pity than reproach. Alas! while he destroys my felicity and repose, he cherishes the idea, that he is laying the foundation of the future happiness of his child."

"Yes!" cried Gomez Arias, smiling bitterly, "by forcing her to waste her life in a cloister."

"No," exclaimed Theodora, "he does not suppose me capable of such a terrible resolution; he is ignorant that my affections are irretrievably bestowed on another, fondly imagining that I shall not long be insensible to the merits of the husband he has chosen."

She fell on the ground, and clasping the knees of her lover, proceeded with redoubled emotion—"Oh, Lope, I know but too well my own weakness! Take, therefore, compassion on my distress, urge me no further, and do not avail yourself of the tenderness and self-devotion of one who adores you, to render her a cruel and delinquent daughter."

Gomez Arias was powerfully struck with the earnestness of her manner; he never imagined he should meet with such opposition from a heart so enthusiastically devoted. He could not but admire the generosity and nobleness of feeling which thus voluntarily condemned itself to a life of solitude and despair, rather than deviate in the smallest degree from moral rectitude. Yet he was inwardly mortified at her superiority, and would fain have persuaded himself that her scruples proceeded rather from a deficiency of passion than from a sense of honor and filial duty. He looked on her with a mixture of compassion and disappointment as he endeavoured to raise her from the ground.

"No, never," she cried, "never will I rise till you grant my request."

"Rise, rise, Theodora," said he gloomily, "and listen to me for the last time.—Since it is your desire, I will no longer, press a sacrifice I was naturally bound to expect from your repeated, and apparently sincere, protestations of regard. Since you will have it so, I must yield. I will begone immediately; but if you are to be for ever lost to me, think not I will tamely submit to my wrongs. I will seek out the cause of our misfortunes, and if he is the valiant knight report speaks him, I shall then find the only solace left me in my desolation, that of taking ample vengeance or falling nobly by his weapon. And now," he added after a short pause, "farewell Theodora! Farewell, for we part for ever!"

"No, you cannot," frantically cried Theodora, "you must not leave me thus. Oh Lope! you were always tender, and generous, and kind.—

Never did you in the slightest manner wound my heart till this dreadful night."

"True," replied Don Lope, "and never till the present moment could I doubt your love."

"Oh Lope! Lope! and is it to your Theodora you speak thus! In pity recall those dreadful words."

"Silly girl," vehemently exclaimed Gomez Arias, "what do you require of me? Or what is it that you wish? You have chosen your path, let me now take mine, unless you force me in my anguish to curse the hour when I first beheld you."

"Curse the day you saw me!" As she uttered this exclamation an involuntary chill crept over her, which seemed to have frozen the springs of her heart.

"Theodora," he now said in a tone of sad reproach, "dry your tears—you will soon have bitter occasion for them. May you enjoy that repose which you have for ever destroyed in my heart—Farewell! Farewell!"

As he said this he gently strove to disengage himself from her hold. The struggle was too powerful for her nature, and like the poor bird when under the magic influence of the serpent, yields itself to the destructive charm, Theodora, unable any longer to combat with her overpowering feelings, threw herself into her lover's arms, and exclaimed passionately upon his bosom—"No, no, dear Lope, we will not part. Let it be as you will." She paused, and then added with solemnity—"It is decreed that I must be wretched, but you at least shall never have reason to reproach me."

Gomez Arias clasped her fondly to his breast, and in the transports of his joy, endeavoured to draw a glowing picture of their future happiness.

"My dearest Theodora, hush your apprehensions and unreasonable fears. At the first opportunity we marry. Your father will at last relent, and even if he should prove deaf to the appeal of nature, the love and gratitude of Gomez Arias will supply the loss."

"Oh that is my only consolation," she interrupted with eagerness. "Love me, Lope, love me even as I love you. No, no, that is not possible. But, oh, if thy love should ever decrease—deceive me! in pity deceive me! Do not let me suspect the dreadful truth—No, let death first conceal from me so terrible a secret."

Gomez Arias again tenderly essayed to calm her agitation, and then urged the necessity of quitting the place with the utmost expedition. She made no longer any resistance, for she had advanced too far now to recede, and leaning on her lover she was almost carried along the garden.

Gomez Arias quickly made a signal, and a ladder of ropes was thrown from the other side. At the sight Theodora could scarcely restrain the agony of her feelings. A crowd of thoughts distracted her mind—a load of anguish was upon her breast, and had it not been for the support of her lover, she would have fallen. Gomez Arias bore the trembling girl across the wall, but as she stood for an instant on the summit, she cast a long melancholy look on the home of her innocence and childhood—the now deserted abode, of a venerable parent, and with a heart throbbing with anguish, she intrusted herself to the protection of her lover.

CHAPTER X.

Where is she?
I wish to see my daughter, shew her me;

* * * * *

You have betrayed me; y' have let loose
The jewel of my life: Go, bring her me,
And set her here before me.—
Beaumont and Fletcher.

The next day arrived—a day of sorrow for the unfortunate Monteblanco. Seated on a ponderous chair of rude workmanship, the old *caballero* waited for the appearance of his darling daughter, to pay her morning devoirs, and receive his blessing. He waited patiently for some time, but his mind becoming fraught with more than usual anxiety, he called lustily to the duenna,—he called again, and again, but to no purpose. The pious old dame was deeply engaged in her orisons, and her mind occupied with other affairs than appertain to this sinful world. She appeared at last, her eyes half closed, her lips moving fast in the fervour of her devotions, and her long skinny fingers employed in a manner equally devout, as with the most exemplary industry, and solemn sedateness, she let fall in measured intervals, one by one, the large black counters of her rosary.

"The Lord be with you!" ejaculated piously the duenna.

"Save you, good Martha," responded Don Manuel.

"And may the blessed Virgin forgive you Señor, for thus disturbing an humble sinner at her prayers."

"Amen!" answered Don Manuel; "and now Martha tell me where is my daughter."

"*Ave Maria!*" continued the duenna, as another counter fell.

Monteblanco, who expected quite a different answer, was however kind enough to give the customary response to the salutation.

"*Santa Maria!*" muttered he with a movement of impatience, raising nevertheless his eyes to heaven. But it so happened that the devotion of the old cavalier was obliged to give way to his paternal solicitude.

"Martha," he therefore cried, "put aside your beads, and tell me, in goodness tell me, if my child is indisposed."

"Holy Virgin!" exclaimed the duenna, "what brings that into your head, Don Manuel?"

"If not," demanded the father, "how does it happen she has not yet appeared?—Where is she?"

"In bed, God help her," replied Martha, "for she very naturally concluded, that a lady who had spent the night in an amorous colloquy, could not be expected to rise over early the next morning."

"In bed!" echoed Monteblanco, "in bed! shame, why it is past seven," he added, somewhat ruffled at the idea. "What! has she passed an indifferent night?"

"Not that I know of, unless indeed that she may have been a little too zealous in her midnight devotions: the grace of the Lord be upon her for a sweet, innocent child. Bless her soul, she could not be otherwise after the holy counsel which I, a miserable sinner, have endeavoured to instill into her tender mind."

"Martha, Martha," seriously observed Don Manuel, "I do not entirely approve of this excess of devotion."

"Ah!" ejaculated the duenna. "That is exactly what I say to her, but she is very scrupulous in her religious exercises."

"Well Martha, you must moderate her zeal, and make her understand that the views of heaven will be much better realized, by yielding implicit obedience to the dictates of a father; and now," he added in a more familiar tone, "go, and bid her come, for I expect Don Antonio de Leyva every minute."

The duenna went out muttering a *Gloria Patri*, which was exactly finished by the time she got at the other side of the door. She then hastened to the chamber of her charge, by no means pleased with a somnolency that exposed her to any rebuke, however trifling.

Gomez Arias; or The Moors of the Alpujarras.

"Oh you sluggish girl," she began. "*Dios me perdone,*[1] what means this? Are you not ashamed to be in bed at this time in the morning, and allow a christian matron like me to be disturbed at her prayers on your account? This comes of your nocturnal meetings; I must put a stop to them; they may be very refreshing to the heart, but cannot contribute to the health, nor to the good keeping of the soul; up, up *perezosa,*[2] and never more expose a kind duenna to your father's rebukes; up, immediately, Don Manuel is waiting." Receiving no answer, she took it for granted, being not a little deaf, that Theodora was replying with the various excuses which were naturally to be expected, under similar circumstances. She continued, therefore, without troubling herself as to their import. "Nay, nay, attempt not to exculpate yourself, for it is very wrong to expose me thus, because I am so amiably inclined as to overlook your frailties with christian charity. Holy Virgin! I shudder when I think to what perilous compromises my unsullied reputation is daily exposed by the tenderness of my disposition. What is it you say?—Eh?—What?—you are silent then, well child, after all that is the wisest thing you can do; it pleaseth me to see you thus humble, for humility, like charity, covereth a multitude of sins." The good duenna proceeded in this strain for some time, without receiving any check to her eloquence, till at length, surprised at such an excess of contrition, she grew impatient, flung the windows wide open, pulled the bed hangings aside, when to her utter consternation she found the object of her intended visitation vanished. The surprise of the duenna was strongly pictured on her shrivelled visage, as the dismal truth obtruded itself upon her mind. The wrath of Monteblanco, and the blot upon her own dear reputation, as the natural consequences of this disaster, took possession of her mind. She first uttered something between a whine and a discordant cry, meaning thereby to indicate at once her emotions of anger and sorrow. Then she began busily to invoke the protection of all the saints in the calendar. But the saints, though very holy personages in their way, are by no means the proper persons to consult respecting the discovery of stray damsels. She appeared to place more confidence in her own exertions than in their assistance. She commenced a scrupulous search in every part of the chamber, under and round about the bed, and waddling out of the apartment, she left no corner in the house unsearched.

---

[1] God forgive me.
[2] Sluggard.

Astonished at the duenna's activity, and puzzled to discover the cause, the servants flocked around her, but to all their inquiries she gave no other answer but interjections and exclamations, and such harsh guttural sounds, that they began to suspect that the good dame had fairly lost her wits.

The garden was now explored, but alas! with no better success, and the perturbation of poor Martha's mind baffled all description.

It was some time before she could determine what course to pursue, balancing in her mind whether it would be more prudent to avoid the impending storm by flight, or boldly and confidently to encounter her master's ire. Flight certainly is the method preferred on similar occasions; but then by adopting it she would tacitly confess herself guilty, and her tender reputation would be sullied with an indelible stain; by bravely encountering, on the other hand, the irritated father, she could stoutly deny all cognizance of the affair, and boldly call on all the saints of Heaven to assert her innocence, witnesses to whose testimony Martha always confidently appealed, being satisfied they would have no inclination to contradict her.

Acting upon this idea, she left the garden, instilling into her parchment features all the surprise and grief that she could muster up at so short a notice.

In the meantime Monteblanco, heartily tired of sending message after message, resolved to seek himself the cause of the duenna's protracted absence.

"Martha—Martha," he cried, as soon as he saw her—"In the name of the devil, what means this?"

"Hush, Don Manuel!" replied the duenna, with great solemnity of manner—"Hush, venerated Señor; for sure enough the evil one has been at work."

"What!" exclaimed the astonished Don Manuel, "explain yourself, and quickly."

"Holy Virgin!" proceeded the dame, "that such a thing should happen in my time!"

"In the name of God—Martha," cried again the father, in agony, "tell me what misfortune has happened."

"Oh!" whined the duenna, struggling hard to force from her old eyes a couple of rebellious tears, "ask me not, for shame and sorrow will choke my utterance."

"May all the curses of Heaven choke you! Woman, what have you done with my daughter? Speak—speak, or by *Santiago de Composte-*

la, I will so belabour thy shrivelled form, as to reduce it to atoms in less time than you can say your *credo*."

The duenna had never before seen her master in so terrible a passion, and she almost repented not having followed her first impulse to fly. She inwardly cursed that tenderness for her reputation, which had brought the more substantial part of her person into the present quandary. A vigorous defence was the only alternative now left her.

"What have I done with your daughter!" she exclaimed, with a look which she meant to be expressive of indignant surprise.—"May the Lord help you!—what should I have done with your daughter?"

"Where is she then?"

A pause ensued.

"Where is she?" demanded again the agitated father, with redoubled emotion.

"Alas! I know not—she is gone to all appearance—May the light of Heaven, and her guardian angel conduct her steps!"

"Gone!—my Theodora gone!" cried Don Manuel in the height of affliction.

"I conclude that to be the case," added the duenna, with assurance, "for she is nowhere to be found."

The desolate father appeared thunderstruck at this intelligence. He smote his venerable forehead, and plucked his grey beard in the anguish of despair. Then he vented the most bitter reproaches against the ingratitude of his daughter, and cursed the day that gave her birth.

Whilst he was thus vainly indulging in the paroxysm of grief, the duenna kept crossing herself with such active fervour, that the repeated and rapid motion of her hand at last caught the attention of the sorrowing and abstracted father.

"Oh, thou vile hypocrite!" he exclaimed, darting a furious look—"Thou beldame!—Is this the way thou hast answered the confidence reposed in thee?—I have nurtured a serpent in my house—I have set the ravenous wolf to guard the lamb! Accursed beldame! Thou art an accomplice in my daughter's flight."

"Holy Virgin of the Conception!" ejaculated the offended Martha, "that such foul aspersions should be thrown on my character, after sixty years of rigid penitence! May the Lord forgive you, Señor, as I do"—and she crossed herself with redoubled zeal.

"Forgive me, thou imp of the devil!" thundered Don Manuel, astonished at her assurance.—"Forgive me!"

"I an imp of the devil!—I, who had an aunt who died in odour of sanctity, in the convent of Santa Clara—I, who am second cousin to

Fray Domingo, one of the most religious as well as most celebrated preachers of the day!"

"May the curse of Heaven fall on thee, and him, and all thy race."

"Do not swear," interrupted Martha; "Oh! do not swear—you fright me—I shall faint."

"Avaunt, thou detested hag!" continued Don Manuel.

"*San Pedro y san Pablo!*" cried the duenna.

"Thou poisonous crocodile!" replied Don Manuel.

"*San Jose bendito!*" responded the duenna.

"Abominable fiend!" returned Don Manuel.

"*Animas benditas!*" answered the duenna.

This extraordinary litany, however, was at length cut short by the arrival of Don Antonio de Leyva. He was not a little surprised at the scene which presented itself, and was for some time unable to obtain an explanation. When he at length arrived at a knowledge of the affair, his astonishment and sorrow were exhibited in the most lively manner.

"Alas!" he cried, "I could not but suspect from my first interview with Theodora, that her affections were fixed on another object."

"Oh, no, no," eagerly replied Don Manuel—"you are far from the mark—she cannot love any one—how could she form an attachment without my knowledge?"

"Then," said Don Antonio, sighing, "it was to avoid my addresses that she has sought a refuge in flight."

"*Jesus Maria!*" interposed the duenna—"Do not say so, Don Antonio—how could she possibly object to so accomplished a cavalier?"

"Good dame," answered he, "it is not difficult to account for her dislike; and I must acknowledge with painful sensations, that I am chiefly to blame for this unfortunate occurrence."

"No, no," cried Monteblanco, pointing to Martha; "the person chiefly to blame in this affair, is that detestable hag.—See how she crosses herself, and rolls her eyes to impose upon our credulity; but it is all over—I have been too long the dupe of her affected piety, and seeming austerity of manners; my eyes are at length open to conviction, and I see the despicable creature in her true colours."

"What reason," observed de Leyva, "can you assign for Theodora's strange resolution, unless it be dislike to me, or love for another."

"Alas! I know not what to think," answered Don Manuel; "my mind is bewildered, and all my conjectures may prove wrong. Perhaps some hastiness in my way of proceeding may have influenced her determination. But I do not despair; she may yet be brought to a sense of her duty; if not," he added despondingly, "the happiness of my declining age is blasted, and heartily shall I wish to be numbered with the dead."

Monteblanco by these means sought a medium between accusing his daughter of downright criminality, and confessing to young de Leyva that his suspicions concerning Theodora's aversion to the intended wedding were not entirely groundless.

He was unwilling also to relinquish the thought of having so excellent a son-in-law, and he believed Don Antonio to be possessed of all those qualities which are capable of enslaving the affections of women, even the most fastidious. He, therefore, prudently resolved, in case of his child's return, to allow her due time to consider the proposal, which he had been so anxious to carry by parental authority, hoping that she would at last be brought to acquiesce in his wishes, by the constant assiduity and numberless accomplishments of her suitor.

Under this impression, he readily accepted the services proffered by Don Antonio, for the recovery of Theodora, and for speedily concerting the means.

"Don Manuel," exclaimed the gallant de Leyva, "spite of your kind and courteous asseverations, I cannot but consider myself the cause of your daughter's leaving her home. This reflection and that tender sentiment which Theodora was as capable of inspiring as I am susceptible of feeling, makes me perhaps a principal in this melancholy event. It is with heartfelt sincerity, therefore, that I offer my assistance. Let us first endeavour to restore the lovely fugitive to her deserted home, and then let not the shadow of compulsion actuate her future determination."

"I shall be happy," replied Don Manuel, "to profit by advice dictated at once by affection and prudence. Theodora," he added after a short pause, "cannot have departed from this city, and we shall probably find her either in a convent, or at the abode of one of her relatives. However, to insure all precaution, I shall forthwith send despatches to Granada, and the neighbouring towns."

Saying this, Monteblanco made a movement to retire with his young friend, and casting a look of anger on the duenna, he said as he passed—"Thou mayest well tremble, miserable sinner that thou art!"

"Tremble, forsooth!" returned the stately dame, with great dignity of manner. "Innocence has no occasion to tremble; and now it only remains for me to quit a place where my virtue and honesty have so unwarrantably been called in question."

"When thou dost quit my house," said Don Manuel, "it will be to be shut up for life in a convent, there to do penance for thy sins, and to profit by the holy example of that good aunt that died in odour of sanctity."

Left to herself, Martha began seriously to reflect on the unpleasantness of her situation; the threat of a conventual seclusion sounded harshly to her ear. She fancied it would be more advantageous to society that her good offices should continue in requisition, than that they should be for ever lost by an untimely adoption of a contemplative life.

"Oh, that ungracious Gomez Arias!" she exclaimed, in her perplexity.

"What wouldst thou with Gomez Arias?" said a well known voice.

She turned, and saw before her the object of her exclamation.

"Blessed be the Virgin! It is he, sure enough. What brings you here, Sir? Where is my young lady?"

"Where is she?" inquired Gomez Arias, with feigned anxiety.

"Nay, nay, your arts are thrown away on me; I know that Theodora, poor silly thing, has eloped with you. She loves you, in very truth, she does; and when a woman really loves, it is unaccountable what a number of fooleries she will be tempted to commit."

"Well," returned Don Lope, "supposing she has intrusted herself to my protection, she only followed the dictates of pure affection; surely there could be no harm in so doing."

"Under favour, Don Lope," observed the duenna, "but there is. Not forsooth in loving you; but yet, there is a crying injustice, an unpardonable cruelty, in leaving me to suffer for it without a——"

"Reward, wouldst thou say?" interrupted Don Lope.

"*Valgame San Juan!* But you misapprehend me strangely. I am not mercenary; heaven knows my only concern is for my safety, threatened as I am."

"Threatened! in what possible manner?" demanded Gomez Arias.

"With nothing less than a convent."

"A convent," repeated Don Lope, smiling, "to so devout a dame, methinks, can have no terrors."

"Aye in troth, I am devout," replied the duenna, "and yet I feel nowise inclined to be immured between four walls. What merit would there be in the sacrifice of an old, poor, decrepid piece of mortality such as I. No, it is the voluntary seclusion of young, rich and beautiful virgins that delights the divinity."

"Most prudent Martha," gaily replied Gomez Arias, "I greatly admire and applaud your discretion. Never ought so worthy, so valuable a matron to be lost to the world. No, thou wert born to be the consolation of gallant knights and amorous damsels; it would be really unpardonable to permit thy seclusion, whilst thou mayest yet tend thy services to lovers. No, no, God forbid thou shouldst go to a nunnery."

"The Lord bless you, good Señor," returned Martha with humility; "but you over-rate my poor deserts."

"By my sword! that modesty becomes thee mightily. But we must lose no time. Attend vespers this afternoon, there thou shalt find my conscientious valet, who will give thee proper directions and assistance to effect thy escape, and ample means to pass the remainder of thy precious life in some distant city of Spain, free from the blessed idea of conventual retirement."

"That will I do, most generous Don Lope, and be thankful withal."

"But stay," added Gomez Arias with mock gravity; "there is one objection to this arrangement."

"*Virgen de las Angustias!*—What is it, Señor?" demanded the duenna, in visible alarm.

"Why!" answered Gomez Arias, "only that thou must sacrifice somewhat of that dear, unsullied reputation by following such a course."

"Alas, Señor!" exclaimed she of the nice reputation—"That is too true; willingly would I preserve it entire, but feeble mortals are not bound to do more than their strength can compass."

"True," rejoined Gomez Arias; "thine argument, most venerable Martha, is a very plausible argument, and very consoling withal."

At this moment a noise was heard. The duenna started. "It is my master, and Don Antonio," cried she. "Hence! begone, Don Lope, they must not see us together."

"Fear not, most respected dame," said Gomez Arias; "I am no college gallant, no unskilful tyro in the affairs of love; I depart but to return in due time."

"Return!" echoed Martha; "to what purpose?"

"To cover thy threadbare reputation," said he laughing; "it appears of so tender a texture, that it is likely to be torn piece-meal, if not remedied in time. Besides, I must protect my own, should it be necessary: a good pilot, even in a calm, must prepare against foul weather."

"Our Lady's blessing be upon your head!" said Martha, "for a right prudent *caballero*."

"Well, mind to give thy assistance at vespers."

"Ah, my good Señor; my devotion requires no stimulus."

Gomez Arias made his exit, just in time to prevent a meeting with the aforesaid gentlemen. They had been busily occupied in devising the most efficacious means to insure success in their researches. Don Manuel appeared more composed in his demeanor, for he placed much confidence in the influence and abilities of his ally. Hope, that with its cheering ray lights us even on the gloomy borders of the tomb, now in part dispelled the heavy cloud that overshadowed the deserted father's heart.

Don Antonio took an affectionate leave, and after repeating his cordial offers of assistance, departed.

Monteblanco, when left by himself, felt his wrath again revived, at the sight of the duenna; he therefore renewed his threats of a convent.

"Don Manuel!" said the duenna, with a most sanctimonious look, "I am innocent—innocent, as the child unborn: yet if it so pleaseth Heaven, that I should be immured in a cloister, the Lord's will be done; a convent has no terrors for me; alas! a poor humble sinner can desire no better abode; but think, Señor, how galling it is to be forced by compulsion to embrace a state, that ought to be embraced out of spontaneous inclination; allow me at least a few hours to arrange my worldly concerns, and I shall be ready to obey your commands."

Saying this, the female *tartuffe* retired to her chamber, to prepare for her secret departure.

CHAPTER XI.

Tu puoi pensar, se'l padre addolorato
Riman quand'accusar sente la figlia,
Si perchè ode di lei quel, che pensato
Mai non avrebbe, e n'ha gran maraviglia.
Ariosto.

Ben se'crudel, se tu già non ti duoli
Pensando cio ch'al mio cor s'annunziava:
E se non piangi di che pianger suoli?
Dante.

Whilst the unhappy father was absorbed in his recent misfortune, and endeavouring to beguile the tedious hours, by directing researches in all quarters of the town, where there was any possibility of his daughter having taken refuge, he was surprised with a visit from Gomez Arias.

"Pardon my intrusion, Señor," he said with much courtesy; "my anxiety for the fate of an honorable gentleman, though a rival, will perhaps hold me excused in the eyes of Don Manuel de Monteblanco."

"Sir," returned Don Manuel, "your visits do much honor to my humble dwelling, and stand in no need of an apology."

After the long vocabulary of compliments had been exhausted, Gomez Arias reverted to the adventure in the *Zaguan*, and with apparent anxiety demanded news of Don Rodrigo.

"I have none, Señor," said Monteblanco; "and alas! I am not likely to feel much concerned for the inconvenience of another, at a time when I am myself plunged in deep affliction."

"Perhaps," resumed Gomez Arias, "it may not be altogether right in a stranger to pry into the secret motives of your sorrows; but if I can by any means in my power alleviate them, I should esteem myself particularly honored in meriting your confidence. I but now perceived signs of alarm in the countenances of your servants, apparently not without foundation, and it grieves my very soul to see so honorable a personage in distress. What has happened, noble Señor?"

"Alas! My child—my child!" cried the afflicted father.

"She is not ill?" inquired Don Lope.

"Oh! worse!—worse," replied Don Manuel with emotion.

"Ah!" exclaimed Gomez Arias, feigning surprise. "What?—no—it is not possible—and yet it may be so."

"Eh?" cried Monteblanco, in an inquiring tone of voice, and opening wide his eyes in the eagerness of anticipation.

"My valet," continued Don Lope, "brought me information that there was a rumour circulating about the town, relating to the elopement of a noble lady. As I am a perfect stranger in the place, I felt no curiosity to inquire further into the affair, but I could not then imagine that you, Sir, were the victim of this misfortune."

"Alas! Don Lope! it is but too true!"

Gomez Arias had learnt so well the part he had to perform, that he found not the slightest difficulty in going through it with the most perfect ease, and by this means he insensibly won the confidence of the deluded Don Manuel, who, like many others under similar circumstances, felt a relief in confiding his sorrows to one, who appeared to sympathise with him so sincerely.

"For surely," continued Don Lope, "some one must have been acquainted with this flight. Have you well examined your servants? Depend upon it, Señor, they are generally the instruments and abettors in the rebellion of children against their parents."

"You are right, my honored Sir," replied Don Manuel. "Servants are the sworn enemies of those who give them bread; but though I am disposed to suspect every one of my dependants of being accessory to this treason, I am yet at a loss on whom to fix my suspicions with justice. I am assured, however, that the duenna must have had an active part in conducting this abominable transaction."

"The duenna!" exclaimed Gomez Arias, darting a look full of wonder and well feigned surprise—"The duenna! By my sword, that must be our clue—I had almost forgotten that you had a duenna in your house, otherwise my astonishment would not have been so lively. Duennas are the soul of every intrigue, and you may indeed affirm, with a safe conscience, that yours has not only connived at, but even facilitated your daughter's escape."

"Of that, alas! I am but too confident," replied the father, "notwithstanding her solemn asseverations and canting hypocrisy."

"Ah! the cunning beldame," quoth Don Lope sarcastically. "She has all the arts of her kind, I perceive; but I hope, Señor Don Manuel, that you are not to be imposed upon by such shallow artifices. We must secure the duenna, and examine her well; perchance a few threats will not be altogether unavailing."

"That is precisely the method I have adopted," said Don Manuel.

"And where is the old hag, now?" inquired Don Lope.

"Packing up her trumpery, to depart for the convent."

"Pedro"—then called Don Manuel.

"Your pleasure?" demanded the valet, as he entered.

"Send Martha to me."

Pedro obeyed, but shortly after returned with a most dismal and elongated visage.

"Well, what is the old dotard staring at?" impatiently cried his master.

"Señor, Martha is flown," replied the dependant.

"Flown!" re-echoed Monteblanco, in consternation; "Flown! And how came you not to prevent her departure?"

"Save your honor," returned the terrified Pedro, "we all thought she was quietly shut up in her chamber. She has contrived to escape, the Lord only knows how—she must have vanished through the chimney, or a key hole, like a witch that she is, *Jesus me valga*!"

"That she is a witch I am fully aware, and you are all her familiars," cried Don Manuel with violence. "But you shall rue the moment the hag foiled your vigilance."

Gomez Arias, who had observed a perfect silence, now ventured to remark—

"We need go no further for a positive proof of the duenna's culpability, since her guilt is rendered sufficiently evident by her flight."

"Yes," observed Don Manuel, "but that circumstance affords me little consolation. The means of ascertaining the truth are now lost, by the disappearance of the principal accomplice."

The afflicted old man again gave way to his exasperated feelings; this last stroke quite overpowered him. His pride was sorely wounded, for he was one of those old Spanish cavaliers, who, when deprived of every other satisfaction, took a melancholy pleasure in inflicting his vengeance on the object of his wrath. But even this solitary consolation was now denied him, and the idea that he had been so grossly imposed upon by an old beldame, added to the galling reflections which his misfortune had inflicted.

Gomez Arias exerted his utmost endeavours to sooth his emotion, employing for this purpose all the established maxims resorted to under similar circumstances—maxims profoundly wise no doubt, but which unluckily are often lost upon their object.

"In order then," said Gomez Arias, "to unravel this mystery, it is of the first importance to set about the inquiry from the commencement, in order to discover the authors. We have now the agent of this nefarious enterprise, but we must seek for the actual culprit. There can be no doubt that when a young girl is induced to elope from her home, there is generally a lover who prompts her to so objectionable a measure. Now, Don Manuel, is there no person on whom suspicion may attach with any probability?"

Monteblanco pondered for a while, and then replied—"Really, Don Lope, if there exists such a man, I am totally unacquainted with his person."

"What, are you unable to hazard even a conjecture?"

"I am, Don Lope," sorrowfully answered the father.

"Indeed! this is surprising;—look, Señor, around the circle of your acquaintance, and perchance you may find a clue to guide your investigation."

Don Manuel mechanically looked around, and then shook his head despondingly.

"I would not willingly," continued Gomez Arias, "throw an aspersion on the reputation of any one, but what are we to surmise from the visit of Don Rodrigo de Cespedes? Certainly, there was something unaccountable in his chivalric expedition against me. Besides, why require the assistance of an aged cavalier, when he might have commanded that of more suitable agents for that description of undertaking?"

Gomez Arias met with no great difficulty in deceiving the man he had injured; for one under Don Manuel's distressing situation, is of all others the most easy to be imposed upon. His own wounded feelings, in some measure, paved the way to the deception;—as a man who has lost his purse, is apt to throw the charge on the very first individual who unfortunately happens to attract his notice.

"In addition to this," proceeded Gomez Arias, "we may remark the visible alarm which was stamped on the countenance of the young lady, when our quarrel took place—her anxiety to bring the light—the shriek she uttered on imagining that my antagonist had fallen;—these,

Don Manuel, are strong indications, which may have escaped your observation in moments of anger and grief, but which to a cooler judgment amount almost to certainty. However, it is not my intention to prejudice your mind against Don Rodrigo; my only desire is to warn you."

By such subtle means, Gomez Arias confirmed Monteblanco's suspicions; for when once started, nothing tends more powerfully to strengthen them than a sort of recantation in their author. Accordingly, Don Manuel felt almost convinced of the treachery of his friend. Certainly there was ample room to doubt the justice of such an imputation, if he had chosen to reflect coolly on the subject; but in cases like the present, the best reasons are unfortunately most unceremoniously set aside.

Thus Don Manuel was at once deceiving himself, and casting a reflection on the character of a man who had not the remotest connection with the event, and whose integrity in this instance could still less be impeached than in the case of his having feloniously taken the old mule of the friar, instead of his own beautiful horse, for the purpose of gaining by the exchange.

Monteblanco, after a moment's thought, suddenly grasping the hand of Gomez Arias—"I owe you much, Don Lope," he said, "and I pray you to be convinced of the sincerity of my gratitude."

"Nay, honored Sir," replied Gomez Arias, "you labour under a delusion—you owe me nothing—at least you owe me no favor, and I solemnly disclaim any title to your acknowledgments."

Many and reciprocal were the compliments that passed from this time between the two cavaliers; they mutually offered their services to each other, and Don Lope very prudently afforded to his new friend all the instructions which might tend to render abortive the pursuit and recovery of the fugitive. Shortly after he took leave of the unfortunate cavalier, who was even troublesome in the expression of his gratitude, and whose hopes now began to assume a brighter hue.

CHAPTER XII.

The intent, and not the deed,
Is in our power; and therefore, who dares greatly
Does greatly.
Browne's Barbarossa.

E ben degg'io, di libertade amico,
Meno la morte odiar di quella vita,
Che ricever dovrei dal mio nemico.
Metastasio.

We must now recall the reader's attention to that portion of the history of the rebellious Moors, which is in some measure connected with our tale. The forty chiefs, who had been elected in the revolt of the Albaycin, succeeded, as we have already seen, in disseminating their sentiments through many towns and villages in the jurisdiction of the Alpujarras: their efforts, however, were almost invariably unsuccessful. In most of their encounters, the Moors were either entirely worsted, or compelled to seek for safety in flight; yet they persevered in their designs. Defeats and repeated crosses, instead of subduing, tended only to increase their courage, by adding to the desire of vengeance.

The rebels had already sustained some severe reverses; amongst which the most prominent was the loss of the town of Guejar, which, after a protracted and desperate resistance, had been taken by storm by the combined forces of Count de Tendilla and the famous Gonzalo de Cordova. Most of the Moors either perished in the defence, or were put to the sword by the conquerors; whilst the Castle itself was given up to the flames.

Gomez Arias; or The Moors of the Alpujarras.

The Count de Lerin next possessed himself of the fortress and town of Andarax; and, exasperated at the resistance of the inhabitants, who continued to protract the defence, although without any chance of success, he at length blew up the Mosque, where a considerable number had fled for shelter, along with the women and children.

Thus of the three strong holds of the rebels, Lanjaron was the only one that now remained unconquered, and this indeed appeared to offer a more formidable resistance, chiefly on account of the garrison having el Negro for a leader—a man of mean origin, but extraordinary courage and resolution. These qualities, together with the services which he had already rendered to the Moorish cause in the wars of Granada, had acquired for him the confidence of his countrymen, who had accordingly intrusted him with the command of this important post. He was a man of severe habits, with a natural ferocity of character, which, although not calculated to conciliate, nevertheless succeeded in commanding the respect and obedience of his troops.

The castle of Lanjaron, situated in the vale of Lecrin, was considered a post of the utmost consequence, not only from the strength of its defences, but from the circumstance of being a place of secure retreat to the Moors of the surrounding country. At this moment the fortress was closely beleaguered by the troops under the command of the Alcayde de los Donceles and other chiefs, who deprived the rebels of the smallest communication with their friends of the mountains, and had thus reduced them to an utter state of destitution.

Under these distressing circumstances, el Negro assembled his men, and in a short but animated speech endeavoured to make them sensible of the importance of keeping possession of Lanjaron, till the other leaders had gained time to organise their means of defence in the Alpujarras. The words of el Negro were received with a burst of enthusiasm, and for some time the Moors vied with each other in giving the most heroic proofs of courage and perseverance. As the fortress, however, was completely surrounded, and the means of subsistence began to fail them, as a last hope, they made a desperate sally during the night, but were driven back with considerable loss. The failure of this attempt damped their resolution, and some of the less courageous even murmured against an exploit beset with difficulties, which it appeared next to an impossibility to surmount.

El Negro beheld these symptoms of discontent with heartfelt sorrow, but at the same time with a countenance expressive of coolness and undaunted fortitude. He exerted his utmost endeavour to quell the rising storm, soothing some with pleasing hopes and promises, and thundering horrible threats on the most refractory. The following morning three grisly heads, dripping blood, appeared affixed to poles upon the battlements; but this salutary punishment did not produce the expected effect, for though it appalled the discontented, it inspired not a single spark of valour in their hearts; whilst the Christians, who beheld the ghastly spectacle, augured favorably from this bloody proof of disaffection.

The numbers of the besieged were daily decreasing, until at length they came to an open resolution of surrendering at discretion. The principal men of the garrison, without the knowledge of their chief, had already sent privately a messenger into the camp of the Spaniards to treat about the surrender, and the conspirators had assembled in a clandestine meeting, when el Negro, whom they supposed to be reposing from his fatigue, suddenly came, and threw them into consternation.

"Traitors! what means this?" he cried, with a voice of thunder; "what are your intents?"

"To capitulate," answered one more hardy than the rest, "and save our lives by a timely submission."

"Villain!" exclaimed el Negro, fiercely, "thou at least shall not enjoy the reward of thy cowardice!" And raising his arm, with a ponderous blow of his scymitar, he cleaved the head of the traitor down to the very shoulder, and the body rolled heavily on the ground. His companions stood aghast in speechless horror, whilst el Negro, his lips curling with ire, and casting around a glance of defiance and contempt—"Go," he exclaimed, "go, unworthy Moors, and abandon a cause which you have not the courage to sustain. Go, and live like slaves, since ye know not how to die like men. Senseless, pitiful cowards! Was it for this then that you forced me to be your leader? Was it for this that I abandoned Granada, leaving there, at the mercy of the Christians, all my dearest friends, and severing the tenderest ties that bind man to existence? Go, and accept the proffered pardon. I will remain alone, to shew our countrymen of the Alpujarras, that at Lanjaron there was at least *one* true man—one who knew how to die in the execution of his duty."

He said, and snatching the sacred standard, ascended rapidly to the summit of the battlements, and placed himself by the three heads, which, from their exposure to the sun and wind, had already begun to decay, and presented a most ghastly and loathsome spectacle. The revolted garrison threw open the gates of the castle to their enemies, whilst el Negro, abandoned by all his companions, continued gloomily pacing the battlements. The Christians, respecting his resolute conduct, and willing to save his life, sent a herald to invite him once more to surrender, declaring he had done his duty, and death alone would be the consequence of his further resistance. He received the message with a sneer, in which contempt was blended with sadness and despair; then taking the presented *adarga*,[1] the acceptation of which was a signification of peace, he threw it disdainfully on the ground, and trampled it under his feet.

"Carry this answer to him who sent thee!" and folding his arms, he resumed his melancholy walk.

The Christians now took possession of the castle, and el Negro tranquilly beheld their approach. El Alcayde de los Donceles, willing to make a last effort to save him, cried out as he advanced—"Yield thee, Moor—yield—and accept thy pardon."

"Never!" exclaimed fiercely el Negro; "the Moor will accept no boon from his enemies. Death is now my only resource; but, Christians, do not rejoice; I have been subdued by treachery, not by arms. Do not rejoice, for our resources are still great, and while el Feri de Benastepar and Cañeri live, your oppression shall not be complete."

He said, and with a sudden spring he hurled himself from the summit of the tower. His body falling on a rock below, was dashed to pieces.

The surrender of Lanjaron, and the tragical end of el Negro, were an irretrievable loss to the Moors. They now found it utterly impossible to oppose the superior and better disciplined troops of the Christians with any chance of success, either in open battle or in regular sieges. They therefore resolved to limit their whole means of defence to the mountains, a description of warfare more suitable to their wandering habits, and far better calculated to harrass the enemy, without sustaining risk. Accordingly, el Feri de Benastepar, Andalla, Cañeri, and other chiefs, collected their forces, and assigned to each other a portion of those mountains which they were at once to govern and defend. By this means the Christians were likewise obliged to divide their army into many divisions, and to encounter the rebels in partial struggles. Don Alonso de Aguilar, who had succeeded in com-

---

[1] The Adarga was a peculiar sort of shield or short buckler used by the Spaniards in those times. The presentation of the adarga was equivalent to an offer of peace. It was a practice often resorted to by the persons entrusted with a mission to the enemy.

pelling el Feri to retreat before him, now pursued his advantage, and advanced towards Gergal, where that rebel chief was collecting his adherents.

In the mean time, Don Antonio de Leyva, whom we have left at Guadix, condoling with Don Manuel at the flight of his daughter, was compelled to forego his wishes to serve the afflicted father. His duty now called him to join the army of Aguilar, and act in conjunction with him against Cañeri and el Feri de Benastepar.

Don Antonio's party had already arrived at Guadix, and the gallant young knight, unwilling to procrastinate his departure when the path of honor was open to him, immediately proceeded to take leave of Monteblanco. He found the unfortunate father plunged in deeper affliction than before. In the society of Don Antonio he had found a source of relief, and his departure was productive of the most melancholy sensations. But Don Manuel felt the necessity of the separation, and he was too generous and noble minded to signify his wish to cause any delay.

"Go, my friend, go, where honor calls you," he said, as he threw his arms round de Leyva's neck—"Go, and show by your conduct how worthy you are of the confidence reposed in you.—When the glory of your deeds shall be blazoned abroad, my ungrateful child will feel a pang of regret for the loss of a man so deserving of her affection and esteem."

Here he was overcome with grief, and could proceed no further.

"Señor," said Don Antonio, "do not yield yourself a prey to despondency; but a short time has yet elapsed since the melancholy occurrence that afflicts you, and you have no reason to relinquish your hopes. In all cases be assured, Don Manuel, that you and those who concern you will always be next my heart, and that unless death deprive me of the power, I shall at least see your wrongs redressed, if I can bring no other consolation."

Saying this he hastily disengaged himself from the arms of Don Manuel, and endeavouring to conceal his own emotion, gave the word of command. He bounded lightly on his spirited barb, and the martial display of his men, the glitter of armour, and the seductive prospect of future glory and renown, powerfully contributed to dispel the cloud that hung over him. Yet it was a sad parting, for there was something peculiarly affecting in the sight of a father who, like Monteblanco, found himself in old age isolated in the midst of the world, and bereft of the last dear comfort that still bound him to life. Besides, in the short interviews between Theodora and Don Antonio, both in the last visit and at former periods, she had left a pleasing recollection in his mind. Already the cries of those who bade the party of de Leyva farewell were diminishing on the ear, and the turrets and steeples of Guadix became more obscurely perceptible in the distance. The warriors began now to assume a mastery over their feelings, and the tear of sympathy was brightened in the glow of expectation. Courage and renown took entire possession of those hearts which but too lately had sympathized with the weaker and more tender sentiments of humanity.

The absence of Don Antonio was like a death-blow to the hopes of Monteblanco. Often did he regret the infirmities of age, which now prevented him from grasping his sword; but his arm was grown nerveless, and for the first time in his life the helpless cavalier felt bitterly the recollection that all his brave sons had sacrificed their lives in the defence of their country, not one now remaining to prop the honor of his falling house. Don Manuel was a man, and this transitory feeling of regret was natural to a father under his affliction, who knew not to whom to turn for consolation and advice.

Gomez Arias, who had insensibly won his favor, departed the next day for Granada, in which quarter he had no longer any danger to apprehend. He was anxious to assume his station in the war against the rebel Moors. Monteblanco considered his intention not only just, but highly commendable, and a tear coursed down the old man's cheek, as he took leave of the seducer of his child, and the cause of his present misfortunes.

CHAPTER XIII.

D'une secrète horreur je me sens frissoner;
Je crains, malgré moi-même, un malheur que j'ignore.
Racine.

Señor Gomez Arias
Duelete de mi
Que soy niña y sola
Nunca en tal me vi.
Calderon.

It was a rich and splendid summer evening. The sun was slowly sinking behind the giant mountains of the Alpujarras, whose dark fantastic shadows were gradually lengthening along the plains below. No intruding sound broke upon the soft stillness of the scene, save when the feathered tenants of the forest warbled their evening song, or the tolling of a distant convent bell reverberated through the sombre recesses of the mountains. A soft languor prevailed over the sylvan scenery. The fancifully wreathing clouds, streaked with the red and gold of the lingering sun—the variegated tints of those quiet solitudes—the warm, chequered streams of light that glanced on the broad-leafed tree, or fitfully quivered over the straggling streamlet—the calm repose which reigned over that wide extending landscape, all tended to raise the mind to contemplation, and to interest the heart.

At this tranquil hour, a group, consisting of three persons, were seen slowly ascending a green sloping height, which seemed designed by nature as a first resting place in the severe ascent of the gigantic mountain. The first of the party was a knight of most gallant bearing, and mounted on a shining black steed. Close by his side rode a beautiful damsel, whose long redundant tresses were with difficulty restrained in a fillet of silver lace. She wore a long riding habit; a Spanish hat, ornamented with a plume of black feathers, was hanging gracefully on one side of her head. Having thrown aside the thick veil which had protected her from the scorching influence of the sun, she discovered a fair countenance, to whose delicate cheek the heat and exercise had lent a gentle tinge of the rose. Yet an expression of pensive sadness pervaded the features of the lovely traveller.

At a short distance behind these two personages, rode a man who appeared by his dress and deportment to be their attendant. He sat with perfect nonchalance on a stout Andalusian horse, but by the looks of suspicious alertness, which he now and then cast around, it might be inferred that this apparent ease was not in strict unison with his inward feelings. At the moment of which we speak, he was singing in a *mezzo tuono* the romance of the Marriage of the Cid—

> A Ximena y a Rodrigo
> Prendió el rey palabraymano
> De juntarlos para en uno
> En presencia de Layn Calvo.

"Cease thy confounded noise, Roque," cried angrily the knight, who, as the reader may suppose, was no other than Gomez Arias. "What in the name of Satan can induce thee to sing, when thou hast neither voice nor ear? Give over, for thy confounded harmony is anything but pleasing."

"Señor," observed the attendant; "what if I only sing to please myself?"

"Silence, buffoon; or I shall presently raise a discord about thee, by which all thy future powers of hearing shall be ruefully endangered."

"Pray, Señor, do not deny me this only comfort; I wish particularly to sing at this moment."

"Thy reasons?"

"Because I always sing when I am afraid; there is nothing so efficacious as a song to drive away fear."

"In sooth, such singing as thine would drive away the very devil. But why shouldst thou fear?"

"Under favor, Don Lope," replied the valet, "methinks fear ought to be the most natural sensation at the present moment."

"Darest thou talk of fear, poltroon!" said Gomez Arias.

"By our Lady of the Pillar," ejaculated Roque, "such talk befits both time and place. Are we not in hourly danger of encountering a set of most fierce murderous-looking *ladrones*?"[1]

"Well, and if that were really the case, we have but to defend ourselves manfully. By the soul of the Cid, I would make very light work of a host of such ruffians."

"Well, my honored master," returned the valet, "but be pleased to consider that this is not our only danger, for I trow we are now in the mountains of Alpujarras, where those accursed and rebellious Moors hold dominion. A plague on the infidel dogs! Are they not continually on the watch to spring upon straggling and unwary Christians, and when they do surprise them—"

"Peace, fool, peace!" impatiently interrupted Gomez Arias, "This is not the Alpujarras. Forgettest thou that when we left Guadix two days since, we pursued quite a different route?"

"That I know, Don Lope, but I likewise know that during the night, either by chance or on purpose, we lost our way. Besides I am not so ignorant of the country as to mistake these places, and I would wager my head against two *maravedis*[2] that we are actually ascending the Alpujarras."

The young lady, who had till now observed a profound silence, with a faultering voice exclaimed—"Oh, heavens! are we really in those terrible mountains, and are we indeed in danger?"

"No, my love," answered Gomez Arias; "the danger is not so great as this fool would make us believe."

"No, my lady," retorted Roque; "the danger is not so great, for after all, the worst that can befall us is but to be hung upon a tree, there to dance to the tune of the whistling midnight wind, and to afford a luscious repast to the ravens, and other carnivorous gentry that hold tenantry in these wild passes."

"Heavens!" cried Theodora alarmed.

"Nay, gentle lady," interposed Roque, "the hanging system will only be followed up with respect to my valiant master and his humble servant. As for yourself, the Moors are men celebrated for their gallantry, and would place too great a value on your beauty, to subject it to such rough treatment."

---

[1] Thieves.
[2] A Maravedi was a coin of such diminutive value as to answer to the one-third of an English farthing.

Gomez Arias; or The Moors of the Alpujarras.

Gomez Arias, greatly exasperated at Roque's insinuations, suddenly turned, and, riding up to him, interrupted the course of his oratory with a smart blow.—"Now, rascal," he said, "if thou darest again to give utterance to any of those ridiculous fears, by *Santiago*, the Moors shall not be put to the trouble of hanging thee—So be cautious what thou sayest."

"Say!" humbly muttered the valet, "Blessed Virgin! I have nothing else to say; your arguments, Don Lope, are unanswerable. But I hope, my good Señor, I may be allowed to recite my prayers, since singing and rational conversation are interdicted."

"Pray as much as thou pleasest, sinner, provided thy orisons are inaudible to us."

Gomez Arias now endeavoured to calm the fears of Theodora, who had been greatly agitated by the imprudent remarks of Roque, which tended considerably to increase the depression under which she laboured.

"My Theodora," he said, "is it possible that I cannot remove the continued dejection that preys upon you?"

"Forgive me, Lope," she answered; "the expression of my grief I know is painful to thee, but a dismal foreboding obtrudes itself upon my mind, which I strive in vain to banish. Alas! it is fraught with a most fearful, but indefinite anticipation; a woeful presage that freezes my very soul."

"Hush such foolish chimeras," said Gomez Arias; "it is true that, for greater security of avoiding observation, I have been obliged to seek studiously the most unfrequented paths, and travel through these wild and solitary passes; but our journey draws to a conclusion, and all the appalling images of Moorish ruffians will soon be entirely dispelled."

"Alas! the dreaded sight of those infidels is not the only cause of my emotion," sadly replied Theodora.

"What else can occasion it?" demanded Gomez Arias, with anxiety. "Surely, my Theodora repents not the hour she intrusted herself to the protection of Gomez Arias?"

She spoke not for some time;—a flood of tears relieved her bursting bosom: then, as if struggling to collect her forces which were almost overpowered by sad recollections, she exclaimed—"Oh! never mention the hour of my crime—for crime it was, and a deadly sin, to abandon the best of parents, in his old age; and yet," she added, sobbing, "conscious as I am of my guilt, were the sin again to be committed, for thy sake, Lope, I should again brave the voice of self-reproach.—Gomez Arias, wert thou to read the hidden pages of my heart, there thou wouldst find a tale of boundless love and never-ending sorrow, which no words of mine can describe, but which must embitter the future portion of my existence, unless we speedily obtain the forgiveness of my injured parent."

"Nay, Theodora, this weakness is as unreasonable as it is unjust; nor can I at all imagine why thy future life should be embittered with grief, united as it is with the very being of Gomez Arias."

"I am sensible," cried Theodora, "both of the tenderness and sincerity of your love, and you know full well with what fervent devotion it is requited."

"What, then, can urge your mind to form such desponding anticipations? Have you seen aught in my conduct,—have you discerned anything in my words, that can afford even the shadow of justice to your apprehensions?"

"No, Gomez Arias," she answered; "your conduct to me has always been kind; your words breathing the same solicitude for my comfort and happiness: but you must forgive the weakness and fears of a fond woman's heart. Forgive me, Lope, if these feelings should sometimes create ideas galling at once to my peace, and derogatory to thy constancy and love. I have laboured hard to subdue them, but, alas! the exertion has constantly proved above my strength; I must give them utterance. Oh, Lope," she added; mournfully, "I fear you are not the same. Pardon me,—you are not the same, as when I first surrendered to you all my affections, fondly imagining you were mine for ever."

"Not the same!" ejaculated Gomez Arias; "have my attentions been less constant than from the first rapturous moment when you allowed me to call you my own?"

A deep long rending sigh burst from the bosom of Theodora, and her whole frame seemed to suffer from a painful recollection.

"No," she said, smiling sadly through her tears, "you watch with solicitude over me, and you are lavish of endearments; but, alas! the pure and soul-warm part of your affection I fear is flown."

"By my honor," said Gomez Arias, "I could never have expected these unkind expressions from you."

"Oh! Lope," cried the affrighted girl; "do not heed me; think not of the remarks to which my foolish fears give rise; I am ashamed of them myself. I will no more disturb your mind; no, never more shall the voice of complaint sound in your ears, and call forth the resentment of your wounded feelings.—Ah! Gomez Arias, compose yourself, and be not angry with your poor—your helpless Theodora."

As she uttered this affectionate appeal, her beautiful eyes were fixed on Don Lope, with an expression in which all the tender, all the genuine feelings of her heart seemed to be collected. Gomez Arias was softened; his features relaxed from that sudden asperity which had for a moment usurped the more habitual complacency of his countenance, and he endeavoured to dispel from the mind of Theodora the impression which such unkindness might produce.

They had now arrived at the summit of the little hill. It was a most delightful spot. A sward of short pliant grass carpeted a romantic little plain, skirted on one side by a portion of a forest, through which the sun cast short and interrupted glances of his parting splendour. Above the heads of the travellers, rose in dark grandeur the majestic form of the Alpujarras; and beneath them, as far as the eye could reach, was spread an extensive range of sylvan scenery, intermingled with the habitations of men. Farther, the little quiet villages lay slumbering in the soft blue shadows. The whole of the scene was wrapped in an indescribable charm, that well accorded with the tranquillity of the hour.

Here they halted, and Gomez Arias turning to Theodora said in an affectionate tone, "My love, your tender frame has already endured a greater share of fatigue than becomes your strength. Let us then, in this delightful and sequestered spot, indulge an hour in refreshing and invigorating repose."

Theodora assented in silence.

"Nay," continued Don Lope, "consult your inclination. I will not press you to rest, unless you feel its necessity."

"I have no wish but your own," cheerfully answered Theodora; "you appear inclined to stay in this place—let us tarry then."

Gomez Arias sprung lightly from his steed, and aided his fair companion to dismount. She threw herself into his arms, but as her feet touched the ground, she heaved a sigh, and cast a melancholy look around her.

"How you tremble, my love," said Don Lope; "this is the consequence of that rascally Roque's foolery. I have a good mind to chastise the fellow for the fears he has conjured in your breast."

Roque, who had followed at some distance in silent mood, no sooner heard his name pronounced, than he pricked up his ears like an intelligent dog on the scent for game, and when he heard his master's kind intentions towards him, he ventured to observe—

"Señor, I would not trespass on your generosity; pray reserve your intended favor for a future occasion, when I shall have more specially deserved it."

"Sirrah! be silent; come down, and tie the horses to yonder trees."

The valet obeyed briskly; while Gomez Arias conducted his fair companion to the entrance of the wood; where, arranging a couch under the spreading arms of a huge oak, he invited her to lie down and rest. She was about to accede to his invitation, when they were startled by a shrill and discordant sound accompanied with a heavy flapping of wings, and presently a flight of dull ill-omened ravens issued from their solitary abodes, and hovered about, as if to dispute the possession of their ancient homes with the intruders.

A fitful and involuntary shudder ran cold over the affrighted girl, as with a wild and appalled look she gazed on the recluse birds, which their arrival had disturbed; she clung eagerly to Gomez Arias, as they both sat down on the spot above-mentioned.

"What ails you, Theodora?" demanded Don Lope. "Is it possible that a few ravens can inspire with childish terrors a mind like yours?"

Theodora acknowledged her foolish weakness, but she was far from feeling tranquil and consoled. Indeed when she perceived Roque, with visible alarm, cross himself fervently three times, it added to the excitement of her feverish imagination.

Owls, ravens and bats, have always had an indisputable privilege to excite superstitious fears. Whence they derive this particular claim, it would be difficult to determine, but they are generally considered the harbingers of some dismal event, which is more properly, after all, the result of an over-heated fancy.

Theodora, who since she left the paternal roof had been a prey to that fixed sorrow which the intoxicating transports of love had not been able to subdue, now contemplated, in the gloomy croaking of the ravens, the sad presage of some dire misfortune. She reclined silently with downcast eyes, while Roque was busy in fastening the horses.

"Gently, gently, Babieca," said the valet, caressing the spirited steed of his master; then he muttered to himself—"for we have nothing to fear if we escape safe and sound from this place—So help me God if I did not count thirteen ravens, as ill-omened in every respect of size, color and voice, as a Christian might wish to behold—Well, our Lady *de las Angustias* send us her grace and protection!"

"What art thou muttering there?" asked Gomez Arias. "Thou graceless varlet, hast thou a wish that I should fulfil the promise I made thee a short time since?"

"Señor?" inquired Roque, pretending not to hear.

"No dissembling, thou dog!—What art thou mumbling to thyself?"

"Save you, kind master; sure enough I am only praying, and in so doing I infringe not your commands, since I have your permission to pray to my soul's content, provided it is in a tacit capuchin-like manner."

The ravens having practised their cumbrous evolutions, now sought their rest amidst the deeper gloom of the forest, and all again was hushed, to the great relief of Roque, who forthwith began to devour alone the provisions which, like a careful and sagacious forager, he had provided against the necessities of the journey.

Theodora had laid aside her hat and veil, to enjoy the luxury of repose with greater convenience, whilst her lover placing himself near her, and watching her every movement, diffused by his tender anxiety a transient joy over her features. She soon insensibly sunk into that sweet state of languor which precedes sleep—her beautiful eyes by fits now entirely closing, now gently opening, indicated the gradual absorption of her senses, till at last she fell into a profound slumber. Gomez Arias, who as we have observed stood watching her, like the tender mother over her beloved daughter, now knelt close by her side, and softly pronounced her name—she answered not—he took her yielding hand, gazed over her anxiously, till he was perfectly assured that a profound sleep had completely overpowered her faculties.

"Señor," quoth Roque, "methinks it would be a pity to disturb the slumbers of the poor lady after the journey she has undergone."

"I do not mean to interrupt her rest," said Gomez Arias, in a low voice, "so we must even retire."

Then he rose up with cautious silence, and drawing near his valet, he added—

"Rise, rise quickly, and make no noise."

Roque obeyed, and both having retreated to some distance—"Señor," observed the valet, who cared not again to disturb the ominous ravens, for which he felt an instinctive horror—"Señor, no necessity for retiring further."

"Yes there is an imperious one," replied Gomez Arias, "I can no longer remain here."

"What say you, my honored master!" demanded Roque, alarmed; "surely you are not afraid of the Moors? By my conscience, we should come to a pretty pass if such were really the case."

"Peace, thou wretch!" said Don Lope; "speak not a word, but immediately untie my horse, and as you expect to live, mind you make not noise enough to disturb even the leaf of the tree."

"Señor, I do not understand," quoth the bewildered Roque.

"I must begone," impatiently replied his master.

"Gone, Sir! Why I understood you had determined not to break our young lady's repose."

"Nor is that my intention. She must remain here with thee, till I am out of sight."

"*Cuerpo de Christo!* What ails you my dear Señor; what ails you, in the name of *San Jose bendito*?" exclaimed the astounded Roque, who really imagined his master was beside himself.

"Listen, Roque," said Gomez Arias, "and mind thou religiously observest my instructions. Unavoidable circumstances require that I and Theodora should part; I have been seeking an opportunity of so doing, and assuredly I shall not find a better than the present. It is necessary I should return to Granada immediately, and it would be highly imprudent to hazard the chance of being seen with Theodora, for reasons of which thou must be well aware. A separation, therefore, becomes at this moment indispensable. When I am gone, thou shalt awaken yon sleeping beauty, and accompany her thyself to the said city, where I shall precede you in order to make arrangements for her reception. There is a nunnery, of which my cousin Ursula is the Lady Abbess, where she shall for the present find an asylum. Thou hast only to inform Theodora, that I thought it most advisable to ride in advance to prepare our retreat. Upon thy arrival at the *Torre del Aceytuno* a man will join thee, to whom thou must look for further instruction, and whose direction thou art to follow with confidence. Thy reward shall be proportioned to the magnitude of the service; so now get me my horse, and let me begone ere she awake."

Roque remained thunderstruck as his master revealed to him his cruel intentions; the poor fellow drew his hand across his eyes, as if to ascertain whether or no he was under the delusion of a dream; but as his master in a more imperative voice repeated his injunctions, the reality of his barbarous purpose burst upon his mind.

"No, no, Don Lope," he said in a supplicating tone, "such surely cannot be your intentions; abandon the poor girl! no, you only wish to trifle with my credulity."

"I must begone," resolutely retorted Gomez Arias.

"Why, Sir, assuredly you loved her?"

"I loved her once, but that is passed."

"*Holy Virgin del tremedal!* What say you, Señor? What has the poor lady done? How has she offended you, unless it be in loving you too well?"

"Aye, Roque, thou art a shrewd fellow; she has indeed loved me too well."

"But consider, my honored master, she is more like an angel than a woman; never before did I see a being so kind, so tender and devoted."

"Roque, Roque, be not sententious; I have no time to listen to thy sentimental cant; the qualities which thou praisest in Theodora are precisely those that withdraw me from her.—Haste thee, I say—What is the fool staring at?"

"But, Señor Don Lope Gomez Arias," solemnly said Roque, "consider that common humanity——"

"Humanity!" interrupted his master, "how am I deficient in humanity, when I place her in the only situation that becomes her, since a marriage between us is utterly impossible. But enough; a truce with your remarks; prepare to obey my orders, and take care thou art strict in their observance as thou valuest my regard, or tremblest at the effects of my wrath and indignation. However, to remove thy ridiculous and ill-timed scruples, I must recall to thy mind that I cannot pursue another course, for thou art aware that I am betrothed to Leonor; I must not violate the sanctity of my promise, and thereby lose the favor of the Queen, and incur the resentment of the justly offended Don Alonso de Aguilar."

This last observation somewhat reconciled Roque to the necessity of the measure, the more so as he hoped that, when at Granada, another plan might be devised for Theodora, besides that of conventual reclusion; and finally, as he knew that all further expostulation would be thrown away upon his master, he prudently contented himself with shrugging up his shoulders, and holding the stirrup for Don Lope to mount.

Gomez Arias briskly leaped upon his horse, and was about to depart, when casting a last look on the victim he was deserting, the better feelings of his heart seemed for a moment to struggle for predominance.

There is something peculiarly interesting in the sleep of a young and beautiful woman; the features unruffled by anxiety or care, appear more soft and attractive. The mind of the gazer scans with nicer accuracy her charms, and dwells with fonder attention on each beauty of the lovely sleeper. Besides the consciousness of so gentle, so helpless and so heavenly a form, sleeping in innocent security, confiding in the protection of man, and that very helplessness of her nature, awakens a sentiment of sympathy and tenderness, as undefinable as it is thrilling and transporting. And such was the sleep of Theodora: she was young and replete with charms, and, alas! but too helpless and in need of protection. Her beauteous form was displayed to the greatest advantage; the sportive breeze now playing amidst her luxuriant hair, which occasionally concealed a countenance beaming in loveliness, and hushed in soft repose, imparted a degree of fairy grace and delicate freshness to her charms. One of her arms was carelessly thrown over her, and with the other she supported her head, while, unconscious of the fate with which she was threatened, she slept on in security. And now a tinge of animation illumined her countenance, or a fascinating smile played upon her lips, as she dreamed perhaps, like the fond deserted Ariadné, that her godlike lover was still watching over the slumbers of his beloved.

Gomez Arias still gazed on her—he heard his name in smothered accents escape her tender bosom, but it awakened in him no feeling of delight, for his heart had now resumed its cold calculations of worldly pursuits; perhaps the predominant sentiment of his mind at this moment, was the necessity of immediate departure, lest the imagination of the unconscious victim should master the deluded senses, and call them back to life, before he had time to remove from the spot.

"Lope! my love!" murmured Theodora, and a gentle thrill seemed to agitate her, as she extended her arm, as though she would assure him that whether sleeping or awake, Gomez Arias was the object that predominated over all her thoughts and affections. Yet Gomez Arias stood calmly for a moment by the victim he was deserting, and bidding her a long farewell, rode slowly and silently on his way.

CHAPTER XIV.

El honor
Es un fantasma aparante,
Que no esta' en que yo lo tenga,
Sino en que el otro lo piense.
Calderon.

Honor's a fine imaginary notion.
Addison.

Honor! thou dazzling and wayward deity, how boundless is thy dominion! How widely different the nature and pretensions of thy worshippers! All do thee homage; all gladly and proudly profess themselves thy votaries; all would resent the supposition of being heretical to thy creed, and yet how few truly adhere to the purity of thy precepts! How few are sincere in the expression of their adoration!—nay, how limited the number of those who really understand the essence of thy doctrine! The sanguinary ruffian considers himself as zealous in the service of honor, as the high minded and courageous man who has a sword to avenge the wrongs of his country, and a heart to sympathise with the picture of human misery. All are swayed by the magic word, Honor; for even those who affect to despise virtue, her attractions being of too humble and plebeian a character, nevertheless pretend to revere the name of *honor*, as conveying an idea more bright and consonant with worldly pomp, and at the same time affording a greater latitude for various interpretations. Alas! this very vagueness has something more flattering to deluded mortals, than the strict and definite term, the more heroic nature of virtue.

Honor was the idol of Gomez Arias, who appeared one of the most scrupulous in the observance of its tenets; he could not brook a word, a glance, a smile which might seem derogatory to the essence of its established maxims. Again, his word was sacred and inviolable. The least equivocation in his promise to man might sully him with an indelible stain; but then he would calmly and deliberately, without transgressing his honor, employ all his guile to deceive a weak and unprotected female. Honor would compel him to acquit the debt of the gaming table, even when he was almost justified in impeaching the integrity of the creditor, but as a counterpoise, that same honor, without any dereliction of principle, allowed him to turn a deaf ear to the claims of more humble suitors; claims, certainly more just and sacred, but far less *honorable*.

The rigid adherence of Don Lope to his word, was fully exemplified in the convenient recollection of his engagement to Leonor de Aguilar. He had pledged his faith to that lady, and had undoubtedly been a little too remiss in its fulfilment, but now that he had nothing more to hope from Theodora, he was alive to the sacredness of his promise, and the almost dishonorable nature of any delay.

It was by this and the like sophistical reasonings, that he endeavored to palliate his ingratitude and cruelty towards the hapless victim of his lawless desires; for hardened as he was in his libertinism, and unjust as were his sentiments with regard to women, he could not avoid feeling a pang of conscious remorse at the recollection of Theodora. He had systematically won the confidence of an unsuspecting girl, and when she had intrusted him with her heart's best affections, how was the trust requited? He had despoiled her of her innocence and peace of mind; seduced her from her home; snatched her from the arms of an indulgent parent, and now abandoned her, degraded in her own estimation, and a prey to all the bitterest pangs of shame and remorse, and disappointed love. He had laid rude hands on the tender flower in its opening bloom, and prematurely sipped the sweetness from the blossom, and then unpitying he had cast it by, neglected and forlorn.

It required all the brilliant anticipations of Don Lope's future career, to stifle the unpleasant reflections that crowded upon his imagination, and he endeavoured for some time wholly to dispel such unwelcome ideas, by courting others of a more agreeable nature.

The image of Leonor de Aguilar stood before his sight in all the charms of ripened beauty, surrounded with the dazzling splendors of rank, fortune, and a glorious name. Gomez Arias perceived the advantages of his alliance with Leonor, and the wildest dreams of ambition danced in rapid succession before his mind. He beheld himself the envied possessor of the first lady of the land, the near relative of its most respected warrior, and the honorable expectant of the highest preferment. His pride would be gratified, and his fondest desires realized. He held the cup of happiness to his lips, filled even to the brim; he was bewildered, intoxicated with the sweet beverage, and in the flow of pleasurable expectations, the thought of *her* whom he had made wretched for ever, was soon completely lost.

Alas! the anticipation of the future will always thus overpower the recollection of the past; beauty, honors, glory, and their sparkling attendants, were fearful odds against the love, the solitary love, of a fond and innocent girl—a love which had nothing more to promise, nothing more to bestow. But to return:

No sooner had Gomez Arias quitted the place, than Roque, struck by the decision and promptitude of his master, stood silent and motionless, gazing on the unfortunate and deserted fair. She was tranquilly sleeping; dreaming perhaps of love and joy, and Roque hesitated to shorten the sweet illusion by making known to her the dismal reality. He felt an unconquerable repugnance to be the messenger of such fearful intelligence; for though the valet was accustomed to the unprincipled vagaries of his master, he was not entirely divested of humanity, and he could not but commiserate the utter wretchedness of Theodora's lot.

But now the soft rays of evening were deepening into twilight; darker shadows stole imperceptibly over the various-tinted and drowsy landscape, till at last all was enveloped in one calm uninterrupted blue of night.

The superstitious fears of Roque, as he saw the gloom increasing around, overcame his feelings of compassion, and he began to think of awakening Theodora, when the hollow sound of a horn burst suddenly upon his ear, and momentarily rivetted him to the spot. He looked towards the quarter from whence the blast proceeded, and with surprise and terror he beheld, at a short distance above his head, two men, who, as well as he could distinguish, were arrayed in Moorish attire; presently three or four others made their appearance, and Roque, now dead to all other sensations than those of personal danger, sprung eagerly upon his horse, and fled with the utmost precipitation in the direction that his master had taken.

The Moors, for such they were, saw his flight with savage disappointment; but Roque having the advantage of a horse to facilitate his escape, they considered that a pursuit would be useless. They left him, therefore, hoping that his capture would be made by some other of the straggling parties that patrolled those solitudes.

"The base Christian escapes," said one, who appeared to be the leader.

"Yes, Malique," answered another, "but let us look what he leaves behind."

"By the Prophet's sacred beard," cried Malique, "it bears very much the resemblance of a woman. But she moves not.—What, is she dead? The detested ruffian surely has not murdered her. Let us hasten down and ascertain the truth."

They rapidly descended from the height, and surrounded the unhappy Theodora, who, quite overcome with fatigue, was still sleeping.

"She is not dead; she is only asleep," quoth one.

"And a pleasant apartment has she chosen for her chamber," cried another.

"She is a lovely lady, and gentle handmaids will she have to awaken her withal," observed Malique. "Soft and fair as one of the Houris promised to the faithful in paradise. By the holy sepulchre of Mecca, such a morsel as this would not be disagreeable even to the fastidious palate of our chief Cañeri."

He approached, and for a moment stood gazing over the sleeping beauty, his eyes glistening with savage pleasure; then pulling her gently by the arm,—

"Awake, fair maiden, awake!" he said, in as soothing a tone as the roughness of his nature would permit.

With a fitful start Theodora awoke. She opened her eyes. Oh, horror! horror! Surely she was labouring under the impression of a fearful delusion. Yes, it must be the wild chimera of her feverish fancy. She saw herself surrounded by a band of appalling figures, each seeming to vie with his fellow who should display in his appearance the greatest terror.

The pale moon that now slowly arose from behind the clouds, threw around streams of chilling, unearthly light, which served to illumine countenances still more chilling and unearthly. Strange black eyes, wildly rolling under their darksome covering, were all intensely gazing on her; and horrid grins, which were peculiar to those features, served to increase the natural ferocity of their ruffian aspect. Poorly attired they were,—outcast and rebellious spirits, who had the caverns of the forest for their resting place, and the wild mountain for their country. The tranquil recklessness of their wandering life was depicted in all their movements; and the cold expression of their bronzed features betokened a hardihood in the commission of crime, and in the unwearied pursuit of vengeance.

"Fair Christian, be not afraid," said Malique; "we will not harm thee."

Theodora looked at the speaker and closed her eyes, as if unable to endure the sight. Words coming from so terrible a source could convey no confidence; and kindness and assurances of safety, offered by such a being, seemed a refinement of cruelty, to render dishonor and death more poignant. A broad face, of swarthy complexion, was rendered frightful by an enormous mouth, where large white projecting teeth seemed to be placed more to disfigure than to adorn it. A large scar extended across the face, dividing the eyebrows, and adding new terrors to that already repulsive physiognomy.

When Theodora recovered a little from her first emotion, she became a prey to the most harrowing recollections. Alas! her reason seemed to return only to augment the poignancy of her distress.

"My love! my own Lope!" she franticly cried, "where art thou? Come, come and protect thy poor Theodora!"

The hardened Moors raised a laugh at those piteous exclamations, whilst Malique observed—

"Nay, lady, if that same Lope be thy husband, or lover, call him not; for I presume he is not within ear-shot, and can afford thee no assistance; so be composed, and yield submissively to thy fate, since there is no other alternative left thee."

Theodora heeded him not, for she was absorbed in the ideas that crowded upon her mind. Terrible was the sight of those mountain ruffians, and horrid was the anticipation of her destiny, yet only one melancholy, heart-rending misfortune occupied her every feeling. She was alive to one only calamity, but in that, alas! all the horrors with which fate could overwhelm her were at once combined. She saw *him* not—the man of her heart—her last protector, and the single link that bound her to existence. Gomez Arias was not by her side; had he abandoned her? She could not harbour such a thought in her innocent bosom,—nay, not even in a transitory flash, was the dreadful truth revealed to her. She was at least blessed in this ignorance, but yet Gomez Arias was not present. She thought that her lover had been murdered, but not that he had abandoned her.

Malique now made a sign, and one of his companions untied the horse which had been left behind.

"Come, fair maiden," he then said, addressing Theodora, "thou must mount and follow us."

"Follow you! Oh! heavens, have pity on me!"

"We do pity thee, lady, for we intend to carry thee to a place of safety, where, if thou knowest how to use to advantage the attractions of which nature has been so prodigal to thee, thou mayest perchance experience a lot far more fortunate than a Christian captive has a right to expect when in the power of the oppressed and injured Moors."

"Alas! where do you lead me?" again tremblingly demanded Theodora.

"Even to our chief Cañeri; and we can promise thee that if thy charms are such as to insure his affections, thou wilt be honored with his choice, and perhaps rank foremost amongst his wives."

"Oh! horror," cried the wretched girl, in frantic agony. "Kill me, oh! in pity kill me, before I am overwhelmed with such degradation."

She threw herself on the ground, and fearfully clasped the knees of the ferocious Moor.

"Kill thee!" re-echoed Malique; "no, no, thou art too beauteous, too lovely. Thy grief at present for the death of the man thou bewailest, makes thee call for a fate which some time hence thou wilt thank me to have spared thee: with Cañeri thou wilt learn to forget the lover thou deplorest, for thou wilt find that a Moor can love even more sincerely than a Christian."

Theodora entreated in vain. Deaf to her piercing cries, Malique mounted her palfrey, and forcibly placed her before him to prevent her falling, as her frame shook convulsively, and he began to fear he would shortly have to support a lifeless burthen.

Night's sable pall had now overspread the drowsy earth. The moon no longer afforded her light, and thick darkness hung over those mournful solitudes. The listless silence was only broken by the tramp of one solitary horse; while the suppressed gaiety of the Moors, and the deep sighs that oft escaped from a sorrowing heart, but too plainly told the tale of violence and distress.

A calm cold tranquillity presided over the place. The screech-owl gave one gloomy shrill and prolonged note, and all was still again. But that sound went thrilling to Theodora's heart, like the death-knell on the mountain blast; while the night wind blew fearfully, and the dismal howling was rehearsed by the echoes of the wilderness.

But deserted and lonely as were those dark recesses, more lonely and deserted still was the heart of Theodora. She was a wretched outcast, a solitary being in the world, and she lived on memory alone. Alas! it is in the hour of distress and perilous adventure, that the voice of memory holds more busy converse with the mind. She then tells a long and varied tale, in which the fortunate portion of our past existence is powerfully heightened, whilst the gloomy part is rendered lighter by the weight of actual endurance. In this hour of terror, the remembrance of the happy home which she should never see again, and the tranquil pastimes of innocence which she could never more enjoy, passed in rapid succession before her mind. The first dawning of genuine love—the fervour of adoration, all were fled. The image of Don Lope, rendered still more endearing by his untimely loss, filled up the measure of Theodora's woe, till her heart could no longer support the pressure of so much distress. She sobbed aloud; and the tears which fell from her eyes in some measure relieved her bursting heart. She looked around, and saw nothing but the undisturbed continuance of wild solitudes, clothed in dark shadows; and she heard nought but mournful sounds to add to the wretchedness of her already deplorable lot. The ill-omened bird again shrieked, and the wind howled fitfully; whilst the moon, issuing from behind a cloud, now threw a cold comfortless light, which imparted a death-like hue to every object around.

While thus overwhelmed with sensations of terror at her forlorn situation, she perceived some object of dark appearance hanging upon a tree almost across their path, and waving to and fro at the will of the blast. A glimpse of moonlight now falling upon the place, discovered a human figure: it was indeed the body of a murdered man. Theodora shuddered at the sight: an icy chill crept over her, and she dreaded, and yet was eager to learn what she, alas! too well anticipated.

"The sight appears to unnerve you, lady," coolly observed her conductor, "and I wonder not, for it is a sorry sight for a tender female, and a Christian withal. Yonder scarecrow was, a short time since, a Christian knight, and is there placed as a warning to his fellow-countrymen how they dare provoke the angry lion in his dominions. In each Moor will the Christian encounter a lion;—nay, something even more terrible than the king of beasts; for, joined with the mighty strength and fierce resolution of this animal, we have the reason and wounded feelings of men."

"By the prophet," said one of the Moors, "that Christian well deserved his fate; a more desperate man never did I see!"

"Aye," continued another, "he fought bravely, and we bought his life at the dear price of two comrades."

"I came not till he was dispatched," exclaimed Malique in a haughty tone, "otherwise the combat would not have been long dubious; but you are a cowardly set, and had the Christian been seconded, I suspect that the five who attacked him would have been disgracefully driven back: but he fought alone, his dastardly servant having fled. Pity we could not catch the rascal, for he would have made a proper accompaniment to his master on the next tree."

Theodora listened in frozen suspense, whilst another of the Moors observed, in an under-tone,—

"'Twas unfortunate though, that love should have brought about his death: in his last moment he said something concerning love; and who knows but this young maiden"—

Theodora heard no more,—she uttered a faint smothered scream, and fell lifeless into the arms of Malique.

"Give help! give help! she faints! poor damsel—Get some water from the brook."

They halted a moment, and sprinkling the reviving liquid over Theodora's face, succeeded in recalling her back to life. Malique then endeavoured to administer words of comfort to the distressed girl, but he was utterly unsuccessful; a settled gloom pervaded her soul, and she discarded the very idea of consolation. Thus they continued to travel during the night, till the first gleams of the dawning day brought to their view the outline of a village enveloped in the morning mist.—As they gently advanced, the scene enlarged, and the shade gradually rolling off, a little quiet town became at length perceptible, shining in the first rays of the sun, and fresh with silvery drops of the dew. The sombre aspect of the Alpujarras began to lose its sterner frown in the loveliness and animation of the morning hour. But alas! it brought no comfort to the desponding heart of Theodora. Deep and poignant as her sorrows were, she felt conscious that a yet more dreadful fate awaited her; she was about to be offered a victim to the lawless desires of a ruffian, and an infidel. Death alone could release her from so degrading a destiny; but even death, that last melancholy consolation, was denied to her. She prayed fervently to heaven, and her supplications, pronounced in the sincerity of her heart, served only to console her. No help came: eagerly she cast her eyes around, and clung with fond endearment to the wildest hopes that ever fancy created.—She hailed with a fluttering expectation the least sound, for in it she was willing to fancy a deliverer. The distant tramp of a horse, or the bark of a dog, failed not to raise hopes which tended only to render her distress more poignant by disappointment.

Her mind, worn out in this conflict, began to lose its powers of consciousness, and as they approached the town, she gradually fell into a state of passive despair. She saw without emotion a group of men standing at the entrance, who, in conjunction with some ragged children, as soon as she was perceived, raised an exulting shout.

A Christian captive! a Christian captive!—And presently three or four armed Moors came forward, to whom Malique related his adventure. They then proceeded altogether through the principal street of the town of Alhacen, which was at that time the headquarters of the Moors, who fell within the jurisdiction of the rebel chief Cañeri. The town presented a most dismal and disconsolate aspect; the inhabitants bearing in their appearance a proof of their miserable wandering life, and seeming all prepared to abandon their precarious tenements at the first summons. Indeed the late losses which they had sustained, and more especially the surrender of Lanjaron, contributed, to keep them in a state of continual alarm. This feeling was considerably augmented by the intelligence they had just now received, that Alonso de Aguilar, the most renowned and the most redoubtable of their enemies, was rapidly advancing against El Feri de Benastepar. However, as they had nothing to lose,—no riches to abandon—no pleasures to relinquish—no comforts to forget, the expression of their countenances exhibited a cold resignation, blended with gloomy ferocity.

The party that conducted Theodora having traversed the town, stopt at its extremity, before a house which appeared somewhat in better order than the rest, in front of which several armed Moors were pacing to and fro.

Malique demanded an immediate interview with Cañeri, which was denied him on the plea that the chief was at the moment deeply engaged in a conference with the most important amongst the Moors. Soon after, however, a short broad-faced ugly fellow made his appearance, and with demonstrations of joy welcomed Malique, who was his kinsman.

"By our holy prophet, Malique, I am glad to see thee return with such a goodly sport:—Cañeri is not to be interrupted now, but thou mayest be sure of a good reward."

Aboukar, for such was the Moor's name, then ushered in his kinsman. Every one seemed to pay great respect and deference to the little man; it was with reason, for he acted in no less a capacity than master of the household to the mountain sovereign of the place. Meantime Theodora was intrusted to the care of an old hag, wife to Aboukar, and a renegade Christian. She conducted her ward to a little narrow apartment, where having placed some refreshments, she recommended Theodora to partake of them, and retired.

END OF THE FIRST VOLUME

VOL. II.

CHAPTER I.

Though I had the form
I had no sympathy with breathing flesh;
Nor, 'midst the creatures of clay that girded me,
Was there but one, who——but of her anon.
I said with men, and with the thoughts of men,
I held but slight communion; but instead
My joy was in the wilderness; to breathe
The difficult air of the iced mountain's top,
Where the birds dare not build.
Byron.

Some secret venom preys upon his heart;
A stubborn and unconquerable flame
Creeps in his veins, and drinks the stream of life.
Rowe.

In the recess of a spacious apartment sat Cañeri, indolently reclining upon a pile of cushions, after the manner of the Moors of distinction. He was descended from a family related to the old Moorish kings of Cordova, so that in consequence of his rank, and a certain influence which it obtained for him, he had been elected by the rebels as one of the principal leaders chosen to direct their enterprize. Weak, and vain-glorious, Cañeri evinced the utmost solicitude to maintain the semblance of a splendour which corresponded but indifferently with the poverty of his present state, and assumed an authority that ill assorted with the precarious tenure by which he held his power. Anxious to cling even to the shadow of a Court, he had appointed his officers, and regulated his household, with all the precision and etiquette of a petty sovereign. The mansion which he now inhabited had apparently belonged to some more wealthy person of the town of Alhacen, and had been studiously decorated with all the tapestry and other ornaments which could be collected together; but the faded and tattered condition of the materials, evidently indicated that the days of their splendour had long since passed.

Cañeri was at this moment exhibiting the capricious disposition of a vain and would-be despot. Some half dozen miserable looking figures, who surrounded his couch, constituted his whole retinue, and appeared completely subservient to the ridiculous fancies of their master. But amongst these desperate ruffians, there was a man whose countenance and demeanor were calculated more particularly to attract the notice of a stranger. He sat at the right of Cañeri, and seemed, by the freedom of his language and manner, to possess the unlimited confidence of that chief. On what plea he could found his claim to such a distinction, would have been no easy matter to determine; his countenance being remarkable only for a larger share of calm resolution, deep malignity, and ill-boding ferocity, than those of his companions. A broad and strongly built frame, dark and lowering features, black shaggy beard, and the savage glitter of an eye that scowled gloomily under its heavy brow, gave to his whole appearance a most forbidding and sinister expression. Even when his features occasionally relaxed from their sternness, they only seemed to writhe into a peculiar sneer, which could not be contemplated without an involuntary shudder of terror and repugnance. Yet, even amidst this repulsive exterior, at times there could be traced a few sad remains of noble lines in that countenance, which spoke of hateful passions, long cherished within the breast. There was enough to induce the belief that this man had originally been capable of better feelings, and worthy a more honorable career.

This mysterious being, like the rest of Cañeri's train, was apparelled in a Moorish garb, remarkable only for its poverty and simplicity. But, though his appearance and attire bespoke the Moor, yet the expression of his features by no means corresponded with his exterior; and a penetrating eye could easily discover, that whatever might now be his profession, he had formerly belonged to other creed and nation than that of the Moslem.

"Bermudo," said Cañeri, addressing himself to the personage in question, "thou art unusually abstracted to-day, far more than for some time past I have known thee."

"Bermudo!" exclaimed the other indignantly; "Bermudo! Call me no more by a name so hateful;—a name that brings to my recollection my miseries and my crimes. It is an ominous, a detested sound, that rings in my ear, to tell me that I was once a Christian—an injured man; and that I am *now*——"

"A valiant Moor," interrupted Cañeri.

"A vile renegade!" retorted Bermudo with a sneer. "A renegade; for thou canst not gild the bitter potion, nor will I attempt to disguise my character. I am a ruffian; but I have pledged myself to serve the Moors, and I WILL serve them faithfully, actively, to the last breath of my loathed existence."

"Thy services, indeed, have been most valuable," said Cañeri, "and grateful are the Moors for the interest thou evincest in their cause."

"Tush," cried the renegade; "thank me not. It is not my love for the Moors that prompts my services, but my hatred to the Christians. No, Cañeri, I will not admit acknowledgments which I little deserve. You say that I am brave and active—'tis true. I can endure privations, and encounter dangers; but in so doing, I look not to advance the interests of the Moorish cause, but to serve that of my revenge. No, I anticipate no triumphs; I live merely for the gratification of vengeance for wrongs long past, but too deeply rooted in this heart to be ever forgotten." As he pronounced these last words his frame shook with agitation.

"Calm thyself, Alagraf," said Cañeri, "since thou hast adopted that name, and art now——"

"A traitor!" cried the renegade, interrupting him. "I am a traitor to my faith and country. Nay, do not attempt to palliate a name in which I glory. I well know the vile thing that I am considered. My career is a dark one; and the passion which fires my heart, and nerves my arm, cannot ennoble my deeds of valour, but may at least satisfy my craving: and that is enough—I am a villain; but woe to the man who made me what I am. May the curse of despair, may the venom that festers here (and he forcibly smote his breast) poison and corrode the life of him who planted it in a heart kind by nature, and designed for virtue; but by one bad man driven to revolting crime."

"Thy wrongs," interposed Cañeri, "shall be avenged; and our cause, desperate as it seems, may still prosper. 'Tis true, we have lately sustained many reverses; but el Feri de Benastepar yet lives, and even now may check the proud course of our enemies, and blight the verdant laurels of the Christian's brow. Even now, perhaps, Alonso de Aguilar meets the doom to which his hate to the Moorish name so irresistibly impels him. We have resources left,—our forces may be less; our courage greater."

"Hold, Cañeri," cried the renegade; "if thou wilt deceive thyself, deceive not me,—thou canst not. I abhor the Christians, but why should I deny the melancholy truth that is daily forced upon our conviction? The Christians are our superiors, and we have to oppose to them, only the desperate, the frenzied power which springs from a sense of deep injuries sustained,—of wrongs carefully treasured up for the day of retribution."

"Alagraf!" returned Cañeri, somewhat hurt at the boldness and freedom of the renegade, "whatever may be the motives that urge thee to second our enterprise, forget not that mine and those of my companions originate in a cause more noble and dignified—It is to assert our rights as a free and independent nation."

"That," sneeringly muttered Bermudo, "may be the pretext; but I will neither discuss the merits of our undertaking, nor the justice of our cause. To me, at least, they are just and meritorious. I seek by my own exertions that redress which my humble station could not procure, when matched against those to whom chance, not superior worth, gave power over me."

"Well," returned Cañeri; "whatever be thy motives, thy services have been most acceptable to us, and thy reward shall be proportionate to the value of thy assistance."

"Reward!" exclaimed the renegade, "I ask for no reward; thinkest thou, Moor, I would have been tempted to abandon the most sacred ties of country and religion for a reward?—Thinkest thou that for a bribe I could be instigated to become an open villain?—a thing despised? for ye all despise me, and must despise me,—nor can I feel offended."

"Despise thee!" cried Cañeri.

"Aye, despise me; for such as I must ever be despised, though their services may be most welcome. A reward! and what reward? Some paltry gold, perchance. No, Cañeri; I am at least a bold, not a mean ruffian, and I wish for no other reward save that which I can exact with my own hands. Ah! let me strew the rankest thorns in the path of my wronger! Let me throw a deepening cloud over the brilliancy of his hopes, and envenom all the springs of his affections and happiness! Let me make him a thing to create abhorrence, and heap upon his head the shame and degradation that weigh me down; and when he writhes in agony, let me enjoy his misery and despair, and hear him cry for mercy, and deny it him, as he denied it *her*! Oh! that I may watch his life as slowly it ebbs away, and then in that last tumult of anguish,—in that violent separation of the soul,—let me—let me pour into his afflicted ear my exulting voice, shrieking aloud *Anselma*!"

Callous as was the nature of Cañeri, he could not suppress an involuntary shudder, when he beheld the horrid picture which the renegade now exhibited. It was a fearful sight, for that gust of frenzied passion gave to his whole person the look of a demon: his frame shook violently, and as he grasped his weapon with nervous convulsion, those iron features became fraught with indescribable hatred and revenge. But the storm passed rapidly away, and after a short struggle, the renegade again resumed his look of dark, imperturbable calmness, and relapsing into his wonted mood of gloomy abstraction, he recovered the cold fixed sneer which habit had rendered natural to his countenance.

At this time Malique claimed admittance, and advancing slowly towards the pile of cushions on which the vain-glorious Cañeri languidly reclined, failed not to present all those marks of reverence which so much delighted the chief, who conceived them indispensable to the support of his dignity. Malique, therefore, crossed his arms with the most abject air, inclined his head until it came nearly in contact with his knees, and with all the outward signs of humility made three times the Moorish obeisance. These tokens of submission Cañeri received with the haughtiness of manner peculiar to a despot, accustomed to command respect and adoration from his herd of slavish dependants.

"Malique," he then cried, "what brings thee here? Why am I disturbed in my moments of privacy? What can induce thee to commit so daring a transgression?"

"Pardon me, most potent Cañeri," humbly replied Malique. "Pardon the good intentions of a faithful slave;—I am the bearer of pleasing tidings, although in my zeal to serve my master, I may perhaps have been guilty of indiscretion."

"Speak," said Cañeri, assuming a look of important gravity. "Alagraf, remain—I may need thy counsel—let the rest withdraw."

"Most mighty Cañeri," continued Malique; "as my party was patrolling the mountains last night, some of my men surprised a Christian."

"And of course he met his death?" interrupted the Chief.

"He did, after a long struggle, for a more desperate man we have seldom seen! he now dangles on a tree, like many others of his countrymen, a fit scarecrow to rambling adventurers."

"Proceed—" said Cañeri gravely.

"A moment after," resumed Malique, "chance led us to the spot where another Christian slept in fancied security."

"And didst thou slay the wretch?" inquired the Chief.

"No, most noble Cañeri. It was a female, and therefore I brought her here, for she is a most bewitching creature—such as seldom meets the enamoured gaze of an enraptured lover. The rose in its opening bloom looks not more lovely in the garden of the faithful, than this beauteous captive. Indeed the fascination of her person is peculiarly striking, though at present the gloom that preys upon her mind, tends considerably to diminish the lustre of her charms. Still I thought she might find favor in the sight of our illustrious Chief, and be honored with his smile."

"A young Christian maiden," cried Cañeri, "sleeping in the Alpujarras!—'tis strange!—how came she there? Malique, didst thou learn? Knowest thou the nature of her sorrows?"

"Yes," answered Malique,—"she bitterly deplores the fate of him we slew. Apparently, he was a husband or a lover. At all events the Christian people cannot boast of a nobler or braver warrior."

"Knowest thou his name?" demanded Cañeri.

"I learnt it," replied Malique, "from the captive herself;—it is Don Lope Gomez Arias."

"Gomez Arias!" exclaimed the renegade; starting back in amazement. "Gomez Arias! it cannot be!"

"Such is the name," returned Malique, "that our prisoner gave him, and there is no reason why she should deceive us. In troth her anguish was too deep, and her grief but too lively, to leave a doubt of the veracity of her statement."

"Gomez Arias!" cried again the renegade, "and is he really dead!—dead! Malique, art thou sure?—did he not escape?"

"Escape!" muttered the Moor, "his soul escaped from his body. That is all the escape that I wot of."

"Then," continued the renegade, Bermudo, striking his forehead in a paroxysm of disappointed passion, "my revenge is foiled, my victory incomplete. I, too, could once have taken his life; but he owed me more than his base life could pay. Long have I toiled to bring about a day of retribution, and now my hopes are suddenly crushed, and my vengeance wrested from my hand."

"What means this, Alagraf?" inquired Cañeri, surprised at such uncommon demonstrations.

"Is this thy acute perception!" cried Bermudo, "that thou canst not divine the motive that alone brings joy or pain to this blighted heart?

Dost thou forget that there is only one solitary feeling that can affect it?"

"Yes, revenge!" replied Cañeri, "but then this Christian! this Gomez Arias—"

"Is my accursed enemy," thundered the renegade; "my foul wronger; once my lord and master; and this captive, this weeping beauty, is perchance his affianced bride, the proud daughter of our bitterest, our redoubtable foe. Yes, she must be the daughter of Alonso de Aguilar. And yet," he added, pondering, "how came she there?"

"What sayest thou?" exclaimed Cañeri, with strong marks of pleasure. "Can it be possible? Thanks, thanks to the holy prophet that vouchsafes such reward to the faithful. This is indeed a most precious gage, as it may perhaps be the means of curbing the overbearing insolence of Aguilar; for, destitute as he is of all sympathy towards the Moors, he may yet feel the anxiety of parental love when he learns the situation of his child. Dispatch, quick; Malique, bring forth thy captive, and ask a meed—'tis granted."

Malique withdrew, leaving the chief reveling in delight at the unexpected tidings; and the renegade, with a countenance expressive of deep regret at an occurrence which deprived him of the enjoyment of the one dark passion that actuated his every feeling, and engrossed every thought.

Meantime, the unfortunate Theodora was conducted by Malique before the chief, like a trembling victim for the sacrifice.

"Behold my prize," said the obsequious Moor, pointing to the helpless girl. "I hope it is deserving the acceptance of the illustrious Cañeri."

The gratified Moor made a slight inclination with his head in token of approval, and then in the most scrutinizing manner proceeded to scan the beauties of the afflicted fair, who hung down her head in sorrow and confusion. The renegade made a movement of disappointment, when he perceived that the captive was not, as he had surmised, the daughter of Aguilar.

"What!" said Cañeri, observing his surprise, "does she not merit thy approbation? Methinks, Alagraf, thou hast no soul for beauty: look, look at that lovely countenance; it is certainly bathed in grief, and defaced with weeping; but that does not detract from its charm."

"Fair Christian," he added, in a condescending tone, "droop not thus like the humble and neglected flower of the valley, since thou art called to a brighter destiny; thou shalt flourish like the cultured lily of the garden, for thou hast found grace in the eyes of Cañeri, and he has the power to render thee happy."

These words of kindness, far from tranquillizing the mind of Theodora, served but to increase its agitation.

She hastily shrunk back as she perceived the Moor make a motion to take her hand. Malique, in the meantime, exhibited much satisfaction in having thus rendered himself useful to the pleasures of Cañeri, and thus acquired indisputable claims to his notice and gratitude; for, with the petty despot, as with the greater tyrants of whom he was the miserable copy, the base ministrants to his private gratifications were generally more abundantly remunerated than those who gloriously served their country.

"Malique," exclaimed Cañeri, his eyes glowing with joy, "I am so well pleased with thy zeal, that I will assuredly enable thee to hold the most confidential offices near my person."

Then, turning to the renegade, who was as stubborn in his silence as the chief appeared eager in lauding the attractions of the captive, "Curse upon such apathy, Alagraf," he said with affected glee, "thou art a man of marble, if such a woman is not capable of moving thee."

"Yes," sternly responded the renegade, "I am in sooth a man of marble, and pity there are so few to resemble me: better it were for the prosperity of our enterprize. What have I to do with the charms of woman? they have proved the bane of my existence. Once, indeed, I knew their value, but that is past, and now they are hateful to my sight: they recall the unfortunate and innocent cause of the horrors which surround me. Moor," he then added, "abandon not thyself to such unreasonable joy; for, learn that the hopes which we conceived from the possession of our captive are already vanished. She is not the woman we had supposed."

"What meanest thou?" asked Cañeri.

"She is not the daughter of Aguilar," replied Bermudo.

"Well," rejoined the Moor, "we must then submit to the disappointment; but will this circumstance detract from the charms which you see render her so lovely?" He cast an enamoured glance, as he delivered these words, on the subject of his present delight; and then, very well satisfied with his discretion, he continued—"I can justly appreciate merit wherever I find it; and although certainly the creed and country of our fair guest are in direct opposition with mine, yet that shall not prevent me from paying the tribute which her beauty so justly deserves."

Theodora heard all this with sorrowful resignation; nor was Cañeri by any means satisfied with the success of his eloquence, for he had been accustomed to meet with a more joyous reception from every female to whom he had yet condescended to make advances.

"Malique," he said, turning to the officious menial, "lead this beauteous damsel to one of our best apartments, and see that she wants for nothing that I can command."

He then favored the afflicted Theodora with a peculiar smile, in which, somewhat of the ludicrous prevailed over the tender, and dismissed her from his presence, with a gracious promise of a visit as early as the importance of his affairs would allow.

While Cañeri spoke, Bermudo held his accustomed silence, but he could not disguise his contempt when he perceived the Moor so completely engrossed with the pursuit of his selfish gratification, at a time when affairs of such magnitude were at stake.

"Cañeri," he cried sullenly; "it appears to me that our cause is not likely to derive any great advantage from the possession of that Christian."

"A mind," replied Cañeri, with an assumption of gravity, "a mind harassed with numerous cares, necessarily requires some relaxation.— To thee alone, as a friend, do I speak in these terms of confidence; to any other, I would not condescend to afford the shadow of explanation regarding what may appear strange in my conduct; my actions must not be subjected to the scrutiny of any one."

As he said this, he looked around with an air of offended dignity, as though a signification of his will were sufficient to command respect and obedience; while the renegade made no other reply than a smile of derision.

Cañeri now summoned around him his principal officers, and happy in the beggarly retinue that attended him, he paraded the wretched town of Alhacen, the capital of his scanty dominions. This was more for idle display, than for the purpose of taking vigorous and efficient measures to check the course of the Christians. The garrison was drawn out in the *Plaza*[1] to be reviewed by their commander. They amounted to about eight hundred men, but exhibited a miserable appearance, both with regard to arms and equipment. He harangued them upon the glory of their cause, and exhorted the chiefs to a rigid observance of their duty. Having thus terminated this singular exhibition to

---

[1] The square.

his entire satisfaction, he returned with the same parade to his humble mansion, which, in compliment to its illustrious inhabitant, was now dignified with the title of the palace.

CHAPTER II.

> Mais puisque je naquis, sans doute il falloit nâitre;
> Si l'on m'eut consulté, j'aurais refusé l'être.
> Vains regrets! Le destin me condamnoit au jour,
> Et je viens, o soleil! te maudire à mon tour.
> *Lamartine.*

> I have no dread,
> And feel the curse to have no natural fear
> Nor fluttering throb, that beats with hopes or wishes
> Or lurking love of something on the earth.
> *Lord Byron.*

Returned to his dwelling, Cañeri seated himself to his repast, which, though frugal in the extreme, was nevertheless served with all the etiquette of a sovereign. The taciturnity of the renegade was if possible more marked than ever, nor could he be prevailed upon to partake of the food which was before them. Cañeri felt an invincible desire to dive into the mysterious history of his confidant; an attempt which he had already frequently made, but always unattended with success. As soon, therefore, as their meal was finished, he dismissed the attendants, and turning to the renegade in the most friendly manner—

"Alagraf," he said, "cheer up; let not thy noble spirit droop: think on our cause, and rouse thy energies in proportion to the danger which surrounds us."

"Danger!" cried the renegade, "talk not to me of danger—I am reckless now of consequences;—what is the whole world to me? My hated, my detested enemy is no more;—the only longing of my life is thwarted, and I can feel no longer any interest in the pursuits of man."

"Surely!" exclaimed Cañeri, somewhat alarmed, "thou dost not mean to abandon our cause!"

"Moor!" replied the renegade, in a voice of thunder, his eyes flashing, and his brows assuming an additional sternness—"Moor! is it to me thou darest hold such language? Thinkest thou that being *once* a traitor, my whole existence must be made up of treasons? Suspicious man, know me better; I am a dark and accursed villain; hateful alike to Christian and Moor, but yet I am no deluded wretch, that will stoop to swerve from the path he has once resolved to follow."

"Calm thy temper, Alagraf," said Cañeri, interposing; "I meant not to offend thee, and if I have, I pray thy indulgence: thou art sensible of the friendship which unites us; it is from the zeal of that friendship, that I continually urge the questions which thou seemest to avoid. Great must be the nature of thy sufferings, and powerful the motive which provokes such unusual signs of emotion; yet surely some consolation might be found in trusting thy secret to the bosom of a comrade."

The renegade remained silent for a few minutes; then, as if suddenly adopting a fresh resolution—

"Cañeri," he said, "oft has thine officious zeal, or weak curiosity, fatigued my ears with repeated questions that are daggers to my soul. I will now satisfy thy craving; yes, I will unravel the mystery that hangs around my head. By this concession I may perhaps acquire the right to brood over my wrongs and misfortunes undisturbed and unmolested in future.

"Cañeri," he continued, "all the calamity which is now the portion of the man that stands before thee—all the struggles, the racking throes that torture this seared breast, arise from one solitary cause—the offspring of one crime, and of that crime the unhappy victim who suffers by it is innocent. The rites of religion never blessed my mother's bridal bed, and I was born a thing despised, looked down upon by the proud ones of the land, pointed at by the urchins, and even taunted by the beggar as he went his rounds. But nature, that made me a thing to be contemned, gave me no feelings congenial to such a state. I was endowed with sentiments more noble, and greater powers of mind than those who affected to spurn me. I know not my father, nor was I ever anxious to learn a name to me so full of misery, and which could claim no other token from his child than a malediction. This much I learnt— that my parent was a nobleman; but what unnatural cruelty could induce him to abandon his offspring, I never was able to determine. I was brought up a retainer in the house of the sire of my bitter foe, Don

Lope Gomez Arias, where I was subjected to indignities at which my proud nature revolted, whilst the obscurity of my birth powerfully contributed to exasperate those feelings already too much excited by repeated contumelies and scorn. Wherever I turned my eyes I discovered a dreary waste in the midst of society; for I was an outcast, and I felt no sympathy with the uses of the world. Chance made me a wretch, and nature unkindly gave me feelings and sentiments to heighten the misery to which my existence was doomed. Alas! my dark and repulsive exterior gave an additional motive to justify the dislike with which I was generally beheld.

"Such a life," interrupted Cañeri, "must have been insupportable."

"It might," nobly answered the renegade, "to a weak mind—not to mine, for the very injustice of my fate gave me courage to support it. I rose superior to my misfortunes, and nourished a sensation of mixed hatred and contempt towards my kind: I assiduously nurtured sentiments calculated to make me believe myself independent in the bosom of slavery and degradation.—Yes, I had a beam of cheering hope, a wild and romantic emulation, a noble ambition, to acquire by my own deeds, my daring exertion, that which was denied me by the combined oppositions of birth and station. My pretensions were supported by my pride, and spread a solitary but brilliant light amidst the darkness with which my existence was clouded. In these sentiments I grew, hated and abhorring, despising and contemned. The springs of my heart, which would have sympathised with human nature, seemed to have been dried up for ever. I found myself incapable of any kindly feeling, and my whole being was wrapped in that dismal and isolated gloom which, like the mephitic vapour, tended to paralyze the exertions and blight the fair prospects of life. Alas! I was mistaken; for, to my misfortune, I eventually discovered that I was a man, subject to the weakness of human nature, that the depths of my heart, which I had judged impenetrable to the influence of the softer passions, were soon to be deeply stirred, and that I was fated to experience those sentiments which I had proudly imagined to be foreign to my nature.

"Amongst the numberless beings who conspired to render me wretched—amongst the many whom I was forced to look upon more as natural foes than fellow-creatures, there was one who first beheld me with a genuine and heavenly feeling of compassion, and from that sweet and pure emanation of sensibility soon sprung the most tender and devoted attachment. This being, generous and kind, this solitary exception to the overwhelming mass of hatred that encompassed me, for whose dear sake alone I might forgive my parents for the miserable life they bestowed upon me—this being was a woman—a woman, alas! for our mutual woe! She was as abundant in personal attractions as she was rich in mental beauty. She loved, aye! she devotedly loved the unhappy Bermudo, the wretched outcast, from whom every one else recoiled. She loved him, and she found in that dark form, in that being so degraded and despised, a heart capable of feeling and estimating a genuine passion. Yes, in this desolate wilderness of my heart, not all was then barren, and the kindly feelings sowed by her hand took root and budded forth; I fostered them, and they flourished as vigorously as if they had been cast in a more generous mould. I loved her! Oh, Anselma! Five years have passed since that dreadful moment, but yet the bloody scene is glowing, burning in my memory. I see thy mangled form, thy beauteous limbs broken, and thy long dishevelled hair clotted with gore. Anselma! Anselma! I did not follow thee to thy untimely grave, for I had to plan and accomplish the deed of vengeance.—I cannot weep: the sad fountains of these eyes are long since dry, but my scorched heart still weeps with tears of blood, when the scenes of thy youth, thy love, and thy horrid fate crowd upon my agonized recollection."

The renegade could not proceed; his agitation became terrible, and all the occurrences of his past life were busy in distorting those features and adding to their natural ferocity. Cañeri looked aghast, for his frivolous soul could not easily comprehend the nature of an attachment so fervent, so deeply rooted, as to produce the violent effects which he now witnessed. But his wonder increased as he perceived that gust of uncontroulable passion gradually subside and give place to a kinder emotion than he thought congenial to the being that stood before him. The renegade was again calm. A tear stood trembling in his eye, and that pitying drop spoke of affections long subdued, but not entirely extinct in the breast of him who had but few tears to bestow. Soon, however, his glassy eyes were fixed, and as Bermudo raised mechanically his long sinewy fingers to his burning forehead, his countenance became the index of a mind engaged in scenes far away. It was a deep though momentary abstraction, for as Cañeri gazed in amazement, the renegade awoke from his trance, and became aware of the notice which his emotion had excited. He felt ashamed that a token of weakness should have betrayed him before man, and with a strong exertion strove to smother the commotion which swelled his breast. He dashed away the drop that fain would soften the lurid expression of his eye. His pride succeeded in the conflict: soon that lip recovered its sardonic curl, and his features relapsing into their calm and gloomy ferocity, he then proceeded—

"Gomez Arias, upon whom nature had lavished her choicest gifts, only as the means of following with greater success his licentious courses—Gomez Arias saw the beautiful Anselma. Her attractions and innocence could not escape his observation, and he marked her out for his prey. Curse the day his wily smile first lighted on the unfortunate girl!"

"She did not then," interrupted Cañeri, "fall into the snare of the seducer?"

"No," firmly replied the renegade, "she did not; but the gentle creature knew too well how boundless was the power of her persecutor, and trembled to provoke its influence—not for her own sake, but for mine. Our mutual inclination was no longer a secret; and my presumption in crossing the will of my arrogant master, would have been attended with inevitable ruin. Anselma, sensible of our dangerous position, carefully endeavoured to avoid the threatened storm. It was all in vain; her tears fell fast, and her prayers were uttered in all the fervour of desolate grief; but the barbarian saw those tears unmoved, and heard her piteous expostulations with the coldness of a villain. Nay, he felt exasperated at the resistance with which his wishes were opposed by one whom his pride naturally led him to consider as affording an easy conquest. He had been accustomed, in his shameful career, to meet with little or no opposition; he was base enough to doubt the very existence of female virtue; and was it for a poor humble girl, born his dependant, an orphan from her childhood, and clinging to no other protection than that which could be afforded by such a thing as I, to contradict the vile opinion which the proud patrician entertained?

"Cañeri, I will no longer dwell on this subject. Gomez Arias at length resolved to accomplish by a vile contrivance, what he could not obtain by seductive persuasion. I was despatched on a trifling commission to one of his estates, my presence being an obstacle to his designs; for poor and despised as I was, Gomez Arias nevertheless looked upon me with a feeling of dread. He could crush the reptile, but he feared the sting. I was strong in my very weakness, for as I had but one solitary motive to link me to life; that being removed, my oppressor felt aware my life would then only serve as the price by which I was to purchase revenge.

"I was absent, when one of his miscreants administered some deleterious beverage to the unsuspecting Anselma, the effects of which answered to their utmost extent the wishes of the libertine. An irresistible lethargy oppressed the senses and rendered powerless the limbs of the helpless victim. In that state she was borne to the couch of her undoer, and by a stratagem worthy of the monster by whom it was invented, Gomez Arias triumphed over her passive unconscious form. Happy, happy if the unnatural slumber in which Anselma was immersed, had subsided into the sleep of death. But no, she awoke—she returned to life, only to curse that life which was now covered with degradation. Alas! she had no one to whom she could fly, and under whose fostering kindness she might hide her shame; she had no refuge left—none but death, the last shelter of virtuous woman betrayed. She spurned with indignant pride the glittering offers of the miscreant who wrought her ruin. She recoiled with abhorrence from his loathsome caresses; cursed in bitter agony his unmanly deed, and brooded over her misfortune, until the loss of her reason followed the profanation of her person."

Again the renegade stopt in his recital, as if unable to sustain the painful recollection, and after a pause he continued:—

"Evening was falling as I returned from my distant mission. My heart felt unusually heavy and desponding; as I was passing near a precipice in these very mountains, my ear was struck with the hum of voices, mingled with the discordant shrieks of birds of prey which issued from the abyss below. Presently a flight of those ominous birds came screaming on high, as if scared by some unwelcome intruders, and the hum of voices was converted into a long, piercing, and promiscuous lamentation. With as much activity as the perilous nature of that precipice would permit, I hastened towards the spot, and soon perceived the melancholy cause of the wailings that had arrested my course. Some peasants were with difficulty dragging from that frightful abyss a burthen, which, as well as I could distinguish from the distance, appeared a human body. I approached nearer, and found that it was in reality a human—a mangled corpse!—It was that of my Anselma!"

"Oh, horror!" exclaimed Cañeri, in chilled amazement.

"It was Anselma," gloomily repeated Bermudo; "my love, my only happiness in this accursed world. She had already been dead sometime. Her slender garments were rent, her long tresses torn and stained with blood, and her delicate limbs broken and mangled with the fall. Alas! her beautiful features were now scarcely discernible; the raven had plucked at those eyes that once beamed with affection, and the hungry vulture had lacerated the pure heart, that hallowed shrine of innocence and love and virtue. I did not weep, nor did I utter a single groan; no sign of grief escaped me. No,—the springs of my heart were instantaneously frozen, and with horrified stupor I gazed on the ghastly spectacle. Suddenly my whole frame underwent a revolution. I felt a dreadful pressure on my heart,—a ball of fire seemed rolling in my brain. It was torture intense; the pangs of frenzied agony came over me, and for a time I knew not what I did; but the tempest of passion gradually subsided, and my soul became fixed in that settled and sombre mood, which has been to me as a second nature since that dreadful event.

"The sad remains of the lovely Anselma were consigned to the kindred earth, and I hastened to learn the cause of the appalling fate, which my boding heart already but too faithfully foretold. I hurried to the mansion of Gomez Arias; the truth was soon revealed, but I felt no surprise—I was prepared for the dire intelligence. I reproached Gomez Arias in the most bitter and provoking terms; he answered me with the laugh of contempt. I laid my hand on my sword—he smote me on the face. Furiously I drew the mortal weapon, but was soon overpowered and disarmed by the numerous attendants of my foe. I applied for redress—for justice. I denounced my enemy as the murderer of Anselma. It was all in vain; justice affected to be deaf to my earnest and reiterated appeal. Alas! what redress could I obtain against so powerful an enemy? His constant good fortune had raised him in the estimation of the court; he was brave, victorious in various encounters against the Moors in the war of Granada. His services were rewarded; his crimes overlooked; and I with the sting of shame and revenge and disappointment rankling in my heart, determined to extort with my own hands that redress which the justice of my country had denied me. I made a world to myself in the solitude of my now desolate feelings. Severed from every pursuit, a stranger to every natural tie, I resolved to dedicate all the resources of my soul to the prosecution of the most exemplary revenge. Ever since that time, I have, under the cover of various disguises, hovered about his path, and I had once an opportunity of partly satiating my thirst of revenge; but I let it pass, because the draught would not half satisfy my fevered longing for deeper retribution. It was in the embrace of a deep slumber that I once saw Gomez Arias, and I hovered over his devoted head with the pleasure of the vulture that sees beneath him its defenceless prey."

"And why didst thou not slay him?" inquired Cañeri.

"No!" replied the renegade, "I would not kill him then, for that were no revenge; his soul would flee from this world without the knowledge that it was *I*—it was Bermudo that inflicted the wound. I did not kill him; I reserved his hated life for more exquisite tortures—a more appalling fate, with all the harrowing attendants of remorse and despair."

"And what probability was there afterwards," demanded the Moor, "of prosecuting your intentions with success?"

"That," returned the renegade, "was the constant object of my meditation; but alas! the whole study of my existence is now rendered useless by the unexpected death of my enemy. However, I joined your cause from hatred to the injustice of my countrymen. That hatred still burns, and I will yet find means for vengeance in the detested blood of Christians. Moor," he then added, with sternness, "I am sunk low, low in the depths of crime, and this is thy best security for my constancy to the desperate course I have adopted. My life is solitary and independent, reckless of all results. Lead then to the combat, and where slaughter stains the way, and where shrieks and groans encumber the air, where death is busiest, there! thou mayest exultingly cry, there is the renegade!"

As Alagraf delivered these words, he suddenly withdrew, leaving the Moor plunged in astonishment. Cañeri, however, was soon aroused from his train of reflection by a consciousness of the importance of his station. He prudently judged that too much of his valuable time had already been devoted to a matter of individual interest. He started therefore from his couch, summoned his various officers, and inquired with minute accuracy into the state of every thing in the palace. Satisfactory answers were returned, and the chief received the communications with a demeanor appropriately grave and dignified. He next paraded the town with a display of importance that might well have amused his followers, if indeed they had been capable of feeling anything but concern in their destitute situation.

Again Cañeri returned to his dwelling, and a discussion was entered into with respect to the several articles that composed his dress: his faded turban was retrimmed; his couch arranged with the greatest care, and odoriferous shrubs burnt in the apartment which he honoured with his presence. The duties of the day having been happily completed, the chief resigned himself to his habitual indolence with all the complacency of one who considers himself by situation entitled to the contribution of every one towards his comfort and luxury.

At the close of evening, however, his repose was disturbed by a messenger who arrived from El Feri de Benastepar, announcing that the redoubtable Don Alonso de Aguilar was rapidly advancing, and that they should shortly be obliged to join in combat. He implored

Cañeri to be ready for any disaster that might occur, and to keep his men prepared for all contingencies. This intelligence, as it may be well conceived, threw the Moor into some degree of agitation, and being rather late, he resolved to call into requisition the multifarious powers he possessed of serving his country. He speedily summoned a cabinet council, whose opinions he would condescend to hear, and whose understandings he graciously intended to enlighten. He pompously reclined himself on the cushions, and assembling his courtly retinue, commenced his harangue respecting the plans necessary to be adopted under existing circumstances. His councillors, however, appeared in a very sorry plight to give advice: they looked at each other with woebegone countenances, and their sleepy eyes seemed to concur in one opinion, though they did not actually venture to give it utterance, that the most rational course to pursue, after the fatigues of the day, was to indulge nature with a few hours of refreshing repose. Indeed the judicious and salutary tendency of this measure appeared to meet with such unanimous assent, that after sitting half an hour, both the president and the sapient members of the council very leisurely fell asleep, and thereby testified their opinion, like sensible men, as to the most rational way of terminating a council of state.

The renegade, disturbed in the meditations into which he had fallen during the empty oration of Cañeri, by the sonorous and unequivocal signs of slumber evinced by his colleagues, saw with surprise the conclusion to which they had unanimously arrived, and casting a look of contempt on the sleeping councillors, retired to his quarters.

CHAPTER III.

Ite, caldi sospiri, al freddo core;
Rompete il ghiaccio che pietà contende;
E, se prego mortal al ciel s'intende,
Morte, o mercè sia fine al mio dolore.
Petrarca.

He has I know not what
Of greatness in his looks, and of high fate,
That almost awes me.
Dryden.

Meantime the unfortunate Theodora had spent the day in a continual succession of sorrows. She had been conducted to another apartment, somewhat in better order, where she had been pressed in vain to partake of some food which Marien Rufa with friendly officiousness presented to her. Sad recollections of her past misfortunes left not an interval of repose, and her interview with Cañeri had awakened in her mind a lively sense of danger and alarm. Slowly, therefore, and painfully the hours wore away. She had no alleviation to her distress. The words of comfort which the hag vainly attempted to administer, would have failed to sooth, even from the lips of sympathising friends, much more when surrounded by the avowed and ferocious enemies of her country.

This melancholy day was succeeded by a night still more dreary; for although worn out with fatigue and suffering, Theodora could find no respite in the sweet oblivion of sleep. Alas! the feverish slumber that stole upon her at intervals, was fraught with all the terrors that her present situation could suggest. The phantoms of night in rapid succession pressed upon her bewildered imagination: she saw her venerable father borne down under the pressure of grief, wringing his withered hands in agony, and pronouncing a direful malediction on his ungrateful child. She heard that thrilling voice, broken by age, and quivering with emotion, and on his countenance she beheld the workings of despair. Fitfully she awoke, and struggled hard to chase away the heart-rending vision, and then she sunk again to meet another still more frightful. The wind whistled gloomily through the forest trees; the wild bird screamed his death song; and a spectre rose with sunken eyes and squalid cheek, his wounds distilling blood, and his raven locks clotted with gore. It was her lover—he had left the tree on which he withered like the seared leaf of autumn, and stalked to her widowed couch smiling sadly in death,—she shrieked aloud—the phantom fled, and again in terror she awoke.

Dreams such as these haunted her imagination during the long night. Nor could the cheering rays of the morn impart consolation to her desponding bosom. She heard the mingling voices of nature's simple minstrels hail in grateful chorus the approach of day, and she listened to the various sounds of busy humanity, rising from the drowsiness of repose to life and activity. But her feelings could no longer sympathise with the pursuits of this world. The appalling images which her feverish fancy had conjured up still pursued her, and if these unwelcome guests left her a momentary repose, they were succeeded by others no less chilling to the soul. The heavy measure of her sorrows was yet to be increased by the anticipation of future evils—evils worse than the terrors of slavery or death, for she was in hourly danger of encountering the bitter pangs of shame and degradation.

Cañeri had been inspired by her beauty with a violent but licentious passion, which he had it in his power at that moment to gratify, and this idea agitated the wretched Theodora with the most dismal apprehensions. While she sat pondering on her disastrous fate, and vainly devising means to avert its danger, she was surprised by the entrance of Marien Rufa.

"A good morrow, sweet lady," said the crone; "well, this is a pretty comfortable chamber:—you must have slept soundly."

A deep sigh was the only answer she could elicit from Theodora.

"At all events," continued Marien Rufa, "you must leave off sighing and weeping, for sure enough you can derive no good thereby. Besides, it is meet your countenance should assume a more cheerful expression, since you are soon to be honored with a visit from the magnificent Cañeri. He has been forcibly struck with your charms, and has signified his intentions of coming shortly to pay his devoirs in person. So I am here before-hand to bid you prepare for the illustrious visitor."

The heart of Theodora died within her, as the hag announced this dreaded intelligence, for though we may fancy ourselves prepared to meet a danger with which we are hourly threatened, yet its immediate approach rarely fails to cause an additional pang.

Theodora was cruelly alive to the helplessness of her situation. She cast a hurried glance around, but could find no signs of comfort; yet she fixed her last hopes on Marien Rufa, this decayed piece of blanched mortality, like the drowning wretch who snatches at a withered branch, though conscious of the frail support to which he clings.

From the little previous intercourse with Marien Rufa, Theodora had discovered that her disposition was not altogether so inhuman as her exterior naturally seemed to indicate. Though a renegade, she did not appear completely divested of compassion towards those to whom she had once been endeared by the ties of religion and country; a latent feeling of remorse lurked within her heart, and she did not seem to feel much interest in the affairs of the Moors. These considerations, together with the imminency of her danger, led Theodora to throw herself on the protection of the crone, and beseech her pity and commiseration. But before she could try the effect of her persuasion, the door suddenly swung open, and the dreaded figure of Cañeri presented itself to her sight.

He dismissed his attendants, and waved his hand to Marien Rufa, who slowly retired muttering some half formed inaudible sentences. The door closed, and Theodora shuddered as she found herself alone with the odious and detested Moor.

He approached her mildly, and endeavoured with soothing words to calm her apprehensions.

"Nay, fair Christian," he said, "thou art too much dejected, nor is thy grief reasonable. The chances of fortune threw thee into my power, and thou art now my slave: this, as well as the circumstance of thy belonging to the race of our accursed enemies, might naturally make thee apprehend but indifferent treatment from the Moor. I might, indeed, have delivered thee to the brutality of my soldiers; I might have heaped upon thee all the horrors of such a degradation; but I have taken compassion upon thy youth and beauty (his eyes glistened with savage joy), and instead of that, thou shalt have the honor of being the partner of my own pleasures."

Theodora covered her face with her hands, and her whole frame shook violently, whilst Cañeri, in an agitated and angry tone, proceeded—

"This contempt of my generosity may prove prejudicial to thy future fortunes. Many, many are the women amongst the faithful who would feel proud to accept the offers which thou seemest to treat with unbecoming disregard. But trifle not with the benignity of my disposition; for Cañeri, though an outcast, and a sovereign only of wild mountains and deserted villages, has yet power enough to enforce his commands, and inflict a summary vengeance upon those who dare thwart his wishes. Remember, then, thou art my slave, and deny me not as a lover what I can easily exact as a master."

"I am your slave," cried Theodora, tremblingly, "and it is not my intention either to despise your generosity or dispute your power. I am sensible of both—command me the most menial services, I will do all—nay, take my life; but, oh! spare me, in mercy spare me the degradation which you are meditating."

"Degradation!" exclaimed Cañeri, rising with rage, "degradation! By the mighty Allah! such temerity is unparalleled! Thy youth and ignorance alone can excuse the criminality of such an expression."

Theodora could only answer by tears. But during the pause which ensued, the mind of Cañeri underwent a sudden revolution; from the highest paroxysm of choler, his features gradually relaxed into complete serenity. This alteration did not proceed from a sense of generosity towards his victim, for he was fully determined to carry his designs into execution; but, like a refined voluptuary, he calculated the advantages he might derive from a timely forbearance. He was, therefore, resolved to exhaust every gentle means before he had recourse to the last extremity.

He now took the hand of Theodora, which she had not the power to withhold, and pressing it tenderly between his own, he renewed his suit with much more suavity of tone and delicacy of manner. Theodora suffered perhaps more from this unexpected display of kindness, than from the brutal asperity and violence which the Moor had before evinced. For in cases of extreme danger, violence will sometimes inspire a degree of courage, while condescension and urbanity from those who have the power to command is more distressing, inasmuch as it enervates that strong principle of resistance and leaves in its place the weaker and less decisive resource of expostulation.

But by degrees the patience of the amorous Moor was wearing away with the ill-success of his suit, and starting up suddenly, and looking intensely on the afflicted fair, he made a last attempt to conquer her opposition.

Theodora threw herself at his feet, and embracing them eagerly strove to interest his pity by the intensity of her anguish. Her tears fell copiously and her sobs almost impeded her utterance; but this evidence of extreme distress, in lieu of subduing, only tended to kindle more warmly the fierce desires of the Moor. In his hot distempered veins raged the fever of passion, as he saw that lovely picture of female helplessness prostrate at his feet; her clustering hair floating in loose profusion, and her charms acquiring additional interest from the wild disorder of her situation.

Cañeri glutted his eyes with her beauty, and his whole frame thrilled in a ferment of anticipated raptures. He snatched the fainting Theodora from the ground, almost overpowered with the conflict of her feelings.—As he clasped her in his arms, the unfortunate girl beheld his savage features glistening with joy. She shuddered at their glowing expression, and with a sudden and violent effort burst from his hold.

The heart of the miscreant swelled with indignation and disappointment. He cast a threatening look on the trembling victim, and no longer restrained by any consideration, he again violently seized her.

"Who will protect thee now?" cried the Moor, exultingly.

"Death!" replied Theodora, with the courage of despair.

"Death!" retorted Cañeri, with a mocking laugh; "Death! Surely thou must fancy that I am to be intimidated by the ravings of a woman. No, thou canst not die, even if that were truly thy desire. Thou *shalt* not die, at least till I think thee no longer worthy of contributing to my joys." Theodora clasped her hands in agony; her fate appeared now inevitable. Her unmanly enemy furiously mastered her remaining efforts; her feeble struggles were almost overpowered, and as her senses were about to forsake her, she wildly shrieked aloud for help. At this moment a noise was heard at the entrance of the room; the door, as if by a tremendous exertion of strength, was wrenched from its hinges, and a tall mysterious figure stalked into the apartment and stood motionless with amazement. Theodora uttered a scream of joy at this timely deliverance, while the enraged and disappointed Moor turned fiercely round to ascertain who had the temerity to venture upon such an intrusion.

The towering figure that stood before him seemed a stranger to his eyes. He was enveloped in a long and ample Spanish cloak, and his countenance was almost hidden by a dark clustering feather that fell from his slouched hat.

Cañeri shook with ire.

"What treason is this?" he exclaimed. "A cursed Christian in my very dwelling. Malique! Alagraf! Where are ye, villains? Guards! Seize the wretch, seize him, and drag him to death!"

"Stay!" cried the stranger, in a voice of thunder; "stay! ere thou darest to offer the least violence to me—nay, advance but one foot, and I'll strike thee to the earth."

Cañeri was awed by the noble and fearless manner of the stranger.

"A Christian!" he continued, in a more subdued voice, "and darest thou in my very dominions to utter such vaunting threats? Dost thou forget that these are the Alpujarras, and that I am Cañeri?"

"I am no Christian," replied the stranger: "a Moor, a true Moor am I, but one who blushes to count Cañeri amongst his associates."

"Speak!" cried Cañeri, bewildered, "Speak! what mystery is this? Who then art thou?"

"Know me, then," returned the other, and throwing aside his disguise, discovered a man of tall stature and athletic proportions. On his dark bronzed countenance there was an expression of bold defiance and cool resolution; his eyes were lighted up with the fire of noble courage, and although no tender feeling could be detected in his stern features, yet they were not altogether devoid of generosity. He was a model of mountain beauty, wild, majestic, and free from artful decoration. A simple Moorish tunic, which the most humble of his followers might wear, covered his manly figure, and the only mark of distinction by which his dignity could be recognized was a scarf of green, the sacred colour, and a large buckler on which was portrayed a noble lion, surmounted by the Arabic motto,[1]

Edem pasban derwish est aslan.[2]

Cañeri gazed in astonishment, and almost bereft of the powers of utterance could only exclaim——

"El Feri!"

---

[1] The Persians, and even the Turks, when speaking of a brave man, generally compare him to a lion;—their poetry is full of this simile, and there is nothing more common than to hear them say aslan, lion, or caplan, tiger.

[2] The brave man who protects the helpless is a Lion.

"Yes!" answered he. "El Feri de Benastepar arrives in time to witness the honorable occupation of his colleague in command, whilst our brave companions remain unburied and rotting on these wild solitudes, and the proud Christian pursues us like the hungry tiger, giving us not a moment's repose; whilst our forces have been routed and slaughtered by the victorious Alonso de Aguilar, and the few that have escaped his murderous sword, in conjunction with El Feri, are compelled to seek for safety in disguise and flight; I thought we should meet with succour and assistance in the mountain home of Cañeri—and how do I meet him? Not ready in arms to cover our retreat; not laudably occupied in providing resources for our dispirited soldiers, but meanly courting the blandishments of a Christian slave. Weak and forlorn and despairing, my few brave comrades are stretched on yonder street, fainting through want, and worn out with fatigue. I call upon Cañeri for help, and I find that the power which was intrusted to him for our mutual defence is basely employed, not against the common enemy, but a feeble defenceless female! Shame, Moor! shame! But that I reverence the public voice that named thee chief, and that I desire not to arrogate to myself a retributive justice, I myself would wrench from thee that command which thou shamest, and entrust it to the hands of men more worthy."

Cañeri remained some time speechless and abashed. Amazement, confusion and terror alternately occupied his distracted mind; the taunts and rebukes which El Feri had so lavishly bestowed, roused his anger almost to madness. His heart boiled in a frenzied ebullition to which he durst not give utterance, for he well knew that he himself would be the first victim of its explosion. Convulsed with rage at the imagined insult, he seemed ready to dart upon the arrogant censor of his actions, but the tremendous power of his fellow-chief suddenly paralyzed his arm. It was the fierce mastiff burning to rush upon the terrible bull, yet restrained by the conscious superiority of the noble animal.

Twice the hand of Cañeri was involuntarily directed towards his dagger, and twice some sudden recollection seemed to arrest its progress. And then he strove to conceal the incautious movement from the eagle eye of El Feri; but the inward workings of his soul were easily detected by the keen penetration of that chief. He stood unmoved, and whilst a sardonic smile curled his lip, he said in a voice of dreadful import——

"Cañeri, thou darest not. I see thy dastardly intention, but thou hast not the boldness to practise what thy heart has the baseness to dictate:—another such a movement, and thou liest a corpse at my feet."

As he uttered these last words, his brow was darkened, and his eye flashed with indignation. Cañeri, if somewhat deficient in the manly virtues of a warrior, was amply compensated by the crafty dexterity of a dissembler, and he now perceived the policy of hailing as a friend the man whom he dared not defy as an enemy: he therefore with a mighty exertion stifled his emotion, and his whole appearance became calm and composed. Indeed an expression of mixed repentance and candour varnished his wily and tortuous features, as he proceeded to greet El Feri with words of amity and companionship.

"Forgive," he said, "the unwary ebullition of transient displeasure. Thou knowest the sincerity of my sentiments towards El Feri. But, were these even to be doubted, the welfare of the Moorish cause imperiously requires the sacrifice of all private resentment amongst its chiefs."

"Yes," returned El Feri, "the welfare of the Moorish cause requires union and amity between the chiefs, but these are not the only virtues necessary to render it successful."

He uttered these words in a significant tone, which could not be misconstrued, but to which Cañeri pretended not to give any interpretation.

"Is then our danger so imminent?" he inquired.

"This very day," replied El Feri, sadly, "this very day perhaps our fate will be decided. The victorious army of Aguilar is rapidly advancing against us. We have been completely routed at Gergal, by forces superior in number and discipline, and the few who have escaped the slaughter are indebted for their safety to their knowledge of the mountain passes. We have no time to spare; our men must be instantly put in a state of defence or we shall be surprised unprepared: the hidden situation of this place affords no security, since a traitor Moor is the guide of the Christians; and to his perfidy is chiefly to be ascribed our late discomfiture."

This intelligence threw Cañeri into some confusion, but he soon recovered that coolness and presence of mind which constituted his resources in cases of emergency, and which made up for his moderate share of personal courage.

"Friend," he cried; "it is enough—let us act."

He was on the point of sallying forth, when he was startled by a confused murmur from without, and presently a Moor rushed in, with all the symptoms of fear and alarm.

"Buzcur, what means this trepidation?" demanded Cañeri.

"The Christians are in sight," replied Buzcur.

"The Christians! The Christians!" echoed a hundred voices.

"Let us haste then, and prepare for our defence," exclaimed El Feri; and he rushed forward without even noticing Theodora, for his thoughts were too much engrossed by the public weal.

Cañeri saw him depart with visible pleasure; for though the danger appeared great, yet he did not lose sight of his expected prey, and casting a fierce look on the affrighted girl, he exclaimed——

"The next time we meet, thou shalt not escape me thus."

Then having with promptness secured all her means of evasion, he hastened to join El Feri de Benastepar and his companions.

The feelings of Theodora at this unexpected event were thrown into the highest excitement. Hope now resumed its sway, though mingled with doubt and fear, for the sudden transition from a state of hopeless despair to that of comparative safety, is ever attended with a misgiving of its reality. Her deliverance from the power of the Moors appeared almost certain; the name of Aguilar was the harbinger of victory; yet the anticipation of her rescue caused so powerful a revulsion of feeling, that Theodora nearly sunk under its pressure. When she had a little recovered, she perceived, however, more clearly, that her destiny was still involved in threatening clouds. The Christians came, but they might be vanquished. The name of Alonso de Aguilar conjured up the brightest hopes, but that of El Feri gave rise to as many fears.

Thus the heart of the afflicted girl fluctuated between pain and pleasure, when the clangor of trumpets, the tramp of horses, and all the imposing sounds of military preparations, announced to her the speedy arrival of the eventful crisis.

In that awful moment her ideas piously reverted to heaven. She fell prostrate on the ground, and while her countrymen were fast approaching to join in terrific conflict with their enemies, she prayed fervently for the assistance of her God in favor of the Christian arms.

CHAPTER IV.

Le desordre partout redoublant les alarmes,

* * * * *

Les cris que les rochers renvoyaient plus affreux,
Enfin toute l'horreur d'un combat ténèbreux;
Que pouvait la valeur en ce trouble funeste?
Les uns sont morts, la fuite a sauvé tout le reste.
Racine.

Morir famosos ó vencer valientes
Pompa triunfal ó decorosa pira
Solo os aguarda.
Ercilla.

Great was the confusion into which the Moors were thrown by this sudden alarm: the appearance of El Feri, however, partially succeeded in restoring order amongst the panic-stricken inhabitants, and revived the fainting courage of the soldiers. In a short time, all the Moors capable of bearing arms were ready for defence, whilst the old and infirm, the women and children, busied themselves in collecting their scanty goods, and placing them securely on their beasts of burthen, as they anticipated the probability of a speedy retreat from their habitations. They evinced no signs of sorrow or reluctance at the prospect of abandoning their homes, for they had been too well enured to the uncertainties of a wandering and predatory life, to betray marks of impatience or anger at an event which necessity had taught them to look upon with indifference.

Gomez Arias; or The Moors of the Alpujarras.

El Feri, having placed himself at the head of a brave and chosen party, boldly sallied from the town to meet the Christians, hoping that by a courageous effort, he might check their course, and afford time to his associate in command, the better to organise his means of resistance. The Christians advanced gallantly to the attack, shouting their war cry of *Santiago y cierra España*, which was answered by the Moors with the sound of Allah! illah! allah!

Twice the Christians rushed onwards with impetuosity, and twice they were repulsed with equal fierceness and courage. Again they closed in the conflict, collecting new energies, and exerting their utmost strength. Don Alonso de Aguilar now appeared conspicuous amongst his companions, directing every movement with cool intrepidity, and animating his followers with the example of valorous achievement; his ponderous sword, reeking with blood, gleamed on high, a beacon of victory; and death marked his progress as he waded through the field of strife. The numbers and better discipline of the Spaniards, at length began to prevail: the rebels wavered, and terror soon spread through their ranks. In vain did El Feri exert his utmost powers to rally the discomfited Moors; in vain did his flashing eye kindle; in vain did he labour to animate their sinking hearts; fruitless was the strength of his arm in stemming the torrent that overwhelmed them: his animating voice, as he called to them the remembrance of their country, was lost in the wild confusion which prevailed, and the few that adhered faithful to him, sealed their devotion with their blood. The rest fled for safety, and El Feri was at length compelled to retreat precipitately into the town.

The Christians paused for a moment in their victorious career. They were about to enter the lion's den; as, from the covert to which the rebels had betaken themselves, they could spread destruction through the ranks of their advancing enemies in comparative security. The Christians were likewise aware that the Moors, although defeated, were not subdued; and they had more to fear from their treacherous ambuscade, than from their courage in open fight.

In the mean time, El Feri succeeded in rallying his scattered forces, and in conjunction with those of Cañeri, prepared for a second encounter: he had, however, taken care to distribute the most expert of his adherents in concealed situations, whence they could more effectually annoy the Christians with their missiles. These hidden foes proved extremely fatal to the Spaniards; blows dealt with security, and from invisible hands, laying prostrate many of their gallant soldiers. Don Antonio de Leyva had penetrated into the town, with the unrestrained impetuosity of youth, reckless of all danger; but El Feri and Cañeri disputed their ground inch by inch, whilst the renegade, in another quarter, was making dreadful havoc amongst his former fellow-countrymen.

Night had now began to lour, but the fury of the combatants, instead of abating, seemed to acquire additional power, in proportion as death reduced their numbers. The Moor and the Christian fell, but immediately their places were supplied by others, equally ready to lay down their lives at the shrine of victory or revenge. The town of Alhacen was now become the scene of indiscriminate carnage, and on every side death appeared busy in counting its victims. The Christians, however, advanced slowly, in consequence of the destruction dealt amongst them by the shafts of their concealed adversaries, who had converted every house into a fortress, whence they could with difficulty be dislodged. In order, therefore, to foil this deadly warfare, they had recourse to a still more terrible expedient: they applied the blazing torch to the inflammable habitations of their enemies; a rising gale seconded their intentions, and the greedy flames spreading widely round, the town was soon enveloped in one promiscuous conflagration. Large volumes of red foggy flame pierced at intervals through the dense columns of smoke that rose in undulating sweep, flinging around a pestilential suffocation; whilst the shrill screams of the women, the cries of the wounded, the despairing shouts of the defenders, the howling of the blast, and the crackling of the raging blaze, united in one wild reverberation, that seemed to strike dismay into the heart of the bravest.

But the frenzied courage of the Moors, instead of yielding, acquired new impetus when they beheld their dwellings a prey to the ravenous flames. Furiously they fought by the light of the conflagration, and as the fitful wind flung high the clouds of smoke, and the unresisting fire assumed the mastery, you might see by their dark reflection the grim visages of the infuriate foes distended with rage, and each arm with fearful grasp raising the deadly weapon, flashing upon his adversary: then they were all again concealed in the wreathing folds of the impervious fog which closed upon them.

The principal street of the town now presented a ruinous and desolate aspect; both parties were concentrating their efforts in this spot, and here the combat raged with the greatest violence. Again the blast swept along, bearing before it the masses of black suffocating vapour, but in a clearer interval the eagle glance of Alonso de Aguilar had descried the terrible form of El Feri, now animating his followers, and now darting amongst the foremost of the assailants. He eagerly rushed forward to encounter hand to hand the formidable enemy of the Christians, crying aloud,——

"Turn, rebel Moor; turn, traitor, and receive thy reward from the sword of Alonso de Aguilar." El Feri readily obeyed the summons, and springing upon his enemy, with his uplifted weapon he dealt a tremendous blow on the shield of Aguilar and almost clove it asunder. A furious combat ensued, the results of which were soon lost in a huge mass of smoke. But now a wild cry rent the air; it was the death knell of the Moors, that rung prophetic on the blast—hope affrighted fled from their hearts, for El Feri had fallen. The mighty chief drew his stern features into a condensed expression of resolute despair; his face assumed an ashy hue, and his frozen lip curled with an expression of scornful defiance. Dimly but ferociously his eyes were bent on his conqueror, whilst his sinewy hand grasped firmly the weapon it could no longer wield. The gigantic frame of the Moor was convulsed, and his soul struggled fiercely to recover the lost energies of its frame. El Feri had fallen, but even prostrate and defenceless, he seemed still formidable; for even in its ruins, manly strength and noble courage must ever strike the mind with a sensation of awe.

Don Alonso de Aguilar gazed intently on the foe now lying at his feet. A single blow, and his country would be for ever freed from her most redoubted enemy. But Don Alonso beheld that enemy defenceless, and his arm refused to strike, for his heart was too generous to admit at that moment of political considerations: he turned, therefore, and pursued his victorious course against those who were still able to offer resistance.

Meantime Don Antonio de Leyva had succeeded in driving Cañeri out of the town. Before this chief the houseless Moors fled in confusion and dismay. By the gloomy reflection that reddened the sky, a caravan was now seen moving in irregular groups towards the thickest recesses of the mountains. As the fugitives who composed it looked behind, they saw their late dwellings fast reducing to ashes; but alas! they deplored not the sight of their flaming homes, for they who had adopted the wilderness for their country, cared but little on what spot their habitations were fixed. They left behind pledges far more endearing, in whom their loss was irremediable, for amongst the flying throng, there was not one who had not to lament a father, a husband or a son, whose remains were soon to mingle their ashes with those of their dwellings.

Don Alonso de Aguilar soon put to flight the few that still remained, and he pursued his march through streets obstructed at every step with broken armour, masses of the falling houses, or the more distressing impediments of mangled and bleeding bodies. The fire lighted his steps through that scene of horror, and often his unguided tread was answered by a smothered groan from a dying man, who was still sensible of the rude pressure. He saw many a Moor, grim in the last writhings of death, still betraying symptoms of unconquered hatred; and then he stumbled on the bodies of his valiant comrades, some of whom he recognized,—the bravest of his band! For many were the victims about to perish in the flames, and mingle their ashes in that vast ruin, where Moors and Christians, separated by mutual hate in life, would be finally united in the embrace of death.

Some of the unfortunate wounded mournfully supplicated their comrades that passed over them to terminate their sufferings; and others, who were already deprived of the powers of speech, sent an imploring look of sorrowful import. Aguilar saw the helpless victims he could not assist, and his compassion was strongly excited, as he pressed forward in the pursuit of the flying enemy. Thus he traversed the deserted and perishing town, when he was suddenly arrested by the piercing shrieks of a female in distress.

He paused, and surveying the place, he perceived that they proceeded from a large house to which the devouring flames had already communicated. Don Alonso boldly rushed forward; his pity required no stimulus, but yet it was considerably heightened, when as he approached the building, the cries of affliction were clearly distinguishable in the Spanish tongue. He darted with velocity to the spot, and rushed through the fiery clouds that enveloped the house. He passed the entrance—traversed the court—reached the stairs—mounted them with the eager alacrity of youth, and guided by the distressing sounds, he at length attained the door of an apartment which was strongly fastened. In an instant it gave way to his powerful strength, when amidst the obscure fog that was fast filling the room, Don Alonso perceived a female form kneeling on the ground, in the attitude of one who had abandoned all hope from mortal assistance.

The noise of the bursting door had called the attention of the unfortunate towards that direction, and when she beheld her deliverer, she uttered a cry of joy, and sprung eagerly into his arms. But the sudden transition from a state of anguish and despair, to that of hope and life, was too much for her to bear. Scarcely had the lovely sufferer contemplated the prospect of a rescue, than overpowered by tumultuous feelings, her energies faltered; the blood forsook its channels to return to its fountain source, and Don Alonso de Aguilar received a lifeless burthen into his arms. The danger was appalling, for the flames had already enveloped the house, and the undaunted warrior, more apprehensive for the safety of his charge than for his own, hastened to snatch her from the dreadful spot.

Aguilar supported the unconscious female with one arm, whilst with the other he gathered together the light and flowing drapery with which she was attired, lest the inflammable nature of the material might attract the fire. Thus he reached the summit of the stairs. There for a moment he stood aghast, for the wooden steps had already become the prey of the fiery element, and a descent appeared totally impracticable. In this emergency, Don Alonso firmly grasped his lovely burden, and with a promptness of decision and rapidity of execution congenial to his character, he threw himself fearlessly from the place, and clearing the flaming obstruction, alighted on the floor, without sustaining any injury. Dauntless he pierced through the rolling mist; he gained the entrance, crossed it, and arrived safely in the street.

But now he felt anxious for the beautiful being he had snatched from a fiery tomb; he tore away part of her garments which had attracted the consuming flames, and in a short time he recalled her to a consciousness of life and feeling. It was a lovely girl whom Don Alonso had saved, for the excessive emotion under which she laboured was not sufficient to obscure the charms with which nature had so liberally gifted her.

"Where am I?" she demanded, languidly opening her eyes.

"Fear nothing, gentle maiden," answered Aguilar, "you are with a friend."

"Oh save me! Save me from the Moors," she cried vehemently; not yet entirely aware into whose power she had fallen.

"Those rebels cannot harm you," exclaimed her preserver, "they fly like timorous deer before our triumphant banners, and you are now by the side of Alonso de Aguilar."

The welcome sound of this glorious name acted powerfully on the feelings of Theodora and, perfectly tranquillised, she cried with ardour—

"Thanks! thanks! to that God, who will not forsake his creatures in the hour of peril!" then turning to Don Alonso, she continued,—"The head of the Aguilars will not forsake an unfortunate child of the house of Monteblanco?"

Don Alonso was struck with a well known name; but as Theodora appeared too much exhausted for an explanation, without inquiring into the cause of the strange situation in which he found her, he contented himself with repeating his assurances of protection.

"Duty," he added, "summons me hence, but you shall find nothing wanting on my part to insure your safety. In my house at Granada, and from my daughter Leonor, you will experience all the kindness that may tend to mitigate your sorrows, until you are restored to the embrace of your venerable parent."

He then turned to one of his attendants, and proceeded:—

"Ramirez, you will conduct this lady to Granada: to your protection I commend her, and see that she be treated with all the consideration due to the charge of Alonso de Aguilar."

Ramirez bowed, and singling out an escort of a dozen men, prepared to obey his leader's orders; whilst Don Alonso, taking leave of Theodora, proceeded with his conquering band to join Don Antonio de Leyva. Each took a different way, and in a short time left the ill-fated town to the melancholy possession of the dying and the dead; occupied alone by the few wretches, to whom a spark of lingering life still adhered, and whose sufferings were shortly to be terminated in the general conflagration now fast approaching to its crisis.

CHAPTER V.

La cosa mas alegre que en la vida,
Permite al ser mortal humana gloria,
Es la patria del hombre tan querida
Despues de alguna prospera victoria.
Lope de Vega.

Ah! che per tutto io veggo
Qualche oggetto funesto!
Metastasio.

Granada now presented a scene of animated confusion. The repeated successes of the Christians against the rebels, and the intelligence lately received of the defeat of El Feri de Benastepar, with the total destruction of his forces, filled the inhabitants of that city with joy. Various bands of musicians paraded the gay and busy streets, uniting their harmonious strains with the more solemn sounds of the bells, whilst the joyous laugh, and other clamorous evidences of pleasure, filled the air with a confused yet pleasing din.

It was amidst this tumult of rejoicing, that Theodora entered the city of Granada. Her party had travelled slowly, so that the intelligence of the recent victory had reached the place before them, and they were not surprised at the extraordinary excitement of popular feeling. The animated scene served, in some degree, to draw her mind from its gloomy recollections, for during her journey she had again relapsed into her former state of despondency. She was now traversing the principal streets of that far-famed and renowned city, so long the grand arena of the Moslem's greatness, now the undisputed dominion of the victorious Christian. Every step she advanced exhibited some new object to awaken her curiosity or excite her feelings, such as a stranger must feel upon arriving at a city so lately rescued from the possession of an hereditary enemy.

Relics of Moorish grandeur were every where discernible; every street, every building, nay the very pavement on which they trod, teemed with associations of by-gone glory and departed power. The city was now chiefly inhabited by Spaniards; yet a considerable portion of its population consisted of Moors, who scrupulously adhered to their national costume, strikingly contrasted by its gaiety with the less fanciful but more manly attire of the Christians. The two people widely differed in all points, though now enclosed within the same precincts. Two mortal and implacable enemies, united in apparent friendship, paraded the streets, or tenanted the dwellings of Granada.

The high balconies of the city were hung with costly drapery, and the turrets of the magnificent palaces adorned with a profusion of large waving banners and gay pennons. Every window was crowded with rank and beauty, witnessing the gambols of the merry children or the boisterous recreations of the populace. The streets themselves afforded a quaint and curious spectacle, for in promiscuous and gay confusion were seen the splendid apparel of the noble, and the modest garb of the peasant; the shining armour and waving plumes of the Christian warrior, and the gaudy fantastic habiliments of the Moslem. With them appeared the solemn and lugubrious vestments of the ecclesiastical dignitaries, and the coarse habit and shaven crown of the monk.

Theodora was lost in wonder, so numerous and so whimsically contrasted were these various objects. But amongst this motley assemblage there were some who appeared more capable of interesting her heart and her fancy. She espied those who were no sincere partakers of the general joy, and whose sad eye and clouded brow belied the accents of their tongue. Some, who vainly strove to animate their countenances with a pleasure that was foreign to their hearts. The dejected and down-fallen Moors were among these; for though they had submitted to the Christian government, and admitted to the fullest extent the criminality of their fellow-countrymen, yet they could not but be sensible that it was the defeat and annihilation of their friends and former companions that occasioned these demonstrations of joy. Besides, they felt the pangs of shame and degradation, rendered still more poignant by a consciousness of the superior courage of those whose destruction they were now in some measure compelled to celebrate. To this was added the painful conviction, that although they might outwardly be treated by the Spaniards as fellow-subjects, no true sentiment of esteem and friendship could be awakened in the breasts of those who must always consider them as vanquished enemies. Besides the hatred which rankled alike in the hearts of the followers of the Cross and those of the Crescent, a hatred, which had been hereditary for many ages, was of itself an insurmountable obstacle to the friendly conjunction of two such different people. The Moors were therefore a prey to the most galling reflections, and smarting under the bitterest disappointment, at the very time that pleasure and contentment alone seemed to hold dominion in Granada.

Theodora beheld these unfortunates with a lively sensation of pity, though they had certainly little claim to it. The image of the odious Cañeri was of itself sufficient to banish any kindly feeling; yet they were forlorn and wretched, and this was alone a sacred title to the sympathies of her generous soul. She was, however, soon obliged to recall her thoughts to a subject of individual interest, for as she was doubling the *Plaza nueva*,[1] amongst the various Moors that paraded about, her eyes lighted on one that struck a sensation of dread to her very heart. It was Bermudo the renegade! She could not be deceived in his person, though his outward appearance had undergone a material alteration. The ingenuity which had changed his dress and disguised his manner, could not however alter the peculiar expression of his eye, and the chilling tranquil sternness of his features. Theodora trembled, for she perceived that she had been recognised by the renegade, who intensely fixed his eyes upon her, as though her person powerfully arrested his attention. She turned with terror from the dreaded object, and during the rest of her way, felt an involuntary apprehension at looking around her.

The party of Theodora had by this time arrived at the palace of Don Alonso de Aguilar, but an entrance was not to be effected without considerable difficulty, all the avenues leading to it being crowded with the multitude eager to congratulate the daughter of the victorious warrior. The lady herself appeared for a moment at the balcony, gaily surrounded by gallant knights and pages, waving her silken scarf in grateful acknowledgment of these public demonstrations of respect. Ramirez turned, and conducting his party to the back of the mansion, sought an easier admission by the garden entrance. Theodora was soon ushered into a splendid apartment, while her attentive conductor proceeded alone, to fulfil his instructions to the daughter of Aguilar.

---

[1] New Square.

During the short interval that succeeded the departure of Ramirez, the mind of Theodora was alternately agitated between hope and fear. Not that she had any reason to doubt the reception she would experience from Leonor, but she felt the painful difficulty of affording the explanation that would naturally be required of her upon the arrival of Aguilar, whose return was daily expected. These painful reflections, however, were checked by the return of Ramirez, who taking the trembling hand of Theodora, led her to Leonor's private apartment. They traversed in silence the spacious corridors of the palace, and before Theodora had time to collect her scattered senses, a pair of folding doors were thrown open, and she found herself in the presence of one whom her fervid imagination had almost portrayed as something more than mortal.

Leonor advanced gracefully to meet her guest, and observing her extreme emotion, endeavoured to sooth it by the most friendly expressions.

"So lovely a being," she said, as she led the passive Theodora towards a sofa, "needed not the recommendation of my noble parent, to be received with cordial hospitality by his daughter;—but rest yourself," she continued, "for you must be in want of repose, after the journey you have undergone."

Theodora, notwithstanding this reassuring tone, was unable to give utterance to the acknowledgments of her grateful heart. There was something in the whole appearance of Leonor that contributed to heighten her natural timidity, and even the kindness and affability of the daughter of Aguilar could not entirely dissipate an indefinable sensation of awe, which Theodora felt in her presence. She had been at first sight struck by the imposing and majestic beauty of Leonor, together with the dazzling splendour in which she was attired. Her senses were bewildered in the contemplation of so much grandeur and magnificence.

Indeed Leonor de Aguilar was designed by nature to produce those sensations in minds far more familiar with scenes of greatness and power than the simple and unsophisticated heart of the guileless Theodora. Leonor de Aguilar was a model of that peculiar beauty which partakes at once of the lovely graces of her own sex, with some of the more decided attributes of man. Her form was largely but most elegantly framed, and exhibited a classic boldness of contour that perfectly harmonized with her stateliness of carriage. Her complexion was of a transparent brown, mellowed by the rich rosy tint that played over it, and her large brilliant eyes sparkled with dazzling and energetic fire. Dark glossy tresses overshadowed her oval face, where a beautiful shaped aquiline nose, and lips of the deepest carnation, contributed to give her countenance an expression of striking brilliancy. Yet there was something stern in the resolute flash of her eye, and the bold curl of her lip. A slight tincture of hauteur was likewise occasionally to be detected, through the affability of manner by which she was characterized; and in the very tone of her voice, even when attuned to the softest expressions of kindness and regard, there was a chord that vibrated upon the ear, which told of conscious superiority and masculine genius. Yet these peculiarities were favorable to the commanding style of her beauty, and served to heighten the impression which her natural attractions could not fail to produce.

"But come," said Leonor, after the first salutations, and when Theodora felt a little reassured; "come, I must introduce you to the grand saloon, where some of the first nobility of Spain are now assembled: I am sure," she added with a smile, "those gallant knights will be greatly beholden to me for bringing so lovely an addition to their society."

"Your kind flattery," replied Theodora, "would certainly arouse a feeling of vanity, if any such, alas! still lingered in my heart; but at present sad recollections too severely oppress me to render society desirable: besides, I should feel myself lost amidst so brilliant an assemblage."

"Well," continued Leonor, "I will not impose any exertion upon my fair guest that may not accord with the present state of her mind; let us, however, hope that her sorrows are not so deeply rooted but that, in the kindness of her friends, she may soon find some alleviation. Yet," she added, "if you will not join in our festivities, you will at least be able to witness them, without inconvenience, from your casement. The grand procession will presently move towards the cathedral, to return a solemn thanksgiving for the successes of the Christian arms. The queen will shortly leave her palace, attended with the flower of Spanish warriors, and all the rank and beauty of Granada. And now, my gentle friend," she continued in a kind tone, "I shall be obliged for a time to leave you, as my attendance on the queen is absolutely required."

She then appointed two of her maids to attend on her guest, and renewing her assurances of regard and friendship, she retired, leaving the unfortunate daughter of Monteblanco deeply impressed with gratitude and admiration.

Upon the departure of Leonor, Theodora drew near the window, and gazed on the moving multitude below. The increased clamour of the populace, and an unusual hurrying to and fro, together with the tolling of the cathedral bells, now announced that the procession had left the palace, and was approaching. Soon after, the sumptuous cavalcade came in sight, slowly moving forwards. A magnificent banner was borne at the head of the procession, displaying the cross of Santiago, patron of Spain, gorgeously embroidered thereon, and followed by the knights of that noble military order, in their grand ceremonial costumes. After them, came those of the order of Calatrava, with their brave and renowned maestre at their head. A long train of noblemen and knights, all martially equipped, and mounted on beautiful steeds, succeeded, bearing amongst them the spoils taken in the late conflicts. Isabella herself at last appeared, seated on a superb milk-white charger, with the ease and elegance of a perfect equestrian. She was immediately attended by the Count de Tendilla, governor of the city, and the Archbishop of Toledo and that of Granada, who were to officiate at the cathedral. The splendor of the cavalcade was diversified by ranks of friars and monks of various orders, who moved in regular order, mingling the sounds of solemn anthems to the notes of clarions and other warlike instruments. Then the incense rose to the sky, flinging around a grateful odour, whilst the din and confusion of the overwhelming throng that closed the march, evinced the interest which the scene excited in the minds of the people.

Theodora gazed after the procession until it gradually diminished in the distance, and the clamorous noise was gradually subdued into a tranquil and pleasing murmur. The pageant moved forward to the cathedral, where a grand *Te Deum* was sung, and a thousand voices united in heartfelt gratitude to that awful power which had been so propitious to the Christian people.

Theodora now retired from the casement, and abandoned herself to her former thoughts. The sumptuous display she had just witnessed forcibly recalled her mind to the subject of its constant meditations. Alas! amongst the host of gallant knights that composed the scene, the best and bravest was not there; and the image of her murdered lover, arrayed in terror, rose sadly before the imagination of Theodora. Her attendants, ignorant of the nature of her sorrows, but in the true spirit of female compassion, endeavoured to divert her thoughts to more pleasing channels. The mind may be better weaned from scenes of past distress, by interesting the curiosity, than by a consolation which often, instead of healing the lacerated heart, serves but to increase the torture of the wound.

The kind females, therefore, led Theodora to view the interior of the palace, which, from its venerable antiquity, and the interesting relics of Moorish taste and ornament it contained, afforded a subject for curious investigation. The quaint and fantastic carvings of the cornices of the grand saloon, together with its Arabic devices and decorations, and the mosaic pavement, harmonized strangely with the armorial bearings and heavily grouped emblems of Christian panoplies.

Theodora gazed on these warlike trophies with a listless indifference, but when she came to a long gallery hung round with pictures, both of Christian and Moorish subjects, her feelings were powerfully excited, and she beheld those living mockeries of departed greatness with a deep sensation of awe. Many a picture was there which recorded the faded splendour of the Moslems. Many a scene of the chivalrous tales and amours of the valiant Gazul and the love-smitten Lindaraxa, and other characters now highly prized in Moorish legend. These scenes of private and individual interest were artificially mixed with other representations of a more general and dignified nature. Battles and sieges and valorous deeds of Mahomedan warriors were gaudily portrayed by the Moorish artist, who had taken care to bestow with his pencil a gratuitous splendor upon the exploits of his countrymen, as they passed in review under his hand. These works were succeeded by others of a very different character, in which the Christian artist had ingeniously taken the hint from his Mahomedan rival, and had fairly outdone the infidel in the fierce and indomitable expression of his heroes.

These were followed by a series of portraits, both of living personages and others who were long since dead. Amongst these, Theodora saw the mighty form of Alonso de Aguilar, on whose noble countenance was stamped that commanding expression which brought vividly to her memory the image of his daughter Leonor. There also stood as in life the renowned and terrible Ruy Diaz de Vivar, surnamed *El Cid Campeador*,[1] mounted on his scarcely less celebrated charger Babieca,

---

[1] At the period in which my Romance takes place, the revival of the art of painting was in its infancy. I am aware, therefore, that some scrupulous folks will be apt to find fault with me for having introduced a gallery of pictures with the same confidence as if I were writing a novel of the present day. Yet this seeming anachronism does not exist. The Moors, though they certainly could not boast of a Rafael or a Titian, had exercised themselves in the art,

both actively engaged in the destruction of their Moorish enemies; for it is a received tradition that the animal had an instinctive horror and abhorrence of the infidels, and accordingly never lost an opportunity of exhibiting towards them his patriotic propensities by the force of his bites and kicks. There was likewise the awful and sanctified figure of the apostle *Santiago*, riding like a whirlwind through the air, on his milk-white horse, and accomplishing in his progress those wonderful and miraculous deeds which have so much embellished the pages of the old legends, and from whose rich sources the romancers have derived such heroic spirit and power. The portraits of the Catholic Ferdinand, and his noble spouse Isabella, were also there, together with many other Christian sovereigns and warriors, who had played conspicuous parts in the history of their country.

Theodora unconsciously wandered along until she had nearly reached the extremity of the gallery, when, as she was about to return, her eye suddenly alighted on a figure that thrilled the inmost fibres of her frame. It was *him* she saw, so truly portrayed and so exact in every lineament, that the painted canvas seemed endowed with life. Gomez Arias was there; his bold demeanor, his proud smile, the intelligent glance of his eye—all, all was religiously preserved in that inanimate counterpart of living reality. Theodora gazed and gazed, until her dilated eyes seemed ready to start from their orbits. The unfortunate girl was rivetted to the spot, for she felt a melancholy pleasure in dwelling on the semblance of those handsome features. She descried all the graces of her lover in that perfect memorial of him, and her own vivid imagination imparted to it life and passion. She stood before the picture, till she fancied her lover present, earnestly gazing on her immovable form, and she felt a portion of that happiness which he never failed to create when he whispered the ardent vows of everlasting love.

Theodora remained some time plunged in a tide of feeling, painful yet pleasing, and in the recollection of past scenes she almost forgot the horrid fate of Gomez Arias. She gazed, and in the height of her enthusiasm she was happy; but, alas! how short, how transient was the delusion which, when dissolved, would tend to sink her deeper in af-

---

and, according to some authorities, even excelled in portrait painting. I do not intend to maintain that either the Moorish or Christian artists of the period had arrived at any eminence: for my purpose, it is enough that they did exist at the time: let imagination do the rest.

fliction! The brazen, heavy voice of the cathedral bell suddenly broke the magic charm. Theodora started from her reverie, and all again became a chaos of misery and despondence.

The pageant was now returning from the Cathedral, and once more the tolling of bells and the martial strains rung in the air. Theodora, unwilling to betray her situation to her attendants, returned to her apartment, where she endeavoured to conceal her emotion as well as the high excitement of her feelings would permit.

The generous Leonor soon repaired to her charge.

"Come," said she, as she entered, "I suppose you will at least grace the convivial table, since I could not prevail on you to adorn the procession?"

"Suffer me," gently answered Theodora, "to trespass so far on your kind indulgence as to excuse my absence from the feast. My mind, alas! is in no state to enjoy the revelry, and I should but cast a gloom on the brilliancy of the scene."

Leonor had a superior knowledge of human nature, and an unusual quickness of discernment. She prudently considered that consolation could much better be promoted by a gentle and timely acquiescence with the desires of the afflicted, than by an overstrained and ill-timed attempt to obtrude gaiety on a mind that was not prepared for its admission. Theodora's request to keep her apartment was accordingly complied with. There she passed the remainder of the day in busy communion with her own thoughts, and bewildered in contemplating the conduct that she ought to adopt in her unfortunate situation. Her forlorn heart naturally and affectionately turned to the home of her childhood; her ideas fondly returned to the pure channel from whence they had too long wandered, and momentarily overpowered the terrors which a consciousness of guilt presented to her imagination. Her father would not discard his afflicted, his repentant child. Her offence towards him had been great, but it could not be greater than the parental anxiety, the fond, boundless affection he had ever shown to the only remaining pledge of her mother's love, the sole descendant of his ancient house.

These consoling reflections happily soothed the heart of Theodora. She arose from her despondency with a sudden start of resolution, and determined that on the moment her generous deliverer should arrive, she would acquaint him with her wishes, and crave his assistance to conduct her to the feet of her sorrowing parent.

CHAPTER VI.

> Così gl'interi giorni in lungo incerto
> Sonno gemo! ma poi quando la bruna
> Notte gli astri nel ciel chiama e la luna
> E il freddo aer di mute ombre è coverto;
> Dove selvoso è il piano è più deserto
> Allor lento io vagando, ad una ad una
> Palpo le piaghe onde la rea fortuna
> E amore e il mondo hanno il mio core aperto.
> *Ugo Foscolo.*

It was night, gentle and serene, such a night as in the favored clime of Andalusia is wont to succeed the sultriness of a summer's day. The bright canopy of heaven shone in passionless serenity, emblazoned with its countless stars. The moon flung a solemn light on the tall palaces and stately turrets of Granada, and tinged the citron groves of Don Alonso's garden with a flood of chaste and silvery splendor. The placid beams reposed calmly and unbroken on the bosom of the still lake, or danced fitfully on the bubbling eddies of the limpid water, as it fell on the marble basin with a refreshing sound.

How beautiful this calm! In such a spot as this could the wearied mind taste of the sweet repose of an earthless spirit. But hark! the breathless silence is violated by a low harsh sound. It is the grating voice of yonder ponderous Moorish casement. It opens, and a female form is there wrapped in contemplation; her eye is fixed, her figure motionless. She now raises the trembling fingers to her white forehead, and reclines on her arm, as she watches, with the unconscious gaze of an absent mind, the sportive waters as they played below. She seemed to delight in the soft stillness, and to gather fresh life amidst the mysterious shades that reigned around. Spirit-like, she sat in the frowning window, enrobed in shadow, and the cold whiteness that pencilled out her form, seemed to array it with the character of a living statue.

It was Theodora—the hapless Theodora, who, a prey to the rooted melancholy that consumed her, had left her couch to enjoy undisturbed the luxury of grief. The garden soon brought to her fancy recollections of past scenes, and the source of all her present misfortunes. It was in a garden, and on such nights as these that her meetings with Gomez Arias had taken place, as well as the last interview which had decided her fate, and given birth to all the miseries which followed. Tranquil and serene was all around; Theodora felt a wild and romantic sensation of delight, while gazing on objects fraught with associations of past bliss and present misery. The hallowed placidity of the blue vaulted heavens; the soft whispering of the foliage that slumbered in the cold moonlight; the spectre-like appearance of the tall trees, which stood partly enrobed in shadowy darkness, and partly glowing in serene and chastened splendor; the gentle murmuring of the sportive breeze—all tended to lead her senses into a delusive, but pleasing reverie. She listened, and thought she heard *his* voice. She looked tremblingly as if in the expectation of the appearance of her lover. The thicket of myrtle rustles and shakes, and flings on the air its load of fragrance, when from its green bosom softly steals forward a tall and majestic figure.

Could it be possible? Or had her bewildered imagination conjured up the airy phantom to deceive her? It was *he*—Gomez Arias—and as she gazed intensely, the shadow moved slowly along, lengthening in the moonlight as it proceeded. No delusion was here; it was indeed her lover she beheld, moving with the same graceful manner as when she saw him last in the garden of her father. The phantom approached, not in the unearthly sickly semblance of a tenant of the tomb, but radiant with the joy of a successful lover; his eye beaming with the glow of life. It moved! it passed! 'tis gone—and Theodora, in the complication of her feelings, remained with her eyes fixed, looking intently on the space where she had distinguished the form of her lover.

During some time she remained plunged in a delightful trance, till the solemn knell of a neighbouring convent, summoning the cloistered monks to their orisons, suddenly dissolved the potent charm, and banished the bright illusion for the reality of sorrow. The dear image of her lover had departed, and a veil of gloom seemed to fall over the surrounding scene. An unearthly dullness pervaded the air; the night wind sighed mournfully through the rustling boughs of the trees; the moon threw a colourless light from behind a shroud of clouds, and the semblance of death seemed to reign around.

Theodora could no longer sustain the dreary scene, and she hurried back to her couch, to linger through the night in the unavailing attempt to court repose. Alas! refreshing sleep came not to close her weary eyelids. At intervals, indeed, a heavy slumber stole over her, but so oppressive was its influence, that she struggled hard to regain her senses. The night wore away, and the morning dawned, but it brought no alleviation to her sorrow. At an early hour she rose from her couch, and, as if led by an instinctive impulse, she drew near the window that commanded a view of the garden. There, musing on the vision of her past night, she was surprised by the entrance of Lisarda, one of her attendants. She came bustling in with an air of importance, and apparently with a firm resolution that no opportunity should escape in the proffer of her good services, and in the exercise of her loquacious talents.

"Good day, sweet lady! Save you, my dear lady! How have you passed the night?—Very composedly I trow, for this is a most quiet and sequestered apartment: but, our Lady defend us! how pale you look;—surely, you are not ill?—*La virgen nos valga*.[1] Samuel Mendez shall be commanded here forthwith; for this same Samuel, you must know, is a very sapient leech, and well versed in occult medical science, though a very dog of a cursed unbelieving Jew;[2] he shall be sent for anon; there is no cause to fear him, for the infidel dare not use any of his poisonous drugs to such as you, my sweet lady. The *Samaritano*[3] would answer with his life any mischance to yours; and that is methinks a right way of effecting cures. So permit me to send for Samuel Mendez."

"Thank you most kindly," answered Theodora, "but my disease is not to be removed by the powers of medicine. Alas! it is seated in the mind," she added, smiling sadly, "and there all the science of Samuel Mendez would be unavailing."

---

[1] Our lady protect us.
[2] In those times, when war was the only meritorious occupation of the gentle blood, the Jews, though despised and persecuted, were in some respects men of great consequence in a state. They were not only, as in the present day, the most expert and assiduous in money transactions, but cultivated the science of medicine with much success; when no other career was deemed compatible with honor and glory but the profession of arms or the church.
[3] Samaritan—term of reproach.

"Cheer up, my sweet lady," returned Lisarda, "for this is a time of rejoicing at Granada, and it would be a pity to have one sorrowful heart amidst the revelries of this mansion. Good heavens! we are all mad for joy in the very anticipation of so much feasting and merry-making."

"I congratulate you sincerely," said Theodora, "though I cannot be a partaker of the general joy."

"Oh, but you must," exclaimed Lisarda, "you must be glad, aye, and rejoice too;—and how can you in troth do otherwise, seeing that our master, Don Alonso de Aguilar, is hourly expected in the city?"

"It will indeed," returned Theodora, "throw a beam of comfort into my poor heart to behold my brave and generous deliverer, and to pour forth the tribute of my humble gratitude, which he so justly deserves."

"His arrival," continued Lisarda, with marvellous volubility of tongue, "is the signal of numberless pleasures; for now, thank God and the mighty *Santiago*, the Moors have had such a dressing that they will be in no humour for some time to renew their unruly frolics, and that happy event which we have so long a time been anxiously awaiting will at last be accomplished."

"Yes," said Theodora, mechanically, "peace will be restored."

"Aye, peace will be restored," quoth she of the expeditious tongue; "peace will be restored; and in sooth how should it not? But then that is not the only happiness in store for the friends and retainers of Don Alonso."

As she said this, Lisarda looked steadfastly on Theodora, as if expecting to be questioned about the said happiness, but as she perceived no symptoms of such an intention, she found the necessity of affording both questions and answers, lest the dialogue should draw to a conclusion, a catastrophe much dreaded by the good Lisarda.

"Now, by *San Jose Bendito*!" she continued in the tone of one that is most good-naturedly inclined to give unsought-for information; "my gentle lady, I would venture to assert that you cannot guess the motive of such happy anticipations."

"I cannot indeed," answered Theodora, with indifference.

"Well, I will keep you no longer in suspense, since you evince so anxious a desire to be acquainted with all the particulars."

Theodora betrayed some little impatience at the unconscionable chatter of her attendant; but the giddy maid, heedless of every thing, continued in a tone of great delight—

"So, the Lord save us! but the happiness in question is nothing less than a wedding."

"A wedding!" cried Theodora, with some emotion.

"Aye, a wedding," repeated Lisarda, emphatically, accompanying the stress she laid on the word with a most appropriate movement of her head and hands, as the right one struck the palm of its left companion, in token of asseveration: "A wedding," she continued; "and such a wedding too, that the like has not been seen at Granada for many, many a year. Let them boast of their Moorish gallantry and their infidel marriages—a fig for them! No, no; a Christian for me—a Christian, who will be satisfied with one woman, and in truth why should he not?"

"And who is the fortunate bride?" demanded Theodora, not from any motive of curiosity, but merely to acquiesce in the loquacious humour of her attendant.

"The bride!" exclaimed Lisarda, "the bride! why, who should be the bride?—Have I not already told you?"

"No, indeed, you have not."

"Really," resumed Lisarda, conceitedly, "for a thoughtless silly girl, I am the most unaccountable female in Spain."

Theodora did not attempt to contradict her, as she was certainly a most unaccountable girl for a woman of forty.

"Well," proceeded Lisarda, "before it again slips from my memory, I must acquaint you that the bride is no other than our beloved and most noble mistress, the lady Doña Leonor."

"She well deserves a gentle bridegroom," observed Theodora, with affability.

"She does in troth," replied Lisarda; "and how should she not, being as she is? We have had no lack of suitors—aye, and the noblest. Good Heavens! what ado there has been about it—gallants we have had, clustering about us like bees when they flock around their queen. The bridegroom is indeed a most deserving and accomplished cavalier; and so he should, to be the favored choice of Doña Leonor. However, he is not the one I patronized, and who I hoped at one time would marry my lady—he, alas! was prevented from proceeding in so desirable an engagement, not from any fault of his or mine either, but from an unexpected event that presented the most insurmountable impediment to the marriage."

"And that was—?" inquired Theodora.

"Death!" replied Lisarda: "it being rumoured and readily believed, that the unfortunate caballero was murdered by those blood-thirsty Moors of the Alpujarras; and indeed his long disappearance from Granada makes the unwelcome intelligence to rest on no shallow foundation."

Theodora felt an involuntary chill at this part of her attendant's narration; for the similarity of fate between Leonor's lover and her own could not but be productive of a most harrowing sensation. Lisarda, however, continued, unconscious of the pang she had inflicted.

"And it was a marvellous pity," said she, "for a more gallant and generous cavalier was not easily to be met with in all Spain. So gentle, so brave, so rich, and so generous withal;—now, never did he appear before me, but he needs must force some present or other upon me; and, indeed, spite of my shyness, I found the greatest difficulty in resisting the acceptance of gifts which were offered in so delicate a manner: peace be to his soul! it was always a ring, a gem, a pair of pendants, or——"

"And what is the name of the present bridegroom?" interrupted Theodora.

"Certainly he is a sweet gallant too, and in great estimation at court——"

"And his name is—?" inquired Theodora.

"Though, to say the truth, there are many others equally meritorious. It is not the Maestre de Calatrava; oh, no; his attractions are rather too mature to suit the taste of Doña Leonor."

"Who is he?" again demanded Theodora "A most handsome man, certainly; now—but do not suppose it is Don Felix de Almagro, or young Garcilaso, or Don Juan de—— No,——".

"Well, but, good Lisarda, what is his name?"

"Oh, he bears a most glorious name; but now I think on't, what a thoughtless, silly girl I am; surely I was to bring you a beautiful dress, that my lady ordered for you: sweet lady, you must forgive me; I will run forthwith and rectify my fault."

Then, without waiting for a reply, she flew out of the room. Theodora felt a strange sensation at the intelligence she had just received. A wedding was shortly to be solemnized, at which her presence would naturally be required, and the idea of witnessing a ceremony which would bring to her mind a train of painful associations, failed not to increase her agitation. Then she was lost in conjectures respecting the bridegroom, and she felt impressed with a belief that he could be no other than Don Antonio de Leyva. She felt a dread at the prospect of appearing before him, whom her venerable parent had chosen for her partner in life.

Theodora strove to drive away such unpleasant images, and to divert her attention she hurried to the garden. There she walked to the same spot where the resemblance of her lover had appeared the preceding night; feeling a strange indefinable delight in visiting a spot endeared by the awful visitation of her beloved and never to be forgotten Gomez Arias. In the garden, therefore, she remained some time, now walking amidst fragrant avenues of orange and citron, now resting on the marble edge of the fountain, refreshing her hands and face in the transparent liquid, or gazing on the clear and sparkling pebbles embedded on the golden sand. Her sighs seemed attuned to the soft but melancholy sound of the murmuring fountain, and she was insensibly falling into her wonted train of reverie, when she was startled by the noise of advancing footsteps; she raised her eyes and perceived a man coming directly across the path on which she was standing; to her utter amazement, she beheld in the disturber of her meditations the person, the very person of Roque. The valet himself was rivetted to the spot at this mutual recognition, and his features exhibited a curious amalgamation of sensations difficult to be defined. He crossed himself thrice, uttered a faint ejaculation, and, with wandering eyes and open mouth, he looked and looked again, as if doubting the reality of what he saw. Being at length perfectly satisfied that it was Theodora herself, the unhappy and forsaken victim of his master, he made a hasty movement to leave the place.

"Stay, Roque, stay!" eagerly cried Theodora; "thou surely dost not mean to leave me thus:—What alarms thee? Is it my dejected and forlorn appearance? Alas! it may well awaken thy surprise; for deep and bitter anguish has left its sad traces on my features."

Roque then approached, but not without casting a look around, as if fearful of being observed.

"What ails thee, Roque?" demanded Theodora surprised; "thou tremblest,—wherefore? What mystery is here?"

"*El cielo, San Pedro y San Pablo me valgan!*" ejaculated Roque, again crossing himself.

"Oh!" cried Theodora, clasping her hand in eager supplication—"do not harrow up my feelings with this suspense:—Speak!—"

"Good heavens! my lady, how came you here?"

"Alas!" answered Theodora, "the tale of my sufferings is as tedious in length as it has been deep in sorrow; rather inform me of matters far more interesting to my heart: tell me," she then proceeded, with vehement earnestness, "tell me the circumstances of that horrid event which has doomed me for ever to despair."

"That horrid event!" re-echoed Roque, with a look of marvellous stupidity.

"Ah! Roque, it was a fearful deed, and not in vain did my heart warn me with ominous forebodings."

"Yes, gentle lady," said Roque, in a tone of compunction, "it was a fearful deed, I confess."

"And thou, Roque," continued Theodora, "thou hast to answer for a great share of the misery which ensued."

"Alas, my dear lady! I know that my courage failed me in that dreadful moment, but perhaps I am not wholly undeserving of pardon, for what other course could I then pursue?"

"To fight," resolutely said Theodora.

"Fight," returned the valet, "fight! good God! you would not have had me fight a host of ruffian Moors, would you, lady? A thousand they might have been, for aught I know. Indeed, at the time, I lost my talent for calculation, but they looked as many, and as for poor Roque, whom Heaven has been pleased to endow with a most pacific temperament, thinking of fighting a thousand Moors, he might as well be expected to engage against Satan, backed by a whole legion of his infernal subjects."

"But was it well," rejoined Theodora, "to abandon thy master in the hour of danger?"

"Abandon my master!" exclaimed Roque, "*válgame el cielo!* Under favor, Señora, it was my master that abandoned me."

"Out upon thee, fellow! I thought thee possessed of more manly feelings than to make light with so sad a subject, and introduce an unseemly jest."

"By all the saints in the calendar, lady—but I am in no mood for merriment. I am not in very truth, and may the first jest I attempt to utter strangulate me outright, before it escapes from my lips. But really, with respect to abandoning my master, thank the blessed virgin, that is a crime of which no one can accuse me. A man cannot help feeling shy at engaging in broils and combats, if his star doth not propel him thereto,—and that in verity is pretty nearly my case; but if any one is tempted to question my fidelity, this miserable carcass of mine can bear witness to the contrary, by displaying the honorable bruises I have reaped in the service of my master.—Alack! had I been less constant in following my Señor Gomez Arias, certain cudgellings and beatings without number would not so continually have fallen to the lot of Roque."

"Darest thou speak in this strain," interposed Theodora, "when thou betookest thyself to a shameful flight, at the very first appearance of the Moors, leaving thy gallant and unfortunate master to be murdered at their hands?"

At this unexpected accusation, Roque appeared astounded, and for some time could collect no adequate term to express his surprise. He cast a look of mixed amazement and compassion, shrugged up his shoulders, and, in a scarcely audible tone, muttered to himself:—"Poor thing! may the Lord preserve her—sorrow hath brought this about."

Theodora, heedless of his manner, continued;—"Alas! what was the courage of a single man against the united force of so many enemies?"

"Aye—aye—nothing," responded Roque, "nothing certainly;—but under favor, my good lady, though my master's courage stood ever the fairest test, yet I do not clearly perceive how he is entitled to encomiums for feats which, though he might, he *did* not actually achieve."

"What!" exclaimed Theodora, with warmth, "would you even defraud his memory of its too-well merited guerdon, the possession of a glorious name?"

"Good my lady," humbly replied Roque, "I would not defraud my master of a single *maravedi*, much less of so valuable a treasure as a glorious name. But I am strangely puzzled to determine how I can deprive him of a commodity which in my hands would lose its worth. Nor indeed can I perceive why you bestow such commendations on the deeds of my master, since, in the instance to which you allude, I rather suspect he was in nowise anxious to distinguish himself."

"Thy speech," said Theodora, "is enigmatical, and wherefore it is so I cannot surmise. But his very enemies confessed that he fought bravely, and fell like a hero. Aye, Roque, they further added, that had you not abandoned him in that critical moment, their victory would not have been so easily effected."

"*Santa Barbara!*" cried Roque, more astounded than ever, "the Moors said that? Well it was very kind of the *malandrines* to speak in such good terms of my honored master.—Good God! good God!" he then continued, in a confused incoherent manner—"My lady, pray forgive my impertinence, but will you tell me if I am awake?"

"Awake!" repeated Theodora.

"Yes, my dear lady, for either I must be now asleep, or you must have been dreaming when the facetious Moors favored you with such an extraordinary story."

"Oh, Roque! cease this ribaldry, so unbecoming in thee when we speak of *him* whom thou knowest I so much loved—when we speak of his untimely death."

"The death of Gomez Arias, say you!" exclaimed Roque, retreating with increased amazement. "My master dead?—in the name of Heaven! what say you lady!"—

"The truth;—with these unhappy eyes did I see his murdered body in the Alpujarras:—art thou then, Roque, so ignorant of his fate?"

"Oh, quite so," replied Roque; "this is the very first intelligence I received of such an event;—and I suppose you will tell me next that you have seen his ghost."

"Alas!" returned Theodora, "it was but last night that I beheld his figure as perfectly as when I saw him last in the Alpujarras!"

Roque assumed as much gravity as he was able, considering the difficulty he had to restrain his risibility; and, supposing that the intellect of the poor lady was impaired, in a comic serious tone observed:—"Well, my master is a most wonderful man, that his murdered body should be food for the ravens of the Alpujarras, and his troubled spirit be haunting Don Alonso's garden; when at the same time I saw him myself not long since, in perfect sanity of body and soul, parading the promenades of Granada."

Theodora gasped for breath; she gazed on Roque with astonishment. The valet was in the greatest perplexity; but thinking that Theodora still doubted the veracity of his statement, he again, in a serious tone and asseverating manner, said—"Yes, my lady, you are deceived—my master is alive."

"Alive!" screamed aloud Theodora, and her whole frame shook like the aspen leaf; "alive! where? where is he?"

"In this city, and will come to the palace presently. More I cannot tell you, lady;—permit me now to withdraw, and oh! that you might do the same!"

Roque, as we have already observed, was far from being of a cruel and hardened disposition, and his acquiescence in the unprincipled actions of his master arose more from dread of his character than perversity of heart. He was now strangely perplexed, anticipating the disastrous results which might spring from the unlooked-for meeting of Gomez Arias and the forsaken victim of his satiated passion. He almost regretted having removed the error under which Theodora laboured with regard to her lover's death.

Meantime Theodora, partly recovered from the violent shock which her feelings had sustained, felt a chill of doubt and a vague apprehension of evil that deadened the first impression of transporting pleasure which the certainty of her Lope's existence had produced. She endeavoured to give a solution to the enigma, but met with none congenial to her feelings. The circumstance of her lover being in Granada, and apparently unconcerned for her fate, withered the budding hopes within her bosom, for she fondly imagined that Gomez Arias could never be separated from her but by death. This suspense was terrible, and Roque's demeanor tended to increase her anxiety. She fixed her starting eyes on him, and holding his hand with a fearful grasp, in a voice wild with emotion, she exclaimed:—"Roque! Roque! in the name of Heaven, unravel this mystery."

She hesitated a moment, but the very poignancy of her anguish gave her force to demand—"Did Gomez Arias, then, leave me in the power of the Moors without attempting my defence?"

Roque made no answer.

Theodora became intensely excited, and with the piercing voice of despair:—"Then it is true!" she exclaimed, "your silence confirms my fears!"

A ghastly smile was on her lip, and a deadly paleness overspread her features.

Roque now perceived the utter impossibility of keeping his master's cruelty any longer a secret from his victim: yet he dreaded to acquaint her with the whole extent of her misery; he trembled for the consequences that such an avowal would produce upon her feelings, and he knew that with a fond woman of extraordinary sensibility and elevated sentiments, the death of a lover might be more easily supported than his dereliction. On the other hand it was imperatively demanded by circumstances that Gomez Arias and Theodora should never meet again; for, alas! such a meeting could be productive only of reproach and shame to the former—anguish, despair, and perhaps death to the latter.

Theodora, meantime, read in the agitated countenance of the valet a tale of distress more cruel than any she had yet endured; whilst Roque, who trembled lest, by an imprudent continuance of his interview with Theodora, they might be surprised by Gomez Arias, summoned up his resolution, and determined at once to acquaint her with her lover's treason:—"Lady!" he exclaimed with emphasis, "in the name of God, endeavour to brace your nerves against the dreadful intelligence I have to communicate.—You must forget him for ever;—nay, if you consult the happiness of all those that are interested in your welfare or in his, you will decide never to see him more."

"What mean you?" demanded Theodora, with redoubled agitation.

"Your lover is false, lady; you must fly to your parent, or encounter the peril of being immured in the gloomy seclusion of a convent. Such were my master's intentions towards you, when the arrival of the Moors happened in time to frustrate them. Should he, however, learn that you are at Granada, where your presence may throw invincible impediments in his way, the knowledge would be perhaps attended with disastrous results. I am a poor man, a butt to sustain my master's ill humours, but I will not so far dishonor my feelings as to permit the possibility of your being exposed a second time to the dreaded manœuvres of Gomez Arias. Fly, lady, fly to your kind parent."

Theodora fixed a wild look on Roque, and the horrid nature of his recital seemed to have frozen the springs of feeling. She did not speak, nor was any passion, save that of despair, depicted on her countenance; a settled stupor sat upon her pallid brow, and shone in the cold glance of her eyes.

Roque was moved by the picture of loveliness that stood before him, motionless in the intensity of grief; but he was conscious of the danger he incurred by protracting his stay.

"Alas!" he said in a soothing tone, "you are very, very unfortunate; but consider, lady, the consequences of our being seen together. Allow me to retire, then, and command my services; but, oh, do not by any means appear before——"

He was interrupted by Theodora, who suddenly started before that dreadful name once so endearing could be pronounced.

"Roque," she cried, in a tone and manner that bespoke her possessed of more resolution than could be gathered from the expression of her countenance, "Roque, I will retire; be silent, and let me see you again.—Yes," she added with a voice of presageful import, "it is better I should not see him more!"

She then hastily retired from the spot, and sought the way to her apartment. That feeling so deeply rooted in the female heart—the desire of probing a lover's perfidy to the utmost, determined her to follow the valet's advice. No, she dreaded not the most disastrous consequences; for, alas! what has betrayed woman to fear, when she seeks justice from the man for whom she has sacrificed all! Is it death? Ah! it is her best refuge and only consolation!

CHAPTER VII.

Sierpes apacienta el pecho
De una muger ofendida.
Moreto.

Ah taci! ogni parola
Mi drizza i crini; assei dicesti; basta
Basta cosi, non proseguir.
Monti.

Roque made a precipitate retreat from the garden; for, anxious as the poor fellow was to render any service to Theodora, he still felt no inclination to incur thereby the displeasure of his master, and draw upon himself the full measure of his indignation. The valet resolved to keep a strict silence respecting his interview with Theodora, and he entertained a belief that the fears of the unfortunate girl would induce her to follow a similar course. Thus he flattered himself there was nothing to apprehend farther than the danger of an accidental meeting.

Theodora meantime, a prey to a thousand distracting fears, had locked herself within her chamber, in a miserable state of hopelessness. Tormented with various conflicting passions, she now boldly resolved to meet her perjured lover, and demand an explanation of his cruel and unnatural conduct; but again she was suddenly checked by an instinctive dread which seemed to freeze her powers of action. She despondingly threw herself upon the couch, that gaudy but unconscious witness of her sorrows, and as the briny drops fell fast from their sad fountains, and bedewed the rich silken covering, she exclaimed—

"Yes, it was he himself that I beheld last night."

These few words conveyed a portion of that exquisite anguish that gave them birth.

Gomez Arias; or The Moors of the Alpujarras.

It was a fearful idea: she had seen her lover a nocturnal visitor to that garden, his face decked with smiles, and his eyes replete with pleasure and hope. He was happy, and thought no more of the lost Theodora. He had forsaken her—her whom he had vowed for ever to love, and to whom he had pledged his word to acknowledge her as his own before the world. This was a masterpiece of ingratitude; and yet Theodora hoped that ingratitude, that blackest stain of the human heart, might have prompted the dereliction of Gomez Arias, rather than love for another. To think that she had entirely lost his love, was a pang more cruel than all she had hitherto endured; and this alas! was the phantom which she strove in vain to chase away, and that most obtruded upon her mind.

The loquacious Lisarda was not tardy in making a second appearance: she knocked for admittance, and Theodora, who in her present state was but little predisposed to encourage her unmeaning chatter, felt nevertheless an inward desire for the presence of her attendant. By her means she could acquire a solution of the mystery with which she so much dreaded to be acquainted, and yet was so anxious to learn. She opened the door, and Lisarda no sooner entered than with her accustomed volubility she began—

"Well, well, my gentle lady, you must forgive me certainly; I have neglected you too long; but then consider, my good lady, what a day this is: what with the expectation of my master's arrival, and the preparations for this wedding, the whole palace is thrown into a marvellous confusion."

"Say no more," replied Theodora; "you need not seek to excuse yourself; I am but a stranger here, and have no right whatever to engross the attention of any one, much less on such an occasion as the present."

"Aye, aye," continued Lisarda, "it is indeed a most busy time. Well, the glorious Don Alonso arrives to-day, and to-morrow his beautiful daughter will be led to the altar by her gallant bridegroom. Only think, my sweet lady, what a wedding this will be. The queen and the Maestre de Calatrava, in the absence of the king, are to be the sponsors."

"That mark of the royal favor," said Theodora, "speaks highly for the merits of both the parties; but I am yet to learn the name of the knight who has rendered himself deserving of such an honor."

She pronounced these last words in a faltering tone, and Lisarda, though a thoughtless woman, soon perceived her agitation.

"*Dios nos defienda!*"[1] she cried, "what ails you, dear lady? you look so shockingly pale. Well, it is all your fault for being set against taking counsel; now if you could but be persuaded to admit the visit of Samuel Mendez, God knows how much you would profit by his advice; for believe me, lady, the iniquitous Jew cures better than most of our good Christians."

"I assure you," interrupted Theodora, "that my unwillingness to acquiesce with your wishes does not arise from the circumstance of the doctor being a Jew, but merely because my indisposition can receive no benefit from medicine, whether it be administered by an infidel or a true believer.—So, I pray you mention no more this Samuel Mendez, but rather tell me the name of the future partner of Leonor."

"Aye, fortunate indeed, Señora, you may well call him fortunate, for Doña Leonor is a most accomplished lady, a beautiful lady; and were it not that she is——"

"She is most accomplished," interrupted Theodora.

"She is in troth," retorted Lisarda, "and so dutiful a daughter withal. She is now going to meet her noble father in his triumphant entry into the city, and she will be accompanied by her future husband, and a numerous and splendid retinue.—But, hark! hear you not the tramp of horses, and the sound of trumpets?"

She flew to the window, and Theodora, in breathless anxiety, followed.

"There!" cried Lisarda, with glee, "they are about to depart. Now, see, my lady, Leonor mounts—the bridegroom holds the stirrup."

Theodora cast a terrified look, which shot a pang to her inmost heart—It was Gomez Arias who helped Leonor to mount. Theodora saw enough—but one glance, and all the horrors of her fate were revealed. The deluding smile which had seduced her heart, the traitor eloquent eye which wrought her ruin, were now devoted to another.

Theodora uttered no piercing shriek; neither did sigh or groan escape her; but she silently sank backwards in the tranquillity of horror. She had now nothing else to hope or fear; no throbbing anxiety to forego,—no further perils to dread—the sum of her misery was complete, and dauntless she might encounter any disaster; for this last blow had imparted to her the passive courage of indifference and despair.

---

[1] God defend us.

Lisarda, occupied with the dazzling objects which moved beneath, did not perceive Theodora's situation, and without taking her eyes from the cavalcade pursued her remarks:—

"Now they go—the Lord bless them, how handsome they look! Well, I do not blame my lady's taste, for certainly Don Lope is the most gallant of cavaliers. What think you, my sweet lady? Well, certainly they do say he has many a grievous sin to answer for, in the list of innocent girls he has seduced and undone: the Lord defend them, poor creatures; I pity them. But it was surely their fault:—more fools they for trusting to the fair promises of such a man—what think you gentle lady, am I not right?"

Happily the cavalcade was now out of sight, and Lisarda's observations were accordingly cut short. But she immediately turned to Theodora, who had sat motionless on her couch from the first glance that had acquainted her with the full extent of her wretchedness.

"Well," said the loquacious waiting maid, "what shall I do to divert you, lady? Really I am at a loss. If you are not moved by the splendid sight you have just now witnessed, I cannot imagine what will affect you. Mayhap I might afford some consolation, since you are so strongly bent against the assistance of Samuel Mendez."

"Thank you," said Theodora, raising her eyes towards the speaker, "thank you for your kind intentions, but if anything could tend to the alleviation of my sorrows, it would be perhaps a free and unmolested indulgence of them."

"Oh, dear lady, but we must have no sorrowful faces at the wedding. *Virgen de las Angustias!* that would be dreadfully ominous. Cheer up, sweet lady; there is nothing in the world like a good example, and when you see every one rejoice, I am sure you will not mar the general joy. Cheer up, good lady—better days will come. To-morrow, at the wedding festival, your thoughts, I engage, will be fixed on other objects; such indeed as are interesting to every female who, like ourselves, is yet blessed in the primeval season of youth. Am I not right?"

"Happy!" cried Theodora, in a thrilling tone, "happy!" Then as if to veil the effect which her exclamation might produce, she added, "who can promise themselves happiness in this world?"

"Alack, and that is true!" responded Lisarda, "for many, many are the lovers who are born to be unfortunate and die of broken hearts." She strove to swell her own with a mighty sigh: "And even those who marry, how oft do they curse the day that—but this is neither here nor there."

"To-morrow! and is it really to-morrow, that the ceremony is to take place?" demanded Theodora.

"There is no doubt of it. God have mercy, the ceremony has been already delayed too long. The young lovers would have been united some months since, had not unavoidable impediments retarded the accomplishment of their mutual wishes."

A clamorous shout, and a burst of trumpets now announced the approach of Aguilar to Granada, and Lisarda with giddy steps sallied out, leaving Theodora to the undisturbed enjoyment of her gloomy reflections. The unfortunate child of Monteblanco had now the most unequivocal proof of her lover's baseness and treachery: Gomez Arias was faithless, but what an aggravation of guilt attached to his infidelity! His cold, heartless villainy seemed to surpass all power of conception, and Theodora for some time remained like one striving to recall the fleeting illusion of a horrid dream. Then she clasped her hands fearfully over her swollen eyelids; a few large drops fell on her cold marbled hands, and in those eyes flashed the wild resolution of despair.

A bitter smile now gently curled those parched and pallid lips, and she raised her trembling fingers to her forehead, expressing all the passive agonies of an absent mind. Then suddenly, as if actuated by a powerful impulse, she sprung upon her feet: she cautiously drew towards the casement in a listening attitude, and the names of Aguilar and Gomez Arias which floated in lengthening sound along the air, threw additional excitement on her already distracted feelings. But one day more, and she was to witness the completion of her lover's union with her rival. What a train of frightful associations this image brought to mind!

Dreadful was the conflict that Theodora had to sustain, and in that unequal warfare, her whole frame underwent an appalling change: her eyes glistened, and her hands shook violently, as she threw back with a resolute movement the tresses of her redundant hair. Again she stopped as if brooding over some frightful design; her throat became swollen with hysteric affection; the blood that hitherto had seemed congealed in its source, rushed with impetuosity down its wonted channels, and the blue veins through which the little rivulet of life had gently flowed, now became dark and turbid as the mountain stream. Her eyes shot the lurid flashes of madness; a wild laugh broke the harmony of the purest voice; and a malignant curl usurped the place where heavenly smiles had habitually sat.

Gomez Arias; or The Moors of the Alpujarras.

Theodora, that soft and seraphic being who but a short time since, rich in the charms of native grace and loveliness, had been the star of a happy home, and the delight of a fond and admiring parent—that Theodora was now changed into the fearful semblance of a frantic being. Alas! such was the effect that a few moments had wrought, that the eyes of a fond parent would have in vain endeavoured to recognize his darling child. Feelings utterly foreign to the nature of Theodora, had now taken possession of the shattered fragments of a broken heart, once the shrine of hallowed and mental beauty; and those intelligent, soul-stirring features which nature had bestowed as the interpreters of soft sentiments and kindly feelings, now faithfully reflected the workings of impassioned and frenzied woe.

Alas! it is too often found that the gentle female heart, when rudely lacerated by the perfidy of man, is capable of being wrought, by a powerful sense of injury and intense anguish, to the utmost agony which the darker passions can display.

With irregular steps, which bespoke the confusion of her thoughts, she paced the silent chamber that gave back with hollow sound the measure of her steps, while the vaulted passages of the palace echoed at intervals the deafening shouts that were heard from without.

But the fit of frenzied passion under which Theodora laboured was too violent to last. That fatal crisis was approaching, which generally terminates in the immediate accomplishment of a mad suggestion, or with calmness treasures up in silence some direful resolve. The moment had now arrived when the forces of the suffering victim were exhausted; she suddenly became composed; her mind appeared irrevocably fixed on some act of madness, and despair was stamped in the cold and unearthly expression which at that moment subdued her whole frame, and apparently subjected her existence to a new dominion.

CHAPTER VIII.

Aguarda hasta que yo pase
Si ha de caer una teja.
Quevedo.

Este misterio aparente
Te voy, Señor a explicar.
Zarate.

We think it almost time to retrace our steps, and revert to a character which played a conspicuous part at the beginning of this history. The reader, if not particularly deficient in memory, will perhaps remember a certain Don Rodrigo de Cespedes, who bustled not a little in one or two of the foregoing chapters, though he had the best excuse in the world for subsequently keeping out of the way. It is to him we must return; therefore, patient reader, suffer your attention to be diverted for a few moments from the interest of the present events, and resume your acquaintance with that most deserving and ill-used cavalier. And here, by the way, I may perhaps be allowed to indulge my spleen, by manifesting my extreme dislike to interruptions in general, for there is nothing so vexatious and mortifying as the unpleasant necessity to which an author is obliged to submit of breaking the thread of a narration when it begins to excite some interest.

It is a subject well worthy of notice, that the generality of readers should be of so inquisitive a temperament, that they cannot be induced to take in good part whatever they read, and rely implicitly on the good faith of the author for the correctness of what he advances. By this means, much time and paper might be saved, explanations would be useless, and works would be rendered more compact, and consequently less tedious, which we cannot but consider an infinite advantage to the literary world at large. However, we must take matters as we find them, and as a circumstantial and satisfactory solution is expected by the reader to every incident enveloped somewhat in mystery, let us hasten to comply with the established custom: and now to return—

We left Don Rodrigo with his man Peregil, patiently waiting the leisure of their beasts, sighing, and cursing, and complaining by turns, for want of more suitable recreation. The night was dreary, and the spreading branches of the tree under which our friends had taken shelter, afforded but a meagre accommodation. If their lodgings were comfortless, the supper which they could expect was still more humble and hermit-like;—the bill of fare consisted of some green grass, which though abundantly supplied, presented a most provoking and unrelishing want of variety. We would not venture to determine whether the refinement of their palate stood in the way of their appetite, but it is nevertheless a fact that both master and man left the reverend father's mule and the *mesonero's* ass undisturbed possessors of the repast. The comforts of supper and rest being, therefore, denied to our wanderers, they resigned themselves to their unpleasant situation, and with the patience that necessity imposed upon them, awaited the approach of morning. Don Rodrigo in particular, being thoroughly impressed with the idea that his rival Gomez Arias had fallen in the encounter, was full of inquietude, and excessively desirous to penetrate further into the mountains to a place of security, where he might lie concealed until their safe return to Granada.

Accordingly, scarcely had the first blush of dawn shed a dubious ray over the still slumbering earth, than with much impatience Don Rodrigo hastened to try how far he might rely upon the complaisance of the mule. Peregil followed the example of his master, and having found that the temper of their beasts had been considerably improved by the abundance of their repast, they quickly mounted, and endeavouring to make up for the loss of time by a tolerably brisk pace, they pursued their route towards the thickest and darkest part of the wilderness.

Two whole days did Don Rodrigo and his attendant continue to wander without making much progress, which may perhaps be chiefly attributed to the perverse disposition of the mule and her companion. Indeed the cavalier and his attendant wandered about much in the same manner that a knight-errant and his worthy squire might be expected to do, with this difference only, that the knight-errant would be eagerly seeking for adventures, whereas Don Rodrigo was equally solicitous to avoid them. The poor cavalier found himself in a most miserable plight; his revenge had been satisfied, but more generous sentiments now occupied his bosom. He reflected, with deep-felt remorse, that for the sake of redressing the fancied wrongs inflicted on him by an individual, he had deprived his country of one of its bravest defenders; then again, like most lovers under similar circumstances, he easily conjectured that the female who had evinced such an unequivocal aversion to his addresses, would feel yet more repugnant to accept them, when offered by a man reeking with the blood of her favored lover.

These and many other reflections of the like nature continued to intrude upon his mind; for it is really a matter worthy of remark how very circumspect and thoughtful a man becomes, when by an undue neglect of those same qualifications he has brought himself into an uncomfortable and perilous predicament. They had by this time penetrated into those places which were under the dominion of the rebel Moors. This circumstance was therefore attended with the greatest danger, and consequently their anxiety and distrust became proportionably augmented as they advanced.

However, Don Rodrigo still bore with manly fortitude the unpleasant and dangerous turn which their affairs had taken, whilst the valet, since he could find no other resource, freely gave vent to his complaints.

"Señor," he cried, turning to his master, "so may the Lord defend us, but we are every instant getting deeper into difficulties. Here are we flying from the clutches of alguazils, to fall into the grasp of the rebel Moors; and after all, unwelcome as the appearance of alguazils may be, I should feel very well contented at this moment to be under their special guardianship, rather than sustain the murderous aspect of these infidels. Nay, would to God that I were safely and comfortably incarcerated within the walls of the most obscure dungeon in Granada."

"Let us then look for our way to Granada, and risk the worst from the friends of Don Lope," said Don Rodrigo, who, though possessed of much personal courage and resolution, yet was aware these qualities would not avail him against the enemies which he was likely to encounter by proceeding.

"Aye, indeed," replied Peregil, "let us find our way to Granada, and may the guardian angel conduct us safely thither.—Blessed be the virgin! for a man like myself, endowed with a lively and poetical imagination, I may say, these wild places are exceedingly disagreeable, for they induce me to make strange metamorphoses: my fancy is continually upon the alert to transform every object into any thing save what it really is: at day-break I mistook my ass for an officer, and your mule for a Moor. Alas! we are alike, my honored master; for you, Don Rodrigo, when in a poetic and loving mood, are ever disposed to convert cheeks into roses, and lips into coral, and to find pearls where others only see teeth. Now, Señor, by a similar process, when a fit of poetry and fear comes upon me, I feel marvellously inclined to convert all objects that come before my view—let alone my ass and your mule—flocks of sheep, flights of crows, stray cows, and barking dogs, into so many, ruffian-looking and hideous Moors; and, moreover, I am fully persuaded that my poetry is not a whit more extravagant than yours."

Don Rodrigo, harassed with the combined inconveniences of hunger and fatigue, paid little attention to the absurdities upon which his timorous valet was commenting; but Peregil, emboldened by the passive forbearance of his master, continued in a higher key:—

"A plague on all lovers, say I; a plague on lovers who for a woman, one solitary woman, when there is so abundant a choice of such commodity in Spain, can be stimulated to cut the throats of each other, risk all sorts of perils, and undergo all the miseries that can afflict human nature. Fye! fye——"

"Peace, thou wretch!" exclaimed Don Rodrigo; "profane not with thy foul remarks and scurrilous rebukes, that tender sentiment which thine own gross and brutish disposition is neither competent to appreciate nor enjoy."

"And most humbly," returned Peregil, "do I thank providence for having given me a heart withal so brutish and so gross, since those refined pleasures and feelings which are likely to lead a man into mischief, are in direct opposition to my taste. Now tell me, my honored master, is there any law, either human or divine, which ordains that, because you most desperately love Leonor de Aguilar, and Leonor de Aguilar as cordially dislikes you, I, who am by no means a party concerned in this love or hatred, ought to be exposed to all the united miseries of hunger and thirst, fatigue, dangers, and even death?"

Don Rodrigo, occupied with very different subjects, heard not the flippant observations of his servant, when suddenly, as they were approaching the skirts of a wood, his reflections and the valet's impertinent loquacity were cut short by the unwelcome appearance of a party of the strolling rebels. They sprung eagerly from their concealment, and in a moment stood before Don Rodrigo and his attendant, bearing on their countenances the marks of their revengeful disposition, and the savage pleasure of meeting with a devoted prey.

"Stand!" fiercely cried one of the ruffians.

Don Rodrigo made no reply, but gallantly drew his weapon, and prepared for a resolute defence.

"What! base Christian! darest thou provoke our anger? Thy life shall pay for the temerity."

"The payment," returned Don Rodrigo, "shall not, at least, be easily extorted."

At this the Moors rushed upon the unfortunate cavalier, who though aware of the impossibility of making any successful resistance against so many enemies, defended himself bravely and undauntedly, while Peregil fled with equal speed and terror. The combat could not be long protracted. Don Rodrigo fell covered with wounds and exhausted from the loss of blood, uttering a faint murmuring complaint on his unlucky fate and disastrous love. The ferocious Moors raised his body from the ground, and as it was the custom with those desperate men when a Christian unfortunately fell into their power, they immediately hung it on a tree. There they left him, and shortly after chance led them to the spot where the hapless Theodora slept, forsaken by her unprincipled betrayer.

The flight of Roque, and the remarks she had heard from the Moors on the night she was taken, led that unfortunate girl to believe that it was her lover who had fallen a victim to the cruelty of those barbarians. Thus she bitterly deplored the supposed death of him who was at the very moment accomplishing the blackest deed of ingratitude.

Meanwhile Roque, instigated by fear, and retreating on the scent of safety, shortly overtook his master, who was not a little surprised and alarmed at the discomposure of his plans, when he perceived his valet appear unaccompanied by Theodora.

"Where is Theodora?" demanded he hastily.

"I don't know," sullenly responded Roque; "probably in Heaven by this time."

"What mean you, villain? didst thou forget my orders?"

"Certainly not, but when I was about to put them in practice, some thousands of most desperate Moors came just in time to prevent my laudable intentions. At first, bearing in mind the gallant master whom I had the honor to serve, it was my determination to fight the unbelieving rascals; but upon second thoughts, I discovered it would be more prudent to yield to necessity, and since it was not in my power to save the young lady from falling into their hands, I considered it laudable to disappoint the rebels of one prisoner at least, whom they might perhaps estimate as the most important of the two; and so, instead of making use of my arms, I had recourse to my legs, which members, on more than one occasion, I have found to be the most serviceable part of my poor self."

Gomez Arias mused for a moment upon the narration of his attendant, as though calculating the probable consequences of the event. Even in spite of the uneasiness which he pretended for the fate of Theodora, he could hardly disguise from himself a species of latent satisfaction. The event removed from his way the only impediment by which his ambitious designs could be thwarted. Theodora, in the power of the Moors, would be even more secure than in a convent, and Gomez Arias, without troubling himself about the probable fate to which his lovely and too confiding victim was exposed, continued his journey to Granada, drowning the recollection of his misconduct in the glittering prospect that was now opening before him.

The next day he met with the glorious army of Don Alonso de Aguilar, by whom he was welcomed with a friendly and parental solicitude. He had the good fortune to act a conspicuous part in the encounter which El Feri sustained at Gergal, and which ultimately led to the complete overthrow of the Moors at Alhacen, and the destruction of that town. Don Lope proceeded to Granada with the prisoners, and to offer his services to the queen upon his arrival. He soon found in the resources of his mind specious pretexts to cover his long absence from Granada, and his apparent dilatory conduct, notwithstanding the notification of his safety sent to him by his future bride. But Leonor de Aguilar, though proud and lofty, was still a woman in her affections, and willingly received the most feeble excuses, when urged as they now were by the eloquence of a favored lover.

Thus Gomez Arias, whilst his victim was abandoned to all the horrors of her fate, whilst her venerable father drank deep the bitter draught of affliction—Gomez Arias, the heartless perpetrator of so much misery, now fondly rioted in the anticipated pleasures of his approaching nuptials, and the splendid honors that awaited his union with Leonor de Aguilar.

CHAPTER IX.

Ecco l'ora—Nel sonno immerso giace
——E gli occhi all'alma luce
Non aprirà più mai? Questa mia destra
Per farsi or sta del suo morir ministra?....
Alfieri.

Est-ce une illusion soudaine
Qui trompe mes regards surpris?
Est-ce un songe dont l'ombre vaine
Trouble mes timides esprits?
J. B. Rousseau.

The night was far advanced, and the numerous guests whom the hospitality of Don Alonso had summoned together, began to retire from the joyous scene of revelry and feasting. The noisy pleasure was wearing fast away, and those antique halls no longer echoed with the boisterous mirth of so many joyous hearts; for in Aguilar's palace that night every heart was happy,—every heart save one,—one which, desolate and solitary amidst this world of rejoicing, was a prey to the canker sorrow that had fastened upon its core.

But now the convivial assemblage had retired, and the banqueting hall was left to the undisputed dominion of silence and lonely repose. No longer ornamented with all the panoplies of war, and the verdant and perfumed spoils of the garden, those glittering scenes which dazzled the eyes and benumbed the senses, were now no longer resplendent, but wore that chilling aspect which imparts to the mind a painful sensation of melancholy and regret. Upon the long tables still remained the scattered fragments, remnants of the banquet. Here the sumptuous display of the looms of Valencia were stained with the waste of racy and highly flavoured wines, and there broken goblets and ornaments of curious workmanship were flung around in the reckless excitement of the revellers. The lamps were out, and the few that still glimmered in the sockets served but to heighten with their fitful and scanty light the deserted and gloomy appearance of the scene.

Gomez Arias had retired to his chamber in a transport of delight; the most pleasing reveries thronged upon his mind, and as he paced the silent apartment, he inwardly congratulated himself on the near completion of all his hopes—the speedy enjoyment of his fondest wishes. In this ferment of expectation, not a single thought obtruded to damp his ardour, or throw a partial shadow over so bright a picture. Every thing around him contributed to his felicity,—for alas! he did not see the sorrow that was busily destroying those charms by whose power he had been once captivated: nor did he hear the wailings of that voice designed by nature to convey the softest tones of innocence and delight. No, Gomez Arias had no thought for his unhappy victim—far, far was he from surmising that she was at that moment beneath the same roof.

In this delightful mood, Don Lope threw himself upon the superb couch, to pass the night in the luxurious vision of his approaching happiness. The silence was awful! the dull bluish glare of a solitary lamp flung around the dim splendor of the chamber a charm of melancholy tranquillity; the rich arabesque ornaments, the gorgeous tapestry, on which the heroes of other times stood frowning in gloomy repose, were now partially obscured in solemn shadows that might have imparted a sensation of superstitious awe. More faintly now gleamed the expiring light of the lamp, which looked a cold unearthly beam, colourless and fixed, save when the chilling draft of nightly air found its way through a crevice of the ponderous casement, and animated the languid flame with a dull and sickly motion.

Hushed is every sound, when lo! the door gently opens, and a white figure moves slowly forwards. It is a female form, and the lamp that still glimmered in the room, and another which the nocturnal visitor carried in her hand, revealed a picture which might well chill the heart of the most hardened:—it was a female in the first stage of youth, and in whose lineaments could yet be traced the fading remains of beauty. She grasped a dagger, and she came ready steeled for crime. Murder!—the blackest deed of human depravity, revolting to the senses even when instigated by the revengeful passions of man, but in a young and tender female, unnatural, and full of horror. The figure paused, and cast around a dubious and uncertain glance; her whole frame trembled, and the weapon in her hand seemed ready to forsake its grasp. Alas! those irresolute motions, bespoke her nature: it was woman, woman armed for crime, but woman still. With noiseless step she advanced towards the couch; she reached the spot, and gazed with fixed earnestness on the sleeping Gomez Arias; a thousand gloomy thoughts expand on her pallid brow; her dark eyes gleam with the flame of revenge; her livid lips curl with the bitter smile of despair! With difficulty she draws the oppressive breath, and violently shakes the hand that holds the shining weapon. 'Tis a demon that directs her every motion, and imparts to that melancholy and fading picture of youth and beauty, the darkest hues of the fierce and frenzied passions.

But the gust of rage is passed. She looks again upon the sleeper, and a deadly calm overspreads those features but lately fraught with convulsive passion. Fixed to the ground, she now appeared like an inanimate statue, and apparently forgetful of the dire purpose that had brought her to the spot. Poor Theodora!—child of misfortune!—victim of that intensity of feeling which nature seemed to have designed for thy bane and ruin; thou wert guilty but of a single error, and is then that error so severely to be visited! That heaven which made thee pure, and beautiful, and lovely, did it intend that thou shouldst experience all the horrors of the most malignant fate, as a counterpoise for the possession of so many attractions; or was it only to be exemplified as a warning to others, who, like thee, might be rich in beauty and gracefulness, of the dangers which these gifts bring in their train!

Theodora had been guilty of one crime; if, alas! that deserves the name of crime which is the genuine offspring of the sincerest heart. She had loved, and loved with all the enthusiasm of devoted affection. She had been generous, and unsuspecting, and for this she was betrayed and abandoned. Her injuries had so far wrought upon her distempered brain, that she was now about to commit a crime, for which she would be cursed, despised, and perhaps brought to an ignominious end.

Theodora remained a short time in a doubtful mood, and a heavenly spirit seemed to struggle with the malignant fiend that instigated her. She held the lamp in her trembling hand over the sleeping form of her lover, and by the sickly light she discovered his features as if inspired by some happy dream. His breath came thick upon her face, as she bent over the couch. Smiles were upon his lips, and a gentle motion shook his frame.

"He loves her!" groaned the despairing Theodora,—"he loves her dearly, and I am come to——"

Gomez Arias; or The Moors of the Alpujarras.

At this moment the deep toned bell of the palace sounded the hour, and interrupted her dreadful sentence. Solemnly the peal rung through the place like the death-knell of the perjured lover; but he, unconscious of his impending fate, slept securely and dreamt of love and happiness. For now his lips move, and in the broken articulation of deep but pleasing sighs, the name of her who occupied his mind, burst from his swelling bosom. It was the name of Leonor; the baneful sound went piercing to Theodora's heart, and roused all the furies that held dominion there. The kindly feelings which had returned, now withered fast away. She starts with frenzy; she grows paler, and revenge alone prevails; her bosom rises and falls with fearful emotion; wildly her eyes roll. She resolutely grasps the dagger; the moment is arrived; one blow, and the despoiler of her happiness would cease to exist: she fiercely raised her arm, but at the instant all her strength withered: nerveless she dropped the weapon from her powerless hand: no! she could not strike; for she was a woman maddened by deep injuries, but she still loved her betrayer, and the fountain of her gentle nature again bedewed her heart. She could not strike the man who had, without remorse, inflicted on her the pangs of a thousand deaths: she smiles in bitterness, and hangs over the couch of her unconscious lover, her clustering hair loosely flowing over the pillow; a piteous sigh escapes her, and, bending lower, she kisses the lips that had betrayed her.

Gomez Arias awakes.—Is this a vision? Surely a phantom mocks his sight; the spectre of *her* he had forsaken stands before him: it is indeed the image of Theodora,—but, alas! how changed! A short time only had flown since last he saw her, and yet so altered was that form, that were it not for a consciousness of guilt, with difficulty he would have recognised her whom he had once idolized. Gomez Arias thrilled as he gazed on the nocturnal visitor; in her pale features could be traced no sympathy with life; a clammy dampness bedewed her brows; a chilling apathy sat upon her countenance. One of her hands now mechanically fell on the feverish breast of Don Lope, and the cold, cold touch imparted a thrill of horror.

In speechless amazement Gomez Arias looked on the mournful figure, and in her glazed eye he beheld one large tear, that, overwhelming the eye-lid, dropt heavily on his hand. It was the tear of anguish, and the drop, as it moistened the hand of Gomez Arias, awakened in his heart a sad remembrance of violated love and truth.

The first impression of astonishment had now subsided, and Don Lope, in a broken voice, exclaimed—"Theodora! Heavens! is it thou?"

"Yes," she answered, gloomily, "it is the lost, the wretched Theodora, once the object of thy adoration, and now thy curse. But tremble not; the dreadful moment is passed, and I cannot harm thee; for though thou hast cruelly betrayed me, thou art *still* Gomez Arias."

"How came you hither?" demanded Don Lope, with emotion: "What was your intention?"

"Behold!" she replied, with a bitter smile, pointing to the dagger that shone on the ground; "I came to kill thee—I came to deal out a reward but little adequate to the pangs to which thy treachery has eternally condemned me. Oh! Lope! Lope! why didst thou not take from me this wretched life when I was no longer dear to thy heart? I should then have been happy!—Thou didst not—but cruelly left me to the mercy of strangers, when I had *none* to look upon in life but thee."

All the feelings of an injured, yet fond woman now flowed uncontrolled over that heart where the stormy passions had raged before. She sobbed convulsively, and a shower of tears relieved her breaking bosom. Her weeping countenance was upon her lover's breast, and as he contemplated her deep anguish, and the wreck of those charms which, but for him, had still shone in their native grace, a ray of pity dawned upon his heart, callous as he was. There was something so peculiarly distressing in the situation of the unfortunate girl, that all the glowing considerations of ambition faded for a moment from his view, and his senses were alive only to more humane sentiments.

Gomez Arias no longer loved Theodora; but still when he saw the extent of her misery, and felt her warm tears inundating his bosom, pity partially supplied the place of his departed affection. He took the passive hand of Theodora, and gently pressed it between his own—and happy—happy was at that moment his innocent victim at this solitary mark of kindness. It was like a healing balm to her lacerated soul; but too soon she discovered—for what, alas! can escape the acute penetration of a loving woman—she soon discovered that pity alone suggested the consoling token—pity which might alike have been excited by any other object of distress; and, oh! how little does the sedate voice of pity satisfy the craving bosom of one who had such claims to command unbounded love!

Theodora fixed her eyes on her lover, not in anger but in sorrow, and, in a thrilling and piteous voice, she exclaimed—

"I know you no longer love me; but, Oh! heavens! have I deserved this from you, Lope? Your vows I will not recall, for who can forget them? They are deeply engraven in my heart, and I believed them true,—I loved you, Lope—Oh! I loved you as never woman loved before, and how was such affection requited? Alas! had I suffered the most terrible of deaths, it had been kind compared with thy desertion."

"Yes, Theodora," said Gomez Arias, "your reproaches are just; for well I deserve the most bitter that language can invent; but I was compelled to that necessity by obligations so imperative, so sacred, that they may serve to explain, and perhaps, in some measure, to extenuate the disgrace, which my heart tells me I have so justly incurred."

"Oh!" cried Theodora, "could aught in earth oblige you to abandon one linked to you by the dearest of ties?"

"It was the consequence of former guilt," replied Don Lope. "Theodora, I will deal frankly by you,—nay tremble not at the intelligence which I must disclose, for it is now imperiously required.— Curse me, Theodora," he then added with emotion, "curse the man who has accomplished your ruin. When I courted your affections; when I sought your innocent caresses, then—then, alas! I was the betrayer; for it was then that I deceived your unsuspecting heart."

"Oh! Heavens!" shrieked Theodora, "you never loved me then!"

"Yes, I adored you,—I loved you truly,—passionately, but it was my very love that wrought this misery. I had no strength to reveal the terrible secret: I became selfish and ungenerous; for when I breathed to your innocent ear the vows of everlasting affection, when you repaid my profession with undisguised, pure, and disinterested love, even at that time, my hand, my faith, were sacredly pledged to another."

Theodora hid her face in agony, and wrung her hands in despair, but she could not speak; her heart was full even to breaking, and it was with a severe struggle that she faintly pronounced "Leonor!"

"It is too true," replied Gomez Arias. "Previous to my arrival at Guadix, and my acquaintance with you, my honor was bound to the daughter of Aguilar by indissoluble ties; we were betrothed, and on the point of being united, when an untoward accident drove me from Granada to avoid the vengeance of the friends of my discarded rival Don Rodrigo de Cespedes. Misguided by the fever of passion, I forgot my sacred obligations to Leonor. You have already but too dreadfully suffered, and a repetition of such scenes must necessarily increase the anguish of your situation."

This recital threw the hapless daughter of Monteblanco into that exquisite agony which falls to the lot of woman alone to feel: for man, far happier in the diversity of his pursuits; less susceptible in the refinement of sensibility; more divided in his intercourse with society, can never experience that poignancy of feeling excited by shame and disappointed love, which exert their baneful influence over the heart of forsaken woman!

Theodora answered not her lover; there was something so atrocious in his recital, that in spite of the palliation which a fond woman, even when most injured, is anxious to find for the man who has wronged her, she could not cast a shade over the glaring colours in which Don Lope's treachery was depicted: she recoiled from him with a feeling of apprehension, and her countenance assumed a deadly hue as she fearfully exclaimed—

"And you left me then to perish in the mountains?"

"No, Theodora," eagerly cried Gomez Arias; "no! such intentions never entered my mind; of that at least I am innocent: it was my purpose to have placed you in a convent, and I availed myself of your sleep to spare you the pangs of a separation. Having instructed Roque how to act, I proceeded onwards to make the necessary arrangements for your reception in the religious asylum the Moors surprised you; Roque fled: of the rest I am ignorant, and how I find you here is more than imagination can conceive."

"I came," said Theodora, bitterly—"I came to be a witness of your joyful wedding: it is to be celebrated to-morrow, and I am yet in time."

There was something evil-boding in the tone of these words, and an involuntary chill crept over Gomez Arias as he fixed his eyes on the sufferer.

"Yes," she continued, "it is necessary that the ceremony should be attended at least by one of your victims—the triumph of Leonor will then be more brilliant; and I," she added in a faltering tone, "I shall also enjoy one satisfaction——"

Struck with horror, no less at these words than at the manner in which they were delivered, Gomez Arias looked wildly on Theodora; but was unable for some time to give utterance to his thoughts.

"My poor life," continued Theodora, "must always be an obstacle to your happiness, and it is meet I should make the sacrifice at the foot of the altar, at the time of your union with the choice of your heart."

Don Lope was fixed in deep abstraction; a thousand thoughts rushed across his fevered brain; he raised himself from the couch; a copious suffusion bathed his distended brows, and every thing bespoke the dreadful conflict of his feelings. He saw all his prospects of grandeur fall like the baseless structure of a dream: on the point of snatching the golden treasure, he was arrested as effectually as if by the hand of death. Perplexed with the most distracting thoughts and boisterous passions, he for a time appeared even unconscious of the form that came to nip his hopes in their blossom: but soon a light seemed to illumine his over-clouded imagination, and his brow brightened as if actuated by a sudden resolution.

"Theodora," he said, with a solemn and energetic tone—"Theodora, I will no longer dissemble with you; I have been cruel, barbarous as never man was before: yes, to-morrow I am to be united to Spain's proudest daughter, and all that ambition and glory can offer in dazzling perspective to the ardent imagination of man, all, all is to be fulfilled. But, alas! Theodora, I cannot endure your distress; your tears, your anguish rend my heart, and awaken that affection which was never completely extinguished. Dared I but hope for your forgiveness, how willingly would I make the sacrifice of these glittering bubbles, and return to that path where alone I can find peace and happiness. Theodora!" he continued after a pause, "can you forgive me?"

This appeal was made in a tone so subdued and pathetic, that a conviction of its sincerity was readily admitted by the sorrowing Theodora.

"Forgive thee!" she exclaimed, in a voice thrilling with emotion, whilst a rich glow of animation overspread those pale features: "Forgive thee, Lope! Can Theodora deny you!"

Earnestly she raised her clasped hands to Heaven, and, in the genuine abandonment of an enthusiastic heart,

"Oh God!" she exclaimed, "thy mercies are boundless. Dear Lope!" she continued, "can I do otherwise than forgive you!" and the tear of joy glistened in her eye. "Your returning love will repay me for all the agonies I have undergone. And now you must forgive me—for did I not even now come armed for your destruction! Oh, horror! I came to murder thee—in this spot—sleeping as thou wast! But ah! pardon me; I was then a poor distracted woman, a despairing maniac, and——"

"Stay, my Theodora; reproach not thyself for an act of which I was the cause; it was a fate that I too justly merited. But no more of that. Listen, dear girl, and follow my injunctions, as upon their strict observance depends our future happiness. To-morrow night I will conduct you to your poor deserted parent: together at his knees we will implore forgiveness. He will not be invulnerable to the tears and supplications of his child; and I will forget the wild dreams that have so long tyrannised over my kinder feelings, to fix all my thoughts upon love and Theodora. To the happy termination of these designs, however, you must be willing to pay attention to my instructions."

"I will do all!" emphatically cried Theodora.

"Well," returned Gomez Arias, "take heed that thou keepest silence with reference to our meeting and resolves;—closed in thy chamber, thou must appear an uninterested stranger to whatever may be proceeding without. It will require the utmost delicacy and ability to disclose my determination to the proud Aguilars, when the arrangements with them are so far advanced. It is an insult they will never tamely brook, and all my policy will be necessary to defer, at least for some time, the terrible explosion of their indignation."

"Oh, Lope," exclaimed the fond girl, in a transport of tenderness, "I will—I will obey you faithfully! Your slightest wish shall be to me a law."

The tide of rapturous feeling overflowed her heart. Intoxicated with happiness, she threw herself beside the couch, fervently clasped the passive hands of her repentant lover, and tenderly pressed them to her throbbing bosom. But those transports beat coldly responsive within the breast of Don Lope; for pity and a sense of duty are but poor and inadequate substitutes for the glow of passion. Still, however, recollection brought to his fancy raptures past and endearments since flown; and memory perhaps made him cherish the present by vividly recalling the past. But it was like the melancholy regretful pleasure which is experienced by one who revisits the scenes of his childhood. He may indulge in the recollection of those departed joys, but his mind is estranged by other feelings, and can no longer enjoy those pleasures which formerly constituted his happiness.

The morning was now fast approaching, and a separation became indispensable.—Theodora made a hasty recital of her adventures and withdrew, replete with returning joy; for she had passed a few moments with greater delight than perhaps she could ever again experience in this world—those blissful moments when hearts severed by destiny, or alienated by misfortune, again unite in the genuine bonds of revived affection.

CHAPTER X.

Oh! what a jewel is a woman excellent!
Beaumont.

Mais qu'aisément l'amour croit tout ce qu'il souhaite!
Racine.

I humbly offer my advice (but still
Under correction), I hope I shall not
Incur your high displeasure.
Massinger.

Oh, Woman! lovely devoted Woman! Of what mysterious particles could nature have formed so strange a being—made up, as it were, of contradictions, and yet deriving from that very inconsistency its principal attraction. Uncertain and wavering, but amiable in that very weakness. When impelled by affection or smarting under highly excited feelings of injury, thou art capable of the most noble enthusiasm, or the darkest exhibitions of passion. Man, proudly arrogating to himself a despotic sway over the higher walks of intellect, and the wild and luxuriant fields of imagination, has left thee undisputed sovereign of the empire of the heart! He is often happy to avail himself of that more delicate discrimination, an instinctive feeling with which nature has gifted thee, though jealous of permitting thee to share in his power. Woman! thou wert born to grace and smooth the rugged path of life; the advancement of one endearing sentiment is the prized object of thy existence, and its successful termination thy reward. Debarred by nature and education from the glittering pursuits of ambition; incapable by the delicacy of thy frame, and the softness of thy nature, of following the rude pastimes, and participating in the laborious and dangerous avocations of man, thy whole being is wrapt in the charm of that one feeling—love! A feeling the most congenial to thy nature—blissful in the possession, and often but too fatal in its effects. Man seeks thee as a friend, to treat thee like an enemy. Thou lovest—he triumphs! and then he spurns thee because thou hast been kind. Base and degrading contradiction of human nature!—that because man is endowed with greater powers of attack, than woman has strength to resist, in the unequal strife, odium and shame should attach to the victim, whilst the betrayer acquires a false lustre from his unmanly triumph!

But Woman! such is the angelic essence of thy being, that while capable of feeling with poignancy the shafts of ingratitude and neglect, thou art still ready to pardon, and ever disposed to forget, when repentance makes an appeal to thy compassionate and gentle heart.

Such a woman was Theodora!—After having borne the extremity of sorrows, which seemed to surpass the strength of human forbearance, instigated by madness and despair, she had grasped the dagger in that soft hand little adequate for a deed so dark; like the midnight assassin, she had entered the chamber of her wronger, bent upon the commission of crime. But the sight of *him* who was once so dear disarms her—she cannot accomplish the deed of guilt, and the sudden repentance of her betrayer, like a potent charm, soon dispels the evil passions to which she was a prey. Only a few words of comfort had Gomez Arias spoken before the voice of sorrow was hushed in her heart. Nay, the man who had wounded her so deeply, was endeared by his very cruelty; for, alas! Theodora felt she loved him *now* more tenderly than ever.

She had forgotten the former treachery of her lover, and, incapable of anticipating the possibility of a renewal, she retired to her chamber to revel in her happiness, and await the coming of the day in anxious expectation.

In the meantime, Gomez Arias was pacing his apartment in the utmost impatience and agitation. Scarcely had Theodora withdrawn and the first impulse of pity subsided, than the sense of the danger to which his ambitious projects were exposed, rushed upon his imagination, and silenced every other consideration, save that of their accomplishment. Morning came, and still found Don Lope measuring his chamber with an irregularity of step that well bespoke the disorder of his feelings. Sometimes he paused and pondered upon an idea which seemed to offer him security, and then he rejected it as unavailable. Then he muttered half broken sentences, and then again suddenly composed himself into a saturnine tranquillity. After this he raved like a madman, and bitterly cursed the unfortunate Theodora as an insurmountable impediment to his views; forgetting that it was by the guilty indulgence of his own unworthy passions that he was now entangled in the intricate perplexities which surrounded him. The ill-fated victim of his guilt, fortunately for her short-lived happiness, heard not the ungenerous reproach. Alas! she was fondly indulging in the supposed kindness of her lover, and longing to clasp him in her arms; whilst the object of her endearment was at the same moment ungenerously contriving how to disengage himself from that embrace.

His present deceit was the natural consequence of the system he had adopted. To relinquish the brilliant prospects which presented themselves to his ambition, merely to listen to the voice of justice, and give redress to the injured, was too great an effort, encompassed as he was with the thousand conflicting passions that silenced the murmurs of neglected duty. His aversion to Theodora now acquired additional strength from the dilemma in which he was involved. He had never for a moment contemplated breaking his engagements with Leonor; he was unwilling even to calculate upon a possibility of such an event, for his honor and pride were both too deeply interested; yet it was of the most urgent necessity to delay the ceremony, and how to conciliate these matters was the source of his present uneasiness. What pretext could he assign plausible enough to justify so extraordinary a resolution?

A thousand plans suggested themselves, all of which he discarded as unavailable: he was apprehensive that night would surprise him before any arrangements could be entered into with regard to Theodora; and to attempt any coercive means of conveying her from the palace of Don Alonso would be madness. At all events he must avoid any interview with Theodora whilst his conduct might be subjected to observation; for at such a time the attention of all the household would naturally be directed towards him.

In this perplexity he was surprised by his faithful valet, who came in the morning, according to custom, to receive his orders. Roque entered, and was not a little surprised to observe his master's abstraction.

"Good morrow to you, Señor," said he, making an humble bow, and advancing towards the musing cavalier; but Don Lope made no answer whatever, nor did he take the slightest notice of his salutation.

"There!" continued Roque. "*Dios me bendiga!*[1] my precious master is in a most thoughtful mood. I had always the power of rousing him from his meditations, but now they appear too powerful for my humble abilities." "Don Lope," he proceeded in a louder key, "good morning to your honor," and he accompanied this Christian-like wish with as many noisy demonstrations as were compatible with good order.

"Oh!" cried Don Lope, suddenly starting, "is it you, Roque?"

"The same, Sir, at your service," replied the obsequious valet.

"Curse thee!" returned his master, "why makest thou that noise?"

"Thank you, dear master, that is a most amiable morning salutation; it augurs well too on a wedding-day."

"Pshaw! my wedding-day!" cried Gomez Arias, impatiently; and he again relapsed into his train of reflection.

"Eh?" ejaculated Roque; "I wonder what is in the wind now; all is not right, I perceive. Señor Don Lope, may I so far intrude on your most important meditations, as to demand what has sent your wits a wool-gathering so early in the morning: surely your dreams have not been unpleasant—for my part I cannot bear terrible dreams; they are ominous, particularly on the eve of a wedding——"

"Hold thy foolish chatter," interrupted Gomez Arias; "it is not a dream that troubles me, but a reality, a most mortifying reality. Roque," he then added in a more familiar tone, "I am involved in a labyrinth from which it will be no easy matter to extricate myself."

"I am very sorry, good Señor; for my part, I can very well conceive that a prudent man has cogent reasons to ponder and reflect more than a philosopher, when he is on the point of being entangled in the labyrinth of matrimony. Yes, Sir, I allow it is a most dangerous experiment: it is a voyage menaced with all sorts of foul weather, and surrounded with shoals, quicksands, and rocks, so that——"

"Roque, a truce with your cursed metaphors," cried Don Lope, "or I'll blow such a storm about thine ears, as to surpass all description."

"Sir," replied the valet, "if you dislike storms, I have not the smallest affection for them, so I'll even hold my tongue."

"Roque," said Gomez Arias after a moment's silence, "I am threatened with the loss of the rich treasure which I have so long and so arduously toiled to obtain."

---

[1] God bless me.

"Treasure, Señor!" cried the wondering valet. "*Cuerpo de Cristo!* Treasure! Be pleased to explain: I was not aware that you expected a rich treasure; from what quarter is it to come? My dear, dear master, I suppose you will then pay me all my vails."

"Here's an infamous sinner!" exclaimed Gomez Arias; "an unconscionable dog, to be talking of money and filthy wages when his master is labouring under the most perplexing dilemma in which ever mortal man was placed. Roque, I do not see what prevents me from shaking thy rascally form to atoms."

Don Lope, in his anger, made a step in advance, while Roque prudently made one in retrograde.

"Don Lope," cried the retreating valet, "as I hope for salvation, it is not my wish to offend: you appear in a terrible passion, and there is certainly some mystery at the bottom: something preys upon your mind, and if you would make me acquainted with it, perhaps I might devise a remedy for the evil."

"You cannot, Roque," returned his master, somewhat composed; "you cannot contrive to defer this wedding!"

"*Virgin del tremedal*," ejaculated Roque, crossing himself, "and is it come to this at last? So you have discovered some imperfection in the beauteous bride; some failing of which you were ignorant; better before the ceremony than after. But it would be a marvellous pity to spoil the feast, after the splendid preparations made to celebrate it with the state and decorum to which it is entitled. Lord bless us! a curious business we should make of it. But never mind; perhaps it is for the best after all."

"Now, Roque, hast thou finished? Who in the name of *Satanas*[1] can hear with patience thy everlasting foolery! I do not intend to postpone the celebration of the wedding from inclination, but because I am so compelled by unavoidable circumstances."

"What say you, dear master? surely nothing has happened."

"Yes, something, and most extraordinary; thou wilt be astonished at what I have to relate, Roque."

"Proceed, Señor; hold me not in suspense, and I can verily assure you, that nothing is wonderful to me."

"I have seen," continued Gomez Arias, in a solemn tone,—"I have seen Theodora!"

---

[1] Satan.

"Theodora!" echoed Roque, affecting surprise. "Seen Theodora! in your dreams, perchance, my good master."

"I have seen her," returned Don Lope, "as plainly as I now see thee. Nay, I have spoken with her."

"Where, Señor Don Lope?"

"Here, in this very apartment."

"You astonish me," proceeded Roque, "and yet I cannot say it is so very strange, neither; for I, myself, saw her—that is, I dreamt I saw her—and dreams, you know, my honored master, are often the precursors of realities."

"Enough," cried Gomez Arias; "we must now think on the means of averting the danger."

"The danger!" quoth Roque; "in the name of *San Pablo*, what danger do you apprehend?"

"Oh, Roque! I am threatened with the worst of evils."

"*Virgen Santa!* what say you, Señor?"

"Theodora expects me to relinquish the intended wedding, and depart hence with her, or she will expose me at the very altar."

"Indeed!" exclaimed Roque! "what, is not the gentle lady already tired of rambling? Good God! I should have imagined she had had too many mountain adventures to be longing to take another trip with you."

"Roque," said Gomez Arias, "we must remove this girl out of our way."

"Our way!" quoth the man of confidence—"our way, my good Señor? she is not in my way, by any means."

"No, buffoonery, Sirrah! you have chosen ill your time for jesting. Now listen, varlet. This Theodora must be disposed of; the urgency of this measure is obvious."

"Very obvious," responded Roque.

"The sooner the better," continued Don Lope, musing.

"Exactly," rejoined the valet.

"And how this is to be accomplished," muttered Gomez Arias, "without exciting suspicion among the household, I cannot conceive."

"Nor I," returned Roque.

"It is really the most distressing circumstance," continued his master.

"Uncommonly distressing," echoed the confidant.

"Of course," proceeded Don Lope, "I must employ stratagem; the wedding must be delayed; I will boldly accost Don Alonso. I shall merely demand one day, and in that short interval, every thing must be arranged, some way or other."

Don Lope uttered this last observation with the most imperturbable *sang froid*, and the conscientious Roque, wisely reflecting that under the head of disposing of cumbersome damsels, there were some ways not altogether in accordance with the dictates of conscience, ventured to observe——

"Pardon me, Don Lope, but I hope that in the premeditated disposal of this troublesome commodity, you do not mean to use any violence; for the Lord knows that the poor lady is already but too deserving of compassion."

"Thou art an impertinent, officious fool, Roque."

"That may be," coolly retorted the valet. "But be pleased to observe, that from the very commencement of this adventure—from the very first moment that you poured your sweet poison into the ear of this innocent young creature, I strenuously set my face against such proceeding; something whispered to me, that it would ultimately be productive of the most disastrous results; time will show that forebodings are sometimes to be credited. So be pleased to recollect, Señor, how often I remonstrated with you about this melancholy business."

"I do, Roque; and I suppose you likewise recollect what you gained by your eloquent remonstrances?"

"Oh, Sir," replied Roque, "favors they were, so deeply engraven, that it would be difficult to efface them from my remembrance."

"Well," continued Gomez Arias, "know, Roque, that I am at this time just in a humour to treat you with a renewal of such like favors, if you do not immediately put a stop to your droning and most impertinent reminiscences. I do not ask your condolence and regret for what is past, for that now cannot be remedied. I want thy shrewdness and invention to aid me in the present emergency. Violence I will not employ, so let your scruples be at rest. I must now see Don Alonso, and prepare the way for ulterior plans. Roque, I recommend thee to preserve a strict silence on the matter, if thou art not entirely disgusted with life. Now begone,—and meet me two hours hence at the *Plaza Nueva*."

Roque made a low bow of assent and withdrew; whilst Gomez Arias, assuming as much resolution as the importance of the occasion demanded, left his apartment to meet Don Alonso de Aguilar. Scarcely had he quitted his chamber than he beheld, with no little emotion, the bustle and activity which prevailed over the whole palace, on account of the expected festivities of the day. Here were maids, in fine attire, tripping gaily along, simpering and smiling, and all good nature and amiability. There ran servants in gorgeous dresses parading about in their respective departments, and assuming importance in proportion to the degree of responsibility which they were to take at the festival; and handsome pages were seen carrying bridal favors in large and beautiful silver salvers. Then came a crowd of friends, eagerly making their way to Gomez Arias, and offering their congratulation to the happy bridegroom; while the bridegroom, so congratulated, bore on his countenance an expression of any thing but happiness. Nor were these tokens of kindness confined alone to friends; for the fame of the wedding had attracted a proportionate number of hungry bards and minstrels who came at an early hour to greet the bridegroom with their songs and rhapsodies, whilst Don Lope, as it may well be supposed, responded to their love ditties and congratulations with most hearty curses.

He traversed the long galleries and spacious halls of the palace, already besieged with numerous visitors—some attracted by the splendor of the festival, and others by the odour of savoury and delicious things that would grace the convivial board—indeed, from the number of intelligent artists employed in the preparations, the *connoisseurs* in culinary science augured favorably of this department of the feast. Don Lope with difficulty escaped the compliments and embraces of his *soi-disant* dear and respected friends, and making his way through this mighty army of parasites, called to one of the servants, and caused himself to be announced to Don Alonso de Aguilar.

He found the warrior already attired for the ceremony, and girding on a most magnificent sword, which he only used on solemn occasions. After the first salutations had passed, Gomez Arias remained for a few seconds pondering within himself the best means of breaking to Aguilar the disagreeable communication with which he came prepared. A consciousness of the imposture he was meditating, rendered his situation in the highest degree embarrassing, and his habitual self-command seemed almost to have abandoned him at this critical moment. The old warrior perceived the constraint of his manner, and was struck with the singularity of a conduct so much at variance with the usual courtly ease and style of Gomez Arias.

He waited therefore for some time in expectation that Don Lope had something to communicate; but as the young cavalier appeared in no haste to signify his wishes—

"Don Lope," at length, said Aguilar, "you are really too thoughtful for a man on his wedding-day."

A pause ensued; and the affair becoming more perplexing every minute, Gomez Arias found the urgency of adopting a decisive step. He summoned, therefore, all his adroitness, and with much deference and respect he said to the father of Leonor,—

"Don Alonso, an unexpected event has just been imparted to me,—and the distress which my feelings have sustained, has no doubt excited your surprise,—but before the ceremony proceeds, however great my reluctance, it is imperatively required that I should communicate with you, and solicit your advice in this difficulty."

"Proceed, Señor," said Don Alonso; "though allow me to observe, that any communication of importance ought to have been made before this day."

"Don Alonso," resumed Gomez Arias, with firmness, "there are circumstances in life which are not controllable by the will of man. Strange as the request which I am about to make may appear, it is absolutely necessary. Sir, with all the respect which you are entitled to command, but with all the firmness which duty requires of me, I must throw myself on your indulgence, and pray you to defer the wedding until to-morrow."

"What!" exclaimed Aguilar, struck with surprise at so extraordinary a demand; "defer the wedding! Don Lope, what means this?—Surely you do not intend to affront my house!"

"The honor of your house, Don Alonso de Aguilar," answered Gomez Arias, with composure, "is now intimately connected with my own; and it would be unjustifiable to suppose me guilty of such intentions."

"What am I then to think of your strange proposal?" demanded Aguilar—his brow mantling with indignation.

"It is a request," replied Gomez Arias, "that I would never have contemplated of my own accord; and you may well imagine what my feelings must be when I am obliged to postpone my happiness even for one day. Certainly it is no trivial inducement that could prompt me to such a measure; I hope this will plead my justification. I have received a dispatch from my valued friend Count Ureña, stating that he is seized with a mortal distemper, and conjuring me, as I esteem the blessings of a dying man, to repair to his couch ere it be too late. He has a most important communication which must be intrusted to no one but Gomez Arias. The castle of the Count," added Don Lope, "is but six leagues distant, and I shall be back by to-morrow. Now, Don Alonso, I crave your advice: shall I disregard the last request of a man to whom my family are under sacred obligations, or will you allow the ceremony to be delayed till to-morrow, by which means I shall be enabled at once to fulfil the dictates of honor and humanity, without trespassing too far on my own happiness?"

Don Alonso de Aguilar was in some manner reconciled to the necessity of the measure proposed by Gomez Arias, though his pride received a severe check, the effects of which were easily to be discerned in his features.

"But," said he with some asperity of tone, "my permission is not the only one you are to obtain, Don Lope. My daughter must be consulted—have you received her sanction? The Queen also must be forthwith apprized of this sudden change, and I know not how her Highness may be disposed to acquiesce in the alteration."

Gomez Arias promised easily to remove all difficulties with his bride, if Don Alonso would immediately use his influence with the Queen, and urge the necessity of the delay. He was aware that the high spirit of Leonor would, under any circumstances, deeply resent such a measure; still he confidently relied on his own abilities and persuasion to overrule any objection on her part. He hurried therefore to her apartment, craved admittance, which was granted, and found himself before his intended bride, rendered still more beautiful by the costly ornaments with which she was adorned.

"Well, Don Lope," said she smiling, while surveying herself in the mirror, "what think you of my appearance?"

"As of a divinity to whom I bend in adoration," gallantly replied Gomez Arias, and taking her hand he pressed it to his lips with respectful tenderness.

Leonor replied to this mark of her lover's regard with a look of affection.

"But," exclaimed she, laughing, "I cannot compliment Señor Don Lope, upon the taste of his toilet. No doubt he will tell me that his imagination has been altogether engrossed with my beauty, and that he has not bestowed a single thought upon himself: however," she continued in the same strain, "from the respect we owe to the Queen, and the noble friends who will honor us with their presence, it will be necessary to recall the attention of the cavalier, even to so unworthy a subject as himself."

She was still proceeding, when Gomez Arias, who considered every moment he lost of vital importance in the arrangement of his plans, resolved at once to acquaint her with his determination.

"It seems fated, dear Leonor," he said, "that I am to experience a greater share of disappointment than usually falls to the lot of man;

scarcely has the late impediment to our union been removed, and I am on the point of succeeding to my heart's fondest wishes, when——"

"Surely, Lope," interrupted Leonor, with emotion, "your rashness has not again placed you in the peril from which you have so lately escaped—and yet your dress and deportment bespeak something disastrous—Speak—say, Don Lope—let me know the worst."

"Calm yourself, dearest Leonor; there is no danger to apprehend."

He then, in a few words, explained what he had already said to her father, and in soothing terms solicited her consent to what he proposed.

"What need is there of my consent," she said, whilst her countenance betrayed the mortification she experienced, "to a measure that meets the approval of the Queen and my father! Certainly," she continued, "let us defer the ceremony."

There was something in the tone in which these words were delivered, that thrilled to the heart of Don Lope; for the sarcastic smile and the forced tranquillity which Leonor had assumed, plainly indicated that her pride had been deeply wounded, though she affected to treat the affair with indifference. Gomez Arias had recourse to all his eloquence in order to smooth the resentment awakened by his proposal, but Leonor repelled his advances with a resolute dignity of manner.

"Go, Don Lope," she said, proudly, "you are losing time here—consider the state of the Count; and unless you make good speed, he may never know the kind and valuable friend he possesses."

She then called her attendants, and with the most perfect indifference began to divest herself of her ornaments, urging all the time to her future husband the necessity of immediate departure.

Gomez Arias, though reluctantly, was compelled to leave his bride, and hurried away further to promote the accomplishment of the plots which distracted his attention.

Leonor was soon disrobed of her bridal garments, and the disconcerted maids were lost in astonishment at the extraordinary change which had taken place. Nor could they explain the cheerfulness of manner visible in their mistress, when she announced that the wedding was to be deferred. But under the apparent indifference of Leonor, rankled a deep feeling of injury. The same pride that resented her lover's determination, forbade her to exhibit any degree of concern; but though the feeling was repressed, its effects would be more lasting than if expended in reproaches and complaints.

Don Alonso de Aguilar signified the unexpected delay to all the officers of the household, and the amazement of every one may easily be conceived. Every trifling circumstance was discussed, but nothing satisfactory elucidated, save that every individual, either as his interest was concerned, or his curiosity unsatisfied, loudly exclaimed against a change which interfered so much with his profit or pleasure.

CHAPTER XI.

Ambition, like a torrent, ne'er looks back;
It is a swelling, and the last affection
A high mind can put off. It is a rebel
Both to the soul and reason, and enforces
All laws, all conscience; treads upon religion,
And offers violence to Nature's self.
Ben Jonson.

Gomez Arias, after his interview with Leonor, repaired to the place where he had appointed his confidential valet to await his leisure. Upon his way he met the diligent Roque, and briefly related to him the success which had hitherto attended his operations.

"My good Roque," he gaily exclaimed, "our path now seems clear, and we have nothing to impede our course."

"Aye, Señor," returned Roque, "so it appears; but God grant that our course may not yet be obstructed. When he who walketh uprightly must see that he stumbleth not, what chance have we?"

"Well," cried his master, laughing, "in such a case mind thou art not in my way; for assuredly my fall will entail upon thee some sore bruises."

"Bless me, good Señor," cried the valet, jocosely, "do what I may, I cannot guard myself from such peril; for, by some unaccountable mischance, when you *do* fall, I am sure to reap the disagreeable results: however, may the saints protect us in all lawful enterprise, and, certes, there is no stronger law than necessity."

"Oh, Heavens!" exclaimed Don Lope, at this moment, "Roque—look! who is that cavalier in the distance?"

Roque looked as he was ordered, but could perceive nothing that might call for such an exclamation.

"Señor," said he, surprised, "what causes your alarm?"
"Is not that *caballero* going towards our mansion?"
"He may—but what is there strange in that?"
"Surely it is the Count Ureña!"
"He looks very much like him."
"Then I am undone! Run, Roque; dispatch! Detain him."

And without further ceremony, by the smart application of his hand to the back of the valet, he gave an additional impetus to the motives for increased exertion, whilst he himself advanced at a brisk pace towards the object that had so unseasonably disturbed his interesting speculations.

Roque, like a good servant, without losing any time in useless parley, obeyed his master's commands by making the best of his way to the person in question, who in reality proved to be the Count. Gomez Arias, feeling certain that his apprehensions were well founded, suddenly seized him by the shoulder, at the same time calling on him to stay.

"What means this?" cried Ureña, sharply, turning round, not at all pleased with the roughness of the salutation: "who is he that dares——"

"Your friend," answered Gomez Arias, laughing.
"Don Lope!" cried Count Ureña, in amazement.
"The same—but whither are you going?"
"To your house, surely: and now you must confess that I am a sincere friend; for although not entirely recovered from my late indisposition, I could not resist the desire of being present at your wedding; so I posted to Granada, and here I am, in time, I suppose?"

"Oh, quite," replied Don Lope, evidently annoyed.

"But it seems," continued Count Ureña, "that my arrival does not meet with your approbation?"

"My dear friend, you must excuse my apparent want of cordiality, but I have already dispatched an express to your castle to explain matters, and you must on no account be seen in Granada."

"But why?"
"I ask it as a particular favor."
"I cannot comprehend," said the Count, perplexed: then he turned to Roque; but Roque, as if aware that he was about to be questioned, and, conscious of his total inability to satisfy any queries, to save the Count a fruitless expenditure of words, shrugged up his shoulders, and rolled his eyes most expressively.

Gomez Arias; or The Moors of the Alpujarras.

"My dear Count," cried Gomez Arias, "it is of momentous importance that you should not be seen in this city by any of our mutual relations and friends. My peace of mind, my future prospects, nay, my very honor, require this sacrifice from your friendship. I have no time now to enter into explanation; but the enigma will be solved upon your perusal of my dispatch: in the meantime suffice it to say, that your immediate removal from Granada, and your strictly keeping within your house, will bind me to you with a powerful and lasting obligation."

"*By Santiago*, Don Lope," exclaimed the Count, good humouredly, "you must either be crazy, or wish to pass some merry jest upon me. Well, I am heartily happy to see a bridegroom in such spirits."

"No, by my honor," returned Gomez Arias, "I solemnly vow to you, that this step is demanded by actual and imperious necessity."

"Well, well," replied the nobleman, acquiescing, "I will, at all events, comply with your request, whatever may be the motive."

The friends took leave of each other, and Gomez Arias breathed more freely, as he again considered himself assured of the success of his plans.

"Señor," said Roque, "we were just speaking of impediments, and there comes the Count. Now, God send that we may meet no more!"

"Ay, Roque," replied Gomez Arias: "If I think rightly, the most material part of the business remains yet to be done, and it puzzles me strangely how to ensure its success."

"Most prudently said, Señor," returned Roque; "for it is indeed a ticklish point to dispose of a lady, when it unfortunately happens that she is not equally desirous to be disposed of;—but whither are we going now?"

"To the gardens,—for there we shall be unobserved:" then, after a pause, he continued; "Roque, thou appearest uneasy; what is the reason that at every minute thy head is turned backwards, as if in apprehension?"

"Oh, nothing, Señor, nothing in the world."

The valet delivered these words in an irresolute tone, for his master's observations had been just. Roque had for some time betrayed such disquietude in his manner, that at length the attention of Don Lope was directed towards the object of his valet's uneasiness, and he perceived a stranger following them at some distance. It was a Moor, of dark and repulsive appearance, who was evidently observing them, although he affected a total indifference to their movements.

"Roque," said Gomez Arias, in whom the slightest incident now created suspicion, "Dost thou know that strange looking man?"

"Think you, my honored master," returned Roque, "that I am likely to consort with so villainous looking a Moor? What should I do with such an acquaintance? I am a *Christiano viejo*,[1] and my conscience would not allow me to consort with infidels, and particularly when they are so ill-favored as yonder prowling rascal."

"Roque, Roque, thou talkest too much, and the very earnestness of thy manner makes me strongly suspect that thy knowledge of the stranger is more than thou art willing that I should learn."

"*San Pedro me valga!*" ejaculated Roque. "My honored master, how can you thus call in question my integrity? Do you think, Señor, it is really possible for me to use any mystery with my master?"

"Avaunt, thou hypocritical dog!" cried Don Lope; "thou canst not deceive me: however, I am now too deeply engrossed with more important matters; but mark me—should I find out any double dealing, any imposition on thy part, thou mayest well tremble!"

"Tremble!" exclaimed Roque, in a shrill tone, and affecting indifference. "An honest man has no reason to tremble."

And he trembled and quivered like the aspen leaf, which doubtless did not look as if he had yet possessed himself of the attributes of an honest man. They had by this time arrived at the gardens, and Gomez Arias was exceedingly surprised when he observed that the strange Moor had followed them thither, though keeping always the same respectful distance.

"By my honor," exclaimed Gomez Arias, "such conduct cannot be merely accidental. Roque, *maldito*,[2] some mystery lies in this."

"In what, Señor Don Lope?" demanded the valet, with much simplicity.

"Attempt not to impose on me, thou base-born and ungracious varlet. Why does that Moor follow us in this manner?"

"My dear master," replied Roque, "is it in my power to stop the man? What dominion have I over him? These places are public, and I suppose that he, though a Moor, considers that he has the same right to walk here as we faithful Christians. Now, good Señor, could you prevail upon the queen to limit the privileges of those infidels, and allot them a piece of ground for their own use, aloof from all public places,

---

[1] Old Christian.
[2] Accursed.

certainly much abomination and contamination would be spared; and thus——"

"Cease, thou graceless dog!" interrupted Don Lope. "Cease, for I can no longer endure thy interminable prosing; a more talkative varlet never intruded on the patience of an indulgent master. See! there is the mysterious Moor again; and if I mistake not, it is the very same who has followed me already twice before. Yes, surely he is the same, although he has somewhat altered his attire."

"What!" cried Roque thrown off his guard; "has he followed you too, Señor?"

"Ah!" returned Don Lope, "then you have seen him before. Now, rascal," he added, grasping roughly the poor valet by the collar— "Leave off this foolish dissembling, or by *Santiago*, I'll strangle thee on the spot!"

"Sweet master, you surely don't mean to harm your faithful Roque?"

"Art thou, then, prepared to confess thy knowledge of the Moor?" demanded Gomez Arias.

"Like a good Christian, I am always prepared to confess."

"Well, then, begin, thou sinner."

"That is easily said," mumbled out the valet; "but, consider, good Sir, that my sins cannot find utterance, as long as you obstruct their natural egress in this most unchristian manner. In pity, gentle Señor, unloose your grasp a little, or I shall die without confessing at all."

Indeed, the poor valet's face afforded an incontrovertible proof of the sincerity of his expostulations; for his master, though perfectly elegant in all his movements and demeanor, was at no particular pain in observing the strictest rules of politeness when he chanced to handle his luckless attendant. Roque's face appeared by this time in its colour no bad specimen of a well burnished pan—his loquacious tongue protruded from its natural dwelling, and the little buried eyes started out with an unusual degree of animation.

Don Lope, observing his distress, released him with a few hearty shakings; and Roque, after taking two or three deep and lengthened respirations, began to examine his person, to assure himself he had sustained no damage, and then applying his hand to his collar—

"*Virgen Santa!*" he cried, "here are fine doings! Oh, my honored master, what have you done! There is my beautiful—my best *gorgue-*

ra[1] completely destroyed—torn to tatters—absolutely spoilt for ever—past remedy. Oh Lord! Oh Lord! Such a fine *gorguera*, too, of the very best lace, and worked by the pretty and dignified fingers of Lisarda—and what will she say? What will she say when her loquacious abilities are called into action by no less a subject than the total destruction of her superb *gorguera*?"

"By all the powers of darkness, Roque," cried Gomez Arias, "but I would confidently match thee against all the Lisardas in the world."

"Señor Don Lope, a fine *gorguera* is perhaps unworthy of your eloquence; for, in sooth, you reserve your powers of tongue for more deserving objects. But consider, Sir——"

"Sirrah!" interrupted Gomez Arias, "I have no time to waste upon your foolery. I perceive your drift; you want to elude my examination; but now, Roque, be explicit or—— how often have you seen that Moor?"

"Much oftener than I could wish," answered Roque.

"Then he wished to form an acquaintance with you?"

"Apparently he did; but you know, Señor, we must not always trust to appearances."

"How did you meet his advances?"

"I did not meet them at all, Don Lope, for I kept advancing myself all the time, and as it happened that we adhered constantly to the same regular pace, we had a fair chance of going round Spain without ever coming into contact."

"Roque, thou art a shrewd villain," said Gomez Arias, who, perplexed as he was at the moment, could not help smiling at this conceit of his valet; and reflecting that, with such a fellow, he was more likely to succeed by gentle means than by actual force—

"Now, Roque," he said, "I am willing to give you credit for what you say, and you ought to deal frankly with me in return."

"Aye, Sir," replied Roque, very coolly, "upon the matter of credit we are even."

"Even upon credit! how, Sirrah?"

"For my wages," composedly answered the valet.

"Roque, you may one day go too far," returned Don Lope; "I may laugh at your fooleries, but they do not always fall in accordance with my humour. However, as to the point in question,—it appears that the Moor had really sought your acquaintance?"

---

[1] A kind of ruffle or frill, worn formerly round the neck—a collar.

"Yes, I must allow that," replied Roque; "but with the proviso that I am in no way accountable for the fancies that either Moor or Christian may take to me, as long as I do not give any encouragement, which is precisely the case in the present instance."

"Well," said Gomez Arias, "this matter shall be investigated at a future period, for I must attend to more important affairs; and now, Roque, tell me what your fruitful invention has conjured up to rid me of the troublesome object of my disquietude."

"My fruitful invention, Señor, as you are kindly pleased to term that faculty, which at other times you most unceremoniously treat with contempt;—my fruitful invention, Don Lope, has conjured up——"

"What, my good Roque?" eagerly inquired his master.

"Nothing," drawled out the valet.

"Provoking idiot," exclaimed Gomez Arias; "I know not what induces me to retain such a dull brute about me."

A pause followed, and Don Lope, quite at a loss on what course to determine, seated himself on one of the stone benches concealed by the trees that overshadowed the place. There he began to muse, whilst Roque, unwilling to disturb his reflections, betook himself to examine the unfortunate *gorguera*, and heave many a ludicrous sigh over its melancholy fate.

"Roque," cried Gomez Arias, after a short lapse, "I see no remedy but placing Theodora in a convent."

"Aye!" answered Roque, "it will all be right, provided she consents."

"Consents! By my troth, thinkest thou I shall put myself to the inconvenience of consulting her inclination?—No, Roque; unless some better plan be instantly devised, I must even resolve upon the convent; for the time passes rapidly away, and this girl must be disposed of to-night."

"Could you not contrive to send her to her father?" demanded Roque: "Poor thing, she is so very unhappy that——"

"Send her to her father!" returned Gomez Arias. "Art thou mad, Roque?—or is it thy wish that my fortune should be ruined for ever?"

"Neither one nor the other," rejoined the valet; "but it strikes me as plainly as day-light, that before we contrive to shut up this bird in the cage, her continual chirping will call some one to the rescue, and then I do not see any chance of mending our fortune; but, by-the-bye, talking of mending, I wonder if I am likely to find any for this most innocent and ill-treated *gorguera*?"

"A thousand curses on thee and on thy *gorguera*!" cried Gomez Arias, impatiently; then, assuming a calmer tone, he continued—"With regard to thy fears that she may call for rescue, that inconvenience may be easily obviated."

"*Santos cielos!*" exclaimed Roque, with visible affright—"You surely do not mean to cut off her tongue?"

"No," answered Don Lope, "that fate I reserve for yours, unless you contrive to keep it under better control."—He then added—"By sending Theodora to some nunnery in a remote city, such as Barcelona or Saragossa for example,—the air must be sharp, indeed, that can convey thus far the sound of her complaints."

"But, Señor," asked Roque, "is the young lady to be conducted to the said remote city by magic, or is she merely to be led in the ordinary way; for if this last be the case, what deception can you use subtle enough to lure a bird that has already been caught once in your snares?"

"That is true," replied Gomez Arias, "but I must risk a distant danger, to ward off a more immediate one. I do not entirely flatter myself that this unfortunate business will not come to light some time; but if I cannot avoid the storm, I am anxious that, ere it explode, I should at least be under good shelter."

"Well, Señor," said Roque, "it is a very delicate piece of business, and I really cannot harbour the presumption of offering you my advice. I shall obey your commands, as in duty bound, provided they are not in too direct an opposition with my conscience and——"

"And what?" inquired Don Lope.

"*Lavabo inter innocentes manus meas*," solemnly chaunted the valet, at the same time affecting to wash his hands.

"*Lavabo inter innocentes*, indeed," exclaimed Gomez Arias: "here's a conscientious sinner with a vengeance! So you cannot light upon some feasible design?"

"No, in very truth I cannot."

"Then who in the name of Satan can extricate me?" cried Gomez Arias, in despair.

"I can!" answered a deep and determined voice.

Gomez Arias started, turned round, and with amazement beheld the mysterious stranger standing, with folded arms, looking calmly upon him.

"And who art thou?" demanded Don Lope, "that presumest thus to intrude upon my privacy?"

"Good Heavens! who should it be?" said Roque, not allowing time to the stranger to give an answer; "why, my honored master, you piously invoked Satan, and his diabolical majesty sends you forthwith one of his emissaries."

"Stranger!" proceeded Gomez Arias, not heeding his valet, "what is thy name?"

"To know that were superfluous," coldly answered the Moor, "and in nowise necessary towards the acceptation of my services."

"And what assistance canst thou afford me? I know thee not—and yet those features should not be entirely strangers to my eyes."

"It is possible that they are not," replied the stranger, unmoved, "nor is your countenance altogether unknown to me."

"Who then art thou?" demanded Gomez Arias.

"Surely a Moor—a worthless Moor!" bitterly returned the renegade; for it was no other that now addressed Don Lope;—nor did he feel apprehensive of discovery, altered as he was by the conflict of his passions, continual sufferings, and even by the dress which he had adopted to baffle the penetration of Gomez Arias.

"Whoever I may be," continued the renegade, "is of no consequence; I come to render you service—are you disposed to accept it?"

"I cannot," firmly replied Don Lope, "from an utter stranger, without previously knowing the motives by which he is actuated."

"What!" exclaimed Bermudo, affecting surprise, "cannot you guess my motives? Certainly, I do not pretend to deny that by assisting you *now*, I chiefly mean to serve myself. You surely cannot expect more from a perfect stranger, as you call me. Look at me, Christian!" he added, stifling the conflict which was working in his bosom at the very sight of his foe; "behold, I am a Moor—a miserable Moor. And what else but interest could prompt a destitute, a desperate man to proffer his services to the proud and rich ones of the land?—Love, or esteem, or gratitude, think you? No, never! My own interest I consult—consult yours, and decide."

"Interest!" cried Gomez Arias; "there is something reassuring in that word. I like to hear a man talk of his interest, for then I am tempted to believe in his sincerity. What, then, canst thou do for thy interest, Moor? Let us hear in what manner thou art able to serve me."

"I can do much," replied the renegade: "You, Don Lope Gomez Arias, are at present involved in a most distressing predicament?"

"I am."

"And the source of your disquietude is a woman?"

"Proceed."

"Her name, Theodora?"

"Thou art indeed instructed in this affair—how cam'st thou by the knowledge?"—and he cast a terrible look on the trembling Roque.

"Señor," cried Roque, "as I hope for salvation, I——"

"Silence, Sirrah!" exclaimed his master.

"Nay," observed the renegade, "blame not yon trembler; it is true that I applied to him before I resolved upon offering you my services personally; but from fear, or some other reason, he paid no regard to my proposal. I therefore waved all further ceremony, and knowing the crisis to be at hand, I have seized this opportunity to address you."

"And what proposition hast thou to make?" demanded Don Lope.

"To remove from your path this obstacle to your ambition; to rid you immediately of Theodora."

"Fiend!" fiercely cried Gomez Arias, "thou darest not propose murder to me?"

"No, Christian," calmly returned Bermudo "dark as my form may be, and unseemly as my features are, yet I would scorn to imbrue my hands in the blood of a woman: no, though a ruffian, I am not yet sunk to the despicable wretch you suppose me. Theodora shall not suffer any indignity from me, but merely be removed from Granada."

"And what security wouldst thou afford of thy adherence to this promise, should I be inclined to enter into arrangements?"

"Security! the most firm and unbounded—the love which a Moor has conceived for her charms."

"What! art thou then the admirer?" sneeringly asked Gomez Arias.

"No!" indignantly exclaimed the renegade—"see you aught of that in me? Can the signs of any tender sentiment be traced in my visage?"

"Well," muttered Roque, "methinks he speaks very sensibly."

"I cannot love," repeated the renegade; "but a Moor, my superior in rank, one whom I have bound myself to serve, is powerfully stricken with the beauty of her you now wish to discard; he will treat her with every consideration, and, in defiance of all disadvantages, is bent upon gaining her love."

The eyes of Gomez Arias glistened with satisfaction as the renegade made these overtures, but still he paused before he came to a determination. He eyed the stranger with the scrutiny of a man resolved to analyze every feature, endeavouring to trace if any line of treachery were discernible; but he beheld nothing to awaken his suspicions. That dark brow was smooth and calm: for well aware of the examination to which he should be subjected by Gomez Arias, Bermudo had prepared himself for an interview on which the success of his plans intimately depended. Thus, his countenance evinced nothing but a gloomy composure, from which expression Gomez Arias could gather no trace of the deeper designs that had urged him to proffer his services.

"Are you resolved?" inquired the renegade, after a pause.

"Where lives the Moor to whom Theodora must be committed?" inquired Don Lope. "Does he inhabit this city? For in this case all further communication on the subject would be needless."

"No," answered the renegade, "he does not dwell in Granada, though not far from it at present: more you shall learn this night, should you be disposed to admit my proposals: but you must decide forthwith, as I shall be obliged to take my measures accordingly."

He folded his arms and gazed on Gomez Arias with seeming indifference.—Don Lope felt a moment's hesitation: there was something in this mysterious transaction that imparted misgiving to his mind; but the shortness of the time at his disposal, and the imminency of the danger, quickly silenced his rising doubts. Roque, who perceived the inward conflict sustained by his master, attempted, by a gentle remonstrance, to persuade him to discard the Moor's offer, but Don Lope indignantly repulsed the presuming valet.

"Sirrah!" he said, "I need not thy counsel; if, when asked, thy humility will not permit thee to give it, I marvel at thy presumption to offer thy opinion now."

"Moor, what are thy conditions?" he continued, bracing all his energies to a firm resolution.

"The price I shall expect," replied the renegade, "you are sensible must be commensurate with the importance of my assistance."

"Certainly," exclaimed Gomez Arias, with a sneer: "what you consider a just remuneration will no doubt be some exorbitant extortion."

"Christian!" retorted the renegade, "to show you that I place confidence in the magnitude of my service, I shall leave the reward entirely to your generosity,—and now listen. At midnight you must be with Theodora at the extremity of *El cerro de los Martires*;[1] the distance is short from Granada, and can therefore soon be traversed. There I will wait for you, and there you may likewise meet the noble Moor that employs me."

---

[1] The Hill of the Martyrs.

"I am resolved," cried Gomez Arias. "Yes, I will meet you at midnight then"—and rising, he was about to withdraw, when the renegade gently detaining him—

"Stay," he said; "I must have a pledge to present to my master."

"What dost thou demand?" asked Don Lope.

"That ring," returned Bermudo, pointing to one that sparkled on the hand of Gomez Arias.

"I cannot part with this gem; it is a bauble, but one I must preserve; ask for another boon three times as valuable, and it shall be granted thee."

"One does not hinder the other," said the renegade, dissembling. "Think you, Don Lope, that the difficulty from which I disentangle you merits no other reward than a paltry ring? I must have it for a pledge, and it shall be returned in due time for gold."

Gomez Arias cast a look of contempt on the Moor, who, thoroughly prepared for his part, most efficaciously assumed the appearance of the mercenary he was then undertaking to personate.

"Well, what is it you resolve," he cried, with a malicious smile—"to part with a ring, or keep the woman you detest?"

"Take it!" disdainfully replied Gomez Arias, throwing the required pledge on the ground.

The renegade humbly inclined himself to take it; but he could not so completely master his feelings as not to betray some marks of the pleasure he felt at the possession of so precious a gage. Gomez Arias, however, erroneously attributed these symptoms to the avaricious disposition of the wretch who appeared willing to undertake any service for gold. He again cast a contemptuous glance on the Moor, and making a sign to Roque, abruptly left the place. The renegade gave a loose to the joy which swelled tumultuously in his bosom; he kissed the ring with wild demonstrations of pleasure, and looking in the direction that Gomez Arias was gone—

"Now," he exclaimed, "my time is coming, and soon, proud Spaniard, wilt thou feel the power of thy bitterest enemy."

CHAPTER XII.

Cielos en que ha se parar
Tan dificultosa empresa?
Lope de Vega.

Quoi! tant de perfidie avec tant de courage?
De crimes, de vertus, quel horrible assemblage!
Voltaire.

After the defeat of his companions at Alhacen, and the total annihilation of their hopes and resources in that quarter, Bermudo the renegade had prudently fled to Granada. He knew he should be in greater security in that city, from the mixed intercourse of Moors and Christians, than by continuing in the wandering habits of a mountain life, now circumvented with numberless dangers from the active searches which the Christians were making to destroy every rebel that might be surprised lurking in suspicious places. The same course had been pursued by a considerable number of the dispersed Moors, whilst others, less enterprising or more cautious, had concealed themselves in obscure caverns and hiding places.

The renegade was one of the first that had arrived at Granada; and prudently mingling with the crowd of joyous Christians, feigned to be exceedingly interested in the solemnity of the day, when his attention was forcibly attracted by the appearance of a cavalcade in which he recognized an object already familiar to his sight. Great as his surprise was, he could not entertain a doubt that it was Theodora herself, Cañeri's fair captive, who now unexpectedly struck his view. An impulse of curiosity induced him to follow her, until he perceived that she was safely lodged in the mansion of Aguilar. From that instant, Bermudo had unremittingly devoted his time to investigating this occurrence. He learnt with pleasure that his hated foe was still alive. Nay, he had actually seen him; and, fervently bent on prosecuting every scheme that might hold out a probability of forwarding his views of vengeance, he had succeeded in his first inquiries to the full extent of his wishes. He had learnt the approaching wedding of Gomez Arias, and, remembering the circumstance of Theodora's lamentations and despair on the supposed death of that individual, he naturally concluded that there was some mystery, which, if discovered, might be easily converted to his own advantage.

He had therefore artfully sought an acquaintance with Roque, the acknowledged servant of Gomez Arias, and partly by insidious questions, and partly by his own penetration, he had drawn the conclusion that Theodora was the forsaken mistress of Gomez Arias, brought by chance to the very scene of his expectations, and who, if apprised of her lover's treachery, would afford a powerful obstacle to his views. The renegade therefore seized the favorable opportunity which presented itself, to accomplish the ruin of his hated foe, and determined to neglect no means of accomplishing the revenge which had been his solitary pursuit for many years. But his plan of operations was as deep and intricate as the motive that directed him was dark and diabolical. Finding that Roque absolutely refused to open his proposal to his master, he resolved to break the matter to him in person, and with this intention had proceeded to the public walks, as already mentioned. His artful and wily behavior, assisted by the distracting position of Don Lope's affairs, had betrayed the latter into that snare which the renegade had so cunningly devised, and which, if followed up with success, would lead the unwary Gomez Arias towards a labyrinth, in the mazes of which his destruction might be easily completed.

Thus Bermudo could not conceal his inward satisfaction when he found himself possessed of the ring of Gomez Arias—a ring which he well recollected had been the gift of Queen Isabella,—a precious gage, which, in the process of his fiendish machinations, might contribute materially to their successful termination. While on the one hand the renegade was thus awaiting with anxiety the result of every move in his diabolical game, and Don Lope on the other was congratulating himself upon the speedy close of his heartless compact, the lovely but unfortunate subject of both speculations was happy in comparative tranquillity at the palace of her preserver.

In perfect obedience to the urgent and repeated injunctions of her lover, Theodora kept herself in seclusion in her apartment. Implicitly confiding in the promises and vows of Don Lope, and fondly indulging in dreams of future bliss, she nevertheless felt a degree of disquietude, natural to the high excitement into which her feelings had been thrown. The morning came—the morning of that eventful day, and the commotion which prevailed throughout the palace, failed not to interest Theodora, although the cause admitted of various interpretations. Now she fondly imagined that Gomez Arias had already sought an interview with Aguilar, and made the necessary disclosures; and then again she shuddered at the idea that the fond wishes in which she had indulged might never be realized.

This state of anxiety and suspense was fortunately interrupted by Lisarda, who burst abruptly into the room with looks of visible alarm. She turned about without ceremony, and before Theodora could collect her thoughts to inquire into the reason of this perturbation—

"*Santos Cielos!*" she exclaimed, "here are fine doings! that it should come to this! fye—shame! precisely at the very moment that— — well, before I would consent to be treated in this manner, I'd suffer my eyes to be plucked out, and my tongue torn from the very root. After so much preparation! Lord! Lord! to disappoint a whole family and throw so many honorable people into confusion!"

Here the good Lisarda was compelled to take breath, of which Theodora most opportunely availed herself to inquire into the cause of the disturbance.

"Now, gentle Lisarda," she said "tell me what has happened? No disaster to the family; I hope?"

"Alas!" screamed out Lisarda, perfectly recovered from her exhaustion, "your hopes, lady, unhappily, cannot prevent the disaster, for truly a most terrible disaster it is,—fraud and insolence, and most abominable perjury is in the case, I am sure. Yes, the family has been treated this morning with the most untimely and vexatious incivility. Such a breach of delicacy and decorum never did I witness before. *Virgen Santa!* how will this end? The Lord knows that I, for my part, never felt tranquil on the score of the gallant.—No, no; I always said Don Rodrigo for my money—but that is neither here nor there; the evil is done, and we must stand the results. Really it is provoking—such a beautiful dress I had prepared, and now to defer the ceremony!"

"Defer what ceremony?" eagerly inquired Theodora.

"The wedding to be sure," responded Lisarda. "What, did I not tell you before?"

"In sooth you did not."

"Really? God defend us! I am a most thoughtless silly girl, that is certain. Why, my good lady, what should be deferred but the wedding?"

"And that is the misfortune, then, which has occasioned such uncommon signs of regret?" demanded Theodora, scarcely able to conceal her inward satisfaction.

"To be sure, lady; and by my troth, it strikes me that the subject is well worthy the mortification it has caused us all. Good heavens! had the accident happened to you, my sweet lady, perchance you might not be inclined to endure it so philosophically. But the Lord save me! if you do not appear to rejoice in this calamity!"

"Rejoice! heavens! what do you mean?" cried Theodora, blushing deeply, and striving to conceal her emotion. "What can induce you to suppose I could have so perverse a disposition, as to rejoice at an event that is evidently annoying and distressing to my kind and generous benefactor?"

"Dear lady, take not amiss my observation, but as sure as I am a Christian, and hope for salvation, you are much altered for the better since yesterday."

Having communicated the news of the palace to her fair charge, the good Lisarda bustled away to learn further particulars. Theodora soon after received a visit from the noble Don Alonso, on whose countenance were strongly depicted the signs of displeasure. Theodora easily divined the cause, and though she rejoiced in the termination of an event, in which her happiness was so deeply interested, she could not suppress a sensation of generous pity, at the idea that she was the immediate, though innocent, cause of her benefactor's disappointment.

With the simplicity congenial to her nature, she more than once during this interview felt a strong desire to throw herself at the feet of Aguilar, and frankly to avow the whole of her melancholy tale; yet she was restrained from following the genuine impulse of her heart, when she recollected her lover's absolute command. Thus, although her delicacy and frankness were hurt at the duplicity she was compelled to use towards one by whom she had been rescued from the most appalling fate, she stifled the suggestions of sincerity, to observe implicitly the wishes of a man who was even then planning her future misery and misfortune. Nor was this the only trial that Theodora had to sustain. She had been obliged to resist the invitation of Aguilar, who repeatedly pressed her to make her appearance in the grand saloon, and she had the mortification of suspecting, that an unfavorable construction was put upon her denial. They might attribute to female caprice, or a want of proper feelings for a generous benefactor, that which in reality was the mere effect of a sensitive mind and a devoted heart.

Theodora underwent all these trials with patient resignation, in the fond expectation of a speedy deliverance from her present irksome situation. In this uninterrupted succession of doubt and fear she spent the long and tedious day, and hailed with transport the arrival of night, which was now enveloping in her sable mantle the proud turrets and lofty buildings of Granada.

CHAPTER XIII.

> Per gli antri, e per le selve ognun traea
> Allor la vita, nè fra setà, o lane
> Le sue ruvide membra ravvolgea.
> *Metastasio.*

At a short distance from Granada there is a place called *El cerro de los Martires*,[1] which traditionary lore had invested with most appalling histories. This place abounded in deep caverns and subterranean vaults, in which it was a received tradition that the Moors used in former times to shut their Christian captives, and make them undergo dreadful torments. By the vicissitudes of fortune, however, these dungeons were now converted into secure retreats by the fallen and dispersed Moors. Several of these lurking places had already been traced out by the unwearied perseverance of the Spaniards, or betrayed through the treachery of mercenary Moors, but there still were some remaining which baffled every research, and whose existence known only to some of the principal and most faithful Moors, were in no danger at least of immediate discovery.

To these subterraneous habitations a considerable portion of the shattered forces of Cañeri had repaired, whilst some of the bolder party of El Feri de Benastepar had fearlessly sought refuge in Granada, where, in despite of the severe decrees promulgated by the queen, and the examples made of those who had infringed them, the rebels never-

---

[1] On the hill of the Martyrs, so called from the supposed cruelties that the Moors had exercised against the Christian prisoners who fell into their hands, Queen Isabella caused a chapel to be erected, which became the object of many a pious pilgrimage.

theless found shelter and protection from their fellow-countrymen. Thus while the rebellion seemed quelled to all appearance, it was not entirely extinguished. A secret fire still slumbered under the ashes, ready to burst forth when a master hand could be found to raise the flame. But the want of unity amongst the Moors, and the general dispersion which had ensued after the destruction of their last town, seemed to offer an insurmountable bar to the organization of a second revolt. Besides, the death of El Feri had struck the hearts of his followers with dismay, and there was no Moor of sufficient talent or enterprize to supply his place.

Things were in this state, when at the close of a sultry day three men were seen cautiously traversing the path which led towards *El cerro de los Martires*. The foremost, who appeared to act as guide, from his robust and athletic make, and the lowering expression of his countenance, might be easily recognized as Bermudo, the renegade; the others were strangers, and apparently disguised. They proceeded onwards, slowly, and with care, until at length they stopped at a sequestered spot, overgrown with brambles, and surrounded with high and widely spreading trees, whose sombre foliage offered an impenetrable barrier to the light of day. They plunged into the midst of this wilderness, and presently the renegade blew a soft and hollow blast, when the thicket suddenly seemed to move, and discovered an aperture which had hitherto been concealed. The two Moors, for such they were, and their guide, then descended through the opening into a deep and winding subterraneous passage. After a descent of a few minutes, they found themselves in a spacious vault hewn out of the solid rock and illumined by a solitary lamp, which afforded only light sufficient to render the darkness more dismal, and to give an indistinct view of forms and countenances naturally repulsive, rendered still more so by apparent want and exhaustion. About a dozen men and two or three women were reposing at length in different parts of the cave, without any other covering than their tattered dresses, and bearing on their features an expression of resolute despair.

At the further extremity of the cavern, which was somewhat elevated, and rendered more tenantable by several pieces of an old carpet, reclined a man of better appearance, whose apparel had evidently not undergone such severe service as those of his companions. This personage it might easily be supposed was the chief of those who, from their exterior, might, without any great deviation from the rules of inferences, be denominated a gang of desperate robbers. But it seldom happens that robbers in the vicinity of a rich and populous city are to be found in a state of such utter destitution; and if such were really the case, it might puzzle the beholder to discover what possible inducement they could have to continue in so unprofitable a profession.

As soon as the renegade and his two companions entered that cheerless and uncomfortable dwelling, all those woe-begone and lugubrious countenances suddenly acquired a degree of animation. It was not without reason; for the renegade and one of his companions laid down some provisions, whilst the other stood with his arms folded, a calm spectator of these proceedings, contemplating with deep attention the group before him.

"Alagraf! Malique!" cried the seated personage above designated: "Who is that stranger?"

"Fear not, Cañeri," whispered the renegade, "this is a friend—nay, perhaps the sincerest adherent and the bravest supporter of the Moors in their present condition."

"Certainly from his proud bearing in our presence," replied Cañeri, with offended dignity, "one might, indeed, be led to suppose him a person of consequence, did not those unseemly habiliments contradict such a conclusion."

The stranger answered not, but contented himself with casting a look of mingled pity and scorn on the mighty potentate of the cavern. The chief, however, was prevented from inquiring more minutely into the pretensions of one who appeared little disposed to pay him unqualified deference, by the shrill and croaking voice of Marien Rufa, who at that moment was actively engaged in heaping a redundance of abuse on the devoted head of her husband Aboukar. The squabble, as far as it could be ascertained amidst the confused din, originated in some provisions which the provident Aboukar, in his capacity of ex-master of the household, judiciously concluded ought to come by right under his control; accordingly, *secundum artem*, he had entered on his official duties by secreting a portion of the said provisions for his own private use, before they were either served up to Cañeri, or finally distributed amongst his hungry and rapacious band. Marien Rufa had observed the sly larceny, but what in the name of conjugal regard could have induced the crone to so unkind and unmatrimonial an action as the exposure of her own husband, is not easily to be determined. An upright and indulgent person might be tempted to believe it was a proper regard and tenderness for the purity of his character; but others, not quite so considerate, would suspect, and perhaps with a nearer semblance of truth, that the unamiable spouse was instigated by a less honorable motive. It was a fact, not to be contradicted, that Marien

Rufa and her once beloved Aboukar, at present detested as cordially as they had formerly loved each other; which curious phenomenon in the condition of matrimony is not of such rare occurrence as to need any particular investigation into its nature or origin.

As soon as Cañeri observed the disturbance, conjecturing from the character of the belligerents that the commotion was likely to increase apace, he rose suddenly from his seat, an action which clearly indicated the extent of his indignation, and with vehemence exclaimed—

"Silence! What means this disturbance? Slaves, is this your respect for your chief? Explain; what is the cause of this unwarrantable breach of decorum?"

No sooner had Cañeri uttered the word "explain," than Marien Rufa, conscious no doubt of her explanatory talents, in a most discordant tone began:—

"Please your Mightiness, the cause of——"

"Stop, stop," cried Cañeri; "I do not wish *thee* to explain." Then, turning, he demanded an explanation from Malique, who, in a few words, corroborated the statement of Marien Rufa respecting the ugly trick of which Aboukar stood accused. Upon this, Cañeri, after pondering some time, and gently striking his forehead as if to conjure some luminous idea,—

"Malique," he cried, "bring hither the source of contention."

The provisions were immediately placed before him, and the sapient chief, after putting aside a portion for his own use, wisely proceeded to give his judgment.

"Here, Malique," he said, "distribute these amongst you all, except the convicted culprit and his accuser."

This retributive justice was greatly applauded by the surrounding party, whose looks clearly indicated the high opinion they entertained of their chief's wise decision; although their ravenous hunger might have, indeed, contributed somewhat to the enhancement of their approbation. The renegade and the new comer stood silent spectators of the scene, but they could not disguise the expression of their contempt both for the degraded state of their companions, and the foolish importance with which the vain-glorious Cañeri comported himself.

Peace being thus restored by the chief's sagacious intervention,—

"Now, Alagraf," he said, "what tidings dost thou bring from Granada? Will thy expectations be fulfilled, and my wishes crowned with success? What further inquiries hast thou made relating to Theodora?"

"I have not been idle," sullenly answered the renegade.

"And yet," returned Cañeri, "I fear exceedingly that our mutual hopes will be disappointed."

"Not so, Cañeri," retorted Bermudo; "but this is no time to enter upon that subject, for another of greater importance has a previous claim to our notice."

"By the holy Prophet!" exclaimed Cañeri, with displeasure, "I should imagine that an affair in which I am interested, is, of itself, sufficient to command immediate attention: Explain, then," he added impatiently, "that which concerns me most."

"Moor!" cried the renegade with anger, "thou surely must forget that I am not thy slave: no, by my sword, I will not speak of these matters until I think the time befitting."

Cañeri was thunderstruck at this open act of insubordination; he rolled his eyes in choler, and looked on his band as if appealing to them to chastise the insolence of the renegade. But though those bold words had thrown the Moors into some consternation, yet no one dared to move a step, so much were they awed by the composed demeanor with which the renegade gazed upon them.

"Alagraf," said Cañeri, disguising his indignation, "are then my injunctions openly to be disregarded before my people?"

"Cañeri," answered the renegade resolutely, "you urge me too far, and you ought to know me better."

A murmur of discontent prevailed among the band, which was about to break forth against the renegade, when, suddenly, their movement was checked by the stranger Moor, who advanced towards them in a threatening attitude.

"Peace!" he exclaimed; "peace! ye abject, paltry slaves!"

"And who art thou," demanded Cañeri, trembling with rage, "that darest thus arrogate to thyself the power of dictating in my presence?"

"I am, Cañeri," answered the stranger haughtily, "thy superior in all, except in vice."

"Seize him!" roared out Cañeri. "Seize the wretch!"

"Stay!" cried Malique, interposing; "lay not your hands upon that man.—Most mighty Cañeri," he then added, addressing the indignant chief, "Mohabed Alhamdem, our opulent brother at Granada, has intrusted that Moor to our care, commanding us to lead him hither; he has most important matters to communicate, and, if the word of Mohabed is to be credited, it is from this stranger alone that the Moors may expect their salvation."

"Who, then, is this mighty personage?" demanded Cañeri, with a scornful sneer.

"He will himself inform you," replied the renegade. "Cañeri, you know how firmly I am devoted to the Moorish cause; why then was I insulted when it was only to advance the interests of that cause I spoke? But let that pass; I am no pettish boy to quarrel with my associates for a word uttered intemperately in an unguarded moment."

He held his hand in token of reconciliation, and then continued:—"Theodora, if appearances amounting almost to certainty deceive me not, will be yours, ere long."

"Is it possible?" exclaimed Cañeri. "When?"

"To-night or never," replied Bermudo. "Shortly I shall disclose to you all the particulars of my transaction; and now let us examine on what resources we can depend for a renewal of the insurrection."

"Resources! None," said Cañeri, "Our surviving men are dispersed and worn out by repeated misfortunes; most of our chiefs are dead, or have passed over to Africa, and the only man who had the power of rallying the straggling Moors, he who alone succeeded in imparting confidence to his followers, El Feri de Benastepar, is now no more: fallen by the arm of Aguilar, he shared the fate of those brave men who mingled their own ashes with those of Alhacen."

"El Feri de Benastepar is not dead," cried the renegade.

Cañeri and his men started from the ground with an instinctive impulse of returning courage, and all, with one accord, sent up an exclamation of joyful surprise.

"But where is the chief, then?" demanded Cañeri.

"There!" replied Bermudo, pointing to the stranger.

"Yes," said he, throwing aside his disguise; "yes, Cañeri, in this humble garb, which necessity has compelled me to adopt, do you again behold El Feri; conquered by Alonso de Aguilar, but miraculously rescued from the grasp of death to redeem the tarnished glories of the Moorish name; to close again in combat with the proud Christian chief, and, with the assistance of the holy Prophet, to doom him to that untimely death which he vainly imagines he has inflicted on me."

A simultaneous murmur of approbation ran through the surrounding party; even Cañeri, jealous as he was of the superior power and glory of El Feri, hailed with real satisfaction his unexpected appearance amongst them; for in the imagination of Cañeri were revived those hopes of asserting the station of fancied dignity from which he had been hurled by the late overthrow of the Moors. He again clung to the fond idea that the Moslem cause would ultimately triumph, and then he of necessity must succeed to a conspicuous share of power, to which he conceived himself entitled by his distinguished birth.

Thus the Moors, whom, but a moment before, we have seen in the lowest state of dejection, now flew to the opposite extreme: they pictured to their fancy the wonderful powers of El Feri, and the magic influence which his name would possess in calling again his countrymen to arms, while the desperate nature of such an undertaking, and the obstacles with which it was on every side beset, vanished altogether before their sanguine expectations.

The renegade beheld this general emotion with more signs of discontent than satisfaction; he argued little advantage to be derived from men, who could so easily pass from the depths of despondence to the summit of hope; for to a man like himself, endowed with strong passions, but accustomed to watch progressively their workings, such sudden transitions betrayed a weakness utterly incompatible with desperate enterprises.

"But how," now inquired Cañeri, addressing El Feri, "has thy precious life been preserved?"

"When I fell by the arm of Aguilar," returned El Feri, "it was more from the excessive fatigue which I had for several days endured, than from the nature of the wounds inflicted—they were not mortal; and as I lay extended and helpless on the ground, I thought upon my country, and my heart sunk within me when I considered that my life, which might still have been preserved to her service, would soon, alas! be lost in a fiery grave. The town was deserted—nought was heard but the crackling of the flames, and the groans of those that were dying around me. Our enemies were gone, and I, collecting my small remaining strength, with much difficulty contrived to drag myself from that place of desolation. At length, exhausted, I sunk under a tree, and there, for want of timely assistance, I might have breathed my last, when, to my joy, I observed two or three of our party, who had escaped in the general confusion, advancing towards me, and the hopes which had almost abandoned me again began to revive. My preservers removed me immediately to a place of security, and administered all the remedies that their limited means could afford. When I had sufficiently recovered my strength, in various disguises we arrived at Granada, and made ourselves known to Mohabed Alhamdem: at his dwelling the plan of a second rising has been concerted, and I am come here to ask your support to the undertaking."

"Noble and beloved companion," replied Cañeri, "next to the pleasure of seeing thee alive, comes, certainly, that of hearing thy proposal. I rejoice that, notwithstanding our little trivial disagreements, thou hast thought of me in the hour of an important crisis: command me freely, and command all mine."

As he delivered these words with his habitual affectation of dignity, he looked around upon his reduced followers, who all inclined their heads in token of blind acquiescence.

"And is this all thou canst command, Cañeri?" asked El Feri.

"No, not all; for at a moment's notice, I can assemble a considerable number, now prudently scattered in little parties, the better to avoid observation. They lie concealed in some neighbouring caves, and will at the first summons readily obey my orders. But what are thy designs, my noble friend? Dost thou contemplate the surprise of some fort? or hast thou in meditation a second expedition to the *Sierra Nevada*?

"Neither;" replied El Feri: "my plans of operation are now widely different; I mean to strike the blow far from the city of Granada: more I will impart to thee at a future period. Art thou well determined to second my exertions?"

"Yes," answered Cañeri, bowing his head. "In the name of the holy Prophet, I swear to follow thy instructions."

"Well then," returned El Feri, satisfied, "this very night I set out for the *Sierra Bermeja*, attended only by Mohabed and a servant: that opulent Moor has enthusiastically joined our cause, and several of his friends, slow to contribute with their persons towards the result, have at least liberally assisted us with their gold. Thou, Cañeri, must not tarry here, but with the utmost expedition march to Alhaurin, a town neglected by the Christians, which thou wilt easily surprise; this is to serve as a rallying place for all those who may flock to our standard. I am assured that the mountain inhabitants of the *Sierra Bermeja* are prepared to join me,—thus, while the proud Spaniard triumphs in security, and rejoices at the supposed death of El Feri, he will suddenly dissolve the charm, and summon his enemies again to encounter the effects of his wrath and vengeance. And now, Cañeri, remember that Alagraf and Malique are the only persons through whom we are to communicate: so to your post, and there await my further instructions. Farewell! and when we meet again, may victory have rewarded our exertions!"

He said; and the two chiefs taking friendly leave of each other, El Feri, without delay, returned to Granada. Cañeri, scarcely able to contain his joy, rose and paced around the cave as if he were already dictating from his palace at Alhacen.

"Now, my brave followers!" he cried, suddenly halting, "be prepared to march at a moment's notice."

Such an injunction was perfectly useless; for it so happened that his gallant followers had no other preparation to make than to rise and march, having no baggage to encumber their operations beyond the very slender equipments which they carried on their persons.

"But!" exclaimed Cañeri, in the midst of his exultation, "Alagraf, if we depart immediately, how is thy promise concerning the fair Christian to be fulfilled?"

"Fear not, Cañeri," answered the renegade; "I have promised you that Theodora will be yours to-night or never."

"Or never!" re-echoed Cañeri, dismally shaping his face into most unwarrantable elongation: "Or never! We have yet some time to remain, and I would gladly wait for such a prize."

"It wants," observed the renegade, "but an hour to midnight,—the time approaches,—my heart feels confident Theodora, will soon be in your power, and I shall then have the means of accomplishing my revenge."

CHAPTER XIV.

Si! m'ingannai: scerner dovea, che in petto
Di un traditor mai solo un tradimento
Non entra.
Alfieri.

Le cruel, hélas! il me quitte,
Il me laisse sans nul appui!
Berquin.

"In the name of Heaven, Don Lope," said Roque; "let me again conjure you to pause before you finally resolve upon this undertaking: my heart misgives me strangely."

"Thy heart," replied Gomez Arias, "is a most impertinent monitor. Simple man! what other course is left me to pursue?—Is it thy wish that I should relinquish the most glorious prize, at the very moment of its attainment, from a pusillanimous fear of consequences? Already so far advanced, must I shrink from an honorable alliance with Leonor? By heaven! I cannot; I will not. Prudence, consistency, honor, forbid!

"But, saving your displeasure," interposed Roque, "methinks that same honor of which you appear so tenacious, cannot urge you to betray an unfortunate girl into the hands of infidel Moors. And although your present situation is certainly fraught with difficulties, there may yet be found some other way of proceeding with regard to Theodora, not altogether so frightful."

"No, Roque, none. We have now no longer time to think; we must act, and act without wasting a single precious moment.—Go, dispatch, deliver this letter to Theodora, and conduct her to the place that I have already pointed out. The night is fast advancing; dispatch; and be faithful in the discharge of my orders. This step is unavoidable, and to its necessity even thou thyself wilt be reconciled, though at present it may awaken in thy bosom a foolish sentiment of pity, or fear, I know not which."

Roque attempted no farther expostulation, but heaving a sigh, and casting his eyes to heaven, proceeded to the discharge of his commission, whilst his master hurried to the solitary spot where he had decided they should meet. Roque, in that wavering mood so natural to his character, alike unfit for good or evil, made his way to Don Alonso's garden, deliberating within himself on the course he ought to follow. Pity and remorse, at intervals, made him shrink with dismay from the picture of wretchedness which the unfortunate Theodora presented to his view. There was something so iniquitous and unmanly in betraying the unsuspecting and lovely victim, that the feelings of the valet, though far from being refined, revolted from the participation: once or twice he had even resolved to acquaint Theodora with the premeditated plot, but these momentary impulses of his better feelings were soon checked for want of strength to follow up the generous suggestion. The awe with which Roque beheld his master, and the dread of the results which his disclosure might produce in the mind of the victim, powerfully contributed to silence the voice of conscience. Then he hoped that the marriage once over, measures might be taken for the security and comfort of Theodora; and finally he fondly admitted the hope, or rather forced his rebellious mind to encourage it, that Gomez Arias would relent at the sight of the unhappy girl, and that he would then fix upon some other expedient less distressing and criminal.

In this conflict, he arrived at the palace, and entering by a private gate into the garden, he approached the window of Theodora's apartment. The anxious girl, who had been all the day on the alert, immediately descended, and stood by the side of Roque.

"Where is he?" she eagerly cried, upon meeting the valet.

"Prudence," replied Roque, "has obliged him, much against his inclination, to keep aloof; but here is a letter which will explain his motives, and the course that you are immediately to adopt."

Theodora ran over the contents of the letter in a trepidation of anxiety, and closed the perusal of it by imprinting the fervent kisses of love and devotion on the vile instrument of treachery.

"Let us make haste," she then said, and without waiting for Roque to lead the way, she hurried through the garden upon the wings of affection. The valet's heart misgave him, when he beheld her speeding with such haste to her destruction. He contrasted the devoted confidence of Theodora, hurrying to the fatal spot, with the duplicity and heartlessness of Gomez Arias tranquilly awaiting her arrival. Roque led her towards the place appointed; nor could he suppress a tear, as he listened to the artless language in which her full heart indulged during the way, in the fond expectation of being again united to her lover, and obtaining the forgiveness of her beloved parent. They arrived at length at the place. It was a beautiful night, unsullied by a breath of wind. The eager eyes of Theodora were strained to catch as soon as possible a sight of the dear object of her solicitude. She perceived at the further extremity a man enveloped in a cloak, and standing beside three horses. She gazed intensely; her bosom throbbed with emotion,— forward she hurried—she flew; and in a moment, with all the enthusiasm of her fond nature, threw herself into the arms of her lover.

Gomez Arias received the tender pressure with feelings hard to be defined. Distracted with conflicting passions, he appeared unable to act the part which he had judged necessary in this critical moment, while the loving Theodora, despite of her infatuation, could not but observe the coldness and restraint evident in his manner.

"What ails you, Lope?" she said, soothingly "are you not happy?"

"Happy! yes, Theodora, I am happy; but be not astonished at my disquietude: for alas! in my distracting situation I can feel no otherwise; the step which I am about to take——"

"Oh! I am sensible!" cried Theodora, earnestly, "of the extent of the sacrifice; I know the glorious prospects you relinquish by renouncing the hand of Leonor. Yes, I am indeed, aware of all the distressing circumstances that may ensue from the resolution you have taken. But, oh, Lope! will not the unutterable love, the fervid devotion of your poor Theodora, afford you some requital for the advantages which your honor obliges you to abandon?"

She looked fondly in his countenance. A tear stood trembling upon her eye, but in her lover's she beheld no sign of mutual tenderness. He coldly assisted her to mount, and bidding Roque follow, for some time they continued their route in silence. Theodora, however, in the gentleness of her nature, was disposed to deceive herself, and without hesitation attributed her lover's strange behaviour to the difficult situation in which he was placed. Nor could she feel hurt when she considered that it was for her sake that Gomez Arias exhibited this disquietude. She had secured the most important object of her life, and was not so selfish or unfeeling as to reproach him with a conduct which she hoped would soon be changed. But the arguments of reason are not always in accordance with the suggestions of feeling. Her mind commanded her to be satisfied, but her heart, in acquiescing with those dictates, was not entirely at ease, though she sedulously endeavoured to conceal her emotion from Gomez Arias. Her efforts, however, were not always successful, and the deep sighs that escaped her bosom, naturally attracted the notice of her lover. He, therefore, artfully strove, by bestowing some passing tokens of affection, to reassure the victim he was leading to the sacrifice. But the art of man, though it may succeed in imitating the various passions which agitate the human breast, is rarely successful when he attempts to feign the more tender sentiments of the heart; for cold must always be the language addressed to one, who has been the object of a fervid passion, when that passion is unhappily extinct. No powers of art—not all the force of imagination can call into life fresh flowers on the barren waste of a heart that no longer loves.

As they approached *El cerro de los Martires* Theodora suddenly began to sob aloud, and Gomez Arias foresaw the dreadful scene he should have to sustain before he could finally disengage himself from the sorrowing girl.

"Theodora, why do you weep?" he asked in a tender tone.

"Alas! I know not," she answered. "But my heart is heavy—I feel as though some misfortune were impending. Whither are we going?—surely this is not the road to my father's mansion? Lope! Lope! whither are you leading me?" she inquired, in a thrilling voice of distress.

Steeled as it was against compassion, the heart of Gomez Arias felt moved at the question. Roque was exceedingly affected, and a groan escaped him as he piously ejaculated—"Heaven protect her!"

Theodora heard the exclamation; for nothing that bodes ill can evade the acute sense of misery.

"Thank you, good Roque," she said, mournfully. "But why call on the protection of heaven? My own Lope, are we in danger?"

Gomez Arias did not answer; for a feeling akin to remorse arose within him, as he thought on the treacherous duplicity he was about to practice against one whose very existence seemed to depend upon his love. They had now crossed *El cerro de los Martires*, and were ascending a little slope, when suddenly three or four persons sprung from their concealment, and checked their further advance. The moon shone brilliantly, so that every object could be plainly distinguished, and Theodora saw with dismay the forms that were moving towards them, as if with the express determination of intercepting their passage.

"They are Moors!" she exclaimed. "Oh, heavens! what can they want in this solitary place at the dead of night? Surely they must be some of those desperate people, who have been left houseless and forlorn in the late rebellion. Alas! they will retaliate on us all the horrors which they have suffered. My dear Lope, if we must die, it will be at least some consolation to meet death with thee."

She looked earnestly on her lover, but could trace no emotion in his features; they were composed. The present feelings of Gomez Arias partook of no alarm, and the unfortunate Theodora felt a fearful presentiment, as she perceived the unmoved expression of his countenance; for though the bravery of her lover might not allow him to dread the approach of death, for his own sake, yet, surely, her own danger ought to create in his mind some sensation of anxiety. In this frightful agony of thought, Theodora remained until they came up with the individuals who had awakened her fears. One of them now detached himself from the group, and advanced to address Gomez Arias, who had checked his horse to await his coming. What was the horror of Theodora when she recognized in the person that stood before them, the dreaded form of the renegade! She uttered a faint scream; and had not Gomez Arias prevented her, she would have fallen to the ground.

"So, Don Lope," said the renegade, "you have kept your word: I could expect no less from the noble Gomez Arias."

"And who are thy companions?" inquired Don Lope.

"There stands," replied Bermudo, pointing to Cañeri, "the illustrious Moor of whom I spoke—so the sooner we proceed to our arrangements, the better."

The mutual understanding which appeared to subsist between Gomez Arias and the renegade, and the heartless manner in which the last words were delivered, left not a doubt in the mind of Theodora, that some treacherous design was in contemplation. Her fears were soon confirmed; for Gomez Arias, turning to her, in a tone of pity, began—

"Theodora, I will not attempt to palliate the conduct which necessity obliges me to pursue; but the circumstances in which I am placed admit of no alternative. We must part for ever—nor can I for a moment prolong a scene, which must be so distressing to your feelings. It consoles me, however, to think that I can place you in the care of those who have pledged themselves to treat you with every consideration."

Saying this, he threw himself from his horse, and found no difficulty in bearing to the ground the yielding form of Theodora. She could not speak; amazement had absorbed all the powers of her mind, and benumbed the principle of will and action. She stood wildly gazing on vacancy, like one conscious of labouring under a dreadful dream, and striving to awake from the painful illusion. But when Cañeri advanced, when she actually saw his hated figure standing before her with a smile of exulting joy, she seemed suddenly to regain all her powers of recollection.

"'Tis he!" she cried franticly, "'tis he. Oh! horror!"—She ran wildly towards her lover.

"Oh, Lope, deliver me from him."

"No, young lady," returned the Moor, "you must now come with me."

"Oh, heaven!" she shrieked, "no, no, he cannot—he will not thus abandon me!—Oh, Lope!—my dear—my own beloved!—undeceive this barbarous, this abhorred Moor."

She appealed to her lover in the fervour of deep anguish,—he turned from her to depart; the moment was bitter; he felt the rankling pangs of remorse. The wretched girl clung to him,—he made one desperate struggle to disengage himself.

"Moor, take her," he cried with throbbing emotion, "but oh! deal thou more kindly by her than I have done. Here," he continued, "receive this, and see that she is treated with the regard which her beauty merits, and her misfortunes deserve. Act faithfully to thy pledge, or dread the worst effects of my vengeance."

He threw a large purse of gold upon the ground, which Malique lost no time in securing, whilst Cañeri, addressing Gomez Arias,—

"Christian," he said, "I fear not thy vengeance, and I value not thy gifts; the word of a Moor is plighted; I love the beauteous female, and these considerations will afford the best security for my conduct."

He then advanced to take the hand of Theodora, but she flew from him with a look of wildness that might have moved the very stones to pity.

"Oh! no, no, never! Gomez Arias, you may be cruel, but cannot be infamous.—Oh, do not, do not deliver me into the hands of the detested enemy of our country—the ferocious, the false Cañeri."

"What!" exclaimed Gomez Arias, surprised, "is this, then, Cañeri, the rebel chief?"

"The same," replied the renegade, interposing; "will that be an obstacle to our agreement?"

Gomez Arias remained a few minutes in silence; he felt an inward disquiet he could not well explain; the name of Cañeri had awakened a new and painful sensation; it recalled to his mind the edicts of the queen, which he was on the point of violating by holding intercourse with the rebel; but again he thought that the elevated situation to which he would be shortly exalted might sufficiently secure him against any danger, should even this transaction ever come to light, of which he could not foresee the slightest probability.

Meantime, poor Roque, who perceived the hesitation of his master, ventured to approach him, and with a voice agitated with fear,—

"Oh, my dear master," he said, "if it is not too late, let us retreat from this dreaded spot; do not conclude this hellish treaty, for be assured it will prove the destruction of your fortunes, if there is an omnipotence above or justice amongst men."

It was too late; the heart that could not yield to the voice of its own conscience, was not easily to be moved by the expostulation of a dependant. Gomez Arias had now advanced too far to retrace his steps; it was a fearful deed, but he relied with implicit confidence on its being for ever buried in silence. Then, without further delay, he made a sign to the renegade in token of agreement, and turned towards Granada.

Theodora became frantic; with a desperate effort she flew to her lover; a dismal, harrowing shriek quivered through the inmost fibres of her heart; and then she spoke not, but clung to Gomez Arias with the fearful might arising from despair. Her face was hidden in his bosom, her pulse beat not, and the spark of life seemed extinct. Gomez Arias gently endeavoured to extricate himself from her firm embrace; she again became conscious of his intention, and in the paroxysm of agony she exclaimed—

"Barbarian! have I deserved this from you?"

Roque now sobbed aloud like a child, and Gomez Arias himself was moved; but the renegade, fearful of the results of the scene, advanced to claim his victim.

"Oh, my honored master!" cried Roque, "does not this harrowing picture of despair move the kinder feelings of your heart?—you once loved her tenderly, and were it only for the remembrance of what she was, spare her now."

Gomez Arias felt the rebuke; it soured his temper and confirmed him in his purpose. He was indignant at the freedom of his dependant, and darted on him a withering look of displeasure. But Roque, who had now acquired a strength of mind and courage, of which his nature till then had seemed wholly destitute, in a bold tone began—

"Shame to the man who calls himself noble, and can behave in this manner towards a helpless woman! Don Lope, this is a fearful deed, and, mark me well, the time will come at last, the time of terrible retribution."

The brow of Gomez Arias grew black as a storm, and every suggestion of pity at once vanished.

"Villain!" he cried, in a voice choked with rage, "is it a base born varlet like thee, that dare utter such threats to me! Moor—" he added, turning to the renegade, "take this fellow into your charge, and see that he does not return to Granada; I will reward thee well."

The renegade gave a token of assent, and made a sign to his companions to secure him.

"And what right," said Roque, indignantly, "have you to sell me thus? I am a free born man, and a true Christian."

"Roque," replied Gomez Arias, somewhat more composedly, "I have often warned thee that thy indiscretion would at length bring thee into trouble and disgrace. Thy offence merits even a more exemplary punishment, which I will spare in consideration of thy former services. Away with him, Moors," he added, "and take him to the distant country whither you are going, for here he may prove dangerous to me."

"Aye," returned Bermudo, in a voice of import, "we will take him in charge, for as you say, Don Lope, he may indeed be dangerous to you."

These words, though nothing in themselves, were uttered with a mysterious meaning that sounded ominous to Gomez Arias. He felt as though a cloud was darkening over the ambitious prospects which had seduced his mind and perverted his heart; the voice that spoke rung in his ear like an awful warning of which he had some strange recollection. Again he attempted to escape from the scene. One sudden powerful effort, and he loosened himself from the grasp of Theodora: the despairing girl fell to the ground, and raved aloud, and pronounced a curse on her betrayer. Then in the furious impulse of madness, she snatched at the dagger that glittered in the girdle of Cañeri, with the determination of closing her wretched existence; but her deadly intention was thwarted by the renegade, who arrested her arm in time to prevent the fatal deed.

Gomez Arias now sprung upon his horse, and Cañeri took the hand of Theodora; but she furiously darted from him, and sought to fly after her lover, who was speeding fast away.

"Oh stay!" she continued, crying in a tone of agony; "Oh stay, Lope! complete your work—in pity kill me. One crime more will not make you unacceptable to her you love. Return! return! oh Lope, in the name of heaven!—Not for me, but for the love of Leonor, do not leave me thus! Oh Lope, do not leave me thus!"

Gomez Arias; or The Moors of the Alpujarras.

Gomez Arias, as he sped away, heard the piteous appeal dying faintly on the wind, and he plunged the rowels into his courser's sides, to escape the harrowing sensation which such accents produced. Soon the mournful cries were lost in the distance, and the wretched Theodora, at length exhausted and overpowered, fell senseless on the ground. The Moors easily succeeded in bearing her away, while poor Roque, who followed close, seemed, out of pity for her, to be reconciled to his own fate.

END OF THE SECOND VOLUME

VOL. III.

CHAPTER I.

> Nul ne sut mieux que lui le grand art de séduire;
> Nul sur ses passions n'eut jamais plus d'empire,
> Et ne sut mieux cacher, sous des dehors trompeurs,
> Des plus vastes desseins les sombres profondeurs.
> *Voltaire.*

The pathetic and heart-rending lamentations of Theodora rung ominous in the ears of Gomez Arias long after he had ceased to hear them; but as he drew near Granada, and beheld its stately edifices, ambition again dazzled his imagination, and he welcomed the bright images which rose before his view to dispel the gloomy tendency of his present thoughts. The stately turrets of the Alhambra enlarging upon his sight, awakened the most flattering ideas in his ardent mind. Proud of the regard with which he was honored by his gracious sovereign, and truly estimating the high connexion he was about to form, he naturally anticipated the most brilliant and honorable career. The last lingering suggestion of remorse, which told him of the cruelty and ingratitude by which he had paved the way to his advancement, now grew less powerful, and conscience, that terrible monitor of the human heart, hushed her enfeebled voice, bribed by the rich prize offered for future silence.

Don Lope secretly applauded the dexterity with which he had extricated himself from all his dilemmas, and rejoiced at having parted with Roque, who now could only be considered as a witness of his crime. By handing him over to the custody of the Moors, he was safely rid of a troublesome servant, whose frowardness in future he must have tolerated as the reward of secrecy. Besides, there was a further probability that the loquacious disposition and impertinent sallies of the valet, would ultimately draw upon him the ill-humour of some sullen Moor, who, not inclined to relish his jests, might pay with a few inches of a poniard the freedom of his tongue. With regard to Theodora, Don Lope could entertain no fear of her escape, being under the guardianship of one who appeared to be a captive to her charms. Meantime his wedding with Leonor would be celebrated, all his views accomplished, and then if a decree of wayward fate interfered with his flourishing honors, he would already have power to set aside the past, and to make his way clear for the future.

In this pleasing anticipation, Gomez Arias arrived at Granada, and awaited impatiently for the auspicious morning that was to terminate his fears, and crown his fondest desires. Early in the morning, therefore, he flew to the mansion of the Aguilars without changing his dress, and bearing in his appearance all the hurry and derangement of a hasty journey. He found Don Alonso in the apartment of Leonor; but the welcome he received from the object of his attachment was certainly not given with the warmth of an affianced bride; nor did the countenance of Aguilar betoken any very friendly reception. Don Lope felt this coldness, but he perceived the urgency of sustaining his equality of character, whatever might be the nature of the peril with which he was threatened. Affecting, therefore, not to notice the unsocial cast of their meeting, in a gay and lively tone addressed himself to Leonor—

"My dear Leonor," he said, "in my impatience to greet you, I may appear guilty of a little indecorum," looking upon his dress; "but you will, perhaps, on that plea pardon my presenting myself before you in a manner so irregular."

"Oh, Don Lope," answered Leonor with a sarcastic smile, "I can forgive you any thing, for my nature has become of late so indulgent, that I find I could pardon offences much graver than a mere breach of manners."

"Your goodness I never doubted," replied Gomez Arias; "but methinks you look rather uneasy; surely you are not indisposed?—the noble Don Alonso too! Nay, has any thing occurred during my short absence to cause your disquietude?"

"Certainly," returned Leonor coldly, "nothing has happened that *ought* to cause disquietude. But, surely, Don Lope," she added sarcastically, "your sudden departure, and the summons of our mutual friend Count de Ureña, might have held us in some little anxiety. Moreover, other small circumstances have contributed to cause a transient uneasiness."

"But you must not," interposed Don Lope, "suffer yourselves to be discomposed on account of our friend Ureña, for I am happy to say he was considerably better when I left him."

"Then," cried Aguilar, "it is as I suspected."

And rising from his seat with an expression of dark displeasure, without further ceremony he quitted the apartment. Gomez Arias was struck at such strange behaviour; but soon recovering his surprise,—

"What means this, Leonor?" he said in an angry tone: "Why am I treated thus?"

"Don Lope," returned Leonor, "surely the malady of your friend has somewhat affected your understanding. We can have no right to interfere with the actions of my father, particularly as I have already told you some accidents have occurred lately to ruffle his temper."

"And what accidents are those, in the name of heaven?"

"Are you really, then, so ignorant of the events which have taken place since you were imperiously summoned to attend your friend?"

"Perfectly ignorant," replied Don Lope.

Leonor looked steadily in his face, and making a sign of impatience which she was unable to restrain, proceeded—

"It is surprising that the Count has not informed you."

"Of what?" interrupted Gomez Arias, astonished. "In the name of heaven, explain yourself, Leonor."

"Now, do you not think," continued she, in an affected banter, "it was highly ridiculous in a man of so grave a deportment as the Count to play such boyish tricks? Can you really believe that, shortly after your departure, a message came from him, to announce his intention of surprising you by his attendance at your wedding."

"Certainly," replied Gomez Arias with visible marks of emotion, "the Count's conduct is strange; what his intention has been I really cannot conceive: but at all events, it ought in no manner to entail on me your noble father's displeasure."

"Why, Don Lope," said Leonor significantly, "you are not such a novice in knowledge of the world, as to expect that a man's displeasure should be strictly confined to the object by which it has been caused. Besides, Don Alonzo has other reasons: our fair guest, who was so sacredly beholden to him, is gone."

"What fair guest?" demanded Gomez Arias, with feigned curiosity.

"Did you never hear me speak of her?"

"If I did, I really do not remember."

"And what is become of Roque?" abruptly demanded Leonor: "he did not attend you upon your departure yesterday, and search has been made after him without effect. Is he ill?"

"Why, to say the truth, his health is rather precarious," answered Don Lope, "and he has so repeatedly been entreating me to allow him to retire to Toledo, where I believe he has a brother or sister, that I was at length obliged to consent to his wishes; which, in sooth, I did the more willingly, as he was growing of late so careless and impertinent, that his attendance became more troublesome than serviceable to me."

"Why, Don Lope," returned Leonor, "you must have been strangely surprised that he should wish to quit your service precisely on the eve of your wedding day. Moreover, you will be still more amazed when I inform you that it was this identical Roque that eloped with our guest Theodora de Monteblanco."

"Impossible!" exclaimed Don Lope, affecting to be thunderstruck.

"Repollo, our old gardener," continued Leonor, "saw them leave the palace, and instigated by a feeling of curiosity, followed them at a distance, as well as the speed of their pace would permit. He saw them at length halt at the public walks, where another person awaited with horses. But this is the most extraordinary part of the tale, for the gardener said that the person who was so complaisantly attending upon the fugitives, appeared so exactly to resemble you, Don Lope, that he would swear to the identity, were he not certain that you set out in the morning for the seat of Count de Ureña."

Great as was at all times Don Lope's presence of mind, and prepared as he seemed for all contingencies, this last intelligence somewhat deranged his composure; a circumstance which did not escape the keen and scrutinizing eyes of Leonor.

"The insolent rascal," cried Gomez Arias after a pause: "It was for this then that he appeared so anxious to quit my service; but I told you that his behaviour had become of late most impertinent, and even arrogant. The reason is now plainly discovered. But after all, your fair guest, as you are pleased to call the lady-love of this unseemly knight, is most to blame. What, in the name of Lucifer, could possess a woman of noble family to elope with a base menial? Was she devoid of all shame?"

"I suppose so," replied Leonor: then, in an expressive tone, she added, "But shame has been completely set aside in all the turnings of this iniquitous affair."

She fixed a significant look on Gomez Arias, whilst the astounded cavalier, aware of the perilous nature of his situation, merely assented to the truth of her observation. Leonor, eager to pursue her clue in ascertaining how far Don Lope was implicated in the transaction, continued,—

"But is it not surprising, Don Lope, that this groom of Roque should in every respect so much resemble you?"

"My dear Leonor," replied Gomez Arias, laughing loudly, and affecting good humour, "it is certainly a sad misfortune to have so unprepossessing a likeness, but we must submit with a good grace to that which is out of our power to remedy. But I dare say the rascally groom is not after all so perfect a resemblance of your devoted admirer as the besotted gardener would make us believe; how could the old dotard distinguish objects so well, at the distance he confesses, and at night? It would seem more probable, by his prowling abroad at such an hour, that a free potation of wine had so far acted upon his senses, that he saw the marvellous story he has related, in a reverie whilst sleeping under the friendly shelter of a ditch."

"Nay, Sir," replied Leonor, "we have no reason to doubt the testimony of an honest and faithful servant, who has no interest in the invention of a tale to deceive his benefactor."

"Well," returned Gomez Arias, "I will prolong the discussion no further than to express my concern that you should bestow your affections on one who has the ill-fortune to resemble a vulgar groom. But I hope this circumstance will not abate the tender regard with which you have condescended to honour one who lives but in your smiles."

Here Gomez Arias attempted to pour forth the most ardent protestations of unalterable attachment; but he was shortly interrupted by Leonor,—

"Nay, Don Lope," she cried, "spare yourself the trouble of uttering a single word more, either to convince me of the sincerity of your love, or in extenuation of your conduct, for I can very well imagine beforehand what you would say."

"That is no miracle," replied Gomez Arias, "your discernment is not too hardly taxed to perceive the emotion which I scarcely wish to conceal, and must of necessity easily imagine the expressions that such feelings must dictate. But pardon, if in a day like the present, my passion oversteps the bounds of common love; for the delirium of bliss that possesses me cannot be manifested by the usual demonstrations of cold-hearted mortals. A day that unites me to the most exalted, as well as the most lovely, of her sex, is surely—"

"Hold, Don Lope," gravely interrupted Leonor; "I will not now dwell upon the respective merits of your passion—for I have a favor to ask, and it is your time to grant a request which, perchance, may sound strangely to your ear."

"I need not say that the wishes of my charming Leonor can meet with no opposition from me," politely answered Gomez Arias.

"Yesterday," continued Leonor, "notwithstanding the fervour of your love, you requested that the wedding should be deferred one day. Now, you cannot deny me a similar favor, and I have particular reasons for desiring that it may be further postponed for a month."

"Heavens! what say you? A month! a whole month!"

"Yes, Sir," cried Leonor with emotion, "a month—a year, if circumstances require a further delay—'tis alike indifferent to me."

Saying this she abruptly left the apartment, leaving Gomez Arias in indescribable consternation.

"I am ruined!" he cried after a pause: "the forced indifference which Leonor has imposed upon herself during this interview, and the burst of feeling that marked her departure, leave me no room to doubt that her suspicions are excited. But shall I tamely submit to this reverse of fortune, after the many and cruel measures I have been impelled to adopt for the success of my designs? No, by heaven! I will not."

He then remained sometime buried in a musing attitude, balancing in his mind the most prudent course to pursue in so difficult a situation.

"Boldness and indifference," he said at length, "alone can insure safety. From Theodora and Roque, I have nothing to apprehend. I will forthwith send instructions to Count de Ureña; nay, I will partially open my heart to him, since his co-operation is now become indispensable to the furtherance of my plans."

After this, Gomez Arias sought another interview with Leonor, and with a proud and offended demeanor, informed her that he was perfectly willing to concede her request. Then, without waiting for an answer, he abruptly left her presence. He next repaired to Aguilar, and bitterly complained of the material change he had observed in him as well as in his daughter Leonor.

"If," he added, "you have reasons to impeach my integrity, speak aloud, Don Alonso, and give me an opportunity of removing the foul slander. But if it is a caprice, or a late repentance in her choice, that induces your daughter to adopt this strange behaviour, let her speak frankly—Gomez Arias is above the thought of constraining a woman's inclinations—and she shall be at once released from all engagements."

Don Alonso de Aguilar was struck with the generosity and manliness of Gomez Arias, and gave credit to the apparent sincerity of his words. The noble mind of Don Alonso could not conceive it possible that guilt should assume so perfect a resemblance of candour. The disappearance of Theodora, and the events which had attended her departure, were certainly well calculated to awake a suspicion that Gomez Arias was implicated in that affair; but as nothing positive could be adduced to prove his participation, Aguilar did not feel inclined to proceed with inconsiderate hastiness in an affair calculated materially to injure Gomez Arias in the estimation of the world. Leonor was naturally more irritated than her father at the least shadow of duplicity in the conduct of her lover. Thus she had requested the wedding to be deferred for a month, during which interval a proper investigation might be made.

Gomez Arias did not lose time in calling all his abilities into requisition, for his case was desperate, and it was necessary that the remedies should partake of the same character. He continued his visits to the Aguilars, but not with the same confidence as heretofore; and as he witnessed the high degree of esteem in which Don Antonio de Leyva was held, both by Don Alonso and his daughter, he affected to look on Leonor with offended pride, while he bitterly insinuated that it was a growing attachment for young de Leyva that had induced her to consider with suspicion, and treat with coldness, the conduct of a sincere lover.

Leonor, however, continued in the same frame of mind, insensible alike to his expostulations and bitter sarcasms. Deeply had her pride been offended, and deeply she had determined to resent the affront; nor could her sagacity and penetration permit her incautiously to trust the soft words and blandishments of a man whose notoriety in gallantry, she began to suspect, did not originate in idle rumour.

Meanwhile the irritated Don Lope spared no efforts to place his own conduct in a favorable light, and endeavoured to cast the imputation of caprice on that of the Aguilars. He complained constantly in terms of acrimony of the ungrateful manner in which his affection had been requited, and vowed vengeance against de Leyva, whom he accused of most criminal and ungentlemanly duplicity.

Contending feelings kept him in a continual turmoil, and he earnestly wished for an opportunity that might divert both the court and himself from a subject of which he was so disagreeably the hero.

Fortune again favoured his desires, by bringing about an event as terrible as it was altogether unexpected.

CHAPTER II.

The battle is their pastime; they go forth
Gay in the morn as to the summer's sport:
When evening comes, the glory of the morn,
The youthful warrior, is a clod of clay.
Home.

The streets and squares of Granada were thronged with a bustling and confused crowd. Here groups were assembled talking earnestly, and evincing all the signs of surprise and terror—there others were running about as if the dreaded event was actually come to pass. A continual hum was heard in every corner of the city; every tongue was eloquent in telling, and happy was he who could obtain an attentive listener, where all were eager to assume the part of orators. Indeed the cause of these demonstrations was important: several expresses had arrived, announcing the insurrection of the Sierra Bermeja, with the additional calamity that the terrible El Feri de Benastepar, whom they all supposed to have been slain, was not only safe and alive, but with the means of renewing a desperate warfare, and actually possessed of a force sufficiently strong to enable him to march upon Granada.

The town of Alhaurin, and several villages in the vicinity of the Sierra Bermeja were likewise in arms, and the rebellion seemed rapidly to extend throughout the whole of the surrounding country.

The rage of the Christians on receiving this intelligence was greatly increased by the insolent carriage of their fellow-citizens of the Mahomedan creed. Indeed, they evinced, in the triumph of their demeanor, the workings of smothered hatred, that only waited an opportunity to explode. Granada itself would have become a scene of tumult and bloodshed, had not Count de Tendilla speedily resorted to measures of precaution to insure public tranquillity. Various bands of veteran soldiers patrolled the streets, where the confused murmur of discontent, or the whispering group of sedition, was heard on all sides.

The queen was highly incensed at this fresh instance of the refractory and turbulent disposition of her new subjects. Her former edicts were again proclaimed through the city, not only against the aiders and abettors of the rebels, but even against such as should hold communion with them, howsoever slight or incidental.

The indignation of Alonso de Aguilar was strongly depicted on his noble and manly features, when in the presence of the assembled court he grasped the standard of the cross, and in a tone of resolution and enthusiasm—

"By the holy sign on this banner," he cried, "and by all the honors of my house, I swear not to return to Granada until this accursed rebellion is rooted out, and the promoters brought to punishment. Ere this month be past, El Feri de Benastepar, or Don Alonso de Aguilar, shall be numbered with the dead."

A shout of enthusiasm answered the noble sentiments of the warrior, whilst the queen issued orders that the next day all disposable forces should depart for the Sierra Bermeja, under the command of Aguilar, his son, Count de Ureña and Don Antonio de Leyva. The troops of Jaen and all Castile were likewise ordered to hold themselves in readiness to march under the Alcayde de los Donceles and Count de Cifuentes.

Gomez Arias seized with avidity the opportunity which fortune thus offered him to signalize himself, and found stronger claims to the esteem and regard of his sovereign, on whose features he had lately observed a degree of coldness which little accorded with her former cordiality. He did not regret his being excluded from the number of chiefs under Aguilar, though his pride might feel a temporary wound. For he considered that his reputation would not be materially increased whilst acting in subordination to such a chief as Aguilar. His gigantic fame would engross almost all the glory, and its splendour would naturally throw into shade the lesser stars of his unequal rivals. He rejoiced, therefore, that his exertions were unfettered by a superior, and his ardent and ambitious mind soon worked out a plan of operations against a quarter of the revolted territory which had been neglected in the hasty dispositions already made.

He now boldly sought the presence of the queen, and requested her authority to embody a division to act under his command, a boon which his reputation as a soldier fully justified him in demanding. Isabella, to whom Don Lope's courtly manners and gallant bearing had always been pleasing, was happy to afford him an opportunity of distinguishing himself, and the cloud that obscured her brow was soon dispelled by a gracious smile as she wished him success in his expedition. Indeed, justice required that the request of Gomez Arias should not be denied, for while most of the Spanish chiefs, his brothers in arms, were about to share the dangers and glory of so honorable a war, it would have been utterly inconsistent that Don Lope, who ranked amongst the foremost in courage, should remain in obscurity.

Gomez Arias immediately made his arrangements with the usual ardour of his character, stimulated by ambition and the desire of forcing upon Leonor a conviction of his superior merits, by adding to his fame without being indebted to the proud family of the Aguilars. He summoned to his ranks all the friends over whom he possessed power, and the retainers of various noble families with whom he was in alliance. But these being volunteers, whom their zeal or hatred to the Moors had instigated to take up arms, could not be put in a state to depart from Granada with the regular army of Don Alonso de Aguilar.

The troops of this noble veteran were prepared to march. Previously, however, to their departure from the city, they piously bent their steps towards the cathedral, where divine service was performed with great pomp, to propitiate heaven in favour of its servants. The archbishop delivered an eloquent oration inculcating on the Christians their duty, and the glory of their enterprize; pointing out fame and honour to the survivors—an eternal crown to those who should fall in defence of their country and religion. The banners of the army were then blessed, and the various divisions directed their march towards the gates of Elvira, by which they were to leave the city.

It was a clear and beautiful morning; no lowering cloud defaced the serene brilliancy of the sky, and the sunbeams sporting on the polished helmets and glittering trappings of the army, were reflected in a thousand curious rays.

The trumpets, clarions, and other martial instruments, poured their brazen voices in wild and animating strains, while the shouts of the multitude, assembled to behold the departure of the Christian soldiers, floated promiscuously along the air. The walls of the city were thronged with spectators, whilst others, more active or more interested, followed the army down the Vega. It was a scene at once splendid and interesting, to behold the army marching gallantly to the field, followed by a multitude all unanimous in imploring the benedictions of heaven on their brave countrymen.

Amongst the dense crowd that gazed upon that martial array, what passions were called forth—how many latent affections kindled—and what sentiments of glory displayed! The magnificent pomp and the spirit-stirring dignity of war, at the same time that it elevates the soul to deeds of heroism, fails not to awaken in the breast a corresponding sentiment of awe.—Alas! while the warrior, in all the enthusiasm of courage and self-devotion, marches with eager strides to the paths of victory, perhaps of death, how many tender hearts swell high and beat fearfully for the dangers which they themselves cannot perceive!

Amongst that overpowering multitude might be discerned the venerable father, a lingering spark of noble fire still lurking in his dim eyes, and his withering frame receiving new energies as he gazed on the military display. A sigh of regret escapes him, for the perilous and glorious scenes in which his age forbids him to bear a part. His outstretched palms are clasped in fervent orisons to heaven, not for the safety of his child, but that his conduct in the field may be worthy of a man and a Spaniard.

There was also the affectionate spouse contemplating the marching army in silent sorrow; her eyes swimming in tears are intensely fixed on that numerous mass of warlike spirits, where *one*, to her dearer than all the world, was speeding from her side. On one arm some innocent, perhaps, lay in sweet slumber, whilst another urchin, with years enough to gaze with delight upon the glorious scene, evinces his pleasure at the animating prospect, and with infantine exultation looks upwards to his mother, wondering to see her bathed in sorrow, for to his unconscious heart no cause is there for grief; and yet his tears flow because his mother weeps.

Farther, perhaps, more lonely, on some high turret, on some distant eminence, striving to hide her sorrows from the eye of the world, is seen the trembling virgin, whose pure heart has received the first impression of love, and whose charmed ear has listened with fondness to the soft tale of promised bliss. Now, with restless and agitated glance, she surveys the numerous host in the vain hope of distinguishing the dear object of all her tenderest affections, torn from her arms to exchange her smile for scenes of bloodshed and desolation. Alas! how numerous and various are the fears that agitate her gentle breast! She may never more see him: he may sleep his last sleep on the field of horror; or he may return triumphant but false to his vows, with a proud heart, to scorn the love of her who mourned for his absence.

But women, likewise, there might be seen more high-minded and more heroic in their thoughts and feelings; some who, like Leonor de

Aguilar, offered their tears at the shrine of glory and patriotism, and who, while they trembled for the life of the object of their affections, were still more anxious for his honor; some, whose passion received a spark of heavenly fire that elevated them above their kind, and who gloried in the sight as they beheld their lovers marching onwards to fame and victory.

Such scenes, such sensations, with others which as powerfully affect the heart, but which the pen would vainly attempt to portray, are generally attendant on a departing army. Fear, perhaps, holds its dominion in the breasts of the many and interesting beings who are left behind; but hope steals gently forward, and gilds with its bright illusion the most fearful anticipations.

Meantime the soldier marches on gaily and reckless, and with a light heart he takes his farewell of those whom he is, perhaps, doomed never more to behold; and the tears that accompany his departure, tears of sympathy and affection, will soon, alas! be changed for the bitter drops of grief and despair.

CHAPTER III.

Mer ;Ce sont là de mes moindres coups,
   De petits souflets ordinaires.

Sos. Si j'étois aussi prompt que vous,
   Nous ferions de belles affaires.

Molière.

No nos rompas la cabeza
Hombre——Pero Ay Dios mio!
Pored un freno a mi lengua;
Y ojala que esta no fuese
La menor de mis flaquezas.
Cruz.

"*Valga me el cielo!*" exclaimed Roque, "Oh Maria, oh Rufa! Oh Rufa, oh Maria! nearly a week have I been with you, and yet I cannot, for the soul of me, believe what I see. There must be witchcraft in this; to find the old crony of my late mother, *que en paz descanse*![1] to find Maria Rufa, whom I had supposed dead, and her soul dwelling with the saints, amongst the rebels—amongst the Moors I mean, and herself a Moor: well, nothing shall make me wonder for the future."

Such were the words that our reader's friend Roque addressed to dame Aboukar, as they were advancing toward the town of Alhaurin in a cavalcade, of which they made a part. The venerable and sour spouse of the ex-master of the household, was rather nettled at the valet's im-

---

[1] May she rest in peace.

pertinent freedom: he had been during the way most assiduous in favouring her with the benefit of his remarks, which he happened to convey with such an extraordinary licence of tongue, that the dame's patience, which it is believed was not of the most enduring kind, at last became completely exhausted. With much tartness and asperity, therefore, in a discordant voice, she exclaimed, "Out upon thee, most saucy and ungracious varlet; curb that licence of tongue, and learn to behave in a proper manner to thy elders and betters."

"Sweet dame," quoth the valet, "I do not by any means desire to dispute that first quality; you are certainly my elder by some good thirty years; but at the same time, most matronly and venerable Marien, I beg leave to differ in opinion on the second part of your assertion."

Then, as if afraid of being overheard, he muttered, in an under tone, "I am a good Christian and ever was."

This observation did not escape Marien Rufa, who heaved a deep sigh, and cast on Roque a look of mingled shame and resentment. She felt sorely the rebuke, but notwithstanding the valet's impertinence, the friendship she had entertained for his mother induced her to consider him with some degree of interest, and prevented her from discharging on him the whole weight of her indignation.

"Roque, Roque," she observed with sourness of aspect, "methinks you ought not to be so enamoured of the sound of your own voice, for that most unfortunate propensity to prating has brought you to the present pass: remember that it was on account of your growing sententious, that your master so unceremoniously dispensed with your services."

"Well," pertly cried Roque, "I suffer for having spoken truth, and I glory in what I have done. By all the saints, since I reflect on the flagrant injustice of Don Lope's conduct, and am become a martyr to my rectitude and compassion, I find that I am endowed with a degree of courage and resolution of which I was far from imagining that I was possessed. And now," he added, drawing near the dame, "now will you condescend to favour me with the particulars of your apostacy from our holy religion. What, in the name of infatuation, could entice you to take a step so detrimental to the interests of your soul? *Virgen Santa!* once no one was to be found more assiduous at the ceremonies of our religion; you were in very troth the most devout *beata*[1] of the whole

---

[1] A devotee.

parish, and now here's a change, in the name of *Satanas*! Oh, Maria Rufa, you have surely been bewitched."

"Alas!" cried the crone, ludicrously rolling her eyes in attempting the pathetic, "you say right, Roque; I was verily bewitched."

"*Santa Barbara!*" exclaimed Roque crossing himself, "and by whom were you bewitched?"

"By that most powerful tyrant."

"What tyrant?" demanded Roque, drawing closer, and casting a suspicious glance around. "What tyrant, Rufa?"

"Guess, Roque, and spare my confusion."

"Spare my guessing," returned the valet, "and with respect to your confusion, I dare say it will not overwhelm you. Now, tell me the name of the terrible tyrant."

"Love," replied Marien Rufa, affecting much disorder.

Roque forthwith burst into an immoderate fit of laughter that startled the cavalcade.

"Love! the Lord defend us!—how could such a guest enter so homely an habitation! Love! here's a pretty object for Cupid to exercise his pranks upon. Now, I do verily believe there is witchcraft in the tender passion. *Miserere! Miserere!* and who was the happy mortal attracted by your matured charms?—whence came the man blessed with the good taste necessary to set a just value on your miraculous attractions? That most beautiful elongated chin—that capacious mouth—those lack-lustre eyes, and shrivelled complexion—that most polite and well-educated nose, which is continually bowing to the neighbouring chin; in fine, those long shaggy tresses of hair, which, if we must judge by their consistency, bespeak thee endowed with the strength of Sampson."

Scarcely had Roque made a stop in his harangue, in order to take breath, than Marien Rufa, exasperated beyond bearing at the caricature he was drawing, with a wonderful alacrity lifted her clenched hand, and dealt the facetious valet such a tremendous blow on the ear, that he fell stunned from the donkey which he bestrode, and lighted on the ground with such violence that the whole place rung with the noise.

"There," cried the hag, "there's a convincing proof that my hair has not imposed on your credulity with regard to my strength."

Roque was completely reclaimed from his waggishness by the unexpected visitation of the Sampsonic fist, and for some time utterly forgot the use of his tongue. The notice of the whole cavalcade was attracted by the mishap of the luckless valet, and the energetic exclamation of dame Aboukar. The Moors that served as escort were seized with a fit of wondering mirth, and even the renegade, who was the chief of the party, spite of his habitual sternness, relaxed his rigid features into something like a smile. The tenant of a litter that was carried in advance likewise stopped to inquire into the reason of the commotion.

"Roque, what is the matter," demanded Theodora (for she was indeed that lady), when she perceived the valet rising from the ground in the greatest confusion.

"Nothing, my lady:" answered Roque, wofully; "the Lord defend us, but we have in our party a devil incarnate, under the semblance of a woman. Good heavens! here's such a concert ringing in the side of my head—such a hissing and whizzing never did I hear. O, Maria Rufa!" he then proceeded, in a humble tone, "what a flame you have imparted to my poor face! If it is a sample of your amorous fires, I am amazed you are not actually reduced to cinders!"

"That will teach you," said Maria Rufa, pacified, "to put a proper restraint on your froward tongue."

Roque for some time after kept a profound silence, for though he affected to treat the matter with jocose indifference, yet he was in no manner satisfied with the mirth and merry sayings which his adventure had occasioned. At length, however, his curiosity prevailed, and almost forgetting his recent disgrace, he again in a friendly manner accosted the Amazon.

"Now, Rufa," he said, "I hope you entertain no rancour against me for what has passed?"

"By no means, good Roque," answered the hag grinning, "I am perfectly satisfied, and I hope you are the same."

"Quite," returned the valet, "quite; so let us say no more about it, but rather tell me, if no ways disagreeable, the origin, progress, and final results of your passion."

"Alas! Roque," replied the old sybil, "it was unfortunate in its results."

And she heaved a profound sigh, whilst Roque, in most sympathetic unison, uttered a dismal groan.

"Console yourself," he said, "with the reflection that your case is pretty general in this sinful world. But what is the name of the amiable barbarian, the sweet monster, the bewitching, yet cruel oppressor, that excited the tender sentiments of your virgin heart, and turned you from the true faith."

"What! you are yet unacquainted with my husband?"

"Husband!" ejaculated Roque, "so there was a husband in the case! Oh, then I am not surprised."

"He treats me like a brute, as he is."

"Indeed! that is astonishing," cried Roque, "wonderfully astonishing, considering the means you have in your power of enforcing proper behaviour on the unruly. And pray what is the name of your brute?"

"You might have perceived it before: it is Aboukar."

"Aboukar!" exclaimed Roque; "Now, indeed, my wonder ceases—Aboukar! Oh the sweet creature! with his pretty lobster eyes, and most awful and portentous proboscis, which seems for all the world like a fine ripe tomato displayed on a copper platter."

But here Roque thought it prudent to make a retrograde motion, as he looked at the masculine arm of the dame, and remembered the little relish she had evinced for his talent of drawing portraits, and the manner in which she remunerated the artist.

"So Aboukar is your husband!"

"Alas! yes," answered the ancient, "we have been married now these five years."

"*Valgame San Roque!*" cried his namesake. "What a dull dog have I been!—five years married—certainly I ought to have discovered that long ago by his treatment."

"Treatment!" re-echoed Marien Rufa, a little incensed, "What treatment?"

"Oh! I mean no harm," replied Roque, "conjugal treatment, that is all."

"Roque," resumed the crone, modulating her croaking voice to something like a human sound, "Roque!" and she suddenly stopt, and looked the valet steadfastly in the face. "Well?" said Roque, surprised at the pomposity of her manner.

"Roque, my child, are you a kind and compassionate soul—a thorough good Christian?"

"A very good Christian," responded Roque, "though a humble sinner. But methinks such a question comes with ill grace from the mouth of a renegade."

"I will confide in thee, Roque," returned Marien Rufa, "I am an unfortunate woman, and alas! might I hope that my repentance were not too late? Roque, thinkest thou that there is truly a hell as terrible as it is depicted?"

"Worse, worse, a thousand times worse," replied Roque. "All the torments which you may have suffered in the company of—— But do you allow me to abuse your husband safely?"

"As much as you please," answered the gentle spouse.

"Well," resumed Roque, "all the torments which that most abominable, ugly scarecrow of a rascally unbeliever has made you endure, are nothing in comparison to the tortures you are doomed to suffer when you are compelled to leave that miserable carcase, and that time you must be aware cannot be far off. Then consider what a life you will lead in those dark regions, where, by the bye, you will be eternally tormented with the sight and company of your ungracious consort."

"I am sensible of my errors, but if I have sought your confidence, it was with the view of exciting your compassion, not your reproaches."

But Roque had insensibly got into a very oratorical mood, and, without heeding the hag's remonstrances, proceeded:—

"Now, Rufa, consider for a moment, who but the devil could tempt a matron full half a century old, without a sound tooth in her head, the head itself being unsound, to look kindly on the most perfect sample of ugliness, and a ruffian Moor to boot: this is enough to make you despair of salvation—But no, the blessed Virgin forbid! I think, and charitably hope, that by a vigorous course of penance, and wholesome castigation, properly and soundly administered, by a frequent use of discipline, constant fasts, devout prayer, donations to the poor, of whom I am one, and the like pious exercises, I really think your sinful soul may be snatched from the perdition to which it has been brought by that infernal Aboukar, your most confounded lord and master; therefore—"

"Roque," interrupted ruefully Marien Rufa, "whether you are in right earnest or only playing the fool with me, I cannot determine; but my situation is such as to deserve the pity of every good Christian."

Roque had, indeed, a peculiar inclination to a ludicrous banter, even when dwelling on the gravest subjects, which might put on his guard a person of quicker intellects than the dame of Aboukar.

"Rufa," he said, "pardon me if, in my admonitions, I cannot impart to your troubled spirit that unction which becomes the important subject that dictates them. Now, provided you will tell me the manner in which you intend to proceed, perhaps I may be able to help you with my good advice."

"Well, child," replied Marien Rufa, "I wish heartily to be reconciled to the church, and for this purpose we must contrive to fly from these accursed Moors."

"Very well," replied Roque, "so, you are resolved to abandon your matrimonial misery?"

"Oh, yes, Roque," retorted Rufa, "my conversion is very sincere; I have so many motives to quit the wretch. Oh, he is indeed a barbarian! Think, Roque, such a sweet partner as I have been to him, and now to neglect me for a little Moorish hussey not worth a *maravedi*. Oh, the faithless Aboukar—the wicked man! Yes, Roque, I wish as soon as possible to be reconciled to the church."

Roque, though far from being a deep divine, could not but significantly shake his head, when he perceived the motives that brought about the conversion of the apostate love-smitten dame. However, the idea of flying from the Moors very much tickled his fancy, and he was determined to adopt the step, provided it could be carried into effect without any great risk to his precious person, and that his mistress Theodora should be a partner in the flight.

Thus he was indulging in the most agreeable reverie, when his fair penitent disturbed him by uttering a most discordant sound, which the valet soon perceived to be a failure in the imitation of a groan. The eyes of the hag exhibited terrible signs of displeasure, as she turned round to some object that called her attention, while writhing her uncouth features into a most diabolical grimace. She thundered out an oath which made Roque invoke *Santa Maria*; but he was not a little scandalized when he discovered that the occasion of the hag's indignation was her frolicsome husband, who, without the least regard to her presence, was carrying on, in the presence of his wife, a little coquetry with a Moorish girl.

"There," cried the ill-treated spouse, "there is a traitor—how I could belabour the barbarian, and pluck that vile creature's eyes out! Oh, Roque! I have been a sad sinner, and I fervently desire to be reconciled to the church."

"Well, well," said Roque, "but first tell me on what foundation do you build hopes of an escape. We are, that is my mistress and myself, so narrowly watched, that it will be no easy task to evade the vigilance of our guards. It is true that by the interference of the renegade I am allowed a free access to Theodora, and the lady herself is treated with much courtesy; but at the same time I have observed that some cursed Moor or other is constantly watching our motions. Moreover, good dame, I must undeceive you, should you have relied on my courage for some desperate plan. I will not fight a single Moor. My humility will not permit me to exercise a business for which I consider myself utterly unfit, both for want of practice and natural inclination."

"No, child," replied the crone with a sneer, "I was never foolish enough to place any great hopes on your bravery; but I trust we shall find means to forward our plans without such assistance. To me," she then added, "all the secrets of the Moors are known, for they consider me too much interested in their cause to doubt my fidelity. Don Alonso de Aguilar is rapidly advancing against El Feri and should he succeed in his expedition against *Sierra Bermeja*, as it is more than probable he will, Cañeri, Mohabed, and the other chiefs will not be able to withstand the forces which are already sent against them. We must take advantage of the confusion to escape, lest they should carry us with them to Africa."

"*Cuerpo de Cristo!*" cried Roque, "and is that all your wise head can devise? Well, I hope you are not overpowered after such an effort of imagination; but really I cannot give you credit for the contrivance."

They were now entering Alhaurin, where Cañeri had preceded them two or three days before, and they halted at the entrance of a large mansion, which appeared, by the guards patrolling in front, to be the abode of the chief. Meantime the renegade helped Theodora out of her conveyance, and led her to the apartments allotted to her use. She was no longer a prey to the frenzied passions that had so long stormed her breast. The keen intensity of affliction, insulted and indignant pride, were now lost in the gloomy resignation and cold apathy to which they had given place. The severe trials she had undergone had impaired the beauties of her person, and poisoned her warm and generous feelings, but still Theodora was lovely and interesting. She had lost the brilliant beauty of a girl blooming with youth and happiness, but she had acquired the chaste graces and loveliness of sorrow. Alas! even in those sad memorials of fading beauty, enough yet remained to make her an object of interest, and keep alive the passion which Cañeri had conceived. The load of grief and despair which had weighed her down at the last proof of her lover's treachery, was succeeded by a mood of deadened resignation. This calm, however, appeared presageful of some dire intent, and accordingly, for the first two or three days, she had not been left a moment alone, and every instrument of death had been carefully removed from her reach. The attentive services of Roque partly reconciled her to her dreadful situation; for it is consoling, even in the lowest depths of affliction, to meet with *one* sympathising being, however humble his station, however weak and limited his means to afford comfort and redress. In the midst of her barbarous enemies, she was permitted the attendance of a Christian, and this circumstance, trifling as it was, imparted some solace to her oppressed spirit. Besides, Cañeri had abstained from importuning her with his loathsome protestations of love. This forbearance of the Moor arose from the renegade having stipulated, that in engaging the affections of Theodora, he should resort to no violence in her present sorrowful condition.

Thus Cañeri had limited his addresses to a bare manifestation of respectful regard, foreign indeed to his nature, and borrowed only from the necessity of acquiescing with the wishes of the renegade, who had boldly declared he would oppose any violence employed against Theodora. This favorable disposition of the renegade was a source of astonishment to the object of his solicitude, for she could not forget that he had been the principal agent in the completion of her misery. Did Bermudo intend by these seeming kind offices to secure the prey to himself? or was it really a sentiment of pity that impelled him to the manifestation of this solicitude? Could heavenly pity dwell in that darksome abode, where the most fiendish passions kept a constant habitation? How were such opposite guests to be reconciled?

These surmises kept the mind of Theodora in a state of continual excitement, but as day after day passed, and the renegade, instead of exhibiting the least mark of enamoured sentiments, seemed to grow more respectful in his attention, those doubts began to wear away, and Theodora concluded that some mystery enveloped his proceedings, which she was unable to unravel, and which time alone could clear up.

In pursuance of the injunctions of El Feri, his brother chief, Cañeri, had established his head quarters at Alhaurin, where his party was daily increasing by the Moors who came to join his standard. Cañeri himself had arrived three days before, having left to the renegade the charge of Theodora, who could not be supposed to travel with equal expedition.

Bermudo, therefore, with a few resolute Moors of his band, and the other personages of whom mention has been made in the former part of this chapter, constituted the cavalcade that now entered the busy and thronged streets of Alhaurin, where the ferment occasioned by fresh and numerous arrivals, plainly manifested the rapid progress of the insurrection.

CHAPTER IV.

Some good I mean to do,
Despight of my own nature.
Shakespeare.

Ser. No hay quien socorra, quien valga
  A una muger infelice?
Fel. Si, que decir muger basta,
  Quando infeliz no dixera.
Calderon.

The air of dignity and importance which Cañeri had resumed with his change of fortune, was displayed to an extent that might render him extravagantly ridiculous in the judgment of any sober individual. He already considered himself a sovereign firmly established on his throne, and he took no precaution to disguise the impulses of his overbearing vanity and despotic character. Thus, while he was apparently serving the cause of independence, he afforded an opportunity to his enemies of truly estimating the purity of his intentions.

Cañeri paid a visit to Theodora immediately upon her arrival; but, according to the agreement with the renegade, he limited his attentions to the mere phrases of gallantry and courtly good nature. This ostentatious shew of civility, however, did not arise from a generous disposition, but merely constrained necessity. The renegade was continually present to his thoughts, and though his superior in command he was forced involuntarily to yield that tribute of respect, which resolution and courage are sure to exact from the feeble, however humble the situation in which their possessor may be placed. Besides this, though his passion for the fair Christian had not abated, his heart was now too much engrossed with objects highly gratifying to his vanity and pride, to suffer the charms of a captive to rule there with undisputed and despotic sway. His visits, therefore, were short, and he soon left Theodora to the undisturbed possession of her own thoughts. She no longer exhibited those signs of exquisite anguish or passionate delirium. Keen and protracted suffering had rendered her in some measure callous to the stings of sorrow. Musing melancholy and listlessness as to her fate disputed alternately the possession of that heart, once so fruitful in every tender feeling, in all the genuine virtues of female loveliness and merit. But, alas! the situation of the unhappy Theodora was, indeed, more distressing than heretofore. Hope now no longer illumined her heart; amidst the darkness which had over-clouded her imagination, no cheering light shone upon her path to lead her from misery. But the dereliction of hope is not the worst enemy of virtuous woman. No, it is the loss of salutary fear, and Theodora was nearly sinking into that lamentable state of indifference which generally succeeds the extinction of youthful hope and affection. Every thing seemed to conspire against Theodora. The secluded and retired nature of her education, and the tenderness of her age deprived her of those auxiliaries to combat her present state, which a woman of greater knowledge of the world, and more advanced in years, would gather from these very circumstances.

Roque had, by order of Cañeri, a free access to Theodora, and he took special care frequently to profit by the permission granted. This was some solace for the unfortunate girl; the interviews with the valet diverted her thoughts by the lively, though ludicrous, pictures which he drew of their future release from their present thraldom. The very night of their arrival at Alhaurin, Roque was giving to his mistress a circumstantial account of his conversation with Marien Rufa, when the door of the apartment swung open, and the renegade boldly entered without any previous announcement. His sudden appearance caused the greatest perturbation and alarm, both to Roque and his mistress. The unseasonable hour of the visit, and the interest evinced by the renegade towards Theodora, were naturally indicative of some sinister intention. Theodora, however, recovering from her first surprise, involuntarily drew back as Bermudo advanced. Meanwhile Roque was at a loss what to think or to do; the flutter of his whole person plainly indicated how ill at ease he was with himself. He looked at his mistress, and perceiving her emotion, felt more afraid, though on what account he was perfectly unconscious. But Roque was not long suffered to remain in uncertainty with respect to his own feelings. Bermudo, with a most haughty demeanor, made a sign to the valet to quit the place, and as Roque deliberated between regard for his mistress and dread for his own dear self, the renegade, to bring about a final determination, laid his hand on his weapon, an argument which completely set at rest the valet's doubts, and convinced him of the necessity of a speedy retreat.

Theodora perceiving how easily Bermudo had succeeded in convincing Roque, and knowing the obsequious manner in which the valet acted when such sort of conviction was forced upon him, deeply felt the danger of her situation, if abandoned by the only being who might interest himself in her fate.

"Oh! Roque, do not leave me," she pathetically exclaimed; "stay—I cannot remain alone with this dark, this terrible man."

Roque cast a melancholy look on his mistress; her piteous appeal went to his heart, but a terrible glance from the renegade seemed to make still stronger impression, for he quickly resumed his retrograde motion.

"He must be gone," said Bermudo resolutely, waving his hand in a most expressive manner, which considerably tended to expedite the valet's exit.

He retired, therefore, and Theodora no sooner found herself deprived of this last frail protection, than with an assumption of fierce dignity:—

"Renegade!" she cried, "what means this intrusion? Were then all thy former marks of regard but the insidious means to cover the real intentions of a miscreant heart? Away!—begone!—I will alarm the place,—yes, I will call on the protection of Cañeri himself, for odious as he is to my eyes, I can never look upon him with the same degree of abhorrence and contempt as I do on a renegade to his faith, a traitor to his country, and the vile minister to a despot's pleasures."

Bermudo heard these bold and severe rebukes without attempting an interruption. Calm and unmoved he suffered the first ebullition of resentment to evaporate, and for some time deigned to make no other reply than a bitter smile of disdain.

At length he broke that dismal pause, and in a slow and deep toned voice:—

"Woman," he said, "thy taunts I will not resent, for partly they are just, and the rest I excuse in consideration of thy forlorn state, and the many sufferings thou hast undergone."

"Oh!" cried Theodora, with a sad smile, "It well becomes you to condole for misfortunes to which you have so largely contributed;—approach me not—begone—I cannot trust a traitor; there is guile and malice in the very proffer of thy kindness;—hence,—or——"

"Hush, lady," interposed the renegade, with indignant pride, "you surely mistake my character. Threats and fears are strangers to this heart. Nay, when it is in some weak moments attuned to virtue, a threat, a solitary threat would banish hence the heavenly inspiration, and the fiend again triumph in its natural dwelling. Therefore, lady, threat me not, for the man is inaccessible to fear, who, like myself, is a beggar in happiness. Rest, lady, rest, and do not by an imprudent act, neglect the opportunity which fortune affords you of escaping the fate with which you are threatened."

There was an air of sullen yet dignified composure on the renegade, as he delivered these words, and Theodora, in spite of her apprehension, was for some time rivetted to the spot, waiting the disclosures of the fearful man.

"I do not pretend," he proceeded, "to command your implicit confidence; I only counsel you to rely on your own judgment and discretion. My character you have drawn in colours dark and glowing, but, perhaps, too true. Yet I must correct an erroneous impression under which you labour; 'tis true I am an apostate—a traitor—and if in the catalogue of accursed crimes, there is a name still more horrid and abhorred, I claim it; but to be subservient to the pleasure of a despot—no, no, you must know me better. No," he added with warmth, "my deeds have been dark, but not dastardly or contemptible; I have drunk deep the cup of crime—yes, I have quaffed it with avidity, but my palate has always been nice enough to scorn the dregs. Had any other than a woman dared to give utterance to the base thought, ere this he would have added one more to the list of those who have fallen by this arm. You are a woman, and a woman in distress; the only consideration that could have restrained my indignation for such an insult."

"What then wouldst thou with me?" demanded Theodora, somewhat reassured by his words and manner.

"To befriend you, not to harm you, for I war not with women; the solitary being that showed the feelings of humanity towards Bermudo belonged to womankind, and the recollection of her virtues and her love for me, would secure her whole sex from the effects of my wrath."

Theodora was struck with this asseveration. She could not reconcile these symptoms of feeling with his previous acts, and his acknowledged character for crime.

"Theodora," resumed the renegade, and his austerity of tone and manner seemed momentarily to acquire a tint of softness uncongenial with his habitual nature; "Theodora, I am a man of guilt; yea, one who plays his part in this detested world without a feeling of remorse—but I cannot harm a woman—and you less than any other of your sex. *She*, like you, was innocent and beautiful—like you, unfortunate—like *you*," he added, with agitation, "like you, the victim of Gomez Arias."

"Heavens!" exclaimed Theodora, "what mystery is this? Oh, speak! I am already but too low sunk in misery, and yet I fain would learn the full measure of the crimes of him who has undone me."

"It would be a difficult," replied the renegade, "an endless task, to satisfy your desire; but you may, perhaps, from your own experience, draw a just inference of his conduct to others. Beauty, innocence, and youth, and unlimited affection, could not save you from his barbarous acts; the rule has been the same for those who like you had charms to captivate his attention, and an unsuspicious, a genuine heart to inhale the poison of his persuasive tongue. But still the fate of poor Anselma surpassed in horror her many rivals in misfortune."

"He loved her once," said Theodora despondingly, "and then forsook her, like me."

"He loved her," darkly returned Bermudo, "with the affection of one, who centres his whole bliss only in the enjoyment of his selfish and degenerate passion. But she spurned him; stratagem and force prevailed. Madness—despair—must I say it? death ensued. Enough—the circumstances of the horrid tale 'tis needless to relate: I have said thus much to convince you of the impossibility of my harming a woman whose fate bears so strong a resemblance to that of my own unfortunate Anselma. Dispel then your apprehensions, and look upon me *now* not as a foe, but as your sole friend and protector."

Theodora gazed on the renegade with mute amazement; the professions of her lover, and his base desertion, had taught her mistrust: her heart was no longer ready to believe any pleasing tale, to welcome every protestation of regard. It was by trusting too implicitly to her feelings that her ruin had been accomplished, and even in her present abandonment she considered those feelings as premeditating another treason. Yet, when she beheld the composure of the renegade, when she recalled to mind that not even a word had escaped him that could be distrusted, she was persuaded to listen to his proposals, if not totally to abide their results. The renegade perceived the state of her mind, and hastened to hush the whispers of suspicion.

"Think you," said he with firmness, "think you that I deceive you?—abandon such a thought; for learn that should I be tempted to harm you, the only object of my life would be blasted; trust then my interest, if you cannot trust my honor. I came to render you a service, which must be reciprocal. Nay, start not; you may well marvel what affinity there can be between an unfortunate and helpless female, and an outcast like myself; yet this seeming anomaly exists—we are drawn together by the most powerful ties that can bind one fellow-creature to another: for we are linked by those of misfortune, and misfortune wrought by the same individual."

"And yet," cried Theodora, "despite of your enmity to the barbarous, unfeeling man, you strenuously seconded his plans; had you not aided him, I should not have been here."

"Perhaps not," replied the renegade, preserving an unalterable composure; "but where would you have been? Have you reflected well on your helpless situation, and the character of the foul betrayer. Ah! call to your memory the last scene of his desertion, and judge by his behaviour then, of what he might have been capable, in order to remove from his path the unfortunate obstacle that impeded his ambitious and criminal career."

"The monster was capable of all!" exclaimed Theodora, with dreadful agitation; for the recital of her lover's perfidy rudely awoke all the dormant feelings of the heart.

"I have saved you from his infernal machinations;" said the renegade. "My conduct to you then appeared barbarous, but my subsequent behaviour must have effaced from your mind those unfavorable impressions. If not, the time is come for you to learn, and me to disclose, the motives by which all my words and actions have been directed. Theodora," he then added, in a firm but soothing tone, "my proceedings have been to you mysterious; the mystery here ends—I have procured liberty, home, happiness for you—revenge for myself."

"Heavens!" exclaimed Theodora, "explain, what mean you?"

"I mean the truth. Be cautious and confident, and not many days shall pass ere you flee from the company of men whom you abhor, and I despise. Ere long you shall return to your deserted home, and enjoy the consolation which a father can confer—a happiness which they say is great.—I never knew it."

"Can this be real?" exclaimed Theodora, with a scream of surprise and joy. "Oh, Alagraf, are you then so generous?" and unable to restrain the swelling emotion of her grateful heart, she fell at his feet.

"Rise, lady, rise," vehemently cried the renegade, "that posture ill becomes you. I cannot sustain the sight. Poor, helpless, innocent sufferer," he then said in a pathetic tone, which in spite of his sternness, he could not suppress. "Poor, poor, forlorn girl—it was thus she begged and supplicated, but he denied her." He suddenly recollected himself, and with an abrupt motion he raised the weeping Theodora from the ground.

"Rise; for by all the powers of darkness, to see you thus more fiercely burns my brain, and my frenzied madness becomes more ungovernable. Woman, I am not generous, I am only just, though some cold mortals might denominate my justice selfish cruelty. But I care not for man or his opinions."

He paused for a moment, and then proceeded in a calmer tone:—

"Theodora, you are now acquainted with my intentions. I only grieve they cannot be put in execution with the promptitude that I desire.—But I must go hence immediately—I must keep up the hellish character which I have assumed, and I am sent to act in conjunction with El Feri; my absence shall be as short as I can make it, and in the mean time fear not any violence from Cañeri. In that quarter you are secure; for the petty despot knows that his death would be the consequence of such a step. And now, lady, keep strict silence on my important disclosures. Roque is faithfully devoted to your service, but much is to be apprehended from his imprudent loquacity, should he be made acquainted with the secret before the time of action. He and any other you wish to point out shall be our attendants. Remember my injunctions. Be comforted, but do not exhibit symptoms of sudden and extraordinary joy, lest you awaken the suspicions of Cañeri; for he is possessed of all the cunning and mistrust which generally fall to the share of a coward heart blended with a despotic mind. Till we meet—adieu! I call for no blessing on your head,—for I can only curse."

He said, and suddenly withdrew.

Theodora for some time was scarcely able to collect her thoughts; the renegade had again revived her drooping spirits, and she ventured to hope once more. She resolved implicitly to follow his instructions, in the anxious expectation of a speedy deliverance from her present miserable and perilous condition.

CHAPTER V.

Un farouche silence, enfant de la fureur,
A ces bruyants éclats succède avec horreur.
D'un bras déterminé, d'un œil brulant de rage,
Parmi ses ennemis chacun s'ouvre un passage.
La Henriade.

Now yield thee, or by him who made
The world! thy heart-blood dyes my blade.—
Thy threats, thy mercy I despise,
Let recreant yield, who fears to die.—
Sir Walter Scott.

The shadows of evening were falling round when Alonso de Aguilar and his gallant army arrived at the plain that skirts the mountain of the Sierra Bermeja. The rebels, with El Feri de Benastepar at their head, who had already been worsted in the plain, had resolved not to hazard another battle, but to keep possession of the mountains, confident of the advantages of their position. El Feri, therefore, having secured all the heights and passes of the Sierra, beheld with inward satisfaction the approach of the enemy; indeed, his situation could not be improved; nature had fashioned an impregnable fortress in the whole circumference of that huge mountain; large masses of rock frowned at intervals around the summit and extended down the sides, and the hollows were filled up with large clumps of trees, the growth of ages. There was only one path by which an ascent appeared practicable, narrow, steep and tortuous, and this perilous pass from the nature of its position might be defended by a handful of brave men; numerous small ravines were likewise observable, by which a laborious and difficult ascent might be attempted, although they were almost choaked with different impediments, being the beds of the torrents which at times poured their headlong course down the sides of the mountain.

The Christians beheld with dread the formidable array which the Sierra presented. The Moors from the adjacent country had flocked to the standard of El Feri, confiding in the prosperous turn which their enterprise was likely to take; they manifested both their hopes and defiance by a prolonged succession of shouts and barbaric yells, which, in lengthened and fearful clamour, were reverberated through the rocky passes and solitary caverns of those mountains.

Alonso de Aguilar was struck with the advantages which the rebels derived from their position, and the attempt to ascend the mountain, crowned as it was with desperate men, might be considered more a deed of madness than an act of true courage; but again he thought of the evil which procrastinated measures often produce in a war of this nature—the longer he delayed the attack the greater the number of enemies he should have to encounter, and if the spark of revolt were not immediately extinguished, the whole province would soon blaze out in open rebellion. Most alarming symptoms of the refractory spirit of the inhabitants had already been manifested during the progress of the army from Granada, and Aguilar well knew that the difficulties he had now to surmount, would increase tenfold each day that he suffered to pass without risking a battle.

Thus, although aware of the desperate character of his undertaking, he nevertheless resolved to engage the Moors in defiance of their superior advantages, relying with the most unlimited confidence on the enthusiastic valour of his veteran troops, whose hatred to the Moors was proverbial, and whose bravery and military conduct he had tried on many a well-fought field.

Under this impression, Don Alonso had summoned Count Ureña, and other principal chiefs, to communicate to them his determination.

"Perhaps you will think," he said, "that the resolution I have formed is desperate, but there is no middle course to choose; we must either return inglorious to our homes, or attack the rebels in their strong hold. An assault must be immediately attempted. Our soldiers burn with impatience to meet those rebellious and ungrateful Moors. It is on the confidence of their love to their country, and hatred to their foes, that I found my expectations. However, we will wait until night has closed; darkness will be more favorable to us in the passive warfare which for some time we shall be obliged to carry on. The shafts of our enemies cannot thus be aimed with such fatal certainty. And now, my brave companions, to your posts, and I hope that when next we meet it will be amidst the shouts of victory."

Aguilar divided his army into three parts, the right wing of which he entrusted to the command of Count de Ureña, the left to Don de Antonio Leyva, whilst he, with his gallant son Don Pedro, determined to lead on the centre to the charge by the more direct ascent, where the chief force of the Moors was judiciously placed.

These three bodies were again sub-divided, as a large mass would afford a conspicuous object against which the efforts of the enemy might be more successfully directed. Thus the different commanders having received their instructions, and the signal being given, various columns advanced towards the mountains from their several points of attack, whilst the war-cry, *Santiago y Cierra España*, was echoed from one to another with inspiring courage and animated enthusiasm. The Moors answered the challenge with wild acclamations, looking on the advancing foe as a devoted prey on which they were shortly to glut their long-desired vengeance. The Christians were, therefore, suffered to proceed unmolested in their course lest, by a premature disclosure of the resources of their enemies, they might be induced to retreat, and thus prevent the Moors from obtaining a complete victory. Slowly, then, the Christians began to ascend the rugged and difficult paths of the mountain. The deafening shouts had for some time ceased, and were succeeded by a dismal and deadly silence. The Christians, therefore, continued to ascend in noiseless progression, until El Feri de Benastepar, judging that the enemy was sufficiently drawn into his toils to ensure success for the artful manœuvres which he had planned, now gave the signal of command, and again the whole mountain rung with an overpowering tumult of cries and yells.

Suddenly the rocks above seemed to be alive, broken into numberless fragments. With dreadful and overwhelming violence their huge disjointed masses rolled from their elevated summits, and gathering a new impetus in their headlong course, rushed down the sides of the mountain, and bounding from point to point with an appalling crash, heaped destruction on the advancing enemy. The ominous and redoubled cries from the summit of the Sierra, rose above the terrific sound of the deadly fragments, and were sufficient to strike dismay into the most daring. Astonishment for a moment paralyzed the Spaniards; yet their intrepidity did not quail in the hazardous moment, though they perceived a heap of mangled corpses swept before them with fearful rapidity. Aguilar could not behold unmoved the destruction wrought amongst his brave followers; and fearing that a second discharge of those terrible missiles might succeed in disheartening them, in a voice of enthusiasm——

"Forward, my brave comrades!" he cried: "those rebels will find that they will sooner tire of hurling rocks than we shall of withstanding them. By suffering we will triumph. On, brave companions, on!"

Aguilar succeeded by his example in instilling into the hearts of his men a degree of maddened courage, which alone could carry them through the obstacles that impeded their course. They accordingly continued fearlessly to advance.

Night had now closed in the most dense and impenetrable darkness. The moon seemed unsuccessfully struggling through a pile of massy clouds, and the scanty light afforded by the dim stars was insufficient to illumine any distant object. Thus the Christians had no means of warding off the dreadful fate which threatened them. They heard, without the power of resistance, the low rumbling sound of the huge rocks that were loosened from their beds, and the crash that followed their ponderous course, as they tore down every object which came before them, mingling all in one vast and promiscuous ruin.

The voice of Aguilar and other chiefs, in hoarse tones, was heard at intervals encouraging and animating their troops, who, wrought up to madness by their loss, had now no other feeling than an ardent desire of attaining the summit, where their enemies lay in security, and quenching their rage in their detested blood. Indeed, the terrors of this dismal and appalling conflict, instead of damping the courage of the soldiers, served only to brace them with redoubled force. Dauntless, therefore, they continued to ascend, unmindful of the cries and groans that rent the air, and although they were sensible that a similar fate might the next moment await themselves. On they proceeded, in the full confidence that some amongst them would ultimately reach the summit, and take ample vengeance for the death of those whom they left behind. Nor did the Moors consider this stubborn constancy and self-devotion without amazement and dread; but El Feri, who read their thoughts, immediately took measures to prevent the consequences with which they might be attended, if he allowed his men to indulge their fears; aware that the best means of keeping up the mettle and ardour of his men was to employ them actively, he ordered a considerable portion of them to descend and meet the enemy boldly in the path. This order was joyfully obeyed, and the Moors rushed impetuously to the attack. Aguilar, who hailed this movement of the enemy as favorable to his troops, by affording them an opportunity of profiting by their superiority, now rushed forward to encounter the charge with increased energy, whilst Don Pedro, with a chosen party, led the van.

The young warrior continued gaining ground; the Moors retreated; and the Spaniards considering this movement as the forerunner of success, boldly pushed on, reckless of the thousand shafts which assailed them on every side. Fresh men supplied, according to instruction, the place of the Moors who retreated; and the wearied Christians had nothing to carry them through the unequal contest but the undaunted courage which had supported them in so many battles. Still they advanced, although the enemy, in spite of the numbers that fell, preserved a fresh and unbroken front, disputing every inch of ground apparently with undiminished numbers.

In the midst of his gallant achievements Don Pedro fell from the blow of a stone, which disabled him from proceeding. His absence soon became apparent; but Alonso de Aguilar pressing forwards to the front, by a desperate effort soon compelled the rebels to abandon their defence, and retreat precipitately to their stations. The Spaniards here halted for a few moments and rallied their forces, on which dismal inroads had been made by the late conflict. Again they advanced in silence and without impediment. Their gallant leader, however, looked on this change with the most gloomy apprehensions; for he conjectured that the Moors were about to renew that system of defence which had been so destructive at the first onset. His suspicions were well grounded. Incontinently another ominous shout rent the air, and the tremendous fragments again rolled down, spreading devastation wherever they passed.

And now, to render the unequal strife more terrific, there fell some broad and scattered drops of rain, announcing the storm which had been gathering in the dark bosom of the swollen and shapeless clouds. Hollow gusts of wind swept through the passes of the mountains, mingling their gloomy cadences with the loud cries of the Moors and the wild lamentations of their victims. And now the pregnant clouds discharged their contents, which poured like an impetuous cataract down the channels of the mountain, whilst from those dark and impenetrable masses fitfully glimmered the livid streaks of lightning, followed by the hollow muttering of the distant thunder. This approaching conflict of the elements Don Alonso beheld undismayed. Boldly he urged on his men, whilst the power of the storm increasing apace, presented additional obstacles to their progress. Nearer the tempest advanced, and the flickering sudden gleams of lightning were succeeded by closely repeated sheets of sulphurous and liquid fire, which in serpentine corruscations illumined those scenes of carnage and devastation, while loud and prolonged peals sounded like the ominous voice of the spirit of destruction riding on the storm, and exulting over the scene of death. But the Spaniards, though moved by the sight of their companions falling around, could not be subdued by the gloomy prospect before them, for it is the attribute of noble courage, while it sympathises with the brave, to continue in the path of honor and duty undaunted and undismayed.

Flash now followed upon flash, and by their livid and unearthly reflection appeared the gallant leader and his band, more resolute in proportion to the fury of the warring elements. The caves and wild recesses echoed with the hollow moaning of the blast, mingled with the shouts of the combatants. Chilling was the scene; more chilling still when the pause made by the raging storm was filled up with the more terrific noise of the falling rocks and stones which came thundering down. Aghast the Christians beheld, by the vivid flashes, the descending destruction; now a block rolled along dyed in the blood of their gallant companions, and again some uncouth and unfashioned fragment had gathered in its career a broken limb, a nerveless arm, or a bleeding leg. The channels were now filled with the water that rushed down the sides of the mountain, forming gurgling eddies around the crushed bodies of the fallen, and mingling their blood with the turbid waters in their descent below.

Such an accumulation of misfortunes began to dishearten the Christians, whose forces were reduced to half their number. Don Pedro, Count de Ureña, and other principal chiefs were wounded, others dead; and an horrific shout on the left, commanded by Don Antonio de Leyva, announced some dreadful catastrophe in that direction.

The renegade, with a valiant reinforcement, had by a dexterous manœuvre cut off the retreat of the Christians in that quarter; and, though they had fought with the most desperate courage, they were completely routed, and the greater number slaughtered on the spot. Savagely Bermudo dealt his blows on his own countrymen, and vented his diabolical feelings on many brave and innocent men to take vengeance for the wrongs he had sustained from one. But few men escaped from this promiscuous carnage, and those few cut their way with frenzied courage through the ranks of the enemy, bearing the bleeding body of their chief, Don Antonio de Leyva.

The rage of the storm had by this time abated, and Alonso de Aguilar, auguring favorably of men who had withstood, undaunted, such an accumulation of terrors, had pushed forward, and was now midway on the mountain. The rebels beheld his progress with conscious alarm, for though his numbers were considerably reduced and weakened by fatigue, yet Don Alonso was about to reach a space of even ground, in which should he succeed, it would render more doubtful the victory which they had till now considered as certain. Still they continued to roll down their destructive missiles, but these had lost their former power; for though some visited the enemy, yet the greater part stopt in their career, impeded by the trunks of trees torn up by the tempest, or stuck in the spots of marshy ground caused by the descending torrents. The Moors, therefore, abandoned this system of aggression, and perceiving that the gallant band of Don Alonso de Aguilar was extremely small, and that it could not receive assistance from the Spanish forces below, they collected a great body, and determined to oppose the further progress of Aguilar, before he could succeed in reaching the little plain. A desperate contest ensued, in which every Christian exerted his remaining strength, and their present position was so far favorable, that the Moors were not able to overwhelm them with numbers. Thus Aguilar, encouraging his men with the better aspect of their fortune, continued fighting desperately, and gaining ground, whilst the affrighted Moors retreated before his amazing efforts.

But the most exalted courage cannot support the body under the accumulated sufferings of wounds and exhaustion, and Don Alonso at length beheld with a look of melancholy resignation, blended with manly fortitude, the diminution of his numbers, and the state of depression under which they laboured. He could no longer hope to accomplish his daring enterprise, nor effect an honorable retreat. The day, which had now shed its first glimmering light, revealed the forlorn condition of his men: he beheld his once gallant army stretched along the path, which was so completely covered with the dead, that it seemed to be paved with human victims. The Spaniards fought still, but their foes were continually supplied with fresh men, and Aguilar foresaw with a pang of distress that the Moors would ultimately triumph. In this emergency he cast a desponding look on his troops below, who would in vain have attempted to assist him, on account of the distance which separated them.

The followers of Don Alonso were now reduced to a very limited number, but he perceived on their countenances the noble expression of resigned courage and high-minded patriotism. A sad smile of satisfaction was on his lip, as with a firm voice, he exclaimed:—

"Christians, this standard must be planted on the highest point we can attain." Then after a pause he added, pointing to the little plain;

"Behold your grave!—-- advance boldly—there is the last stage of our existence—and if any one returns to Granada, he may tell the queen that Alonso de Aguilar has redeemed his pledge."

These words were electric—the countenances of his companions brightened, and they seemed to acquire new vigour from the example of their noble leader. They dealt their blows with increased energy, and after a terrific struggle, they at length reached the fatal plain. There they halted at the goal of their glorious career, and Alonso de Aguilar planting the standard of the cross firmly on the ground, placed himself near a rock which he caused to be surrounded by his men. There the devoted warriors resolved to await their fate.

The Moors now rushed on them from all parts with a ferocious joy. But many were those who fell before they could succeed in mastering the brave and infuriated Christians. Man to man they fought, and round the rock the gallant soldiers gradually fell. The heroism of the Spaniards might protract, but could not avert their fall. Aguilar at length beheld himself alone amongst a heap of his fallen men; his armour was broken in many places, and stained with the life-blood which flowed through the crevices; with his left hand he grasped the remains of a banner, and supported himself against the rock, while his right still continued to wield his ponderous sword. The numerous assailants looked with dread and awe on the redoubtable champion, and for some time seemed to be rivetted to the place. But a host was gathering around to rush at once upon the formidable foe, when a giant figure made his way through the crowd, crying aloud—

"Yield thee, Christian, for the Moors know how to respect courage like thine."

"Yield! Never will I yield to a rebel. I am Alonso de Aguilar."

"Thanks to the prophet!" cried the Moor; "look then on thy irreconcilable foe!—I am El Feri de Benastepar."

Aguilar saw the Moor-chief with the fortitude of a noble heart, and rising superior to his adverse fortune, although covered with wounds, and fainting from exhaustion, he sprung forward to meet the advance of his terrible adversary, whilst the Moors awed by the meeting of such warriors, stood around in breathless silence.

The mighty foes closed in desperate combat. But soon Aguilar conscious of his weakness, retired to his original position against the rock, and in that posture sustained the attack. The fresh and unabated force of El Feri became too powerful for the Christian chief, worn out as he was with the loss of blood, and the fatigue of many hours of battle. Aguilar now perceived that to die nobly was the only alternative he could embrace, and accordingly grasping firmly the banner, he continued a resolute but unequal combat. His exhaustion, however, increased, and as he perceived his end approach, he sprang forward, and with one desperate blow, in which he collected his remaining energies, endeavoured to crush his enemy. But the exertion far exceeded his strength, and the same blow that an hour before would have cloven through buckler and hauberk, now fell almost harmless upon the shield of El Feri. The Moor availed himself of the moment, and before Aguilar had time to recover, the scymitar of his foe had cleft through the helmet of Don Alonso, and sunk deep into the brain. The hero fell; with one deep sigh his noble spirit parted from its clay, and the brave, the generous, the heroic Don Alonso de Aguilar was no more![1]

A tremendous shout from the exulting Moors announced the catastrophe to the Christians below: it sounded through the mountain like the ferocious yell of demons revelling over their victim. El Feri stood silent for a moment gazing on his prostrate enemy, and he could not but contemplate with veneration and awe that form which even in death preserved the nobleness and dignity which had distinguished it through life. His helmet had given way, and rolled to some distance on the plain. His black hair silvered with age, and now dripping with his blood, overshaded part of his noble countenance. Shorn of its proud device, his broken shield lay on his left arm, as well as the remains of the banner which he had sworn to defend with his life, whilst his right arm still retained that sword once the terror of the Moors, now lying harmless on the ground. Thus fell Aguilar, and the exulting Moors flocked round his corpse, led by an instinctive curiosity to behold the prostrate warrior so long the object of their dread.

---

[1] History describes Don Alonso de Aguilar as one of the most valiant and renowned amongst the celebrated warriors of that period. His death has been the subject of many and some very good ballads or romances, but it is better known and appreciated among the reading portion of the Spaniards by the description given by Hurtado de Mendoza in his work entitled, "Guerra de Granada." It is a masterly composition. Indeed the whole work passes amongst the literati as the most elegant and classic piece of Spanish history.

CHAPTER VI.

Inter their bodies as becomes their births:
Shakespeare.

Few, few shall part where many meet,

* * * * *

And every turf beneath their feet
Shall be a soldier's sepulchre.
T. Campbell.

The victory of the Moors was complete; and as they had been long accustomed to reverses, so unusual a success elated them beyond all bounds of moderation. They considered their independence as now firmly established, and could scarcely be restrained from rushing, like a disorderly horde of conquering barbarians, on their enemies below, and ravaging the country round. But fortunately El Feri joined to great courage and activity the rare endowments of a prudent and sagacious chief. He foresaw that the present success, if not followed up judiciously, would prove more prejudicial than favorable to their cause. It was not by a confused depredatory system that this first victory should be followed up; for their cause could only be ultimately benefited by improving their present advantages. Besides, the fierce courage of his followers, arising rather from a sense of injuries and revenge, than real military bravery, was ill calculated to sustain the superior numbers and better disciplined bands of the Christians. Nor could El Feri be so far dazzled by one solitary success as to attribute solely to their conduct and courage that result which was chiefly to be ascribed to the advantages of their position, combined with a series of fortunate circumstances that had assisted them against the Christians. He knew that the intelligence of this victory would excite those of his countrymen who were as yet lukewarm in the cause, to take up arms and repair to that mountain which was now the cradle in which their infant liberty was to be rocked. He wished to preserve and improve this situation without risking the danger of another action, until he possessed ample means of insuring success. A precipitate movement now might involve the Moors in difficulties capable not only of retarding their triumph, but even of rendering fruitless the effects of a first victory: Gomez Arias was likewise marching with a powerful army, and it would be madness to abandon the strong hold of the Sierra for the sake of hazarding an encounter, when as yet they were in all respects inferior to their enemies.

El Feri, therefore, strongly deprecated the design formed by Mohabed of advancing at present against the Spaniards. But Mohabed, flushed with pride and little conversant with military affairs, could only be prevailed upon to defer his sally from the mountain for two days; and El Feri, considering the baneful effects which any disagreement amongst the chief leaders might produce, prudently acquiesced in his decision. He hoped that in the meantime he should have an opportunity either of dissuading his brother chief, or at least of organising a more systematic and powerful invasion.

Whilst the best warrior in the Moorish ranks was deeply interested in forwarding their views, his disorderly and savage followers were affording proofs of their wanton cruelty and insubordination. El Feri saw with disgust and sorrow, that the men he led to the field adhered not to the principles which they pretended to profess. He perceived that his army more resembled a horde of undisciplined barbarians than true and sincere patriots; that the gratification of private animosity and revenge had a far greater preponderance in directing their exertions, than the heroic impulses of noble enthusiasm and public spirit. He had been himself stimulated to take up arms solely by pure and patriotic sentiments, without the least alloy of personal interest, or the indulgence of a revengeful disposition. He, therefore, bitterly lamented, for the sake of his country, when a secret voice whispered to him, that he was less the leader of independent men, panting for liberty, than of a lawless discontented rabble, better deserving the name of rebels than that of liberators. Alas! how often is the lustre of a good cause darkened by the private interests and vices of its agents!

The attention of El Feri was however diverted towards a tumult in that part of the mountain where the mighty Aguilar had fallen: he hurried to the spot to inquire into the cause of the commotion, when he saw the noble form of his redoubtable foe ignominiously placed on an eminence, round which men, women, and children were crowding, to glut their eyes with the bleeding spectacle. While their savage disposition was gladdened with the sight, they heaped maledictions on the dead. This dastardly ebullition of revenge was more particularly displayed by the weaker portion of men, and by the refuse of women. Women, fashioned by nature to indulge every kindly feeling, and tender sentiment of compassion for the fallen—women, when they have overstepped the barriers of their natural delicacy, become more lawless and cruel than the most hardened of men. An old hag was, with wanton mockery, striving to close the eyes of the warrior; another was trampling under her foot the cross which she had wrenched from his breast; and a dirty urchin was rending his venerable locks, whilst some miscreants, not satisfied with these profanations, in base revenge plunged their weapons into the lifeless clay. But still there were some whom the great Aguilar inspired with terrors even in death, and they shrunk from the inanimate corpse, as if it were ready to start into life, and wreak vengeance for the outrages sustained. Flushed with indignation at the sight, El Feri soon dispersed the vile and motley crowd.

"Base, pitiful wretches," he cried in anger, "it well becomes your cowardly nature thus to insult in death, the man you dared not look on in life. Aye, quench your valour on that unconscious body, for those weapons are unworthy of warring against the living, which cannot respect the dead. Avaunt, miscreants! tempt no further my just anger."

The affrighted crew shrunk back in confusion, but one more daring than the rest ventured to exclaim—

"He was the mortal foe of the Moors, and of El Feri de Benastepar——"

"In life he was," sternly replied El Feri; "but death reconciles the bitterest enemy—for enmity must lose its fire in the cold precincts of the grave."

"The Moor and the Christian," retorted gruffly the other, "even in death, must be irreconcilable; even in the frost of the sepulchre, the hate of such foes must not be extinguished.

"Cease, miscreant!" fiercely returned El Feri, "or by the mighty Allah, a single word more, and a blow from the scymitar of El Feri shall be thy only answer."

In speechless terror they all retreated, when El Feri turning to one of his followers—

"Do you, Moraz," said he, "and some of your brave companions, pay the last honors to the noble Don Alonso de Aguilar."

The Moors obeyed the orders of their chief, and forthwith a grave was dug at the foot of the rock. No funeral pomp—no military honors graced the obsequies of the great Aguilar—no chaunting priest was there to rehearse the service of the dead—no friend to weep over his loss—no grateful dependant to raise the closed hands in prayer to heaven; but in silence his enemies laid him in his humble grave, and strewed the earth over his warlike form. What, though no sculptured marble was there to point out the noble dust that lay beneath; the name of the warrior will live in the hearts of his countrymen, and will be handed to posterity as long as the records of Spain shall exist. But, in the absence of the pomp which marks the burial of the illustrious, Don Alonso received the most honorable tribute that can adorn a warrior's grave—the manly and venerating tear of his mortal foe; for, as the earth covered for ever the remains of Aguilar, the silent tear of noble feeling fell on it from the eye of El Feri de Benastepar.

Meantime the Christians at the foot of the mountain were making a precipitate retreat, carrying with them a number of their wounded companions, and leaving behind a terrible monument of their bravery and misfortune.

How imposing is the calm, when the warm activity of action gives place to the desolate repose of death! Now, the din of strife is over; no longer the brazen notes of the trumpet swell in the wind—no longer the echoes of the mountain rehearse and fling back the warlike sounds. Hushed is the voice of command and animation—mute the cries of victory or defeat. Even the howling blast, which lately, with its fitful voice, increased the terrors of the scene, is now softened into a low and mournful murmur, emblematical of the dismal tranquillity that reigns around. The smiling face of nature is blotted and defaced by the truculent works of men. The rich and reviving green that carpeted the ground, now presents to the view an ensanguined plain, and the smiling flowers, emblems of innocence and peace, bear no longer in their calice the pearly moisture of the morn, but display the crimson evidence of man's hatred to his kind. The soft grass is not now ruffled by the welcome pressure of living individuals, happy in the joyous dance, or gently reclining under the sweet influence of slumber, but by the weight of ghastly corpses.

It was a sight fearful to behold! not a sound was heard; an unnatural sadness prevailed over the scene; a thousand warriors lay there in the silence of the grave, but in those colourless features still lingered a tinge of the last feeling by which they were animated—the last passion that raged within; the brow stiffened into gloomy fierceness—the eye intensely fixed with bold resolve—the firmly clenched hand—bespoke the various sensations in which they were surprised by death. Tranquil and extended lay some who had received the summons without a throb; surely the blow was struck, and swiftly fled the spark of life, whilst others, in the violent contraction of the muscles, and the writhing expression of pain, indicated how fearfully the rebellious soul had grappled with the destroyer, before she could be dislodged from her tenement. Death levels all distinction, and here were seen men of various ages and ranks, so widely separated in life, promiscuously mingled in the last repose. Youth and age alike indifferently strewed the plain, and the silvered locks lay beside the flowing tresses; the pale hue of protracted life, with the rosy healthful tints of commencing and hopeful existence. Spring had mixed its blossoms with the falling leaves of autumn. No distinction of rank was here; by the noble chief lay the humble soldier—their attire alone could distinguish one from the other; and even this external ornament would soon be destroyed, and all, all would be amalgamated in one general indiscriminate dust.

But still that period was not arrived, and the encampment of corpses, fresh in death, appeared most like an army of sleeping warriors; but for the bloody tokens and fearful disorder which drove away every image of natural repose, it seemed as if their departed spirits still hovered within the bodies which they had lately abandoned. But alas! too soon the harbinger of fading and helpless mortality would speed to dispel the melancholy charm. The carrion birds were now hurrying to claim the undisputed inheritance of that prey which a short time since had been the receptacle of so many feelings and affections, while a thousand hearts were doomed to weep for the occasion that afforded joy to the gloomy and filthy revellers.

The routed Christians, meantime, were fast retreating, whilst the news of their defeat and the fate of Aguilar spreading swiftly around, soon reached the stately city of Granada, for misfortune is a most expeditious traveller. The heroic Isabella felt an indescribable shock at these unwelcome tidings; even victory, if purchased with the death of Don Alonso, she would consider a reverse, but attended, as it was, with complete overthrow, it created the most lively sensations of indignation and sorrow. She made a solemn vow in the presence of the archbishop her confessor, and her nobles, that she would neither wear linen nor sleep on her royal couch until that daring rebellion had been annihilated, and its agitators brought to retribution. She next gave orders that all her troops should march against the rebels, and a numerous army was soon collected, both of veterans and volunteers.

Meantime the grief of Leonor for the death of her father was exhibited in a striking manner, but still in a manner worthy a branch of that noble tree. She found a generous consolation in the name bequeathed to her by her departed parent, and she fondly cherished the halo of glory that surrounded her father's life, and now must adhere for ever to his memory. The queen, anxious to contribute to the mitigation of her sorrow, had kindly invited her to the palace, that by a temporary absence from her own dwelling she might be relieved from the sight of objects, which continually brought to her mind a train of painful associations.

CHAPTER VII.

Padre mio, caro padre,
E tu ancor m'abbandoni!
Guarini.

I know not how to tell thee;
Shame rises in my face and interrupts
The story of my tongue.
Otway.

Bermudo, the renegade, having received instructions from El Feri soon after the affair of the Sierra Bermeja, returned to Alhaurin, where he found Cañeri in an extacy of uncontrollable joy. His late extravagance had of course been considerably augmented by the news of the recent success. So elated were his spirits, and so confident did he feel of the happy results which would attend all the future operations of the Moors, that, forgetting a secret dislike he always entertained to actual strife, he talked of heading a body, and meeting the Christians, who were rapidly advancing upon Alhaurin: but the renegade brought different injunctions from El Feri, who was now looked upon, by common consent, as the supreme arbitrator of the Moorish cause. Cañeri was ordered, unfortunately for the display of his present ebullition of valour, to fortify himself in Alhaurin, and prepare a retreat for Mohabed, in case the rash expedition of that chief against Gomez Arias should prove unsuccessful.

All El Feri's persuasions had been thrown away upon Mohabed, who, quite inexperienced in war, and highly flushed by their recent victory, had descended the Sierra Bermeja with a strong division to offer battle to the Spaniards. Cañeri submissively followed the orders of his brother in command. Indeed in his present exhilaration of spirits, he would submit almost to any thing, except to renounce the outward show of dignity, for Cañeri was one of those good-natured soldiers, who can be satisfied with the shadow, whilst other leaders possessed the substance of power.

In every age and country, there needs must be warriors of all descriptions; some are designed by nature to encounter perils, and acquire a name to be enrolled in the temple of immortality, and there are others whose noble achievements entitle them to the same honor, though traced in different characters; there is also a third class of military men, who, being neither sanguinary nor heroic, are yet intended to shine in a more peaceful warfare,—generals of undoubted military capacity, of extraordinary genius for the enactment of regulations and orders, with a clear judgment for the various qualifications of staff officers, and bearing an exceedingly martial and appropriate carriage in courts, reviews, and parades. Now, to this last class Cañeri most assuredly belonged: his talents for military parade and shew no one could dispute. He now approached the renegade, and in as affable a manner as his arrogant dictatorial manner would permit:—

"Alagraf," he said, "these are joyful times for the Moors."

"Provided they last," coldly returned the renegade.

"Last," rejoined the Moor, with indignant surprise. "Behold!" and he pointed to his men, all arrayed and equipped in a martial style, as they were standing in review, "those men are not likely to tarnish the laurels already culled by their companions of the Sierra Bermeja. But you are ever sullen, Alagraf; no victory, no fortune can efface the gloom which pervades every action of your life."

"Yours, at all events, Cañeri," replied the renegade, sneeringly, "is excessively gay; the love of your country must certainly be great, since it can occasion such extraordinary marks of satisfaction for a temporary success."

"My country and religion are dear to me," returned Cañeri, with dignity, "very dear, and sacred. But then," he added, relaxing, "my heart is not wholly absorbed in the love of my country."

"That I believe," replied Bermudo, significantly. "It will easily admit of division, and in the distribution of your lore, I dare swear you have reserved a considerable share for yourself."

Cañeri laughed affectedly, then drawing nearer to the renegade, and taking him gently by the hand—

"My friend," he said, "much as I love myself, still have I a store left for such as love me well, and when a lady fair——"

"Eh!" exclaimed the renegade, "what lady fair is this?"

"Oh, Alagraf," returned Cañeri, unable any longer to contain himself, "I am the happiest of men—Theodora—the beautiful Theodora has at length yielded to the soft persuasions of love, and it is to you, my good Alagraf, that I stand chiefly indebted for such favorable results."

The renegade started back in visible consternation. Cañeri's words sent daggers to his heart. Could it be possible? the amiable and elevated Theodora, sunk to the base minion of so worthless a character! and all his plans overturned for ever! It appeared unaccountable—impossible. Theodora could not look kindly upon the object of her late mortal abhorrence.—Such a transition was abrupt—unnatural—unless, indeed, her reason had fallen a sacrifice to her accumulated distress.

Terrible thoughts coursed over the troubled and darkened brow of the renegade, whilst his whole person manifested strong marks of the passion that agitated his bosom.

"Alagraf, what means this emotion? why, you appear thunderstruck."

"Yes;" replied the renegade, assuming his composure, "with surprise. But you said it was to my good offices you stood indebted for your success. Now would you favour me with the particulars of such an extraordinary conquest?"—

"Aye, my friend," returned vauntingly Cañeri; "Fortune is very capricious. She never works progressively, but by starts, and then according to the mood she is in, a man is either overpowered with misery or with bliss. Some time since both the affairs of my country and those of my heart went on desperately; the scales are now turned, and I am blessed in a double triumph.

"But," cried the renegade, "the nature of your triumph I would fain learn."

"It is complete," replied Cañeri with complacency.

"Complete!" re-echoed the renegade with emotion—"complete! how?"

"At least by anticipation," returned the Moor. "Complete by anticipation. Nothing is yet concluded."

The renegade recovered from the suspense of agony.

"The triumph of which I speak," continued Cañeri, "is yet to come, though it is already beyond a doubt. Theodora, until now so resolutely bent against me—Theodora, who at the very sight of me shrunk back with horror and abhorrence—Theodora at last receives me not only without reluctance, but even with kindness. My visits no longer create disgust and dread, and every symptom foretels a speedy and grateful termination to my fondest hopes." He then added with conceited vanity,—"And I marvel how else an affair of this nature could terminate? Theodora was a lovely woman, a woman in affliction; but she was a woman still, and could not be expected to continue eternally in the same mind. Constancy in any thing is against the very nature of woman; perseverance is a foe she could never successfully withstand."

To this sapient observation the renegade made no reply. A glance of scorn was the only sign by which he evinced his value of the chiefs opinion. He allowed him a free range to his hopes, and when the vain Moor had satisfied himself with aerial happiness, the renegade in a bitter bantering tone wished him joy of his conquest, and hurried away to certify upon what basis were founded the expectations of the Moor.

Cañeri retired to his couch, when to his waking dreams succeeded those of night, which though not wilder in their nature, were still by their flattering prospects the source of unspeakable satisfaction. He rose, therefore, the next morning if possible in greater exhilaration of spirits than before, and immediately sent for his confidant the renegade; but his confidant came not, and Cañeri was in absolute necessity of a person to whom he might communicate his hopes and his plans. Malique was accordingly ordered into his presence.

"Malique, where is Alagraf?" inquired the chief.

"Alagraf!" exclaimed the astonished Malique; and he remained for some time as if struck by a thunderbolt.

"Alagraf!"

"Alagraf! yes Alagraf," repeated impatiently Cañeri. "What means this confusion? speak. Where is the renegade?"

"The renegade is gone," answered the trembling Malique.

"Gone!" echoed Cañeri with superadded agitation.—"Gone! where? when? to what purpose?—gone! without my knowledge!"

"The purport of his mission," replied Malique, "I know not; nor was I made acquainted with his departure until this morning. The guards of the night allowed him to pass. Possessed as Alagraf was of your secrets and unbounded confidence, it was naturally supposed that he acted under your instructions: his egress from the town therefore caused neither surprise nor alarm."

"My instructions!" cried fiercely the chief; "I gave him no instructions; it is an act of insubordination. That man was ever too proud; his accursed Christian blood still remained in his veins, when his mouth pronounced a recantation of his creed. He renounced his country; but could not renounce his character. By the mighty Allah! he shall severely suffer for this breach of discipline if Cañeri has power amongst the Moors. Yes, he shall feel the bitter consequences of his imprudence upon his return."

"Return!" cried Malique, despondingly, "If he acted not according to your orders, I much apprehend he will never return; for his companions in flight leave no doubt as to the motives that have directed him."

"Companions!" exclaimed Cañeri, in breathless anxiety. "What companions?"

"Even the fair captive, and the menial Roque," replied Malique, after some hesitation.

"What! Theodora gone! gone with the renegade!—hell! furies!—unsay those words, Malique! tremble for the villains that allowed him to leave the town—nay, tremble for your own life!"

The fury of Cañeri knew no bounds, upon the confirmation of Malique's intelligence. He stamped and raved like a madman, and plucked his beard in very ire: then, in the summary way of distributing Moorish justice, he caused the chief and two or three of the guards of the night to be slaughtered in his presence. Indeed, Malique himself would have shared the same fate, had not the private interest of the Moor superseded his frenzied revenge. But Cañeri considered Malique as totally devoted to his person, and he was loath to part with a man of whose aid and counsel he stood in greater need than ever. Thus the life of Malique was spared by the despot, as those of many other humble slaves had before been and will again, by their despotic masters, not for the services which they have already rendered, but in consideration of those which they might still afford.

"Malique, quick," cried Cañeri, "take the best of my troops, the fleetest of my horses, and speed after that accursed renegade; bring him, dead or alive;—alive, if possible; and ask for any recompence, any, how great soever, which I can grant.—Begone!—fly!"

In a moment the faithful Malique with a chosen band was mounted, and in a moment they started rapidly with the velocity that a hope of recompence or a dread of punishment inspires. They sped in the direction reported to be taken by the fugitives, but it was too late; the renegade had devised the necessary precautions to insure success in his undertaking. He had the advantage of a whole night's journey, and had besides prudently changed his route as soon as he found himself out of sight.

Thus the efforts of Malique proved as abortive as the ravings of his master. After a day spent in fruitless pursuit, the party was compelled to retreat before an advancing band of Christians, and returned to Alhaurin, to witness the extravagant rage of Cañeri, who was alternately the prey of shame, disappointment, and vexation. Indeed, all the Moors evinced signs of discontent at the disappearance of the renegade. Some, because his presence animated their courage, and others because they dreaded the despotic temper of Cañeri, now rendered doubly formidable by this untoward event. All the Moors were, therefore, in dismay at the flight of the renegade, all but one, and that was Aboukar, who found with no less surprise than joy, that amongst the companions of the runaway was included his spouse, Marien Rufa.

Meantime, the fugitives were rapidly approaching the town of Guadix, the native place of Theodora. But with what throbbing hearts the travellers proceeded on their journey, and how different were the feelings that gave expression to their features! A thousand sensations agitated the bosom of Theodora; fear, hope, and filial love, alternately disputed the mastery, whilst the countenance of the renegade evinced nought but a dreary isolation of feeling; revenge alone reigned in his heart uncontrolled, and undisputed. The two inferior personages were likewise indulging in reflections consonant to their nature and habits. A vacant joy, a happy riddance from a state of fear and thraldom, predominated in the heart of Roque, whilst a curious amalgamation of gratified spite and returning superstition claimed that of Marien Rufa. But, however different the sentiments by which they were actuated, the travellers evinced an equal joy when their anxious look caught the first glimpse of Guadix, which now stood before them softly enveloped in the twilight shadows.

"Welcome! dear lady," cried Roque, joyfully, "once more behold your home."

Home, delightful thrilling word! It went to the heart of Theodora in a tumultuous flow of pleasing, yet painful sensations. She now returned to the scenes of her innocence and happiness, but it was also the theatre of her disgrace and sorrow. What agitation did she feel as every well known object presented itself with powerful associations to her mind. Already she descried the stately appearance of her father's mansion, rising majestically in the shades of approaching night. Though distant she clearly perceived every object, every feature of the surrounding scene.

Tranquil and quiet the country and the city lay in religious silence, and the gentle hum of humanity that softly stole upon the ear, and the tinkling of a bell, or the social bark of a dog, every well-known sound struck with a congeniality of feeling on the trembling heart of Theodora. She returned to her home like the happy traveller after a lapse of many years, to whose memory charged with numberless objects that have intervened since his departure, these infant scenes must return in a confused, fading, yet pleasing sensation of delight. Theodora came; she drew near the place of her birth with anxiety and dread. Around she beheld every object as she had left it. Nature had proceeded undisturbed in her accustomed rotation. Green were the fields, and the boundless heavens still displayed their majestic grandeur. Yet, all around, to the eyes of Theodora, bore a tint of strangeness she could not well define. Alas! the change was not in those places, but in the tone of mind with which she considered them. Guadix and its gardens, and its groves, and its fountains, were still the same, but Theodora was changed. She had left those happy scenes in all the glory of youth and beauty. She returned experienced in grief in the beginning of life, and bearing in those heavenly features the iron stamp of premature decay. She had left them in the wild delirium of love,—in the intoxicating bliss of a first all-powerful affection, lavishly bestowed, and abundantly requited. She returned with a heart desolate and forlorn, the pure springs of which were envenomed by the baneful effects of passion, and embittered with shame and grief. She had left them in the happy society of a fond lover, full of present joy and glowing hopes of future happiness. She returned full of disappointment and remorse, under the protection of an apostate, the dark enemy of her country. These sad images obtruded upon her mind, and to such dismal thoughts was superadded the load of fear and anxiety arising from the uncertainty of her offended parent's reception. She was his only child, tenderly loved and cherished; but yet, would not this very love offer obstacles to a reconciliation? Would not her father's unbounded kindness serve to set off in blacker colours her own cruel ingratitude?

With these gloomy ideas she at length reached the threshold of the paternal dwelling. There was a melancholy calm that smote her heart—the ponderous casements were closed—a dismal silence prevailed, and as they entered the *Zaguan*, the echo of their steps was sent back in a mournful sound that seemed to rebuke the intruders. The old favorite dog of Don Manuel lay in a corner dozing a dull slumber, and Theodora, as she fondly called him by his name, received no sign of pleased recognition. The animal slowly raised his head, and mechanically fixed his heavy eyes on the speaker, but he neither leaped briskly to hail an old friend, nor resented the approach of an unwelcome stranger. The servants, too, were long in making their appearance, and when at last Pedro, the old major-domo, advanced to meet the party, he bore on his countenance deep lines of affliction: for some time he gazed vacantly on the strangers, and then in a harsh, inhospitable tone, inquired their business.

"Pedro!" said Theodora, with faultering emotion; "Pedro, don't you know me?"

At the sound of that voice Pedro started, and made the sign of the cross—he gazed in astonishment, applied his hand to his dim eyes, and then in a sort of wild stupor—

"*Santo cielo!*" he exclaimed, "Is this a dream, or a miracle? Surely it must be an apparition!—My lady Theodora, here!"

"Yes, good Pedro," mournfully replied Theodora, "this is no delusion. I am, in truth, Theodora, thy young mistress. But the announcement shocks you! What means this confusion?" Her emotion redoubled—she trembled and had scarcely strength to cry—"My father!—where is my father?"

Pedro heaved a sigh, and shook his head despondingly—"Alas! your father!"

"What! speak!" shrieked Theodora, struck with horror—"He is not dead!—Speak!"

"No, not dead," replied the old man, "but it seems that heaven sends you to close his eyes, and witness his departure from this world.—Oh!" he added, sobbing violently, "sorrow hath bowed down his venerable head: since his daughter fled from him, this has been the home of grief and desolation."

Theodora covered her face with her hands; the consciousness of her guilt came with additional force to pierce her heart, as the melancholy results of her dereliction were revealed to her. Roque and Marien Rufa were much affected, and even the stern features of the renegade seemed to be softened by a tinge of pity.

Theodora now could be detained by no consideration. The powerful impulse of nature rose superior to the suggestions of fear. She hurried to her father's chamber—she crossed the long corridor and reached her own saloon without opposition. There she threw a melancholy glance on the objects around, and heaved a bitter sigh when she beheld every thing in which she formerly took delight remaining in the same situation as when she had left them. Her books were scattered about, and her guitar was thrown carelessly upon the sofa where she had last sung a mournful romance previously to her meeting her lover in the garden. It was a rapid glance Theodora cast, and yet, alas! what a world of keen sensations did it produce. Every thing around bespoke the disconsolate tranquillity of a deserted home. Theodora at length gained her father's apartment; the door was closed, but she listened, and distinctly heard the murmur of disease. She gently knocked; an old female attendant opened the door—Theodora rushed in, and threw herself at the feet of Monteblanco's couch.

"Oh! my father!" she cried, and her agony denying her the powers of utterance, silent she sank by the bedside; yet the violent respiration and the smothered groaning which escaped from her bosom but too plainly told the full measure of her sorrow.

"Who is this?" feebly inquired the old man, as those sounds of distress snatched him from the feverish and troubled slumber of disease.

"Your daughter! your guilty, your unfortunate Theodora! Oh, my father, I come but to crave your forgiveness and die."

Prostrate and weakened as Don Manuel was, the sound of his daughter's voice, and her pathetic appeal, awakened all his latent feelings, and gave a new impulse to his decaying frame.

"Theodora! my child! my child!" he cried, raising himself on the couch; and as the sombre reflection of a dim lamp fell on the form before him, he was chilled with horror and amazement. He saw his Theodora; for the eyes of a father will always recognise his child, spite of the blasting influence of misfortune in disguising the features. He recognised his daughter, but alas! how changed was that model of female loveliness and beauty. Sunk was that eye, and quenched its pure and brilliant fire; the smile of innocence had fled from those lips, and the soft delicate tint of her countenance was chased away by a deadly paleness. But still Theodora was interesting and lovely; still Monteblanco gazed on her with the tender fondness of a parent. He rose superior to the malady which confined his withered frame to the couch of sickness; the film of decaying nature was upon his eyes; but yet he fixed them intensely on that fading form that bore the resemblance of his once-beloved child. He could not speak, nor did his daughter attempt to break this pause of dreadful solemnity. Her overpowering grief burst with impetuous effusion; in briny showers the tears fell, and her bosom seemed ready to break under the pressure of heavy and tumultuous groans. Monteblanco was moved to tears; his parched eyelids, which appeared unused to these testimonies of sympathy, were bathed in moisture. He wept, while in soothing accents he endeavoured to raise his daughter from the ground. But she struggled to preserve her humble position.

"Oh, my father!" she cried in an agonizing tone, "your kindness will kill me more than cruelty. I am unworthy of so much tenderness; forgiveness, only forgiveness, is the melancholy boon that the wretched, the guilty Theodora craves from her venerable and injured parent."

The recollection of some dark dream seemed now to absorb the senses of the old man. The debility to which sickness had reduced his mental and physical powers, and the overpowering efficacy of a first impression of pleasure and surprise, had entirely banished from his mind the dreadful image of a parent's just indignation. At first he only saw his lost child returned to his arms, nor in that moment of agitation did he recur to the cause of her absconding, to the state in which she returned. All the sensations which might naturally spring in the bosom of an injured cavalier were deadened by the more powerful feelings of a father's love.

But now that the first emotion had subsided, and that the voice of the guilty Theodora sounded distinctly in his ear, the attention of Don Manuel was promptly recalled to images of a painful nature. His daughter's desertion and the misery consequent on this first act of guilt, rushed upon his mind in deepened and aggravated colours. He rudely drew back the hand which the unfortunate Theodora was bathing with her tears, and in a tone of indignant feeling—

"Say," he cried, "art thou come to hasten my departure from a wretched state of existence?—Speak, guilty as thou art; unfold the horrid tale; and when I am doubly cursed, when I have seen thee thus forlorn and blasted by guilt and misfortune, then let me die!"

"Oh my father," she exclaimed with heart-rending emotion, "I am a criminal daughter—a wretch unworthy of the name I bear—yes, I amply merit your wrath and malediction. But oh! in pity do not deny me your forgiveness, for I have drunk deep of sorrow; if my guilt has been great, so have likewise been the tortures that have rent the heart of your child, since the moment of her first transgression."

"Unfold to me those horrors," exclaimed the desolate father, in a frantic tone; "perhaps their disclosure may break my heart, and bestow on me the only comfort I can now expect—yes, speak, and let the last words I hear from my daughter be my passport to the tomb!"

"Father, speak not thus—on me alone let the vengeance of the offended heavens fall—I alone must expiate the guilt, for shame cannot be joined with the name of Monteblanco; but you, oh! father, live—live to support the dignity of that name."

"You have disgraced it," interrupted Don Manuel, "but I will hear tranquilly—ere I deeply curse, I will deliberately examine the extent of your guilt."

He seemed suddenly to acquire a dreadful composure, and Theodora, as soon as her emotion would permit, told in the strains of deepest woe the particulars of her sorrowful history. It was interrupted repeatedly by her disconsolate father: rage, pride, pity, and resentment, by turns swelled his breast, according as the circumstances related excited those different feelings. But when the harrowing recital was finished, his character seemed to assume a tone of energy uncongenial with his present state of malady. Family pride, a sense of degradation and of injury unrevenged, rose paramount in his mind, and stifling for the moment all the pleadings of pity and parental tenderness, he felt an equal degree of horror and resentment against the betrayer and his unfortunate victim.

In the first impulse, therefore, of his rage, Monteblanco fixed his despairing eyes on his daughter, and in a tone of bitterness, enough to break the fibres of her heart, he cried out imperiously—

"Begone from my sight for ever—begone, and let me die in peace—let me descend to my grave without the additional pang which the presence of an ungrateful child inflicts upon me—rise and begone; and may the stings you have planted in this withered heart, and the shame you have heaped on my head, be your companion to the latest moment of your ignominious life."

"Oh horror! horror!" shrieked Theodora: "Father! father, you do not—you cannot curse your hapless child. Oh! my expiation has been boundless—the justice of Heaven itself must be satisfied, and the heart of a father cannot deny forgiveness to the poor wretch whose miseries are far—far superior to her guilt. Oh pity me!—grant me your pardon—repulse me not thus from your heart, and I will immediately speed to bury my sufferings and my shame amidst the gloom of a cloister."

She ceased, and the wildness of her manner, a fitful tremor that shook her frame, and the unearthly hue that overspread her already pallid countenance, exhibited in glowing tints the havoc that such deep anguish had made. Her trembling arms were extended, and the thin cold fingers clasped in agony; loosely her dishevelled tresses fell on her father's couch, as in the earnestness of grief she appealed to him for mercy.

Monteblanco looked on her, intensely looked on that harrowing picture of distress, and felt the burning tears that descended in copious streams from their swollen springs. The vivid signs of her repentance, and the excess of her affliction were inconsistent with depravity. Error more than guilt was there, and Don Manuel could not behold unmoved his once beloved daughter, the pride and solace of his declining years, reduced to her present state of utter wretchedness. Dreadful was the conflict which the noble and high-minded cavalier had to sustain between the stern dictates of worldly prejudice, and the tender pleadings of nature. But happily to the father's honour, nature at length prevailed. He was softened, and in an extacy of mingled grief and affection, he clasped his sorrowing child in his trembling arms.

Monteblanco appeared now partially relieved from a load of anguish. He consoled the poor forlorn culprit that pathetically clung to his protection, and his fondness for the once beautiful and accomplished Theodora, seemed to return with additional force for the unfortunate being that stood before him.

But now new feelings took possession of his breast. As he gazed with a melancholy joy on his restored child—as he considered with the smile of sadness the mournful devastation which one man's treachery had wrought there, all his thoughts were forcibly drawn into one predominant idea, whilst the decaying energies of his frame received a new impulse to second the resolutions of his working mind. The cold and unnatural atrocity of Gomez Arias burned in his brain; he felt the agonized throb of his injury run corrosive through his veins, and impart an uncontrollable desire of revenge; the fever of excitement rose superior to that which had laid him prostrate, and he seemed impatient at the weakness that confined him to his couch.

"Before I die, poor suffering mourner," he said, turning soothingly to his daughter, "I shall see your wrongs redressed, and my insulted honor amply revenged; this sacred duty links me yet to life, and I hope fervently in God that my existence may be protracted until that period."

The renegade was there; for when revenge was the word, how could Bermudo be absent from the essence of his life? Theodora, overpowered with the emotion which her meeting with her father had produced, retired to compose her disordered spirits, and in the mean time, Don Manuel had a short but terrible explanation with the renegade: in few words this man of darkness unfolded his powers of seconding Monteblanco's plans of vengeance.

The heated mind of the old cavalier, though in need of no stimulus, nevertheless gathered fuel from the insinuating eloquence of the renegade. A plan was concerted, and an immediate appeal to the queen resolved upon; but the state of Monteblanco's health did not allow him to put in execution his determination with a promptitude consonant with his feelings. The renegade was therefore prudently concealed for the present, to avoid the danger of inquisitive curiosity, whilst the only obstacle that retarded the departure of Monteblanco for Granada, was the sickness which still confined him to his couch.

CHAPTER VIII.

> Crece el tumulto, y el espanto crece:
> Y todos le abandonan—uno solo
> Fiel se presenta, y con valor perece.
> *Anon.*

Don Manuel de Monteblanco has already been described as a man weighed down by years and the iron pressure of infirmities and sorrows. The disappearance of his daughter, in whom all his thoughts, all the affections of his heart were solely centred, tended to fill the measure of his misery and reduce him to that gloomy state of despondency with which his lost energies and increasing age in vain attempted to struggle. Totally unsuccessful in his endeavours to discover the retreat of Theodora, time at length reconciled him to his state of desolation, but it was the resignation of despair; that feeling which makes man acquiesce with gloomy calmness in the decrees of fate, and look with tranquillity on the approach of death as the happy termination of his sufferings.

Don Manuel had sent despatches, and made diligent inquiries to recover his daughter, but in vain. Martha, the old duenna, from whom he might have obtained a knowledge of the truth, had successfully baffled his pursuit, the sanctimonious hag having embarked at Barcelona, for Italy. The vessel was wrecked, and it was supposed she perished, as no information of her could be afterwards obtained. Don Lope Gomez Arias had all the time kept up a correspondence with the deluded and ill-fated father, who, far from harbouring the least suspicion against the betrayer of his daughter, considered him as one in whose advice and services he could implicitly confide. Thus in proportion as the intelligence from Gomez Arias grew more cold and less frequent, the hopes of the old cavalier decreased, until he was at last reduced to a state bordering upon distraction. He lay prostrate on the couch of sickness; it was presaged he was doomed never more to rise. Slowly death was stealing over him, and all his friends and dependants bitterly deplored the causes which contributed to render so miserable the last days of the good old cavalier. Indeed, it appeared as if the angel of death hovered round his fated mansion, and awed all its inmates into a melancholy tranquillity. At this time the sudden and unexpected appearance of Theodora worked a powerful revolution in the feelings of the family, whilst the frame of Don Manuel, instead of sinking under the weight of the impression which it produced, seemed to revive. His latent feelings were roused from their gloomy torpor, the slumbering energies were called into action by the powerful excitement of new ideas, and the mind rendered buoyant in proportion as new projects called for the exertion of its faculties. The unparalleled effrontery and cruelty of Gomez Arias formed the source from which the drooping frame of Monteblanco gathered life. His wrongs, instead of accelerating the progress of death, seemed instantly to check its strides, while the desire of revenge so powerfully operated on his mind, that it warmed the torpid energies of decaying mortality.

Three days had scarcely elapsed since the arrival of Theodora, when Don Manuel already considered himself equal to the exertion of a journey to Granada. The distance was short, and his feelings would not allow him a longer delay; for he conceived every dilatory suggestion to be as detrimental to the success of his design. The renegade, instead of checking Monteblanco's views, contributed to encourage them by his instigations.

Early, therefore, on the fourth day, every thing was prepared for their departure. Theodora habited herself in robes of deep mourning, and departed from Guadix with her father and her former companions in flight. The presence of Roque was indispensable, and Marien Rufa went with the pious intention of being reconciled as soon as possible to the church, by the Archbishop of Granada.

Whilst our travellers are journeying towards that city, let me entreat you, kind or unkind reader, to suffer them to go in peace, and accompany me in another direction. We must now revert to the Moors, whom we left in high excitement at Alhaurin, though the rage of Cañeri at the flight of his captive had considerably damped the joy produced by their victory.

The disappointed Moor roamed about like a discontented mastiff, growling and casting around his revengeful glances; whilst his dependants, awed by his ferocity, cared not to encounter the ebullition of his wrath, but timidly skulked away: strange phenomenon of human nature! Amongst those Moors there was not one who did not inwardly despise the petty despot; not one that was not endowed with a greater share of personal courage, and yet they all trembled before the man they contemned, and shrank from an object invested with no other terrors than those which they had voluntarily conferred upon it. Where lies the spell of a tyrant that enables him *alone*, hated and contemned, to tyrannize over his fellow creatures! However, the Moors had now a respite from their fears, for the approach of the Christians compelled Cañeri to forsake the gratification of his petty malice, and direct his thoughts to the public danger. The town of Alhaurin, which he commanded, was well garrisoned, and had a plentiful store of provisions; and yet the mind of the chief sadly misgave him. Every moment straggling Moors arrived, who depicted, in the most lively colours, the terrible appearance of the Christians. These reports, and the names of the gallant chiefs who headed the enemy, failed not to depress the hearts of those who a week before had looked upon their triumph as certain, imagining that the lustre of their glory was beyond the possibility of a blemish.

In the mean time Mohabed, contrary to the advice of El Feri, had descended the Sierra Bermeja with the Moors under his command. El Feri had expostulated with his brother chief, but could not persuade him to postpone an attempt which, planned with haste, and executed with rashness, could only be attended with disaster. The Moors, though possessed of courage, were unskilled in the discipline of war, and better calculated, therefore, to harrass the Spaniards by detached bodies, in petty skirmishes, than to oppose them in the open field. Mohabed was callous to all remonstrances; and this want of unity in the chiefs, proved a mortal blow to the Moorish cause. El Feri saw with grief his companions descending that mountain which, to them, had afforded a strong hold, and a secure home, to risk, by an act of imprudence, the advantages which they had already gained.

Mohabed boldly directed his course towards Granada, in which direction Gomez Arias was said to be advancing. The enemies shortly came in sight; but no sooner did they come within hearing, than the Moors sent forth a wild shout of exultation, which was answered by the war-cry of the Christians, who were burning to revenge the defeat of their countrymen in the Sierra Bermeja.

Gomez Arias beheld the advance of the enemy with transports of joy. He hailed an opportunity of avenging the death of Aguilar, and of acquiring, by a brilliant act, fresh laurels to sanction his ambitious and enterprizing schemes. Besides the many deceitful stratagems to which he had resorted on account of Theodora, his unsatisfactory conduct on the day of his intended wedding, and a degree of mystery that remained over that affair, had combined to throw a shade over his character which he was anxious to remove by the *eclat* of a military exploit. The hope of victory, the desire of retrieving the late disgrace of the Christians, and the sweet whispers of ambition, produced a state of wild excitation he could scarcely restrain. His soldiers were equally impatient to signalize themselves, and every one awaited the moment of action in a ferment of expectation.

Gomez Arias made choice of an advantageous position near *Rio Gordo*, and there resolved to receive the attack of the enemy. Meantime Mohabed, as if to forward the wishes of the Spaniards, hurried on without considering the fatigue and exhaustion to which his men were reduced by a forced march. The Christians, in their turn, beheld the approach of the rebels, as an approaching holocaust to the spirits of those who fell in the Sierra Bermeja with the gallant Aguilar. Don Lope commanded his men to sustain the first attack without moving, and then, taking advantage of the confusion excited by a repulse, suddenly to charge their enemies with the united advantages of discipline and courage. His wishes succeeded to their utmost extent. The Moors rushed on to the charge in a blind and disorderly manner, totally heedless of the consequences of their want of organization. The Spaniards suffered the attack with the greatest coolness and intrepidity; when their fiery courage, acquiring additional stimulus from having been compressed, now spurred them on, and, with their entire force, they fell on the confused and crowded masses of the enemy with an overwhelming shock.

A dreadful carnage ensued. Terror had succeeded the first ebullition of courage, and the Moors perceived their own rout and confusion only when it was too late. Mohabed exerted all his powers to rally his panic-stricken followers, but it was in vain. Disorder and dismay every where prevailed, and the Christians obtained a victory as easy as it was complete. The greater part of the Moors were slain in the field; a few only escaped to carry the disheartening tale to their companions. The rest, with their chief, Mohabed, fell into the hands of the enemy.

The news of this disaster caused the wildest consternation amongst the rebels at Alhaurin and the Sierra Bermeja. El Feri de Benastepar, grieved but not surprised at the unfortunate results of Mohabed's rashness, was active in repairing the loss, but his numbers being so much reduced, he was now more fully confirmed in his design of confining their warfare against the Christians to the Sierra Bermeja. With the vigour of a superior character, he did not feel dejected by this overthrow, as he had not been wildly elated by his previous success. Not so with Cañeri: the total rout of Mohabed, described in the darkest colours by those who had succeeded in effecting their escape, began to awaken apprehensions for his own safety. His fear was considerably aggravated by the arrival of the Alcayde de los Donceles, who, by forced marches, had suddenly made his appearance before Alhaurin, to which he immediately laid siege. The disorder and discontent of the Moors hourly increased, and the absence of the renegade was severely felt.

At this moment the Alcayde de los Donceles sent a herald to summon the rebels to surrender, promising a full pardon should they be willing to lay down their arms and deliver up their chiefs. But in case they neglected to adopt in time this conciliatory measure, it was threatened that they should all be put to the sword, and the town reduced to ashes. Discontent and insubordination now prevailed amongst the rebels. The sense of their danger—the formidable array of the enemy—and above all, the unpopularity of their chief, Cañeri, conspired to render a great portion of the troops willing to accede to the proposals of the Alcayde.

Soon a numerous and powerful cabal was formed, and the malcontents, deciding that their cause was desperate, agreed to surrender. In a large body they proceeded to the palace, and insolently demanded that the gates of the town should be opened to the Christians. Cañeri, and some of his adherents, aware that they were made an exception to the amnesty, were naturally anxious to defend the city, as the only means of averting their fate.

Cañeri, no longer an unruly despot, now crouched to the danger like an abject slave, and in a piteous tone began to expostulate with the mutineers. It was a striking contrast to see the man, who lately was the terror of all, converted into so gentle an animal as to astonish even the Moors when they contemplated the cowardly being who had held them so long in dread. They were not moved by his entreaties; for the supplications of a despot, instead of awakening sympathy, serve only to augment the rage of mankind, by placing in a more striking light his pusillanimity and unworthiness, and the shame of having suffered so despicable a thing to tyrannize over and oppress them.

The uproar and insubordination increased as the term allowed by the Alcayde to effect a surrender was drawing near. All obedience was now disregarded, and a party of the most turbulent resolved to put their chief to death, and, by this means, propitiate the favor of their enemies. Accordingly, with wild exclamations and terrific yells, they surrounded the mansion of Cañeri, and insolently summoned the few Moors who still adhered to him to give up the despot, or that they would immediately commit the palace to the flames. Cañeri, pale, haggard, and trembling, stood like a convicted culprit in the scene of his former brief authority, bewildered with fear, and without knowing what course to pursue. To escape was utterly impossible, the palace being surrounded by the infuriate Moors, and the town beleaguered by the Spaniards. In this emergency he cast an imploring look on his followers, and saw with despair the limited number of his adherents. In vain he attempted to harangue the infuriated throng from the window; he was driven back by a shower of stones and other missiles. In this suspense and agony he remained some time, during which he had the mortification to behold his few remaining friends gradually deserting his side in proportion as the danger became more imminent. All was tumult and anarchy, and the cries which proceeded from without, predicted to Cañeri's ears his approaching and terrible fate. To the curses heaped on his devoted and abhorred person, succeeded the appalling threats and the wild savage laugh of exultation over his near downfall. Those who were formerly the most abject of his slaves, were now more particularly conspicuous in manifesting their revengeful disposition.

The outward gates had now given way to the ponderous hammers with a terrible crash, and the frenzied mutineers rushing impetuously in, traversed the hall and gallery without opposition, and directed their course to the apartment of the chief.

The wretched Cañeri, alike unable to meet his death like a man, by opposing his rebellious soldiers, or to prevent by his own hand the ignominy which threatened him, awaited in stupor the crisis of the bursting storm. Aghast he rolled his starting eyes, glazed with agonized terror; and he saw himself deserted in that dreadful moment by all his dependants. All had forsaken him—all but one man; he alone, in spite of the fate which inevitably awaited his adherence to the fallen chief, still remained faithful to his side: it was Malique. There is an instinctive fidelity, existing sometimes in the most unrefined and barbarous minds, honorable to human nature,—the uncouth Malique was of this stamp; he had received no favors from his master when in prosperity, yet he now scorned to abandon him in adversity.

Cañeri looked at him, and in spite of his forlorn and perilous situation, could not but be moved at the sight of the faithful Malique. The noble minded Moor stood by his side, his scymitar drawn, and evincing on his countenance no signs of terror or dismay. Cañeri, frail as was the protection that could be derived from a single man, still fondly clung to hope with the sordidness of a cowardly mind.

"My faithful Malique," he cried in a tone of agony; "Is there no hope?"

"None," replied Malique, sadly, but resolutely: "none, but to die like brave Moors; draw your weapon, noble Cañeri, and perish as becomes your race." The trembling chief answered with a groan, for the mutinous soldiers had succeeded in bursting the door of the apartment, and now with a dreadful clamour poured in, eager to strike the first blow at their wretched and defenceless chief. Their very impatience retarded the accomplishment of their fell desire, for as they thronged the narrow passages, some were thrown down, the impatience of the one impeding the progress of the other.

His suspense between life and death was protracted by the confusion; and the miserable Cañeri suffered the additional torture of hearing for some time the appalling heralds of his fate, before the blow was struck. The door burst open, and the savage eyes of his enemies glared upon their victim, and the glitter of their weapons struck fearfully on his sickening sight. He stood gazing with the petrified look of despair; Malique boldly advanced and placed himself before his master, with the resolute courage of one who has determined upon his part.

"Malique," cried the foremost of the conspirators, who happened to be one whom Cañeri had favored; "Sheath thy weapon; we seek not for thy life." Malique made no reply, but with a single blow he levelled the traitor with the ground; he then sprung fearlessly amongst the rebellious crowd, and after having laid prostrate two or three of the most infuriated, he was himself struck down, and met his death with the courage of a soldier, and the coolness of a man, who dies in the discharge of his duty.

Grown desperate by the very impulse of terror, and moved by the sight of Malique bleeding at his feet, Cañeri assumed a courage arising from desperation, and as the mutineers closed round him, he dealt several blows with a stubborn resistance that might have done him honour in the field. He was, however, soon overpowered, and fell covered with innumerable wounds. His head was immediately severed from the body, and being affixed to a long pole, the disorderly and motley crowd now proceeded to the camp of the Spaniards, bearing before them the bleeding and ghastly token of their surrender.

The whole town now became the scene of indiscriminate riot; men and women, old and young, ran about in a tumult of hope and fear, whilst the discordant shouts of the soldiery, and the appalling sight of the procession, bearing the ensanguined trophy, greatly contributed to increase the confusion.

El Alcayde de los Donceles having taken the necessary precautions to insure the safety of his men, in case of treason, now entered the town of Alhaurin amidst the acclamations of his late foes; the chiefs of the rebels had already been secured, and the disorderly multitude taking advantage of the proffered pardon, soon evacuated the place, and dispersed in every direction.

Meantime the Alcayde, having left a garrison in the town to prevent any further trouble, proceeded towards the Sierra Bermeja, the last and only refuge of the Moors; for the little villages where the fire of sedition yet burned, were too insignificant to engross his attention. The Christians therefore continued their march towards the dreadful spot, where the spirit of the noble Aguilar seemed to hover, in expectation of redress, and where the terrible El Feri, the most valiant of the Moors, still kept his ground.

CHAPTER IX.

Cuan breve y cuan caduca resplandece
Nuestra gloria! Cuan subito, en el punto
Que deleita a los ojos, desparece!
Herrera.

Che piu si apera, o che s'attende omai?
Dopo trionfo e palma

* * * * *

Luto e lamenti, e lagrimosi lai;
Tasso.

 Granada, lately the seat of mourning, was again converted into a scene of indiscriminate joy. The recent victory obtained by Gomez Arias, and the defeat of Cañeri which had so closely followed that advantage, awoke the most pleasing sentiments in the minds of the inhabitants. They almost considered the rebellion as at an end, assured by the late successes, and awaited with impatience the triumphant entry of Gomez Arias and his conquering band, now rapidly approaching towards the city. The court was assembled, and displayed the heroic Isabella in all the insignia of royalty. Surrounded by all the principal personages in Spain, she awaited the arrival of the victor, anxious to offer him her congratulations and to bestow upon him adequate marks of her royal favor.
 The grand saloon of the Alhambra, where formerly the Moorish sovereigns dictated their laws, now afforded a different, though no less striking display. The dazzling glitter of armour and the sumptuousness of official dresses, blended with the gay and richly ornamented attires

of the ladies of the court, presented a picture at once beautiful and imposing.

At this moment a rumour was heard at the extremity of the long hall. It proceeded from the guards, who appeared anxious to deny admittance to some person who, with a feeble though piercing voice, was heard continually to exclaim—

"Justice! I come to the Queen! Justice! She cannot deny it to an unfortunate noble!"

The queen was moved by the appeal, and ordered that the supplicant should be admitted without delay. Scarcely were her commands obeyed, when a venerable old man, in sable robes, and bearing on his countenance deep traces of grief, slowly and solemnly advanced towards the throne of the queen. He supported, or rather was supported, by a young female, likewise in mourning, and wearing a veil, which reached almost to the ground, thus concealing her beauties and her sorrows from the curious gaze of the spectators. Two other figures followed closely, a man of strong athletic proportions in a Moorish garb, and a thin curious-looking individual, apparently of inferior station.

Solemn silence prevailed, and every one seemed anxious to learn the cause of this extraordinary appeal. But when the stranger reached the throne he was immediately recognised by the queen and several of the nobles, who could not conceal their astonishment at the sight. "Monteblanco!" involuntarily and simultaneously escaped from several voices in the some breath.

"Yes," replied he, kneeling with his daughter at the foot of the throne; "the wretched Monteblanco comes humbly to crave justice from his sovereign. Before his grey hairs descend with sorrow into the tomb, he collects his weak remaining strength to seek redress from the powerful, and to interest in his behalf the feelings of all the noble and generous. Pardon, most noble and gracious Queen—" he then added, addressing Isabella, "Pardon, if I come in a day of glory and jubilee, to damp with the tale of woe the joy that reigns around. But behold the picture of an aged father, wounded and insulted in his best affections—a noble family dishonoured—the only scion of that family reduced to the lowest state of obloquy and shame. Such a picture may well call the attention of the just, even from objects of dazzling interest. Yes, I may be pardoned for intruding my misfortunes on my Queen—my generous Queen, from whom alone I can expect redress."

"You shall not demand it in vain," replied the queen; "all times are sacred to the solemn appeal of justice, and in the court of Isabella, every other consideration shall be postponed to satisfy its demands.

Monteblanco, you have been guilty of no intrusion; speak confidently—unfold the particulars of your grievances, and trust that nought on earth shall induce the Queen to deviate a single step from the sacred path of justice."

"Gracious Queen!" cried Monteblanco, "that hope has been my sole inducement to prolong my miserable existence. I am injured deeply; injured in the dearest feeling of a nobleman and a Spaniard. The honors of my family, gained by a long line of illustrious ancestors, have been foully tarnished by one who calls himself noble and a Spaniard, but who is alike unworthy to rank as either. I will not enumerate the services of the Monteblancos to interest our Queen in behalf of their affronted house; still, whilst the lustre of their name is on the point of being extinguished, it may be permitted to the last remaining but withered branch of that noble tree, once again to speak of those who are alas! now no more. Oh, Isabella, I had five sons; all—all deserving of the name they bore. Bravely they fought against the Moors, and gloriously they fell before the walls of this city, in the sacred cause of their religion and country. I was left desolate with this only frail but dear support of my declining age."

He cast a piteous look on Theodora, and then continued. "The fate of my sons might draw tears from the eyes of a father; but those tears were unmingled with the bitterness of shame. With pride I remembered that my boys died for their country. Heaven! could I then surmise that in my unfortunate daughter all the former glory so dearly earned should be degraded! Could I ever anticipate that the day should come when the noble fate of my sons would be to me a subject of regret! I am now reduced to envy my country those lives which might now stand forward to avenge the honor of their house. My daughter, blessed with innocence and beauty, gentle and kind in her nature, was the only solace of my declining years—the only sweet and blooming flower that still grew smiling beside the parent stem. Yet of this, my only remaining comfort, I was treacherously and cruelly deprived. A ruffian, honored far beyond his deserts, and rich in the plenitude of power, envied me this solitary consolation. My unfortunate daughter was seduced from her home! Oh heaven! that a Monteblanco should be reduced to confess his shame! She was seduced from the fond arms of her parent under the most sacred promises, and then, in violation of his plighted honor, the miscreant cast her aside to wither in neglect and obscurity. But it was necessary that the most atrocious example of barbarity should accompany his base desertion. In the arms of sleep, the hapless victim was abandoned amidst the wilderness of the Alpujarras. She fell into the power of the Moors, from whom she experienced all the terrors which her forlorn situation was naturally calculated to produce. Fortune threw her again in contact with her betrayer, when the cold heartless ruffian, under the most insidious promises of false repentance, drew her from the house of her protector, that she might be no obstruction to his ambitious career. He again delivered her to the power of the Moors, the rebels whose heads were proscribed, and with whom the guilty man scrupled not to hold communion, in open defiance of the repeated and solemnly promulgated decree of your highness."

Here Monteblanco stopped, and a suppressed murmur of indignation ran through the whole assembly.

"Such an example of depravity," continued the old man, "astonishes you, but your wonder will be increased when you learn that the man who has so disgracefully added treason to his crimes is one high in rank, great in military renown, and honored by the favour of his sovereign."

"Those circumstances," cried the queen, "render his conduct doubly criminal. Monteblanco, your wrongs shall be redressed. Let the guilt be firmly established, and then, were the culprit the first man in the kingdom, the support of my throne—nay," she added, rising in her anger, "were he even of my own blood, he shall not be screened from the rigour of the law." As she delivered these words a cloud of indignation mantled on her brow, and her eyes shot the fire of insulted majesty as she looked proudly on the surrounding nobles and warriors.

A pause ensued, and the splendid train that had assembled to celebrate a victory, now gazed on each other in blank dismay, expecting to hear in the name of the criminal one of their own friends or relatives.

"Pronounce the name of the traitor," cried the queen, "and if he be not here already, he shall be summoned this very moment into our presence, to answer these charges."

"His name is powerful," replied Monteblanco.

"Not more so than my will," nobly retorted Isabella.

At this moment a burst of popular applause announced the triumphant entry of the victorious Spaniard, and the name of Gomez Arias, in the wild strains of a grateful multitude, was repeated by a thousand voices.

"His name?" impatiently demanded the Queen.

Viva! Gomez Arias, *Viva!* again burst on the ears of the Court, and Monteblanco, with bitter emphasis, exclaimed:—

"Hear! hear his name honored with the strains of triumph: hear the name which causes my misery and dishonor, now receiving the glorious reward of the hero! Oh, shame on my withered arm; where is the strength of my youth; and where the sons of my name?"

"Gomez Arias!" cried the queen and the courtiers with one simultaneous cry of amazement—"Gomez Arias!"

"'Tis he!" replied Monteblanco, firmly and indignantly.

A dismal silence then succeeded, and the emotion of the queen became strongly apparent. She felt that, in the person of a triumphant conqueror, she was about to receive a criminal, and that the reward due to his services could not avert the punishment incurred by his guilt. The surrounding courtiers stood aghast, gazing in wonder on the queen. They were well assured of the rigid impartiality which had swayed her conducts through life; and aware that not even all the powerful voices in the country could successfully plead against the claims of the unprotected, or stay the decree of justice upon the oppressor and the criminal.

Meantime Gomez Arias, with all the exultation of a conquering warrior, entered the hall, attended by his principal adherents, and preceded by Mohabed and other captive chiefs. He advanced in joyful expectation towards the throne, when suddenly his course was arrested by a dreadful vision.

Fixed in mute astonishment, he stood, as he gazed upon the group, at the foot of the throne; an ashy paleness succeeded the glowing tints of joy yet visible on his countenance. His confusion became apparent, and was productive of the most injurious surmises in the minds of all around. Yet Gomez Arias raised his eyes towards his sovereign, but from her features he could augur nothing favorable; no encouragement could be traced in their calm and distant expression.

A consciousness of guilt now mastered all his powers of dissimulation, and the nature of Gomez Arias seemed, in a few moments, to have undergone a total and inexplicable revolution. His joyous attendants were surprised at these unwonted signs of consternation; and the sounds of pleasure and triumph suddenly ceased. A deadly spell seemed to have been suddenly cast over the scene, and every one remained in a state of terrible suspense. At length Gomez Arias, striving to conceal his agitation with an assumption of boldness and ease that ill consorted with his manner—"Most gracious Isabella," he cried, "behold the rebellious Mohabed at your royal feet, and accept the humble congratulations and devout attachment of your faithful servant."

Gomez Arias; or The Moors of the Alpujarras.

"Don Lope Gomez Arias," answered the queen, with stern dignity of tone and demeanor, "before we receive your congratulations, and acknowledge your services—before we can consider you with the regard due to the glorious character of a victorious soldier, you must remove certain accusations which have this day been averred against you by the noble and respected individual now before the throne. Answer these serious charges before you claim a title to our gratitude and favor; for not all the splendor of conquest shall throw a veil over flagrant guilt. Approach, and behold those whom you have wronged—mark well the situation to which you have reduced a noble family, and say, what you can plead in justification."

Don Lope cast a glance on the group; but when he perceived his man, Roque, whose presence deprived him of the little opportunity left for prevarication, hope forsook him, and the presence of mind which had served him on so many occasions proved utterly insufficient at this critical moment. He foresaw that any attempt at exculpation would be as fruitless as dangerous. He therefore continued in mute silence, and appeared to plead guilty to the accusation. His countenance, however, gradually cleared, as though a cheering ray had suddenly beamed upon him. He seemed to adopt some resolution so imperiously demanded by circumstances—he regained his composure; but a deep sigh escaped him; it was the last testimony of regret that announced the disappointment of his hopes. No alternative was left; he must relinquish all thoughts of Leonor; and he accordingly attuned his mind to receive with deference the commands which he awaited from the queen.

"Gomez Arias," said Isabella after a lapse of time, "that silence clearly bespeaks thy conviction; the honor of a noble family has been stained. It now remains for you to make all the reparation in your power; and that must be done immediately; for I will not leave this place, nor shall you leave my presence, till I see the victim of your wantonness and cruelty restored to that honor and happiness of which she has been deprived."

Gomez Arias heard these words with apparent respect and humility. Foiled completely in his former hopes, he yet was willing to preserve the favor of the queen, and to effect this it was necessary to deprecate the indignation which his conduct had excited. He therefore assumed all the symptoms of repentance, without any alloy of fear or servility, and casting himself at the foot of the throne, "It would never," said he, "be worthy of Gomez Arias to resist in any instance the will of his sovereign; much less on an occasion when honor induces him to follow her dictates."

"Pity," answered Isabella sarcastically, "that this consideration did not sooner induce you to adopt such a course, for much misery had by these means been prevented. But the evil is already done, and must be instantly repaired.

"Don Lope Gomez Arias," she then proceeded, "This very moment you must plight your hand and faith to Theodora de Monteblanco. You appear fully sensible of the justice of such a measure, and therefore in my presence let the ceremony be performed."

One of the chaplains of the queen was immediately summoned, and before the assembled court, whose looks bespoke their astonishment at this extraordinary scene, the unfortunate Theodora became the wife of Gomez Arias. With trembling steps, and supported by her father, she advanced to the foot of the throne. Don Lope approached her, not only without symptoms of dislike, but even with some appearance of a kindly feeling, the sincerity of which was however of a doubtful nature, as little trust could be placed in a conversion so suddenly effected. Nor did Theodora, blinded as she was by her infatuation, confide entirely in his specious address; but yet the thought of restoring peace of mind to her father, and honor to herself, rose paramount to every other consideration. Amidst the tears that dimmed her eyes, and the lines of sorrow that marked her countenance, some grateful signs of happiness were discernible, like the cheering rays of the sun struggling through the gloom of the clouds.

She received the hand of Gomez Arias tremblingly, with a mixed sensation of joy and dread. Alas! when she took that hand, once so dear, it seemed deadly cold, and the touch imparted to her heart a chill she could not define.

As soon as the ceremony was performed, the queen arose, and with a stateliness of manner that struck with awe the surrounding train—

"Don Lope," she said, "You have, as far as it lay in your power, repaired the injury you have done to the daughter of Monteblanco; you must now answer your Queen, for treason to your country."

Gomez Arias was struck with astonishment, not so much from the consciousness of guilt, as from the suddenness of such an unexpected charge. As soon, therefore, as he recovered from his surprise, with indignant pride he exclaimed: "What! Gomez Arias charged with treason, when he comes to afford the most incontestable proofs of his love and devotion to his country? Where—where is the villain who dares affix so foul a stigma to the name of Gomez Arias? Where is he?—let him appear, that I may confound and chastise the miscreant;"

then looking round with haughtiness, he added, "who dares charge *me* with treason?"

"I dare," cried a voice; and presently the renegade, who, till then, had been concealed from Don Lope, came forward with boldness, and fixing his eyes steadfastly on Gomez Arias—

"I dare," he repeated, "in the face of Spain, and I will make good my charge."

Gomez Arias staggered at the sight; the apparition had burst upon him so unexpectedly, that, unable to contain his emotion,—

"Ah!" he cried, faultering; "what! the Moor here!"

"The Moor!" echoed the queen; "then you know the Moor?"

"I have seen the wretch before," replied Gomez Arias; "but how dares he throw on me so dark an imputation?"

He cast a look of darkening anger on the renegade, but Bermudo returned the haughty glance with a cold sneer.

"Proud man," he exclaimed, "your wrath affrights not me, and humility becomes you better than arrogance. You can as little intimidate me, as you can effectually contradict the veracity of my accusation. Queen of Spain," he then cried in a tone of fearless intrepidity, "and you, ye nobles of Granada, behold in me one of the rebels who has laid down his arms and accepted the amnesty. An eager desire to unmask that haughty man, has obliged me to abandon my companions, and appear within the walls of a Christian city. My motives for proceeding against Don Lope will shortly come to light; but first his guilt shall be established. His conviction and punishment will necessarily follow, if the court of Isabella can boast real claims to that impartial justice, for which the world gives it credit."

These words were delivered with such firmness of tone and manner, that the friends of Gomez Arias began to look on him with mingled pity and amazement. He, however, cast around a glance of indignant contempt; then he preserved a sullen silence, attempting not to contradict the statement of his accuser.

"What answer make you to this charge?" demanded the queen, observing the pertinacity of his silence.

"Answer!" replied Don Lope, with overpowering indignation; "none! Gomez Arias will not deign to answer the accusations of a vile rebel, nor will he afford his Queen and brethren in arms the satisfaction of seeing the established character of a noble Christian put in competition with the base assertions of a villain."

Hurt as the queen felt at the arrogance and insolence couched in these words, she forbore manifesting her displeasure.

"No, Don Lope," she said, "your Queen is grateful, but not more than she is just. You stand accused of treason, but the mere word of that Moor will not be sufficient in itself to induce your Queen, or your brethren in arms, to convict of treason one of the first knights in Spain. We must have proof—evident, irrefragable proofs of the crime alleged against you, before a decision is pronounced."

"Proofs!" exclaimed the renegade, with a sarcastic sneer—"such a demand is too just to be denied; and who would be the presumptuous madman, that dare impeach Gomez Arias without proofs? In the first place, therefore, the Queen will perhaps not question the validity of this." And saying this, he took a ring from his finger, and approaching the throne, added:—

"Your Highness cannot have forgotten this pledge of your regard for Gomez Arias, though that nobleman seems totally to have overlooked such a gift, when he speaks in dubious terms of your Highness's gratitude."

A gloomy joy animated the features of the renegade, as he pronounced these words; a demoniac triumph was visible on his countenance.

The queen felt an involuntary shudder as she received the ring, whilst Gomez Arias stood in speechless suspense, a transitory, but deadly paleness driving the flush of anger from his countenance.

"Moor—how camest thou by this ring?" asked the queen.

"It was," answered Bermudo, "a recompence for the services I rendered Don Lope Gomez Arias. When this gallant knight wished to part with yon noble lady, I was the agent in the transaction; I procured him the interview with Cañeri."

"Cañeri!" exclaimed several voices in consternation.

"Cañeri, aye, Cañeri," repeated the renegade, unmoved. "Could the noble Gomez Arias enter into a treaty with a rebel less than a chief. I was the individual who introduced these personages to each other, and surely for so considerable a service could I expect less than a ring—a ring valuable indeed in itself—more valuable from the illustrious personage to whom it had belonged—more precious still, as I have it in my power to return it to that elevated owner."

The solemn mockery of this speech was suddenly interrupted by the queen, while, with looks of anger and displeasure—

"Peace!" she cried. "You came here to make good an accusation, not to intrude upon our patience with these remarks." Then turning to Gomez Arias, she continued in a tone of mingled sternness and compassion—

"Don Lope, you gave this ring to the Moor?"

"I did," replied Gomez Arias, gloomily, but dauntless.

"An oath," resumed the renegade, "will surely be held sacred with a Christian. Let one be taken by that man," he added, pointing to Roque, who was now endeavouring to effect his escape, as he beheld, with dismay, the unexpected and serious turn the affair was taking, and felt repugnant to criminate his former master, for whom he still preserved a feeling of respect.

"Secure the man," continued Bermudo, "and we will then see how far I am justified in my assertions."

"Silence!" again exclaimed the queen, inwardly grieved at the evidence that was pressing against Don Lope. "Silence, Moor: we need not thy instructions."

A mixture of pity and amazement prevailed throughout the assembly. They met to congratulate a victor, and they were now to consider him as one who had not scrupled to outrage the laws of his country, and for the purpose of accomplishing a detestable crime. So extraordinary and contradictory a situation appeared to some impossible; yet nothing is beyond the compass of the passions when unrestrained in their headlong career.

The feelings of the unfortunate Theodora were such as to beggar description. There she was obliged to stand and witness the accusation of her husband, brought by her means into this dreadful situation. But her dismay was doubly augmented when she observed the queen rise, and in a solemn manner, address the surrounding train.

"Christians," she said, "I bitterly deplore this melancholy event, which changes a day of triumph into one of sorrow. Governor of Granada," she then added, turning to Count de Tendilla, "to you I commit the person of Don Lope Gomez Arias, accused of treason to the state. See that he be safely guarded, though respectfully treated—and you, Don Lope, prepare to stand a trial for your life."

"For his life!" exclaimed Theodora with horror; and she fixed her imploring eyes on the queen.

Gomez Arias heard the decision of his sovereign with more indignation than fear, and in the bitterness of his soul, he said, turning to his adherents—

"My friends, be zealous to serve your country, for you perceive the recompense and encouragement which await you in a day of triumph."

"Don Lope," cried the queen with warmth, "charge not to your country what has been the effect of your unrestrained passions and imprudence; nor carry your insolence so far as to imagine and insinuate that I can wantonly sport with the life of the meanest of my subjects, much less with yours. You shall be judged by your peers, who will not neglect any extenuation in your favor, and it shall be only on irresistible evidence that the decree of justice shall be pronounced."

She then made a signal for the assembly to disperse, and every one retired in deep consternation. A deadly silence prevailed as they slowly left the hall, and to the joyful sounds of popular feeling which had lately been heard, now succeeded the murmurs of grief and astonishment.

As it was feared that the friends of Gomez Arias might be tempted to some rash act, proper precautions were taken, that the public tranquillity should not be disturbed. Mohabed and the other prisoners were confined in dungeons, and Monteblanco and his wretched daughter, by the desire of the queen, remained at the palace until the fate of Gomez Arias should be decided.

CHAPTER X.

A do el favor antiguo? a do la gloria
De mi pasado tiempo y venturoso?
A do tantos despojos y vitoria!
Herrera.

I am merrier to die, than thou art to live.
Shakespeare.

The fatal day of the trial arrived; the evidence was heard, the facts fully substantiated. Gomez Arias convicted of treason and condemned to lose his head on a scaffold! This sentence filled the inhabitants of Granada with indescribable horror. The man, who a few days before had been the theme of general admiration; he, who came victorious, borne on the wings of fortune to the highest pinnacle of honor, was now, by the same capricious turn of fate, shorn of all his dignity and splendor, and condemned to the horrors of an ignominious death. He, who had so long awakened the jealousy of the great, was now the object of general compassion.

Theodora had been schooled in affliction, and familiarized with suffering, yet when she was apprised of the result of the trial, many circumstances conspired to add to the intensity of her grief. She considered herself as the primary, though innocent cause of her husband's untimely fate; all his ingratitude and cruelty; all the treachery of which he had been guilty towards her, were now forgotten, and her vivid fancy, excited by the extent of the danger, now saw nothing but his brilliant qualities, and his untimely fate. Doubly dear was Gomez Arias to Theodora, when she perceived him on the brink of destruction. Hope, however, did not entirely forsake her, though the boding voice of grief, which floated on the air, soon dissolved so enchanting an illusion. If expectation had been great, the disappointment was now doubly terrible; the sentence had been pronounced, and the queen alone could mitigate its rigour by virtue of the royal prerogative. To this last hope Theodora clung with fond expectation; Isabella was humane and a woman; she had, it was true, acquired celebrity by the rigid and unimpeachable justice of her decisions, but could she send to the scaffold, a young and gallant nobleman, to whom she stood indebted for a brilliant victory, without infringing the sacred principles of that justice. She was a woman, and though heroic and high-minded, still nature must have planted in her bosom the genuine attributes of her sex. Pity, humanity, generosity, would stifle the sterner voice of duty, and she could not repel from her throne, the humble, yet noble supplicants for mercy; she would be deeply moved by the tears of one, whom but lately she had made a bride, and whom another word would make a widow. Besides, the application of many intimate friends, and many of the first families in the kingdom, could not be utterly disregarded by the queen, to whom their services had been so important.

These soothing ideas in some measure lulled Theodora's apprehensions, and she successfully combated the idea of losing him for ever. Unfortunate woman! soon she was doomed to learn the fallacy of her expectations! Several strong appeals had already been made to the queen; the first families of Granada had deeply interested themselves in favor of Gomez Arias, but all applications had met with a disheartening and absolute repulse. Nor indeed could the queen be taxed with ingratitude and cruelty, for she adduced powerful reasons in her answer to the supplicants, to prove her inability to comply with their request, without at the same time giving her subjects an example of unjustifiable partiality. A week had not elapsed, since six men had been executed in the *Plaza de Bivarrambla*, on account of the same offence for which Don Lope stood condemned. With this melancholy precedent, even the most sanguine in their expectations began to droop, and the death of Gomez Arias was looked upon as an inevitable misfortune.

Theodora heard the opinion generally entertained with a feeling of horror. In vain she cast herself at the feet of the queen, and there implored the royal clemency with all the fervid eloquence of grief; Isabella received her with tenderness, but allowed the wretched girl no room for hope: Theodora's feelings were wrought to the wildest paroxysm of anguish. She flung herself violently on the ground, and in all the poignancy of her affliction, prayed, fervently prayed for the life of her husband, the mere life, though by incurring banishment, she might be doomed to see him no more; the tears of the unfortunate bride fell profusely; her hands were frantically clasped, and trembled in the intensity of her emotion. It was a picture of distress unutterable. The queen beheld it with compassion—she was astonished at the sight of such affliction in one so injured as Theodora, but she could not remove her sorrows without a partiality in the administration of justice, which it had been the pride of her life to avoid.

Evidently distressed, she kindly bade Theodora rise, but with noble dignity she pronounced those memorable words:—

"As a woman, I might forgive a treason against love; as a queen, I can never forget one committed against my country."

The wretched Theodora was then ordered to retire, but she was unable to obey the mandate. She clung earnestly to the foot of the throne, fondly imagining that as long as she retained sight of Isabella, she could not lose every hope. Again she was invited to withdraw, the queen humanely wishing to spare her feelings another unnecessary shock, but the object of her solicitude was not conscious of the kindness of her motive. An officer of the governor now entering, proceeded to deliver a roll of paper into the hands of the queen. Isabella appeared suddenly agitated as she received the scroll, whilst a ray of horrible light glancing across the mind of the wretched supplicant—

"Oh, in mercy do not sign"—she franticly exclaimed. "In the name of heaven! not yet—do not sign!"

It was too late—the decree which condemned Gomez Arias was signed, and his unfortunate wife fell senseless to the ground.

In this melancholy state she was carried to her father, who, far from being able to afford consolation, was himself a prey to the bitterest woe.

Gloomily the day wore away, and the inhabitants of Granada beheld with horror the high scaffold which was already prepared at the Plaza de Bivarrambla. An universal mourning seemed to prevail throughout the city. Every one felt interested and shocked at the approaching execution, though no one dared to impugn the justice of the sentence, by virtue of which the noble culprit was about to suffer.

After the condemnation of Gomez Arias, a strong guard was placed at the mansion of Count de Tendilla, where he had been confined. He was treated with the utmost deference and regard, the queen having particularly commanded that every attention should be lavished on him; and indeed, until his death warrant was signed, the prisoner had been permitted a free intercourse with his friends and relatives. Thus his prison bore rather the resemblance of a levee of a person in power, than the visits of despairing friends to one in the last stage of mortality. All his friends and companions in arms had been assiduous in these mournful visits, and he appeared greatly pleased with this testimony of their regard. Indeed it was his pride which had brought Gomez Arias into this dreadful predicament, and he was thus highly gratified at the very general interest exhibited in his behalf.

It might be easily seen that he had not yet lost every hope; for to him it seemed impossible that the queen could ever be prevailed on to give her sanction to the sentence. He fondly recalled to his mind the high favor in which he had hitherto been held by Isabella—the different tokens of regard received from her royal hand—the many interviews and even familiar conversations with which he had been honored. To these pleasing recollections he added the intercessions of so many powerful advocates, all eager to solicit the royal clemency in his behalf. Thus, every thing conspired to buoy up the spirits of the prisoner, and to prolong an illusion from which he was soon to be rudely awakened. He was conversing in a tranquil, nay, lively manner, with two or three friends, when Count de Tendilla, followed by the official attendants, entered, and in a sad melancholy tone—

"Don Lope," he said, "I deeply lament the necessity to which I am reduced, of being the messenger of woeful tidings; but part of the pain I feel in such a disagreeable duty, is removed when I have to communicate it to such as Gomez Arias, who have fortitude and courage to know how to sustain misfortune."

"Proceed, Count," answered Don Lope, with a bitter smile, "let me know the worst, and I dare say I shall have that fortitude which you kindly suppose me—"

"Don Lope," solemnly said the Count, "your sentence is confirmed, and you must prepare for death."

"Death!" exclaimed Gomez Arias, with emotion, "death!" Then suddenly composing himself, he continued in an indignant tone:—"Well, I must confess that I am somewhat struck with your information, Count. Certainly, I was not prepared for so much—banishment and confiscation, I could have expected, but I see that I have most erroneously calculated on the favor of our Queen—her generosity, indeed, surpasses my most sanguine ideas."

Count de Tendilla, without seeming to understand this innuendo, proceeded—

"In consideration of your services, Don Lope, the Queen is willing to grant any request you may wish to make. It shall be most religiously observed."

"I am greatly beholden to the Queen," replied Gomez Arias, in the same bitter manner, "but upon my honor, I am already too much indebted to her Highness, and I should be loath to trespass on her indulgence."

"Don Lope," cried Tendilla, with warmth, "you wrong the Queen. At this very moment she deplores the necessity which compels her to sign your death warrant. Had there been any means, any honorable method to save you from your fate, she would eagerly have seized the opportunity. She would willingly forfeit the greatest treasure of her kingdom to save your life.—Yes, for your existence she would sacrifice all—all but her duty."

"And when," demanded Gomez Arias, "is this sentence to be carried into effect?"

"To-morrow;" replied the governor, "but should you like to profit by the favor, a respite of two days is granted."

"No," proudly returned Gomez Arias, "I should feel exceedingly mortified to disappoint the expectations of the public, who, no doubt, are by this time anxiously looking for the preparations of the approaching spectacle: no, let the ceremony take place to-morrow; I am ready." Then, turning to young Garcilaso, who had been his companion in the expedition against Mohabed—

"My young friend," he said, "you are a gallant and most promising soldier, but be careful how you use the favors of the ladies; for not all your services rendered to a queen will compensate the most trivial disregard offered to the woman; and above all, be cautious how you meddle with rings."

Count de Tendilla did not think proper to resent these remarks, for the present situation of Gomez Arias precluded the propriety of replying to the imprudent effusion of his irritated feelings.

"Don Lope," resumed the governor, "I will place your person under no unnecessary restraint, but you must pardon the disagreeable necessity to which my responsibility reduces me of stationing a guard within your apartment."

"The presence of soldiers, Count," replied Don Lope, "was never unpleasant to Gomez Arias; on the contrary, I shall feel particularly gratified; they will, perhaps, tend to dispel the cloud that hangs over my mind by recalling to memory my former glory; besides, they will acquire a new stimulus to serve their Queen by witnessing the encouraging reward she has in store for her servants."

He now folded his arms and began to pace the room with an affected indifference, but his inward feelings baffled even the powers of his superior mind. No man can feel calm and indifferent under such circumstances; it is against the principles of his nature; pride and a due sense of honorable feeling may help him to assume a dignified composure, or ferocity and callousness may adopt an insolent demeanor or a gloomy tranquillity; but real philosophic evenness of mind exists more in theory than in practice. Nevertheless Gomez Arias manifested no symptoms of weak regret, and his exclamations bespoke more his resentment against the queen than the dread of relinquishing life in the midst of a brilliant career. He now seemed to be absorbed in thought and the governor prepared to take his leave, when—

"Stay," he cried, "upon better reflection, perhaps it will be more respectful not to refuse the kind offer of my sovereign; I shall therefore make one request."

"Name it," said Tendilla, kindly; "it shall be granted."

"It is," resumed Don Lope, "that upon my way to the scaffold I may be allowed to head a party of my own gallant soldiers, mounted on my charger and attended with all military honors."

Count de Tendilla gave an involuntary start at so strange a demand, and looked steadfastly on Gomez Arias, as if doubting whether compliance might not be attended with danger. The request might involve the secret of some desperate act, or perhaps only bespoke the workings of a noble pride. However, the governor considered himself justified in granting the favor.

"Your wish shall be fulfilled," he said. "Whatever may be the feeling that prompts you, Don Lope, to make such a request, I and my *own* guard will likewise accompany you."

He delivered these words with great significancy of tone and manner, that Gomez Arias might be sure the governor was prepared, should there be aught in contemplation that might affect the public tranquillity.

"And now," resumed Tendilla, "I must bring you a visitor, Don Lope; one who earnestly wishes to take a last farewell."

"And who is that charitable being?" inquired Gomez Arias, carelessly; "for if I mistake not, all my friends and relatives have already fulfilled that duty."

"It is your lady," replied Tendilla, "the lovely and unfortunate Theodora."

Gomez Arias made a sign of impatient displeasure, and then, in a cold and constrained manner—

"I am sensible," he said, "of her kindness and self-devotion, but I cannot consent; no, I cannot, I will not see her; and I earnestly pray and hope she may no longer require an interview to which I have already given an absolute denial."

This was true. Gomez Arias had obstinately refused to see his once idolized Theodora, nor could all her prayers and entreaties, backed by the remonstrances of friends, prevail on him to alter so unkind a resolution. This determination might have sprung from a feeling of horror for the cause of his death, or of pity for the poignancy of her anguish: perhaps he wished to avoid a scene which was capable of producing nothing but terrible or melancholy recollections.

He evinced, however, no reluctance to see his man, Roque. The poor faithful creature anxiously desired to be admitted; for though the claims of his master to his gratitude were feeble, yet a lively sentiment of affliction and a degree of horror for having been, though unwillingly, one of the instruments to forward the catastrophe, made him desirous of throwing himself at the feet of Gomez Arias.

Tremblingly the poor valet entered, and as he beheld the noble figure of Don Lope standing composedly in the middle of the apartment, he could not refrain from tears.

"Oh! Don Lope," he cried, despondingly, "my dear and honored master, that it should come to this! That ever I should live to see the most gallant cavalier in Granada undergo such a sentence!"

He then threw himself at the feet of Gomez Arias, and clasping firmly both his knees, in a tone of keen anguish continued—

"Alas! my unfortunate master, I will not rise from the ground until you grant me full pardon for the share I have in your death. Heaven knows how unwillingly I have acted, and how sadly I repent the untoward circumstances which reduced me to that fearful alternative."

"Rise, my good Roque," said Gomez Arias. "I freely forgive thee, not only the melancholy necessity to which thou hast been compelled, but even all the other transgressions of which thou hast been guilty in my service, and I dare say they are not a few; however, as I am to undertake to-morrow so long a journey in which, I suppose, thou hast no inclination to bear me company——"

"*Virgen de las Angustias*," interrupted Roque, "how can you, Señor, speak of such dreadful things in so light a manner?"

"Now, Roque," replied Don Lope, "thou must be silent, at least at present, and allow me thy privilege for a time; listen with attention. It is high time to settle my accounts. I am thy debtor, Roque."

"*Valgame Dios!*" exclaimed the valet. "Señor Don Lope, why think of these matters at such a time?"

"The best of times," returned his master, "or you run a fair chance of not being paid at all."

"But I do not want to be paid," cried Roque, sobbing aloud. "I am sure you think too meanly of me, if you suppose I came here with such on intention."

"No, Roque, I well know thy fidelity, and I mean not to offend thee; but thou must not refuse the last bequest of thy master: here, take this," he said, delivering a large purse, which the valet could scarcely be prevailed upon to accept. "And here," he continued, taking a ring from his finger, "receive this as a token of remembrance," and as Roque hesitated to take it, he added, smiling, "Take it, for I can now give rings away without danger."

"Thank you, my good master, but have you no pledge of affection, no last remembrance for *her*?"

"Why," answered Gomez Arias, with affected levity, "she will never forget me. Besides I have nothing worthy of her acceptance—give her my best wishes, and beseech her to pardon me as freely as I forgive her."

Having said this, he wished to turn away, but Roque again interposed, and in a most doleful tone—

"Alack! Don Lope," he said, "remember what I told you at Guadix; my forebodings did not deceive me, for my prognostication has, unfortunately, been but too truly accomplished. Now, had you then—"

"Gently, my good fellow," interrupted Gomez Arias, "gently; this will never do; thou camest here in the humble mood of a sinner, to crave my forgiveness, and now thou hast relapsed into thy former calling by assuming the preacher. In goodness forbear, and leave that task to those who claim it in virtue of their office. And now, my faithful Roque, begone, for I feel drowsy, and an hour's sleep would not come amiss."

Saying this, he bade his servant kindly adieu, and retired to his closet, followed by two guards.

Roque was bewildered, for though he had already had several occasions of forming a just estimation of the character and temper of Gomez Arias, yet he could not comprehend how a man on the eve of death could resign himself to sleep with the ease and composure which his master evinced.

"*Virgen Santa!*" he ejaculated, "did ever man think of sleep at such a time? Why *los siete durmientes*[1] would have been at fault at such a pinch. He is going to sleep; the Lord help him! I am sure I cannot sleep; nay, I don't know whether I shall ever sleep again."

Saying this, poor Roque withdrew, weeping and wondering, and imploring the protection of all the saints in the calendar, for his unfortunate master.

---

[1] The seven Sleepers.

CHAPTER XI.

Voilà le précipice où l'ont enfin jeté
Les attraits enchanteurs de la prospérité.
La Fontaine.

Oh di destino avverso
Fatal possanza! a mie tante sventure
Ciò sol mancava.
Alfieri.

Forget! forgive!—I must indeed forget
When I forgive.
Southern.

Every hope was now extinct—the fatal morning arrived. Theodora, the hapless Theodora, against whom fate seemed to have exhausted all her malice, after a night of restless grief, had left her couch betimes, and in a gloomy reverie was sitting by the casement, her hands clasped together, and her eyes vacantly fixed on the moving groups below.

The door opened, and her father entered—the wretched man was in a most pitiable state.

"My child," he said, tenderly, "my dear child, you must leave this place."

"Never," cried the melancholy Theodora, "unless it is to be carried to the grave. Oh! my poor, my dear father, you will soon have to fulfil that last mournful duty towards your hapless child."

"Theodora, speak not thus; your words are daggers. We must submit to the will of Providence—raise your streaming eyes to that heaven, my beloved, and cherish the fond hope that this life of sorrow is to purchase an eternity of pure uninterrupted bliss. Throw yourself into the arms of religion, and your evils will appear lighter to bear."

"Yes, my father, now my only friend," replied Theodora, in a tumult of agony, "I will consider my misfortunes as a just atonement to offended heaven, for the ingratitude of which I have been guilty towards the best of parents."

"Heaven bless thee, Theodora," returned the affectionate father, "and restore to thee peace and tranquillity; and now grant me a request—you must away with me."

"But whither are we going?" demanded Theodora, "I cannot—I will not quit Granada until I see *him* laid in the ground. I am now his wife, and I shall religiously fulfil the duties of such a character, for cruel as he was," she added, mournfully, "to refuse me permission to see him when alive, he cannot prevent me from showing my attachment when he is dead."

"Theodora," said Monteblanco, "it is not my intention to take you away from Granada. I merely wish you to accompany me to the dwelling of our kinsman, Don Antonio de Leyva. He has repeatedly demanded to see you, but you have always denied his request. You surely cannot dislike him?"

"Father! father!" cried Theodora, in a tone of reproach and sadness; "why this eagerness to renew an intimacy with a man whom I have wronged? Think you that Theodora will be able to sustain his reproach?"

"No, Theodora, such thoughts are far from the minds of Don Antonio and your father. But the gallant young man lies prostrate on the bed of sickness. The wounds he received at the disastrous affair of the Sierra Bermeja, have reduced him to the last stage of debility. He has this very instant earnestly requested to see you; for he has something to announce which may affect the fate of us all."

Theodora answered not, but rising immediately, signified her readiness to obey, and supported by her father, she proceeded towards the residence of Don Antonio. Dismay and confusion reigned throughout the city. At every step Theodora met with some object to impress her forcibly with the dreariness of the fate which was at hand. Busily the moving groups were talking of the melancholy event. She beheld the troops that were collecting and marching about to insure the public tranquillity, and this testimony of the hopeless situation of her husband filled her bursting heart with new terrors. How dismally sounded the trumpets and clarions! And now the ponderous bell of the cathedral sent forth its reverberating tones, and it sounded like the summons of death to Theodora. It struck eight, and in two hours Gomez Arias would cease to exist. A chill seized on the very soul of Theodora, at each stroke of the dreadful monitor, and as if its terrors had not been sufficiently multiplied, a hundred different clocks, with their boding voices, repeated the same sad tale to the agonizing heart of the wretched girl.

Next came the sight of the ministers of religion hurrying about; sad heralds of mortality, in Christian charity, earnestly wishing to offer their prayers for the departing soul, or holding out the example of the approaching execution to the young and inexperienced.

Theodora shuddered at every object she saw—at every sound that struck her ear, and in this state she reached the mansion of Don Antonio de Leyva, which happily was situated at a short distance. She trembled with emotion as she found herself before young De Leyva, nor was her appearance productive of less astonishment to Don Antonio. They were both much altered—she by intense suffering—he by his wounds and lingering sickness. Don Antonio, extremely faint, was reclining on a couch, from which he attempted to rise when he saw his kinsman enter, but was prevented by Monteblanco. The countenance of the gallant young man seemed suddenly to brighten up.

"Theodora," he kindly said, "tremble not thus, for you are in the presence of a friend, a sincere friend; one who bitterly laments having, though unconsciously, been instrumental in your misfortunes. Alas! dear lady, had you placed more confidence in me, perchance so much misery had been prevented. However, this is no time for reproach; the moments speed swiftly away, and we have none to spare. Had you not at this moment arrived, weak and wounded as I am, I was about to be carried to your habitation, though the exertion had proved fatal to my recovery. Theodora, look upon me as a friend—as a dear valued friend, and receive the greatest proof a man can give of pure disinterested regard. Here," he then added, presenting a little casket to Theodora, "take this precious gage; look, it is the portrait of our Queen, given by her own royal hands, when fortune favoured my exertions in the last tournament. The bearer of this gift is entitled to claim any boon from Isabella. Dispatch—present her with this beauteous copy of herself. Reclaim the promise—demand the life of Gomez Arias—it will be granted."

"Merciful heavens!" cried Theodora, overpowered with emotion, "Can it be possible!" Then falling at the feet of young de Leyva— "Generous—generous Don Antonio; is this the way that you repay an injury?"

Gomez Arias; or The Moors of the Alpujarras.

"I might," replied Don Antonio nobly, "satisfy the cravings of a paltry revenge, by leaving my rival to perish ignominiously, when I have it in my power to save him. But no; my heart shudders at such reprisals, and finds joy in contributing to the happiness of Theodora."

Struck with admiration at such noble and manly conduct, Theodora seized the hand of the high-minded Don Antonio, and would have imprinted on it a thousand kisses of gratitude, but he modestly prevented her, urging her to depart.

"My dear Theodora, begone; you have no time to lose. Think that the least delay may perhaps prove fatal."

These words acted like magic on the mind of Theodora. The thought of her husband's danger absorbed every other consideration. She rushed with impetuous alacrity towards the palace, pressing with convulsive firmness the valuable pledge on which all her hopes depended. Upon her arrival at the entrance, the guards, struck with the wildness of her manner, and sympathising with her misfortunes, expeditiously opened a passage, as she exclaimed almost incoherently, that she must see the queen.

Meantime the Plaza de Bivarrambla was thronged with a vast multitude, for the novelty and exemplary justice of such an execution had thrown the people into a ferment. It was long since a nobleman had suffered thus, and no instance occurred to their recollection of a conqueror stepping from the car of victory to the platform of a scaffold.

All lamented the fate of Gomez Arias, and yet most of the lower classes, amidst the feelings of pity, experienced a kind of satisfaction at the idea that so great a personage was doomed to suffer, as well as the meanest of their own class. In the middle of the Plaza rose a high scaffold, covered with costly black velvet, and most of the houses around were likewise draperied with mourning symbols of the sorrow of their owners. A strong body of veterans lined the square, whilst other detached parties of horse patrolled the neighbouring places to prevent any obstruction from the multitude. The hurry and agitation of the people now became extreme; but when at last the tremendous knell from the cathedral gave the mournful signal for Gomez Arias to set out for the goal of his mortal career, a simultaneous murmur of horror rose from the surrounding crowd. The dismal tolling of bells, accompanied at intervals by the sad and hollow strains of trumpets, announced that the procession was ready to move.

Gomez Arias had descended from his apartment perfectly composed. Indeed, no other feeling could be descried in his features but stern pride and resentment. He walked with a firm step towards the melancholy train that awaited him. But when about to mount his horse, he perceived the Countess de Tendilla bathed in tears, approaching to bid him farewell. He kindly thanked this lady for all the attentions he had experienced at her house during the time he had remained there, and having bidden her a last adieu, he bounded on his favorite charger. The spirited animal began to curvet and rear, as if proud of his burthen.

"Gently, gently, Babieca," said his master, caressing the noble steed: "be not impatient, for this is the last time thou wilt carry thy master."

He then looked around, and as he saw a party of his victorious troops, chosen for his escort according to his desire, all plunged in the deepest grief, in a soothing tone he bade them be of good cheer.

Don Lope being determined to set at defiance every appearance of despondency, had assumed an air of martial and dignified composure. His handsome figure never looked to greater advantage than at this disastrous moment; he was attired in a most sumptuous suit, while all the friends and relatives who accompanied him were habited in deep mourning. The procession moved slowly on amidst the confused murmur of the multitude, deeply lamenting the fate, and admiring the firmness of the hero of the dismal tragedy. He was attended by a crowd of the ministers of religion; but two friars of the order of St. Francis attached themselves more particularly to his person. The whole presented a most singularly contrasted scene; for in the same view appeared mingled all the panoplies of war, stirring the soul to martial deeds, and the solemn emblems of religion inviting the mind to abandon the pomp of the world, and turn its thoughts towards eternity. Warriors and priests, banners and crosses, moved promiscuously along, while the subdued blast of clarions united their strains to the deep-toned and gloomy cadences of the chaunting monks.

In this manner the procession reached at length the Plaza de Bivarrambla. At the sight of the scaffold, Gomez Arias gave an involuntary start, for he was unable to stifle the impression which the first view of that dreadful spot made on his mind. He soon, however, recovered his usual composure, and cast an inquiring and intense look on the assembled multitude. Sorrow and consternation were every where visible, but all was tranquil and quiet. The last lingering hope now vanished from the breast of Gomez Arias, and he seemed resigned to the fate that awaited him. The murmur of the multitude was hushed into a deadly silence. Don Lope dismounted, ascended the scaffold, and turning to his soldiers, he said—

"Farewell, my brave companions; this is the last expedition in which we shall meet; but in this, as well as in all the former, Gomez Arias will display the coolness and courage which becomes a soldier." He then with equal resolution was about to bare his neck for the fatal stroke, when a piercing scream was heard at a distance in the crowd. Presently a female form was seen flying towards the scaffold—

"A pardon! a pardon!" shouted various voices; and the multitude joyfully opened a passage to the unfortunate. She ran with frantic speed, until she arrived at length, exhausted, at the foot of the scaffold, exhibiting in the disorder of her person and the wild expression of her features, all the workings of terror, anxiety, and joy. Every one stood mute with astonishment when they beheld in this apparition the wretched Theodora, who flew up the steps of the scaffold, holding aloft in her trembling hand a paper; then throwing herself into the arms of her husband—

"Oh it is not too late," she cried eagerly; "I have brought your pardon. Here! here! You are safe—it is the Queen's signet."

Count de Tendilla took the paper from her hand, and read joyfully aloud the pardon of Gomez Arias. Theodora looked wildly around, her large beautiful eyes fraught with terror: she gazed upon the appalling scene, as though still fearful that the execution would not be suspended.

"Read! read!" she cried vehemently to Count de Tendilla: "it is the Queen's order. A messenger will soon arrive; but I am here first. I came to save my husband."

These few electric words were followed by a shout of tumultuous applause from the assembled throng.

The messenger indeed arrived. Theodora uttered a wild scream of joy, and her feelings, unable any longer to support the efforts she had made, overpowered her, and she fainted in the arms of Gomez Arias.

Even Gomez Arias, that man so hardened to all the tender pleadings of gratitude, was at length overcome. As he beheld her who had returned his coldness with affection, and repaid his cruelty with kindness—as he considered that miracle of love and goodness lying lifeless in his arms, a tear stood trembling in his eye—one solitary tear; but that testimonial of feeling in Gomez Arias was equivalent to years of sorrow in other men. He tenderly pressed Theodora to his heart, and the fond embrace seemed to recall her suspended animation. She opened her languid eyes and was happy; for she saw the object of all her care and affection now watching with tender solicitude her returning life.

"Oh Theodora," cried Don Lope, in a voice almost inarticulate with emotion, "I am unworthy of you. How can I ever atone for so many wrongs? This is indeed a noble vengeance."

The queen had ordered that Gomez Arias should be conducted to her presence, and accordingly, accompanied by the happy Theodora, he proceeded towards the palace, followed by the immense crowd, who rent the air with joyful acclamations.

When they arrived at the palace, they found the gracious Isabella seated in the large public hall, ready to receive them. Her countenance was radiant with delight in the consciousness of having been able to save Don Lope from an untimely end.

"Gomez Arias," she said, "your life is saved by the most fortunate, as it was the most unexpected of incidents. Nobles of Granada," she then added, turning to the surrounding court, "you cannot accuse your Queen of partiality in the distribution of justice. At the moment when Don Lope was approaching the end of his mortal career, this gage was brought to me and the guerdon claimed. It was a pledge of regard given to Don Antonio de Leyva for his conduct at the tournament, with my sacred promise that any boon should be granted to the bearer. Theodora produced it, and I could not resist her just appeal—my royal word had passed. Gomez Arias, you owe your life to the generous Don Antonio de Leyva and your wife. Let then your future life show that you are not insensible of the magnitude of the obligation. To yourself you owe nothing; for had it not been for this happy circumstance, by this time you would have been numbered with the dead. Go, and rejoice with your friends over your fortunate deliverance, and then I will receive you as becomes a victor."

A shout of unfeigned approbation burst from every one. Theodora seemed intoxicated with happiness. She looked on Gomez Arias, and in those features which had so successfully enraptured her young heart, again saw a display of tenderness to recompense her affection. All her sufferings were forgotten; the cup of misery had been drained, and happiness, boundless, uninterrupted happiness, was to be hers for ever. Gomez Arias, moved with kindly and generous feelings which had long been dormant in his heart, had as yet been unable to give utterance to his demonstrations of gratitude. He now disengaged himself from the hands of Theodora, moved forwards, and threw himself at the feet of the queen. Every eye was joyfully turned on him, when suddenly one of the friars, who had attended him at the scaffold, broke from the surrounding group. In his hand gleamed a poniard, and before any arm could arrest the blow, he buried the fatal weapon in the breast of

Gomez Arias, who started on his feet, reeled, and fell at the foot of the throne. In an instant every thing was wild confusion. Theodora, with a piercing scream, threw herself beside her murdered husband, while several leaches hastened to the assistance of the fallen knight.

The queen alone seemed to preserve her presence of mind amidst the uproar that prevailed.

"Seize the assassin!" she exclaimed, and the guards immediately secured his person. He was one of the Franciscans who had accompanied Gomez Arias to the scaffold. He still held in his sinewy hand the ensanguined poniard, and with the savage laugh of a fiend exulted over his deed.

"Now, God be thanked!" exclaimed the leach who had examined the wound of Gomez Arias, "if my skill fail me not, the knight may yet live."

"Never!" cried the friar, in a voice that chilled the reviving hopes of every one; "Never! your skill is vain—the dagger is poisoned."

A shudder of horror ran through the court.

"Man of darkness," exclaimed Count de Tendilla, "fiend under the holy garb of religion, what could prompt thee to such a crime? But a short time since I saw thee attend thy victim to administer to him hope and consolation."

"Yes," replied the friar, grimly, "yes, I did accompany him to the stage of his despair and my glory: yes, I was beside my victim, like the vulture watching for the moment to lacerate his heart. But I went not to whisper hope into his dying ear, or to bid him rely on the mercies of Heaven; no, it was to speak the words of horror; to bid him despair, and point the way to that hell whither soon I was to follow him. My soul was drunk with joy; my heart was wild with happiness: gladly would I purchase with a whole existence of misery and crime those few rapturous moments when I could watch the dreadful workings of his mind, as the last peal of my ominous voice rung in his ear, ere his soul took its flight from this world."

"Peace, wretch!" exclaimed the queen. "Leave thy blasphemy; tremble for the profanation of thy sacred calling; tremble for the punishment which awaits thy crime."

"I tremble at nought," sternly replied the assassin. "No canting friar am I; no preaching monk; but a man deeply wronged, and now amply revenged. Look on me," he continued in a wild tone, throwing off his disguise, "I am Bermudo, the renegade!"

Every one shrunk back with instinctive horror at the well known name; but the consternation increased, when in the person of the apostate was recognised the Moor who had played so principal a part in the condemnation of Gomez Arias.

"Look on me," proceeded the renegade; "look on me, Gomez Arias; behold the man by you condemned to misery and shame—I am Bermudo the outcast, the maddened lover of the unfortunate Anselma. Call back, Don Lope, the powers of thy fleeting soul, and fix its fading recollection on thy crimes and my misfortunes: remember Anselma—remember her frightful fate—your wrongs to me—the despair to which I was driven. But for thee, proud man, I might have been a hero, and for thee I am a traitor and a renegade. But, oh! now thou art laid low—no, not even princely fortune and favour could save thee from the hand of a desperate man. Die, then, die in despair: it is in the hour of rapturous happiness that the blow is struck, and think with agony that it is struck by Bermudo.—Anselma, thou art revenged!"

A wild and savage laugh closed this apostrophe, and the renegade stood calmly gazing on his victim with an expression of ferocious joy: his dark features seemed to brighten in the glare of infernal revenge, and his strong frame shook with the rapture of the fiend that inspired him.

Meantime, Gomez Arias was rapidly approaching his end; the blood flowed thick and heavy through his veins, and the film of death was fast dimming his sight: still his noble features shewed no symptoms of unmanly emotion; but fixing his dying eyes upon the renegade, in a firm tone he said—

"Bermudo, thy hellish desire is but partially fulfilled; I die not in despair; despair is the attribute of cowards, not of Gomez Arias: I feel thy poison burning in my veins, yet my soul takes its flight with calmness. Wretched man," he then added, "may God forgive thee as I do: and thou, dear and last object of my solicitude," he said, faintly addressing himself to the disconsolate Theodora, who, in a paroxysm of agony, was kneeling beside him, "Theodora, injured and unfortunate girl, too late I appreciate thy value; too late I deplore my fault. Oh! if I regret existence, it is because I cannot live to prove my love and gratitude. Forgive me, Theodora! forgive the repentant Gomez Arias!"

His dim eyes were cast tenderly on her despairing countenance, and pressing gently her clammy hand, he breathed his last.

The piercing cries and lamentations of Theodora deeply affected the spectators of this tragic scene: she tore her flowing tresses, and falling on the bleeding corpse, in a wild incoherent tone poured forth her anguish. The renegade himself appeared somewhat moved at the exhibition of her frantic sorrow. The darksome deed was done; his enemy was dead, and Bermudo seemed no longer to live in this world; stupor and apathy were overshadowing his countenance, for the principle that fed his life was now no more.

The soldiers were about to move away with the prisoner, when a minister of religion addressed him:—

"Sinner," he cried, "behold your deadly crime and repent; repent ere 'tis too late; thy mortal career is short; employ it, then, in calming the offended justice of heaven."

"Friar," said firmly the renegade, "my conscience is seared; my soul has no longer sympathy with human feelings; I cannot, will not now repent me of a deed which has been the sole object of my existence. Lead me to torture, and when ye tear this flesh, and suffering nature is unable to sustain the racking pangs, then, even then, my eyes, faithful interpreters of my soul, will tell you I shrink not from my fate; the poniard that struck my foe I might have plunged in this breast, but I disdained to evade the recompense of my deed. Lead me to torture, but mock me not with words of penitence."

"Oh horror! art thou a man and speakest thus!" exclaimed the priest.

"I was a man; I know not what I am; let me return to my kindred clay, and hide from the face of the earth the monster at which ye shudder."

He ceased, and his features stiffened into a horrid tranquillity more appalling to behold than his wildest ebullition of passion. One last savage look he cast on his prostrate enemy, and then, with a firm step, he walked away to meet the punishment due to his crimes.

The wretched Theodora could not be torn from the mortal bleeding remains of her adored Gomez Arias, until the paroxysm of her grief was succeeded by insensibility. In this melancholy state she was borne from the fatal spot, while sorrow and compassion swelled the hearts of every one who had witnessed the events of that disastrous day!

CONCLUSION.

La douleur lentement m'entr'ouve le tombeau,
Salut mon dernier jour! sois mon jour le plus beau!
Lamartine.

Three months had now elapsed since the death of Gomez Arias, and the people of Granada were again rejoicing in the success of the Christian arms. The insurrection of the Moors was now completely quelled; the wise and prudent conduct of the queen had saved the country from the horrors attendant on a fanatical war. The individuals admitted to the counsels of Isabella were in general men of enlightened understanding and philanthropic dispositions, and though some few voices, swayed by fanatical zeal and religious intolerance, opposed themselves to liberal measures, yet, happily for Spain and honorably for her ministers, their objections were over-ruled, and the more beneficial and milder course adopted. A full pardon was proclaimed to the rebels. Moreover it was promised that they should enjoy the same privileges as the Spaniards, and that no compulsory measures should be adopted to make them embrace the tenets of the Christian religion. Free permission was given to every Moor who should prefer passing over to Africa, to remove unmolested, and with full security to his family and property.

These judicious resolutions answered the desired effect. The Moors joyfully accepted the offers of the queen, and the greatest part of them came immediately to lay down their arms at the feet of the Alcayde de los Donceles, and other chiefs who still were carrying on the war. However, some Moors of the higher rank, who refused to subject themselves to the Christian government, retired into Africa, and amongst this number we must count the magnanimous El Feri de Benastepar; for, as no account was received of his death, it was supposed he had abandoned the country.

Thus peace was at length restored, and the city of Granada became again the center of gaiety and happiness, and this was not a little enhanced by the anticipation of the union of Leonor de Aguilar with the gallant Don Antonio de Leyva: the nuptials being only delayed until a due allowance of time had been devoted to the memory of the noble Don Alonso de Aguilar.

Meantime Don Manuel de Monteblanco and his unfortunate daughter had retired to their mansion at Guadix. Shortly after the mortal remains of Gomez Arias had been consigned to the earth, Don Manuel prevailed on his unhappy daughter to abandon a city fraught with such dreadful associations. Theodora submissively obeyed the desires of her solicitous and kind parent, but alas! the sorrow that slowly consumed her heart was not to be removed by change of place: the lovely victim carried within her the deadly poison that was to consign her to an early grave. Theodora became the prey of a deep-rooted melancholy. The kind attention of friends, the tender expostulation of her father, might momentarily withdraw her mind from the subject of her constant meditations; tokens of regard, and the soft caresses of pity might elicit a transient smile; but soon, alas! her mind would revert to its mournful occupation; soon her smile would give way to sadness.

During the day, she wandered about the large mansion like a restless spirit whose duties in life are fulfilled, and who longs to take its flight. Sometimes she took her lute, and in wild and plaintive voice she would sing those romances which Gomez Arias had loved to hear. Then she would ramble through the garden, and visit those spots endeared by the recollection of her love. Sometimes, too, in the stillness of night, a most piercing scream would issue from her chamber, and arouse the unfortunate Monteblanco from his couch, to hush the fevered imagination of his daughter, continually haunted by the image of the murdered Gomez Arias.

Day after day the disconsolate father watched the progress of the malady. Gradually Theodora was wasting in form, and her intellectual powers seemed to share in the wreck of her outward appearance. Nothing could disturb the gloomy monotony of her thoughts. Musing tranquilly, she would pass the hour, and oft in the night when the moon beams fell on the garden, she would be seen gliding along its paths like some fleeting phantom.

In this melancholy state Theodora had continued during some time, when one morning Monteblanco was agreeably surprised to see his child in unusually good spirits. The gloom which sat habitually on her brow had vanished, and a placid smile played upon her lips. Joyfully the venerable parent beheld the welcome change, and anxiously he wished to improve those favorable symptoms of returning health. Theodora told her father that she had dreamed in the night an awful dream. She had seen her husband, not as heretofore, in the fearful scenes of his desertion and death, but his eyes beaming with a heavenly light, bidding her be happy, as he was happy and blessed.

It was the anniversary of the day on which Theodora had left her home. Night came, and Monteblanco saw not his daughter by his side. He waited impatiently for some time, and then repaired to the garden, for he knew Theodora delighted in rambling there.

The faithful Roque, who since the death of his master had attached himself to the service of Monteblanco, took a torch, and accompanied the old cavalier to the garden. Don Manuel called aloud upon his daughter, but his voice was only answered by the sad echoes of the place. He became alarmed, and hastily proceeded to the bower: there he descried Theodora lying on the marble seat, apparently asleep. He approached her, and affectionately chid her for her absence.

"Awake, child, awake," he cried; "surely your delicate health will be injured by the chilling air of night."

He gently raised her arm.

"Roque, bring closer that torch."

Roque obeyed—Theodora indeed slept, but it was the sleep of death.

Struck with consternation, the wretched old man clasped the lifeless body in his arms, and called eagerly on his child by the most endearing of names. Alas! it was too late: the spark of life had fled for ever, and the dull glare of the torch that fell upon her countenance soon confirmed the mournful truth. Pale and bloodless was her cheek, and cold were those beauteous limbs. The angel of death had spread his sable pinions over her dewy brow, and closed her eyes in eternal sleep. The despairing father now strove to raise his daughter in his arms, when something fell from her nerveless grasp. Roque immediately took it up—he gave a start, and uttered a most piteous moan, as he presented the object to Don Manuel. It was the portrait of Gomez Arias. That melancholy testimonial told that the heavenly spirit had lately taken its flight, for it was yet moist with *her* tears, the last effort of her departing soul—the last sad evidence of a *woman's love*.

Gomez Arias; or The Moors of the Alpujarras.

Non come fiamma, che per forza è spenta,
Ma che per se medesma si consuma,
Se n'andò in pace l'anima contenta.
Petrarca.

THE END

Also from Benediction Books ...
Wandering Between Two Worlds: Essays on Faith and Art
Anita Mathias
Benediction Books, 2007
152 pages
ISBN: 0955373700

Available from www.amazon.com, www.amazon.co.uk

In these wide-ranging lyrical essays, Anita Mathias writes, in lush, lovely prose, of her naughty Catholic childhood in Jamshedpur, India; her large, eccentric family in Mangalore, a sea-coast town converted by the Portuguese in the sixteenth century; her rebellion and atheism as a teenager in her Himalayan boarding school, run by German missionary nuns, St. Mary's Convent, Nainital; and her abrupt religious conversion after which she entered Mother Teresa's convent in Calcutta as a novice. Later rich, elegant essays explore the dualities of her life as a writer, mother, and Christian in the United States-- Domesticity and Art, Writing and Prayer, and the experience of being "an alien and stranger" as an immigrant in America, sensing the need for roots.

About the Author

Anita Mathias is the author of *Wandering Between Two Worlds: Essays on Faith and Art*. She has a B.A. and M.A. in English from Somerville College, Oxford University, and an M.A. in Creative Writing from the Ohio State University, USA. Anita won a National Endowment of the Arts fellowship in Creative Nonfiction in 1997. She lives in Oxford, England with her husband, Roy, and her daughters, Zoe and Irene.

Anita's website:
 http://www.anitamathias.com, and
Anita's blog Dreaming Beneath the Spires:
 http://dreamingbeneaththespires.blogspot.com

The Church That Had Too Much
Anita Mathias
Benediction Books, 2010
52 pages
ISBN: 9781849026567

Available from www.amazon.com, www.amazon.co.uk

The Church That Had Too Much was very well-intentioned. She wanted to love God, she wanted to love people, but she was both hampered by her muchness and the abundance of her possessions, and beset by ambition, power struggles and snobbery. Read about the surprising way The Church That Had Too Much began to resolve her problems in this deceptively simple and enchanting fable.

About the Author

Anita Mathias is the author of *Wandering Between Two Worlds: Essays on Faith and Art*. She has a B.A. and M.A. in English from Somerville College, Oxford University, and an M.A. in Creative Writing from the Ohio State University, USA. Anita won a National Endowment of the Arts fellowship in Creative Nonfiction in 1997. She lives in Oxford, England with her husband, Roy, and her daughters, Zoe and Irene.

Anita's website:
    http://www.anitamathias.com, and
Anita's blog Dreaming Beneath the Spires:
    http://dreamingbeneaththespires.blogspot.com

Milton Keynes UK
Ingram Content Group UK Ltd.
UKHW011501250224
438379UK00002B/357